FELO DE SE

Phil Egner

Cover Design
FrinaArt

In memory of my parents

It is a strangely irrational notion that there is something in the very fabric of time which will inevitably cure all ills.

'Letter From Birmingham Jail'
Martin Luther King, Jr.

Say not thou, What is the cause that the former days were better than these? For thou dost not inquire wisely concerning this.

Ecclesiastes - 7:10

Da capo (English: /dɑː ˈkɑːpoʊ/, also US: /də -/, Italian: [da (k)ˈkaːpo]) is an Italian musical term that means 'from the beginning'. Literally, 'from the head…'

Wikipedia

CONTENTS

Title Page

Copyright

The Coroner   1

Richard   17

Carin   107

Gillian   161

Jack   189

Francesca   209

Veronica   247

Da capo   273

Afterword   289

About The Author   291

THE CORONER

"Mrs Pascoe, please!" said the coroner.

Then, as the two women - the wife staring, the mother glaring - unlocked their eyes from each other and turned towards him, qualified that with, "Mrs Pascoe senior".

"An absolute slander!" the mother repeated, quivering with rage. "Totally disgraceful."

The wife remained as calm as she'd been throughout her time on the witness stand, while her indignant mother-in-law was being quietly, but urgently, addressed by the family solicitor. This impression of patience, even perhaps stoicism, the coroner sensed was as much intended to contrast with the older woman's outburst as to emphasise her own veracity.

There had already been undercurrents in her testimony for him to suspect that an old score, or possibly several, were being settled under an oath to *tell the truth, the whole truth and nothing but the truth*. A woman of her obvious intelligence did not drop the kind of bombshell she just had without thinking through the likely consequences.

Outbursts during an inquest were rare. A high-profile case, perhaps one involving corporate negligence, could provide moments of controversy, but such scenes generally had more an air of stagecraft about them than spontaneous anger. Family matters tended to proceed in a more sombre manner.

Unlike a criminal or civil court, an inquest employs an investigative rather than an adversarial process. It's rare for anyone other than the coroner to question witnesses, always conscious that a loved one has been lost in circumstances grave enough to warrant a life being picked apart in public and that few lives are so virtuous as to emerge well from such scrutiny.

"Mrs Pascoe," he repeated, softening his tone. "I'm aware of how distressing you must be finding this. But if you continue to interrupt these proceedings, I will have to ask you to leave the courtroom."

It seemed as if she were about to argue, but her solicitor, now also standing, placed his hand on her forearm. He spoke to her again in that same soft but urgent tone and after a few seconds, with a reluctant shake of the head, she sat down.

"Thank you," acknowledged the coroner with a brief smile and a nod. He turned back to the witness.

"Please," he said to her. "Continue."

* * *

The coroner liked to think of himself as a methodical man. After familiarising himself with all the pertinent documentation - medical records, police reports, witness statements - he was careful to apply that methodology to the specific nature of each case.

Where that relied almost entirely on medical evidence, he would first call on the doctors, surgeons, or nursing staff who'd been directly involved. By taking them through their written statements and where necessary clarifying and expanding, he would not only be seen to be arriving at the appropriate verdict but also supplying the grieving family, friends - and perhaps the media - with a coherent narrative. It was important for them, he felt, to believe that their loved ones had received both the respect which they deserved and the due process of law to which they were entitled.

But where death had been the tragic outcome of a series of events, he would first hear from witnesses to that sequence and in chronological order. Then, where relevant, family or friends who might cast light on the deceased's course of actions or state of mind. And finally expert testimony, whose psychological assessments, medical conclusions and legalistic scrutiny would combine to determine whether the matter was now laid to rest or needed to be referred to other agencies for further investigation.

Prior to an inquest and reviewing the police files and witness accounts, the coroner often had the sense of skimming the text of a play whose performance he was shortly to attend. Characters he could only picture in his mind would soon be brought to life, fleshed out in ways he knew he would occasionally find surprising. Nervously giving evidence - few people are natural extroverts and rarely so under the gaze of the law - and with the truth, like spilt water, frequently meandering into the unlikeliest nooks and crannies.

Robert Pascoe had been found dead in his car two months previously. He'd been a prominent local businessman, a partner in a chain of estate agents who also owned an interest in several related concerns. To all appearances as upper crust as St Hannahs got, whether your criteria be cash in the bank or generations in the churchyard.

Working his way through the witness statements, the coroner discovered Pascoe had spent the evening in the lounge bar of *The Barque*, a hotel and restaurant by the harbour and one which he knew well himself. During the course of that evening Pascoe had drunk to excess, grown argumentative with some tourists - although the altercation hadn't become physical - the result of which was that he had been asked to leave. The landlord offered to call him a taxi, having earlier taken his car keys from him as a condition of continuing to serve him drinks.

An offer declined.

However, it would seem that Pascoe kept a spare set in a magnetic key safe attached under the wheel arch of his car. No one actually saw him drive home, but the car had travelled from *The Barque* car park to the integral garage of his house, a key was in the ignition and the key safe empty.

The electric up and over garage doors were operated by a remote switch Pascoe kept clipped to the sun visor. On approaching the house, he only needed to reach up and press it to drive straight into the garage, from where a glazed side door led into the house itself. A second press on the remote closed the doors. There was no distinct 'Open / Shut' status to this remote fob, the police report noted. Each successive click simply moved the doors to their opposite state.

According to Mrs Pascoe's statement, she and her husband occupied separate bedrooms. With increasing age, his snoring had grown worse and he would often work late at night in his study. Being both a light sleeper and an early riser, Mrs Pascoe found this combination disruptive and a room of her own became the practical solution. For that reason, she had not been aware of her husband's absence from the house that evening.

It was the paperboy who raised the alarm. Making his regular 7am delivery of *The Daily Telegraph* for Mr Pascoe and *The Guardian* for his wife, he heard a car engine running inside the closed garage. With admirable prescience for one so young, thought the coroner, he'd banged on the garage door and when failing to get a response, rang the front doorbell. Mrs Pascoe answered in her dressing gown and together they approached the garage, where Mrs Pascoe entered the door code on a numeric keypad. As the doors rose, exhaust gases came billowing out from underneath and both backed away, coughing.

Once the doors were fully open, the fumes quickly cleared. Telling the paperboy to stay well back, Mrs Pascoe cautiously walked to the entrance and peered inside. After a few seconds, she turned and asked him to use the telephone in the hallway to dial 999 for an ambulance. She waited for him to run into the house and then ventured into the garage. Opening the driver's door, she took her husband's wrist. She found no trace of a pulse and the hand was cold.

The ambulance arrived fifteen minutes later, the paramedics pronouncing her husband dead at the scene and informing her he had been so for several hours. There would have been nothing she could have done.

Working through the medical and police reports, the coroner found little to strike him as unusual, other than one intriguing entry.

The police had recovered Robert Pascoe's laptop computer and given it a cursory inspection for any insights it might provide. They hadn't discovered anything obviously untoward on it, but in a nest of folders marked 'Personal' was an encrypted file, the only such file on the machine. Its title, FDS, didn't offer much by way of explanation but they'd sent the laptop away for a more thorough examination and were still waiting to hear back.

As a rule, after digesting the reports, the coroner would

expect to have a fair idea of the verdict he would later deliver, but in this instance he wasn't so sure. Based on what he'd seen so far, unlawful killing could almost certainly be ruled out, but accident, misadventure and suicide were all very much in play. The reliability of the remote switch could be an issue. Was it possible for it to have closed the doors unexpectedly? Did he perhaps intend to take a few moments gathering his thoughts after what had developed into a somewhat fraught evening out and, under the influence of alcohol, fallen asleep? Or were there as yet unknown factors which the inquest might bring to light?

Robert Pascoe's state of mind at the time was obviously going to be of crucial importance. What had led him down to *The Barque* and why was he drinking to excess? And he was also curious to know - despite Mrs Pascoe's explanation - exactly how long they had been sleeping in separate rooms?

* * *

The inquest opened to few surprises. Although the image of the deceased which emerged from witness statements occasionally suggested two very distinct personalities, didn't we all, reflected the coroner and not for the first time, consciously or not present varying faces to the world under different circumstances? That our families and our work colleagues might hold quite contrasting opinions regarding the strengths and weaknesses of our character.

Robert Pascoe was a businessman and over the years the coroner had acquired a set of assumptions which generally served him well in that regard. The key factors to a successful, self-made businessman would seem to be a capacity for hard work, single-mindedness of purpose and a natural inclination toward duplicity. Intelligence he placed somewhat further down the list, most needing only to be savvy enough to employ someone smarter to do the thinking they'd eventually take the credit for.

But Pascoe was not self-made, he was the grandson of the founder of the estate agency and the coroner also set great store by the adage that the first generation creates wealth, the second stewards it, the third consumes it. And the Pascoe family, it began to emerge, gave little reason to dispute that precept.

"Was Mr Pascoe one of your regulars?" the coroner asked Rod Truscott, landlord of *The Barque.*

"He'd pop in most evenings on his way home," Truscott told him. "A lot of the local business community do. Usually just for a pint, maybe two. Show their face and then be off." He hesitated. "Occasionally he'd get caught up in a session and be there for the evening."

"Was that typical behaviour?"

"Two, perhaps three times a month."

"So, you wouldn't describe Mr Pascoe as a heavy drinker? In your opinion," he added, as Truscott appeared to hesitate.

"Robert," he said slowly, "if he was settled for the night, was someone you kept your eye on."

"Kept your eye on?"

"He was a lovely fellow," said Truscott. "Most of the time."

"Unless he'd been drinking heavily, you mean?"

"Not necessarily." Truscott shook his head. "With some people, yes, you know exactly how many pints it's going to take to flip that switch. When all of a sudden they're somebody else entirely. Robert did have his dark side, but you never really knew what would set him off. Sometimes he could be knocking them back all night long and leave with a wave and a smile. Others, he'd be only halfway down his first pint before turning on someone."

"He could become violent?"

"I never saw that," said Truscott. "But he could get argumentative and that might turn very nasty. And his language..."

Truscott shook his head again.

"On the night of his death, you took his car keys away from him. Was that a common occurrence?"

"It's a common occurrence for any of my customers whose motor's in the car park and who wants more than a couple of pints." He shrugged. "Sergeant Vanner's extremely hot on drink driving and he's not someone you'd want thinking about a license review."

"And that particular evening, Mr Pascoe began an argument and you asked him to leave?"

"It was with two blokes at the next table, down here from London. As soon as he started effing and blinding, I showed him the door. There were ladies in the bar and I wasn't having any of it."

"What exactly transpired between them?" asked the coroner. "The exact words, if you remember them."

As Truscott hesitated, the coroner reassured him with a small smile.

"I'm aware of how inappropriate the language of a late night bar room altercation can appear in a court of law," he told him. "But these are details pertinent to this inquest."

The two visitors, it transpired, had been noisy. Not so much boisterous as assertive, engaging in one of those carefully choreographed conversations which always seem less about communicating with each other than establishing mutual superiority over anyone within earshot.

"I had to go down to the cellar to change a barrel," said Truscott. "So I'm not really sure how the argument started."

But what Truscott had returned to hear was one of the visitors addressing Pascoe.

"You know, we in the advertising profession..."

"Oh, so it's a profession now, is it?" Pascoe had interrupted. "I must have missed that elevation. Tell me, exactly which oath does one have to profess in order to practise? The one about two cunts in a kitchen?"

"That had been it," Truscott told the coroner. "I had him up and out of the front door. Told him that if he wanted to wait outside then I'd call him a taxi, but he just shook his head and walked off."

"How inebriated do you believe he was at that point?" asked the coroner.

"He wasn't unsteady on his feet as he got up," said

Truscott. "But he'd had five or six pints and I'd guess on an empty stomach. That's the kind of thing which tends to hit you when you step outside. Especially into the evening air."

The coroner thanked him for his testimony and called Mrs Pascoe to the witness stand.

* * *

The coroner had found Mrs Pascoe something of a surprise, inasmuch as there was definitely more of the Mediterranean than West Country about her. In her youth she must have been a beauty, he thought, and in middle age was still striking. Above average height, slim and holding herself erect with a bearing that suggested self-confidence rather than assertiveness. Qualities which some men, the coroner knew, would find disconcerting but others a challenge.

"You'd retired for the night when your husband arrived home that evening?" asked the coroner, when the witness formalities had been completed.

"That's correct," said Mrs Pascoe.

"And you had separate bedrooms, which prevented you from noting his absence?"

"Yes."

"Had this been a long-term arrangement?"

"For a couple of years now." She shrugged. "I'm a light sleeper and an early riser. Robert liked to work late in his study and, as he got older, he found himself getting up during the night to use the bathroom. Also, if he'd had a nightcap he tended to snore... Separate rooms were a pragmatic solution. For the working week, at least."

"The working week?"

"Most weekends we'd share a room. And on short breaks and holidays." She gave a small smile. "This arrangement wasn't down to a lack of intimacy. We tried to get away together once a month or so, and have a week or two abroad in both summer and winter."

"I see." The coroner referred to his notes. "You and Mr Pascoe had been married for...?"

"Twenty-four years," she filled in for him. "In the mid-seventies, a friend and I went into partnership to buy a hotel in St Hannahs. Robert was handling the sale, which was how we met."

"Were you living locally at the time?"

Mrs Pascoe shook her head.

"No, in London. But my family had owned a holiday home in St Hannahs since before the war, and so I knew the area well."

The coroner began to question her further to the chronology of her marriage. He'd learnt that the inevitable awkward questions raised during an inquest felt far less accusatory or judgemental when arriving at the conclusion of a litany of fact finding. Bolts from the blue were tactics of prosecution and defence counsels. His route to the truth of the matter lay in keeping witnesses at their ease.

"We heard earlier," he told her, "that your husband would occasionally drink to excess. And could sometimes appear belligerent."

"On occasion," she said.

"Mr Truscott, landlord of *The Barque*, has stated that on the evening of your husband's death he became involved in an altercation in the bar there. And was asked to leave." He paused. "Would you say that your husband had a problem with alcohol?"

Mrs Pascoe considered.

"If you're asking whether Robert was an alcoholic, someone who needed a drink to function, then the answer is no. He'd call into *The Barque* most evenings but that was little more than social lubrication, networking with other local businessmen. And aside from a glass of wine with a meal and a nightcap if he'd been working late, he rarely drank at home." She paused. "The times when he did drink excessively, I always assumed, were down to business problems."

"You assumed?"

"Robert kept his business affairs separate from home life."

The coroner studied her.

"Isn't it unusual for a husband not to confide in his wife?"

Mrs Pascoe hesitated slightly before continuing.

"Five years ago, the estate agency found itself in financial straits. Robert assured me that the situation was temporary and asked me to sell my share in the hotel to bail the business out. Which I did. A year after that, Robert formed a partnership with a rival estate agency."

The coroner checked his notes again.

"This would be with Alan Bradshaw, his business partner at the time of his death?"

"Yes. Both Robert and Alan touted it as a mutually beneficial strategy. A pooling of resources, strength in unity, etcetera. "

"And this was a successful merger?"

Again, that slight hesitation as Mrs Pascoe appeared to consider.

"Two years ago, Robert told me that he and Alan had been offered an exceptional business opportunity involving the purchase and renovation of a local hotel. They had a line of credit in place, apparently, but were in need of a guarantor."

"To be clear, a guarantor for what, in effect, would be a loan?"

"Yes." Mrs Pascoe gave a tight smile. "I own an apartment in central London, which I inherited from my mother. Robert said that I needed to offer it as surety." Mrs Pascoe shrugged. "I refused."

"What was Mr Pascoe's reaction to this?"

"Oh, we had the full gamut of emotions at one point or another. But the upshot of it was that I remained adamant. And from then on, Robert never discussed any of his business dealings with me."

And also from then on, noted the coroner checking the dates scribbled on the pad in front of him, they began sleeping in separate rooms.

"Did this proposed enterprise go ahead?" asked the coroner.

"You'd have to ask Alan Bradshaw that," said Mrs Pascoe.

"But if it did, it's proceeding at a snail's pace for all the visible evidence of it."

"So, you'd be unaware if your husband found himself under pressure during the last days of his life?"

"Business pressure, yes. But..."

She let her voice trail off.

"Mrs Pascoe?" the coroner encouraged her.

"About a week before Robert's death, we'd been visited by a reporter," Mrs Pascoe continued.

"A reporter?" he prompted.

"Well, by profession. But the reason he wanted to see us, he'd explained on the telephone to Robert beforehand, was that he was working on a biography of James Carrington."

"The VC?"

"Yes." She hesitated again. "It was strange, really. Both Robert and I had connections to him, although quite independently. I'd once owned *The Grange* - or half owned it. It was the hotel I mentioned earlier, which I'd sold my share of to re-finance Robert's business."

"This was the house Captain Carrington built in St Hannahs shortly after the First World War?" asked the coroner, recalling that his own father had handled some legal matter for him at one time. A complex character by all accounts, erstwhile recipient of a string of military honours for valour, but with a private life probably best glossed over.

"Yes. And Robert's grandfather, Arthur, had served with him, he'd been the regiment's Adjutant. Immediately after the war they were involved in several business enterprises together and when Carrington decided to build a house in St Hannahs, Arthur moved down here to oversee the project."

"And, presumably, when it was completed he remained in Cornwall?"

"Yes. During that time he'd met Robert's grandmother and they'd fallen in love. Mary didn't want to leave the village where she'd lived all her life and so Arthur began to look for business opportunities in the area. Eventually, the story went, with a loan from Carrington he started the estate agency."

She appeared to be collecting her thoughts.

"Our assumption had been that this visit was purely for research and initially that seemed the case. He was interested in anything that I might have come across at the house - photographs, old paperwork to do with tradespeople, shopkeepers and servants. And the same from Robert - had his grandfather kept a diary, was there any surviving correspondence between Arthur and Carrington?

"But then he asked Robert if his grandfather had ever talked about his war service. Or of his specific duties in the regiment. Robert said that - like a lot of old soldiers - Arthur had been reticent about his wartime experiences. The family had heard a few anecdotes about life in the trenches, but nothing reflective of the horrors he must have seen.

"One of Arthur's duties as Adjutant, the reporter explained, was to sort through the effects of servicemen killed in combat before forwarding them on to their families. To remove anything that might seem inappropriate or likely to embarrass. At this point, the reporter produced a selection of photographs."

Mrs Pascoe gave a slight shake of her head.

"I imagine they'd be considered very risqué back then, nude studies of young women, but by today's standards they seemed relatively mild. In fact, the thing I found most shocking was that each one was bloodstained.

"This was quite an enterprise, the reporter told us. Arthur would remove these photographs from the possessions of dead servicemen and hand them on to his partner, a corporal who would re-sell them to freshly arrived recruits. And with the mortality rate being what it was on the Western Front, the same photographs could pass through their hands on an almost daily basis.

"This corporal kept a diary, according to the reporter. He took out a sheaf of what appeared to be photocopied exercise book pages and passed them over to Robert. 'Dates, names, times, and amounts,' he told him. 'And as you'll see, for the period the figures are substantial - certainly enough to get a fledgling West Country estate agency up and running.'"

"That is outrageous," bellowed Mrs Pascoe senior, rising to her feet incensed. "An absolute slander."

The coroner raised his hand for silence.

* * *

With the courtroom subdued and under the still glaring eyes of her mother-in-law, Mrs Pascoe resumed her testimony.

"Sex and death, he told us," she continued, "always make for good sales. But as this wasn't directly connected to Captain Carrington's story he'd be open to offers to skip over it. Could be to everyone's advantage, he said."

"And what was your husband's reaction to this?" asked the coroner.

"Oh, Robert threw him out, of course. And quite literally, he had him by the collar and frogmarched him to the front door." Again, Mrs Pascoe appeared to be collecting her thoughts. "I only mention it because..."

The coroner waited.

"Over the years, I've seen Robert in a lot of different moods," she said. "And until that afternoon, I would have thought probably the entire spectrum. But that was the first time I'd ever known him to be so... Wounded is perhaps the word I'm looking for. And vulnerable."

"You think this possibly contributed to his state of mind the evening he died?"

"If you mean do I believe my husband killed himself...?" She shook her head. "No. However dark things might have seemed to him, I don't see that as a route Robert would have taken. But if I were to speculate, I'd suggest that in the context of what he'd learnt about his grandfather, the events that played out in *The Barque* that night resonated with him in a far different manner than usual. That as a foreshadow of a scandal perhaps to come, he recognised those actions for the petulant response they actually were. And possibly saw other aspects of himself as if through the eyes of others..."

Her voice faltered.

"I think Robert arrived back home that night in a mood more reflective than angry, and that he may have intended to sit for a while to gather his thoughts before coming into the house. And then, with the drink..."

She let her voice trail away.

"Did this reporter get in touch with your husband - or yourself - again?"

"No. Or if he did, Robert chose not to tell me."

"Did he leave his contact details with you? I've a few questions for him myself," he added dryly.

"I have his card," she told him.

"Would there be anything else which you feel you need to add, Mrs Pascoe?"

"No."

"Then thank you. I'm aware of how painful you must have found this, but your testimony has been genuinely insightful."

She managed a weak smile and stepped down.

* * *

The coroner considered.

He'd intended to adjourn until the following morning, but in the light of what he'd just heard, he was now inclined to make that a week. Give them time to track down that reporter - it was a profession he'd scant respect for at the best of times, forever circling his courtroom like vultures. What the man had done might not have been illegal, but it was disgusting and the coroner relished the prospect of having him on the witness stand and holding his feet to the fire.

The other matter which concerned him was Robert Pascoe's computer. He'd had a quiet word with Sergeant Vanner before today's proceedings began and learnt that it still hadn't been returned from forensic examination. It was difficult to believe that an encrypted file in a folder marked Personal wouldn't have light to shine on Robert Pascoe's state of mind and he made the decision to contact the lab personally and put a rocket under them.

Also, as a result of Mrs Pascoe's testimony, he wanted the chance for a more detailed review of Alan Bradshaw's witness statement, Pascoe's business partner. And see what he could do about getting a look at their financial records before putting him on the stand.

Because what initially had been a vague nagging doubt was now an increasingly strong feeling that there was more to all of this than had first met the eye.

RICHARD

He wasn't wearing a navy blue blazer, or carrying a rolled up newspaper, but I had him pegged straightaway. For all the self-confident poise in the doorway, his slight hesitancy before stepping through into the hotel bar was - consciously or not - the acknowledgement of a last chance to cut and run.

For my part I'd kept to the arrangement, the distinctively pink *Financial Times* lay folded flat on the table and although I'd removed the sandy-coloured suede windcheater - it being warmer in here than I'd expected - I'd been careful it remained in plain sight on the bench seat beside me. He took in the room with a sweeping glance and as he made his way to the bar, his eyes might just have lingered in my direction a fraction longer than anywhere else.

A dozen or so obvious regulars were taking up most of the space at the counter. Men in late middle age, comfortable in tweed and calvary twill, sat on barstools while their wives - quilted gilets and chiffon - were scattered around a collection of small tables. Their accents weren't local, Yorkshire and the South East mostly, and now retired down here I'd gathered from fragments of conversation overheard whilst waiting. Their morning would have been taken up by bowls or golf, a scene played out in lounge bars along the coast from Dartmouth to Dover.

The far end of the room opened onto a terrace overlooking the harbour, where closely packed tables were crowded with holidaymakers. I'd picked a seat midway between, in a deserted expanse of shabby upholstery, worn carpets and scuffed table tops. Hand-drawn posters on the walls invited patrons to an "Eclipse Brunch" celebrating next week's solar eclipse, only visible in the UK across this stretch of southern coastline. More professional designs urged early booking for a "Millennium Banquet" on New Year's Eve, fully five months away, but the departure of the twentieth century was already something the entire country seemed geared up for. My own feelings were mixed, I was old enough for the idea of the year 2000 to still have a flavour of science fiction about it.

He brought his drink over to the table next to mine and sat down alongside rather than facing. Carefully judged, I thought, for soft conversation to remain between the two of us while not meeting each other's eyes.

"May I?" He indicated the newspaper on my table with a casual gesture of his hand.

"Sure," I told him, a couple of strangers engaging in bar room affability.

He opened the paper and appeared to study it.

"ms4912, I presume?" he asked dryly.

I nodded.

"Herostratus."

"Pleased to meet you," I said.

"You know," he continued, "I wish these chat rooms would simply allocate an identity instead of allowing one to indulge oneself. I do regret not following your example and opting for the utilitarian rather than the grandiose."

"A rose by any other name..." I shrugged.

"And speaking of other names," he said, "what should I actually call you? I'm presuming Michael or Mark, but perhaps you prefer 4912 for short?"

"We're supposed," I reminded him, "to maintain anonymity."

"Oh, stuff and nonsense." He gave a disdainful shake of his head. "Unless you were bloody fool enough to pay for that drink with a bank card, who's ever likely to know once today's over?"

"Richard," I told him.

"My, you're doubly cautious, aren't you? Peter, but let's not attract attention with a handshake." He raised his glass to his lips. "Have you come far today?"

"St Hannahs," I said. "Cornwall."

"Not too long a journey. Are you there visiting?"

I shook my head.

"We moved down a while back."

"We... You're married?"

"Yes." My throat had gone dry and I sipped my drink.

"Veronica."

* * *

It's 1970, and a housemate has brought me to an experimental theatre project at the Roundhouse. She has a vague connection to one of the cast members and we've been invited to a private party at a local pub afterwards. Veronica is a striking figure and I overhear someone ask who she is.

"That's Lee Munro's girlfriend," is the answer. The name is familiar, and when I hear, 'Oh, from The Hendersons', *it clicks. She'd been a child actress in a TV series back in the late fifties, early sixties and now, armed with that context, I realise she also played the leading role in the performance we've just sat through.*

In the eighteen months I've lived in London, my notion of queer life has come a long way from the stereotypes of the Midlands council estate where I grew up, camp hairdressers and grizzled bus conductresses. But as a couple, they still defy my expectations. Lee Munro does project an androgynous quality, but more waifish than butch. Veronica's features aren't delicate enough to be called pretty, but she exudes a sultry presence suggestive of a drift net of pheromones trailing behind her and - Sapphic lover or not - most of the girls in the room with boyfriends are keeping a wary eye on her.

* * *

"And is," he asked, "Veronica complicit in this?"

"No."

"I'm sure you have your reasons, but perhaps you should reconsider. A burden shared, in my experience, is considerably more than halved."

I gave a slight shrug but remained silent.

"Barbara," he said softly. "We know the area well and often stay at this hotel." He reached for his drink. "But the choreography begins with her spending this afternoon visiting friends who live locally."

For the first time, he turned and looked directly at me.

"Have you been here before?" With his free hand, he gestured at the room. "The hotel, I mean, not Lyme Regis."

I shook my head.

"Not what it was in the fifties, but fond memories count for a lot, you know." He took a sip of his drink. "And it's also one of the few places left in the town without bloody cameras everywhere."

I had the sense of someone who liked the sound of their own voice consciously reining themselves in and understood his nervousness. I'd even anticipated it, perhaps expected to share it, but the realisation that - as a first impression - I didn't actually like him much, went a long way to alleviating my unease. It made this more of an actual task than whatever else it might have become.

My continuing silence prompted him to turn and stare at me for a second time.

"Do you have children?" he eventually asked.

"No," I told him. "No, we don't."

* * *

Nothing in life prepares you for the loss of a child and nothing so tests a relationship. Past adversities pale into absurd insignificance and however compassionate the circle of friends and family that closes in around you, ultimately it is only the strength you find in each other that determines whether you're going to make it through this together.

Emily's service is a small, private ceremony at a North London crematorium.

"I don't want a fucking shrine," Veronica had said. The funeral announcement in the local newspaper read 'Family only, no flowers, donations to Save the Children', *Emily's favourite charity. But her close friends have been quietly informed they'll be welcome.*

It's an unhurried affair and more people than I expect have taken the opportunity to speak, quite movingly at times, of what Emily has meant to them and how much she'll be missed. Afterwards they linger and Veronica circulates, asking anyone not already invited to join us back at the house.

I notice a small, mousy looking woman during the service, perhaps the only person there I don't recognise. She is unfashionably dressed in a tweed suit, wears wire-rimmed spectacles and her hair is pulled tightly into a bun. I wonder if she might have been one of Emily's schoolteachers.

"Hello," I say to her outside. "Thank you for coming."

"I'm so sorry, Richard," she says, and moves in close to hug me. "I can't imagine what the two of you are going through."

It's the voice I recognise.

"Lee?"

As she steps back, Veronica joins us. She stares for a second and then gives a half choked sob as they embrace. And for the first time today, there are tears on Veronica's cheeks.

"I couldn't not be here," says Lee, softly. "But you've no idea how quickly something like this can turn into a circus once…"

She sighs and lets her voice trail off.

"Thank you," says Veronica. "Will you come back with us?"

"Best if I pass on that," Lee tells her. "Someone's bound to twig, and that shouldn't be what today is about."

"Okay." Veronica hesitates. "How long are you in London?"

"I'm not," says Lee. "I'm filming in Budapest." She gives a slight shrug. "But I went all prima donna on them, so they're shooting around me for the day - there's a jet waiting at Northolt."

"Oh, Lee!" Veronica seems to struggle with her emotions but, after a few seconds, regains her composure.

Lee reaches into her jacket pocket, pulls out a thick brown envelope and hands it to me.

"I've a bolt-hole down in Cornwall," she tells us, "that's totally set up for privacy. When you're on the other side of this, you should head down there." She rests her hand against Veronica's arm. "I know it seems impossible, but you have to begin to heal."

"Cornwall?" I ask.

"All the details you'll need are there." She indicates the envelope I'm holding. "A place called St Hannahs."

* * *

With a sigh, he shook his head.

"Forgive me," he said. "For prying. All our circumstances are unique and you're quite right to remind me that anonymity is key to this." He drained his glass. "Your first outing, correct?"

I nodded.

"My fourth, but previously taking your role, of course." He turned his head again, but this time it seemed more to study me than to stare. "You have to understand that your reaction to the actuality may differ greatly from what you've envisaged. But generally, the less nervous one is, the more smoothly things go."

"I'm okay," I said.

"You're sure of how to proceed?" he asked. "In detail?"

"Yes," I told him.

He laid the newspaper down on the table, casually checked that no one was looking over in our direction, and then slipped a room key with a brass plate attached into the fold. "Room 411."

He hesitated.

"Leave it thirty minutes or so, would you?" He gave a small smile. "There's a... ritual or two I need to go through first."

"Of course," I nodded.

He finished his drink, stood up and without looking back, left the room.

But I knew that whatever might transpire over the next hour, there was no way now I'd be able to get Veronica out of my head.

* * *

It hasn't been how I intended to spend the summer before my last year at art college, but...

The engineering firm Dad works for has a vacancy for a cleaner. Keeping the shop floor swept tidy of metal turnings and the lathes wiped clean of the milky coolant that finds its way everywhere. And once you've worked from one side of the factory to the other, it's time to start over. Still, the pay is surprisingly good and I learn never to underestimate the satisfaction which dull repetitive work can bring, particularly to a troubled mind.

Saturday morning is compulsory overtime. When the hooter blows at half twelve, it's down the pub for most of the blokes there. A pie and a pint and then off to heckle or cheer whichever of the city's two teams are playing at home today. I surprise Dad by joining them this week and myself by enjoying the easygoing camaraderie.

"Sounds like your mother has company," says Dad, as we come in through the front door and hear peals of female laughter. I follow him down the hallway and he pushes open the kitchen door.

"Here they are," smiles my mother. As I step inside, Veronica rises from her chair at the table.

"Hello Richard," she says, as shy and bashful as I've ever seen her. "Surprise."

* * *

A 'Do Not Disturb' sign hung from the door handle. Despite its archaic appearance, the key turned smoothly in the lock and I stepped through into a large suite. A sofa and two armchairs sat in the centre of the room, a TV in the corner and doors led off to presumably the bedroom and bathroom. French windows opened outward onto a balcony with views over the harbour to the bay beyond, sea cliffs and hills stretching into the distance.

One of the armchairs had been repositioned in front of the windows, but far enough back - given the bright noonday sunshine - to be out of sight from the street. From the doorway, I saw Peter's head leaning slightly to one side. Music played from a portable CD player, Mahler and surprisingly good sound quality from a machine so small.

A leather case, similar to the bags doctors carried in the days when they made house calls, was on the floor by the chair. Opening it, I removed a pair of latex gloves and pulled them on. I switched the music off, initially disconcerting as from this moment on the slightest sound has the potential to mean something. Then remembering *'The less nervous you are, the smoother things are likely to go'*, I gave a shrug, walked back over to the door and locked it. I crossed to the windows and drew the curtains. Then I turned to face Peter.

He'd removed his jacket and replaced his shoes with slippers. He seemed peaceful enough. There was no sign of movement and I reached out and felt for his wrist. No pulse, nor one in the carotid artery. To be doubly sure, I took a small mirror from the bag and held it to his mouth.

It remained unfogged.

I sat down on the sofa, allowed myself a calming breath and considered the scene.

* * *

I leave Veronica chatting to Mum and Dad while I go up to my room to change. We're going out for a walk, Veronica's suggestion.

And to talk.

I'm slipping my shoes on when there's a knock at the door.

"Come in," I say.

My mother steps into the room.

"I just wanted a quick word," she says.

"I'm sorry about this, Mum," I tell her.

"Don't be silly," she says, and then hesitates. "Veronica told me that the two of you have had an argument."

I nod.

"Is that why you came back home?"

I hesitate and then nod again.

"Yes."

"You know," she says, "the older you get, the more you realise that the things which seemed to matter so much in the past, everything you got so worked up about, wasn't worth a tinker's cuss when you look back on it all."

"It's complicated, Mum." I shake my head. Could two worlds ever be further apart? *"Really complicated..."*

"I know it seems that way now, love." She sighs. "We've been talking all afternoon. Not about you," she quickly adds, "just, well, nattering."

She comes over, sits down on the edge of the bed and takes my hand.

"She's a really lovely girl, Richard. I only want you to think carefully about things before making any decision."

"Don't worry, Mum." I force a smile. "I will."

* * *

He'd moved an occasional table to stand alongside the armchair. On it sat an empty tumbler and a bottle labelled a German brand of fruit schnapps, but wasn't. I took the glass into the bathroom, carefully swilling it out and giving it a good rinse before putting it back in the glassware cabinet. It had been emphasised that no more than two sips would *'prove effective'*.

The bottle went into the bag.

I lifted Peter out of the chair - I was expecting dead weight but it was almost effortless, perhaps the adrenaline - and laid him face down on the floor. The effects would be symptomatic of his doctor's expectations, I'd been told, so I guessed those would include a sudden convulsion and collapse.

I moved the armchair back to where the marks on the carpet suggested it had originally been placed and did the same with the small table. Switching on the TV I selected a news channel, setting the volume to just above audible. I reopened the curtains and unlocked the door, smudging the key's brass plate with my thumb and leaving it alongside the TV.

I gave the room one last searching look for anything jarring with the scenario I'd been given. Satisfied, I picked up the bag - this was mine now - and cautiously opened the door. There was no sign of movement in the corridor. Stepping outside, I pulled the door shut behind me. I removed the 'Do Not Disturb' sign, folded it in half and slipped it into my pocket.

As casually as I could manage, I headed for the stairwell.

* * *

We walk towards the Rec at the end of the road.

"How did you find me?" I ask.

She turns and stares.

"There are these things called phone books..." Shaking her head. "It's not like you're some secret agent gone to ground, is it?"

I try to think of something to say, but can't.

"So, this is where you grew up?" she asks eventually, looking around.

"Yes."

"I expected it to be more... northern."

"That's the thing about you Southerners," I tell her. "The other side of Luton and you think it's all tripe and whippets."

We get to the Rec and sit on the nearest empty bench.

I wait, pretty sure I know what's coming.

"I'm pregnant." Staring straight ahead, her face impassive.

"Veronica," I begin, but she cuts me short.

"No, let me finish..."

I remain silent

"I love you," she says. "And if that means I have to change what..."

"Veronica," I break in, "I know what you're going to say and," shaking my head, "we both know that's not going to work. And when that becomes obvious, you'll always blame me."

"So you don't even want to try?" There's both disbelief and bitterness in her voice as she turns towards me.

"There's a knotty old piece of northern wisdom," I tell her, "which says that what the head doesn't know, the heart doesn't grieve over."

"Wouldn't that be living a lie?"

"And what your proposing isn't?"

She's silent at that.

"It would work for me," I say. "I could settle for eighty percent of you if the other twenty wasn't being rubbed in my face all the time. Figuratively speaking."

She considers and then shrugs.

"Probably be closer to ninety," she says and I softly laugh.

She leans into me and I put my arm around her.

"Do you really think we can make this work?"

"As long as we keep things real between us, then yeah, the rest doesn't matter." I squeeze her shoulder. "In the end, don't most marriages come down to the two of you against the world?"

"Oh, so we're getting married, are we?"

"Aye lass, if thou's to do summat, then best do it proper."

We sit in silence for a while.

"I'm so sorry about what happened at Pembridge Villas," she says, carefully. "I'd only just found out, bloody hormones."

"It's okay," I say.

"I thought you might want me to get rid of it."

"Of course not." I give her another squeeze.

"That's what I was really worried about - when I came back that night. Then seeing you..."

She straightens herself up, reaches into her pocket for a tissue and wipes her eyes.

"And Richard - thank you."

I turn to her and she smiles at my quizzical expression.

"For not even thinking of asking, 'Are you sure it's mine?'"

* * *

"Lovely motor," said the attendant at the private car park on the other side of the harbour. "Bit of a money pit though, ain't they?"

I smiled and gave him a practised, rueful nod as I paid the fee.

"Got a mate in the trade, like," he continued, handing over my change, less than I'd calculated but I wasn't going to argue. "Always good for spares, if you're interested?"

"Could well be," I told him, experience suggesting this will be the quickest way to bring the conversation to an end. "You usually here, if I wanted a quote?"

He gave a solemn nod.

"Winter and summer, seven days a week," he declared and went on to inform me that whatever I might find myself in need of, from shock absorbers to a reconditioned gearbox 'always a worry on Jags that age', I wouldn't get a better price elsewhere. I left him with an amicable smile, strolled over to unlock the car and, after putting the bag in the boot, slipped in behind the wheel.

The thing about a classic car is that it rarely attracts resentment or envy in the way that a new Rolls or Mercedes does. Okay, it's a Jaguar, but it's also an old one and that does tend to leave people scratching their head about you. Who knew if it had been rescued from a scrapyard or lovingly tended for thirty years in a converted stable on a country estate? Mostly you got the benefit of the doubt.

Except this was neither.

First impression was of a Mark II, 3.8 litre Jaguar saloon,

British Racing Green paintwork, cream leather upholstery, walnut dashboard and all beautifully set off with wire spoke wheels. But to say that it had undergone modification would be something of an understatement.

I'd ordered it from G.K. Jones, a specialist in car conversions who ran his small but very select business from a village hidden away in the Yorkshire Dales. Gerry's talent was to take a British classic from the fifties or sixties, strip it back to bare metal and then rebuild it using the latest technology. Most vehicles of that era had suspensions that would either jar your teeth loose or leave you seasick and even the iconic sports models couldn't keep pace with the turbo-charged saloons now coming out of Germany and Japan. On retiring as a Formula One mechanic in the late seventies, Gerry had decided to fly the flag.

Integrated into the refurbished body shell was carbon fibre. Behind the dashboard were state-of-the-art electronics and shoehorned under the bonnet was a supercharged 5.2 litre engine, thirsty enough to make a necessity of retaining the original twin fuel tanks. And, for all the appearance of refined elegance, it could leave everything but a Porsche or Ferrari standing at a set of traffic lights and cruise the autobahns all day long at three kilometres a minute. Gerry also added his own personal touches - any souvenir hunter giving a tug at the silver cat on the bonnet would be startled by a sharp blast on the horn and the flash of a camera. A second attempt sent twenty thousand volts through it.

Needless to say, none of this came cheap. I could have bought a new Bentley for what it had set me back, but Veronica had been philosophical about it.

Sort of.

"No, I get it," she'd said. "A bit like making it with a movie star you'd mooned over as a kid and pretending all the face-lifts and fillers don't make any difference."

But now I needed to do something about getting rid of it, I didn't want Veronica being ripped off in a quick sale. The easiest solution would be to ask Gerry if anyone on his waiting list might be interested and offer him a chunky finder's fee.

Still musing, I pulled out of the car park and headed for home.

* * *

The meeting with Veronica's parents goes far better than either of us anticipate, which I suspect is down to their having more of a handle on their daughter's lifestyle than she realises. Relief is not entirely masked by Ronald and Marjorie's genuine delight at the prospect of becoming grandparents and while I might not seem much of a catch, they appear more than happy to cut their losses on that score.

But the following week, Ronald invites me to lunch and in its low-key way it's very much a version of 'Exactly what prospects can you offer my daughter?'. *Over the soup we discuss what had led me to art college, the main course is an exploration of the career opportunities awaiting me on graduation - for which he appears to have carried out extensive research - and dessert examines the obvious penury we were heading for. Over coffee, we each silently ponder the situation and by the time he's lighting our cigars, I've agreed to give up college and accept his offer of a job.*

"I'm not exactly sure what," he tells me. "But you're obviously a bright lad and so I'm certain we can come up with something that's of value to the business and of interest to you."

Ronald has a Chartered Accountancy practice, so I find that doubtful. But I'm shortly to have a wife and child to support and my most recent excursion into the job market had me sweeping a factory floor.

We keep the wedding quiet. Veronica invites Lee, but there are stories in the press which, according to Veronica, are down to a bitchy sister dishing out family dirt to a tabloid. 'I'm the last person you need there,' she tells us, before I've even had a chance to feel ambivalent about it.

While we are on honeymoon, Ronald ponders the quandary of what to do with me. He can't employ his son-in-law in a menial capacity, but with no qualifications other than a few A-levels in the arts, he also can't give me a significant role in his business without attracting accusations of nepotism.

On our return, Ronald asks me into the office.

Quite a few of his clients, he tells me, are in the pub trade. One of their constant bugbears is getting a regular stocktake done. Stocktaking, he explains, when combined with bar receipts, is the easiest way of checking whether any of the staff are on the fiddle. He's constantly being asked if he knows of anyone reliable offering this service.

What he proposes is to set me up in a stocktaking business - no professional qualifications are needed to do the job. He has a friend in the trade up in Leeds where I could spend a month doing an internship to pick up the basics, any local firms being unlikely to welcome potential competition.

I'd have an office here, he says, together with the use of his admin staff and so with no real overheads I'll be able to offer competitive rates to build the business up. Once it's turning over a steady profit, we can look at things again.

"Well anyway," he concludes, "give it some thought and ..."

"That sounds great," I say, cutting him off. Great isn't exactly the word I have in mind, but what he suggests doesn't involve being shut away in a room all day long with a bunch of clerks obsessed with football, birds and last night's telly. Being out on the road will probably come with its own levels of the mundane, but it does offer at least a degree of freedom. "Thanks Ronald," I tell him, offering my hand. "I really appreciate what you're doing for me here."

He masks his surprise with a slightly uncertain smile - I guess he's been expecting a harder sell - and stands up.

"Well," he says. "Let's see if we can find you a billet."

* * *

The traffic wasn't as heavy as I'd expected. Occasionally I found myself in a convoy trailing a tractor or caravan, but after a few miles they'd either turn into a lay-by or we'd come to a short stretch of dual carriageway. I'd crossed the Tamar back into Cornwall by mid-afternoon and pulled into our driveway just before five.

Cliff Dene is approached from a cul-de-sac, the last

building before a circular widening of the road allows anyone who's taken a wrong turn to rectify their mistake and be on their way. At first sight it doesn't seem much, a low slung bungalow sitting behind high stone walls, with parking space for five or six cars out front. From this vantage it appears almost windowless, giving the more astute passerby a clue that this is actually the back of the house and what they're looking at is the top level of a four-storey structure, hewn out of a wooded sea cliff in those faraway days when planning permission was barely a mote in a bureaucrat's eye.

Over the decades, the outer appearance has remained almost unchanged. It's a distinctive sight from the town below, a timbered Swiss chalet design that sits well amongst the surrounding trees. The entire top floor is an open plan living area with a wide veranda running around the house and in every direction the views are spectacular. On the floor below is the kitchen, dining room and a study, underneath that are three bedrooms and a bathroom. The ground floor houses a workshop - the original owner liked to tinker and we've still yet to decide what use we could put it to - and a laundry room.

There isn't really a garden, there's only so much you can terrace out of an almost sheer drop. What little needs keeping in check is done by fortnightly visits from the husband of our cleaner, both of whom we inherited from the previous owner.

Veronica's Land Rover was parked at the end of the driveway, together with a Volvo hatchback I recognised as belonging to Gillian Brown, a friend of Veronica's and a teacher at St Anne's, the local secondary school. I pulled up alongside and switched off the engine.

Before going inside, I took the schnapps bottle out of the leather bag and locked it away in the glove compartment. When I had the house to myself, I'd find somewhere safe to get rid of it, but in the meantime I didn't want it lying around.

With that taken care of and a sideways glance at Gillian's car in passing, I opened the front door.

* * *

Most marriages fall into a pattern after a while and ours is no exception, except perhaps of a fuzzier nature than most. In the early days we'd both spend a fair amount of time away from home, myself travelling, Veronica visiting friends and Ronald and Marjorie more than happy to play doting grandparents with Emily.

There is no actual conspiracy of silence here, no point at which Veronica and I sit down to either establish ground rules to be followed or boundaries to be constrained by. Silent mutual consent seems to be working just fine and so leaving well alone becomes our modus operandi. 'I'll be away this weekend' *or* 'I'm out tonight' *would be met with an easy acknowledgement and the understanding that only an emergency would warrant a phone call.*

And mostly it did all work.

* * *

As I came in through the front door, I heard voices and laughter from the veranda. I crossed the room and stepped outside. Veronica and Gillian were sitting side by side, on chairs angled to keep the sun off their faces without sacrificing the view over the harbour. A wine bottle sat in an ice bucket on a small table, between two almost empty glasses.

"Ah, home is the hunter," said Gillian.

"Hi babe," smiled Veronica. "Good day?"

I nodded as she picked up the wine bottle, tipped the remaining contents into Gillian's glass and started to rise from her chair.

"It's okay," I told her, reaching out to take the bottle from her. "I'm going inside to fix myself a drink."

"So," smiled Gillian, "good to see you have him well trained."

I stepped back into the living room and found myself wondering if Gillian had any idea of what she might be getting into here.

Because Gillian was one of those women who, for all of their continual dismissive talk of 'men', do actually seem lost without one. In her case, it was a pleasant enough solicitor who appeared to live most of his life either on the golf course or inside his own head. But she wouldn't be the first *hausfrau* Veronica had taken a shine to who - flattered by the attention - found herself entranced into playing with fire. The thing was, Veronica knew all about shaking up someone's world and so nor would she be the first to get her fingers burnt.

I opened the drinks cabinet, took a beer from the fridge compartment and another bottle of wine. Back out on the veranda I motioned to fill their glasses, but Veronica reached out for the bottle.

"It's okay, I'll do it," she said. "By the way, Alan Bradshaw rang earlier, asked if you'd give him a call." I noticed Gillian's glass got far more of a top up than hers and I also realised that while Gillian was quite tipsy, Veronica wasn't. "Said he needed to see you about something."

"Oh, Mr St Hannahs himself," said Gillian languidly. "You are honoured."

"Okay, I'll ring him back." I nodded towards the ice bucket. "What's the celebration?"

"Gillian's promotion came through," said Veronica.

"Well, the actual interviews were held today, they're required to open up the position to external candidates." Gillian gave a lazy shrug. "But it's been pretty much rubber stamped."

I remembered Veronica telling me that for the last six months Gillian had been Acting Head of her department, following a colleague's resignation through illness.

"Congratulations," I told her, raising my glass. She gave me a smile - and an almost mocking imitation of my toast - before placing her drink down on the table and staring out over the bay.

"This view," shaking her head. "Could you ever get blasé about it?"

Deciding that any host obligations had now been duly fulfilled, I stood up.

"I'd better phone Alan, find out what he wants."

"Okay," said Veronica, "see you in a bit."

Gillian continued gazing out to the horizon.

* * *

We'd first met Alan and his wife Safranka at the local Chamber of Commerce's annual dinner and dance. It had sold out months prior to our arrival in St Hannahs, but the evening before it was being held we'd arrived home to find a message on our answerphone from the Chairman. Firstly, he'd like to welcome us into their community, it was always good to see fresh faces. And secondly, they'd had a cancellation for tomorrow evening's event, a death in the family unfortunately, but which meant they had two tickets available if we'd care to attend. He left a number to call.

"Word's got around that we bought this place for cash," said Veronica. "And donated to the Sure Start programme and Art Gallery. So, they figure we're loaded and probably daft with it."

"I take it we're going?" I asked.

"Oh, definitely," she grinned.

I rang back, exchanged pleasantries, paid by credit card and was informed that we would be sharing a table with a Mr and Mrs Bradshaw and a Mr and Mrs Carstairs.

"Seems odd," I said to Veronica, putting the phone down. "Getting a heads up on who you'll be sitting next to."

"A place like this," said Veronica, "probably has bad blood going back generations. Throw in free booze and they'll have taken more care over the seating than at a mob wedding."

It was the following morning that we'd discovered our cleaner Emblyn's talent for tapping into St Hannah's underbelly. Mention a name, we learnt, and you had a Stasi like overview in the time it took to Pledge and polish a coffee table.

"Mrs Carstairs, nothing's ever good enough for her and he's no better, my Edward says. Londoners they are - nothing wrong with that," a quick glance up at us, "but you can't expect things to be the same and if you did why bother coming here?

"Alan Bradshaw, he moved from up country about ten year ago. Worked for an estate agent in Truro at first, then set up on his own. Did very well and no surprise there, he's someone who can always turn on the charm when he wants to. But a lot of people think he's too pushy by far. His wife's foreign, they only got married a couple of years ago, and in one of them countries on the news where there's been all that fighting. His partner, Mr Pascoe, took his missus out there, but no one else went. The photos were in the Gazette, two pages of 'em and it all looked very romantic, very gypsyish if you know what I mean?"

"Wonder what she's saying about us," said Veronica as we finished getting ready to leave that evening. *"They do seem very nice, but you'd never believe what was in her bedside drawer and I can't imagine what she'd do with it."*

* * *

The dinner was being hosted at St Hannahs Golf Club. Because there hadn't been time to send our tickets by post, we had to wait at Reception to collect them and so our fellow diners were already seated as the waiter led us over to the table.

"Hello, I'm Alan Bradshaw and this is my wife, Safranka." He half rose and leant over to shake hands. Alan was tall, I guessed in his late thirties and with one of those boyish faces which time was going to bleach rather than age. There was a Yorkshire accent which life in the south hadn't taken much of the edge off, but at least it didn't have the tenor - as is often the case - of being a statement in itself.

His wife looked to be maybe ten years younger and was by far the best looking woman in the room. 'Foreign' had said Emblyn and Slavic would be my guess. Sharp cheekbones, a generous mouth, wide-apart eyes and her hair was pulled tightly back from her face before falling in ringlets over her shoulders.

"Harold Carstairs," said the other man. "And my wife, Margaret."

Introductions complete, Veronica and I took our seats.

"I believe," said Alan, "that you know my business partner's wife? Claudia?"

"Yes," Veronica nodded, adding dryly, "We go way back."

* * *

A friend has an invitation to a party over in Notting Hill. At the house, he tells me, of the actor Don Mayberry.

36

"Well, he doesn't actually live there himself," he continues. "But he owns the place."

This house is rented out, apparently, to people involved in the arts and theatre. Aidan McShane, who is beginning to make a name for himself as an artist, has a studio in the basement and Lee Munro also has a room there.

"So, it's bound to be an interesting evening," he says.

Don Mayberry's star is definitely on the way up. In the early sixties he'd been one of those jobbing actors whose face you regularly saw on TV, although would be hard pressed to put a name to. But over the last few years he's appeared in a couple of Hollywood movies that, while not being box office hits, have received critical acclaim. And recently he starred in a TV series about London's gangland, containing scenes of such sadistic violence that questions were actually raised in Parliament.

But as the evening progresses, any celebrity spotters are having a thin time of it. McShane is a no show, nor has there been any sign of Lee Munro. But in the kitchen, seemingly unsteady on her feet with drink, is Veronica.

"She's been away filming for the last month," I hear her say in tones of discontent to another girl, who is looking at her with an expression midway between sympathy and concern. "And now she's off to bloody Cornwall for the week, with the Contessa," she continues disparagingly.

"They're only friends, darling," her companion reassures her, rolling a rich Sloane Ranger cadence around her mouth. "They've known each other for yonks."

"She spends so much time over there, she might as well move in," Veronica snorts. Then, lowering her tone, asks, "You don't have any blow, do you?"

Moving closer and catching her eye, I reach into my pocket and take out a chubby spliff.

"Well," she smiles, "hello there."

I suggest we go out into the garden, but she shakes her head.

"Don's got a thing about dope," she says. "And you never know when he's going to show up. We should go to my room."

"You live here?"

"Yes - I hope you've brought an oxygen mask with you."

She isn't kidding.

We're both breathing heavily by the time we arrive at her door, the final narrow flight of stairs at an almost vertical angle. The attic rooms had originally been the servants' quarters, I guess, and this is reflected by the room's size, more like a large cupboard. But somehow she's squeezed in a small wardrobe, dressing table and single bed, the only place to sit. She flops down with a sigh and pats the coverlet alongside her.

"You were at the Roundhouse a while back," she says, reaching for an ashtray by the side of the bed and placing it on the floor between our feet. "And then afterwards at The Adelaide." She's staring now, just the hint of a smile on her lips. "You were checking me out."

"That night," I tell her, lighting the joint, "pretty much everyone was checking you out."

I take a quick hit and offer it to her.

"I'm..." I begin, but she cuts me off.

"You're Richard," she says. "You're an art student and you share a house in Peckham. You've had a couple of girlfriends since you've been in London and word is you broke up with each of them when you thought things were getting too serious." She shrugged. "I checked you out too... Well, girl talk, I was sorry you didn't come over."

I take the joint back from her.

"I thought that you were with..." I let my voice trail off, my uncertainty is genuine.

"So did I. But it seems that with Lee, when we're together we are, but when we aren't, we're not." She gives a shrug. "I suppose I can live with that."

"Right," I say.

"The thing is," she smiles, and her eyes lock onto mine, "could you?"

"Yes," I tell her. "Yes, I could."

"Good." She takes the spliff from my fingers and places it in the ashtray. *"Because I've just stopped doing serious, too."*

She puts her hands on my shoulders and pushes me down across the bed.

* * *

"Claudia's aunt died on Thursday." Alan slowly shook his head. "They've had to go up to Kent."

"Oh, I'm sorry to hear that," said Veronica, her tone suddenly sombre. "I remember her talking about her aunt and uncle. They were all the close family she had, I believe."

"So this is...?"

I indicated mine and Veronica's places, and Alan nodded.

"Anyway," he said, "let's wish them well, without dwelling."

We all clinked glasses, the Carstairs with a slight hesitation. In the short time we'd been sitting there I'd been picking up on body language and I guessed the Carstairs were in the 'too pushy by far camp' regarding Alan Bradshaw.

"You're in computers, I heard?" asked Alan. "Or is that just Chinese whispers?"

"It was a business that spearheaded remote data gathering," I told him. "I cashed in my share a while back."

"All a complete mystery to me," Alan sighed. "I simply nod along when the kids in the office start explaining it all and hope I don't get found out." He turned to Harold Carstairs. "Do you understand any of this stuff, Harold?"

"Computers?" He gave an almost disdainful shrug. "I don't need to, I have a brain."

"You've a pair of legs, too," smiled Veronica, "but if you have to go to London, you don't walk there."

It wasn't the response he'd been expecting, and he narrowed his eyes at her as his wife pursed her lips. But before he could say anything, Alan turned to Veronica.

"So, how do you and Claudia know each other?"

"She's been a friend of Lee Munro's since they were teenagers." Veronica picked up her glass and took a sip. "In 1970, I was living in a house owned by Don Mayberry. He rented rooms out to actors, artists, writers."

"And which of those were you?" asked Margaret Carstairs.

"Oh, I liked to think of myself as more of a muse," Veronica smiled back at her. "A handmaiden of the imagination, seeding inspiration and comfort."

Under the table I tapped her ankle, just lightly, with my shoe.

"Don was away in Hollywood for most of that year," she continued, "and Lee was managing the place for him. We met, seemed to hit it off," I gave her ankle another tap, "and she offered me a job as her Personal Assistant."

* * *

Veronica and I aren't exactly on/off throughout that summer - it's more always on, but not always there. She'll regularly disappear for a few days, 'Actress Lee Munro and her PA Veronica Hewitt arriving at Heathrow yesterday morning', *might be the caption for a quarter page photo in the Daily Sketch and times are still naïve enough for that to be taken at face value.*

Veronica doesn't so much run the gamut between helpless vulnerability and ferocious passion as blend the two into a heady mix, whose effect on me I could almost believe reeks of necromancy. 'Can't live with her, can't live without her' *may be a smug aphorism, but the reality becomes slow torture.*

The twist is that I don't even regard Lee as a rival, certainly not in the same way that I would another guy, plus I do get what Veronica sees in her. She's smart, funny, genuinely self-deprecating about her celebrity status and if it weren't for the minor detail that she might be giving my girlfriend a better time in bed than I am, I'd probably like her too.

I'm supposed to be going home for the summer holidays, the student house I share is being redecorated. But I want to stay in London and so Veronica suggests moving in with her until the new term begins. Mostly, I have the place to myself, a TV series Lee has a role in proves popular enough to be dubbed into several European languages and it now seems that every other week is a promotional junket to France, Germany or Italy.

All in all, it's not a situation that lends itself to stability...

* * *

"How long were you working for her?" Safranka's English was heavily accented, but her delivery fluent.

"For about a year. Until Richard," she jerked her thumb in my direction, "decided to make an honest woman of me."

Safranka grinned, but Margaret Carstairs eyes narrowed to slits. Fortunately, the waiter appeared at that point with the first course. Amid the distractions of who was being served what, the impetus of the conversation had been reset and Alan now steered it through a fairly neutral preamble of St Hannahs life, with only the occasional barb breaking the Carstairs' passive aggressive facade.

After coffee, the couple wasted no time in departing and the atmosphere around the table noticeably relaxed.

"So," asked Alan, offering me a cigar, "how did you get started in computers?"

* * *

"It's called a TRS-80," I tell Ronald, who is staring bemused at the machine. "It's a computer."

"Exactly how much," he asks, "have you paid for this thing?"

"Just over a thousand," I tell him.

"Good Lord!" he exclaims, which is about as vehement as he ever gets. "To do your typing?"

"Ronald," I say to him, "sit down. I want to show you something."

Still shaking his head, he lowers himself down into the chair alongside mine. I slide a floppy disk into the drive and wait for the program to load.

"This," I tell him, as the whirring ceases and the logo appears on screen, "is called a spreadsheet."

It takes less than twenty minutes for him to be convinced, staring fascinated as I amend a figure and the entire screen recalculates.

"By simply retyping a figure into the calculation," I explain, "you've actually completed that revision through to the final total.

And when you've finished, it's immediately ready to print out."

"Would it be possible," asks Ronald, never slow to catch on, "to have the previous stocktake figures, and the takings, in that calculation?"

"To show projected sales totals against the actual ones? And to highlight discrepancies over a given percentage variation?" I smile. "Sure."

"It would be important to get in quick with something like this," says Ronald carefully. "Package it up as a fixed price service and perhaps approach the large brewery chains with it. Those with tenant landlords."

"I was thinking of doing a course on it," I say. "Get myself up to speed…"

"No," interrupts Ronald, sharply. Then he softens his tone. "It would all be too much to take in quickly, you'd either become bogged down or sidetracked. This is the kind of expertise you need to buy in."

He considers and then indicates the computer.

"Where did you hear about this?"

It had been through Billie, our bookkeeper. Her sister worked for a paper import agency on Fleet Street, bringing in newsprint for the national dailies. The founder's son, Geoff, had recently taken over the business and was a new broom sweeping clean - typewriters replaced by word processors and sales ledgers with spreadsheets. I'd tentatively asked if I could take a look at their systems and he'd been more than welcoming, casting himself in the role of proud harbinger to a new technological dawn and happy to spend a morning walking me through it all. I'd bought the TRS-80 that same afternoon, from a branch of Tandy's on Tottenham Court Road, and had spent the weekend driving myself crazy setting it all up.

"Have a word with this Geoff," says Ronald, after I explain. "Find out who put it all together for him. Then try to get a quote from the company to do the same here."

Which we do.

Then the problem we have, if you can call it a problem, is that Ronald does sell our services to the brewery chains and we are about to be swamped with work.

"We're going to have to start taking people on," I tell him, "and maybe even find larger offices."

Ronald gives me a smile and shakes his head.

"The likeliest outcome here," he continues, "is that this business will become very successful. Taking on more staff might seem the obvious move, but eventually - I'd guess about five years down the road - our largest clients are going to start reviewing the service they're receiving from us and arrive at the conclusion that it's something they could do just as well themselves. And probably for quite a bit less. At which point the plug gets pulled, leaving us with a redundant workforce and a lot of outgoings. Trust me, you wouldn't believe the number of firms I've seen swamped by their own success."

"So what do we do?" I ask.

"Create a franchise company. We'll provide a package to self-employed individuals. The computer, software, a week-long training course and a core client list of pubs in their area to prime the pump."

"You think people will go for it?"

"I have it on good authority," says Ronald, "that the Government is about to introduce what they're calling an Enterprise Allowance Scheme. That anyone who sets up a business with a thousand pounds capital can claim a grant of forty pounds a week for the first twelve months."

He smiles.

"I'd say that with some selective marketing, this could provide a very lucrative income stream, with very little in the way of liability if circumstances suddenly change."

And Ronald, as ever, is absolutely right.

* * *

"By the early nineties," I told Alan, "we were ready to sell. We'd recently incorporated hand-held pocket computers - called Psion Organisers - into the stocktaking franchise and were linking them directly to computer databases via telephone modems. Around the same time, the Government introduced new legislation on the breweries."

"Banning them from owning pub chains," said Alan, and I nodded.

43

"They had to sell off their existing interests and were cash heavy, looking to diversify. We caught their attention because they saw what we were doing as both a link to a business sector they understood well and an investment in future technology. We'd had a few tentative offers before receiving one that we really couldn't turn down."

I leant back in my chair.

"All about being in the right place at the right time," I told him. "Don't get the idea that I'm any kind of entrepreneurial guru."

"I'm sure you're not giving yourself enough credit there," he smiled, but he did leave it at that.

* * *

In small communities, you rarely have much choice over who you'll spend time socialising with, but I think the four of us would have become friends wherever we'd met. Certainly Safranka - Saffy - and Veronica hit it off from the beginning.

She was in the process of setting up a business of her own, a self-catering holiday letting agency.

"I work in industry before," she told us. "Is money for old rope. Holidaymakers pay you to find somewhere to stay, someone with empty house pays you to find someone to stay there. You make brochure and money pours in - you have to be idiot for it not to."

The evening finished with an invitation to a party the Bradshaws were holding the following week.

Veronica had been a bit chary about the possibility of a close encounter with Robert Pascoe's wife, the infamous *Contessa*, and I felt her stiffen when the couple arrived a few minutes after we did. But Claudia appeared genuinely pleased to see us and later, when Veronica and I slipped outside to share a cigarette, she joined us on the patio.

"I'm sorry that we didn't get to know each other that well, back then," she said, obviously aimed more at Veronica than myself. "But life was moving at such a pace in those days."

After a couple of seconds, Veronica nodded.

"Yes," she said. "Most of the time I didn't know whether I was coming or going myself."

"Safranka and I are meeting for lunch tomorrow, down at *The Barque*," continued Claudia. "If you're free, you'd be more than welcome to join us."

"I... Yes, thank you," said Veronica. "I'd like that."

Her husband, Robert, I was less sure about. On arrival he'd been charm itself, but as the evening wore on - and the more booze he was putting away - the geniality grew more argumentative and it was noticeable that people were starting to steer clear.

"Time to go, I think," I heard one woman say to her companion and he nodded. Then, seeing I'd overhead, she raised an eyebrow and said softly, "Don't get into an argument with him."

Veronica appeared with our coats.

"Thank you for a lovely evening," she said to Alan and Saffy, just as the sound of breaking glass came from the kitchen. Alan excused himself and Saffy gave a slight shake of her head.

"Make good your escape," she smiled.

"Are you going to be okay?" Veronica asked her.

"Sure - nothing we haven't handled before." She shrugged. "Our cross to bear, apparently."

"I gather it's a regular occurrence," Veronica told me in the car, driving home. "There's something like a thirty-minute window between him trying to pick a fight and passing out, but nobody bothers sticking around for that to happen anymore."

"And Claudia...?"

"Who knows," she said, turning her head towards me with a wry smile, "what's really going on in any marriage?"

* * *

Veronica and Saffy began to meet regularly for lunch.

It quickly became apparent that Saffy intended to be more than simply a figurehead for the letting agency, despite it presenting far greater challenges than placating property owners over broken crockery. Noise complaints from a neighbouring holiday cottage led to the interruption of a porn movie shoot while, at the darker end of the scale, holidaymakers arrived at a barn conversion to discover a farmer had resolved his wife's infidelities with a shotgun.

"At least you're not bored," Alan had said that evening to his white faced and still shaking wife, handing her a tumbler filled to the rim with vodka.

But what really impressed Veronica was Saffy's adeptness at dealing with local government officials. She'd asked Veronica to go along with her the first few times, worried her language skills might not be up to the intricacies of planning regulations governing farm buildings' extensions in conservation areas.

Somewhat reluctantly Veronica agreed - half expecting a mishmash of flirting and flattery directed at a bemused building inspector - and returned home taken aback by Saffy's adaptiveness.

"In her way, she's actually quite brilliant," Veronica told me.

Saffy displayed a genuine talent for pulling out an overview from a mass of legal documentation and presenting it to a planning sub-committee as beneficial to all concerned. And word started to get around that if you had a holiday property to let, then Saffy Bradshaw was someone who'd look after you.

Veronica herself had displayed a definite restlessness following our arrival St Hannahs, until eventually she began volunteering at the vicar's Sure Start program. Lee was a patron and I guessed had twisted her arm into becoming a presence when she wasn't around. But a couple of mornings a week had now become most mornings and it really did seem to have given her a sense of purpose.

Which left me feeling a lot less worried about what was about to come down the line.

* * *

"Hi Richard."

"Alan, what can I do for you?"

"Well, in all honesty, I was hoping for a favour." Alan

hesitated. "Are you free tonight? Could I buy you dinner?"

I'd considered defrosting something from the freezer, assuming Veronica and Gillian would be heading out with plans of their own. So Alan's invitation, stacked up against an evening of solitary dwelling on a bizarre day, should have been a slam dunk. And would have been, if today's events hadn't been entirely triggered by the last favour I'd done Alan Bradshaw.

Well, whatever it was, I could always say no.

"Sure," I told him. "Where were you thinking?"

"What about the Golf Club?" suggested Alan. "You can usually find a quiet spot for a chat. But look, I'll pick you up from home and run you back afterwards. Say in about thirty minutes?"

"Okay," I said. "See you then."

* * *

The day after Robert Pascoe's death, Alan Bradshaw had arrived at my house carrying a plastic Tesco shopping bag.

"I was really sorry to hear about Robert," I said, as I led him through to the living room. "Do they know what happened?"

He shook his head as we both sat down.

"No, but it's looking like an accident. At least, no one's found a note yet." He hesitated. "Is Veronica here?"

"No, she's gone into town."

"I was hoping you might do me a favour?"

"Sure," I told him.

He reached into the bag and took out a laptop computer.

"You know all about these things, right?"

I nodded.

"This is - was - Robert's. It's going to have to go to the police, but would you take a look at it first?"

"Take a look at it?"

He hesitated.

"Robert was insured," he said. "By the business. We both are. So that if anything happened to either of us, we could buy the other's share from the wife."

"Okay...?"

47

"The policy has a suicide clause in it." Alan slowly shook his head. "If Robert deliberately closed that garage door with the engine still running, then it's worth bugger all."

"Why would he have done that?"

"No reason at all that I can think of, but who knows? The thing is, if he did, I'm going to have to make some moves and pretty smartish. Getting finance in place for starters - unless he and Claudia had some big time marital problems no one knew about, the assumption's bound to be that the business is in trouble."

He indicated the laptop with his hand.

"Robert took that thing with him everywhere…" His voice trailed off. "If I've got a shitstorm blowing in, business wise, I could use a heads up."

"Okay," I said. "Have you had a look at it yourself yet?"

"I wouldn't know where to start." He shook his head. "I don't even know how to switch it on."

"Good," I told him. "It's difficult to do that without leaving some kind of trail."

"Which you can't delete?"

"You can. But then that opens up a whole new set of questions for whoever might examine it."

"Right. You mean, like something that's been wiped clean of fingerprints?"

"Exactly. But there are ways around that." I hesitated and then nodded. "Sure, leave it with me."

"Any idea how long it's likely to take?" He shook his head, apologetically. "I wouldn't want to seem to be rushing you, but I'm guessing someone will be asking about this sooner rather than later."

"Depends how much stuff there is to sort through." I shrugged. "I'd guess that if I don't come across something in twenty-four hours, then it's either buried too deep or there's nothing there."

"Okay." He stood up. "Thanks, I really appreciate this."

"Could you put it back in the bag?" I asked. "There's a

reason for your fingerprints to be on it, but not mine."

"Of course," he said, bending over and slipping it into the shopping bag.

"I'll call you if I find anything," I told him.

* * *

Discipline in the nineteen fifties leans toward the swift and sharp. The slipper, strap or cane are regarded as little more than a tug on the reins of a wilful spirit straying from the straight and narrow. Administered for the most part by those who a decade earlier were crossing minefields under enemy gunfire or huddled in Anderson shelters as high explosives tumbled out of the sky, juvenile angst receives short shrift.

We kids do sense flashes of ulterior motive, although God help anyone trying to untangle the jumble of PTSD, sadism, or possibly worse in play. A Miss Bright at primary school is the very devil with a steel edged ruler and her heavy breathing as she works the back of your thighs isn't entirely down to the effort of holding you in place across her lap. Other perils are even more insidious, but we have herd instinct regarding what to be wary of, that being singled out as favourite or victim carries equal jeopardy.

But mostly you take it in your stride. You get caught, you get belted, you move on.

When you really have to worry is when you get caught and don't get belted. When the adults in your life hold low conversations about you in other rooms and give you looks more pitying than angry.

* * *

A few months earlier, Veronica's laptop died on her. Backup, it appeared, had been regarded as something of a chore and so I contacted Vic, an IT contractor who'd set up our remote data gathering software. Like most people in that line of work - who were good at what they did - he was a bit of an odd fish, but these were skills it was always handy to have just a phone call away. We'd stayed in touch and I was careful to remember him every Christmas.

Vic had put a couple of cables in the post and when

they arrived talked me through salvaging Veronica's photos, correspondence, etc. It was a process still fresh enough in my mind to apply to Robert's laptop.

I carried the Tesco bag into my study, opened a drawer and took out a pair of thin cotton gloves. Vic had insisted I should wear these whenever I had the back of the laptop off, to prevent moisture from my skin getting into the circuitry. Four screws held the rear panel in place and once removed, it easily lifted away. I'd assumed the cables Vic sent me would be generic and a glance at the connection between the laptop's hard drive and motherboard seemed to confirm that.

I unscrewed the back casing from my desktop PC, and once it booted up I went into the date and time settings. I changed the system date to three days ago, and then I plugged one of Vic's cables into the same internal socket I'd used for connecting to Veronica's laptop. Then I unplugged the cable from Robert's hard drive and replaced it with the cable connected to my PC. There was one more cable connected to the laptop's hard drive, the power supply, and I replaced that with Vic's second cable, which had a wall socket transformer at the other end. I flicked on the socket switch and opened up Windows Explorer on my PC. A new entry was on the directory tree, Robert's hard drive.

PCs keep system information in ROM - read only memory - in a chip on the motherboard. Programs and data were stored on the hard drive. Hopefully, what I'd just done had bypassed Robert's system chip and any changes I might make would be dated three days ago, when Robert was still alive. It was unlikely to fool any truly forensic examination, but I guessed a resident IT nerd at Truro nick wouldn't be doing much more than skimming it for drafts of a suicide note, emails and bank records.

I took the gloves off and began pecking at the keyboard, working my way down the directory tree.

* * *

The whole thing begins with an episode of Jungle Jim, *a*

teatime children's TV show. The series features Johnny Weissmuller updating his Tarzan role to that of a white hunter, presumably because now in his fifties a loincloth doesn't present him in as flattering a light as it used to. But mostly the same recurring themes are in play, rescuing shapely but naïve blonds from the clutches of dastardly villains with Germanic accents, aided by loyal natives.

This week's episode features Jim freeing himself from captivity by using a broken bottleneck as a magnifying glass, focusing the sun's rays on the ropes that bind him and burning through them. This strikes both Michael Jones - my current best friend - and myself as somewhat fanciful, and so we decide to put it to the test.

The council estate where we live, still expanding but already the largest in Europe, is far enough from the city centre to border open countryside. A strip of dense gorse, perhaps half a mile long and a couple of hundred yards deep, runs between the edge of the estate and what is known locally as the Brook, a narrow stream which also forms part of the boundary between the city and the county.

As well as being a natural adventure playground for us younger children - an absolute labyrinth construction of pathways has been created over the years - the Scrubs, as this area is called, likewise provides cover for the amorous experimentations of teenagers. While these activities are mainly confined to the hours of darkness, it's not unknown on a summer evening to stumble across two or three boys with a sullen faced girl and be told "Keep movin', youth". *Which of course we do, but the older we get the more frequently we sneak back, ready to risk a beating as we peek through the undergrowth, trying to make sense of what we are watching.*

Michael and I find our way deep into the Scrubs, carrying an empty glass Dandelion and Burdock bottle and an old newspaper. We gather scraps of loose gorse and mix them with strips of torn up paper until we have a mound about six inches in diameter and three inches high.

"Right," says Michael, picking up the bottle and turning it in his hand. We aren't exactly sure what to do with it, unlike with a magnifying glass you can't actually see the stream of sunlight being

focused. We take it in turns, holding the bottle above and to one side of our little nest of kindling.

"See," says Michael eventually, "I told you it..."

With a sudden whoosh!*, the pile ignites.*

Startled, Michael drops the bottle, which lands on top of the flames, scattering embers in every direction. One large piece reaches a densely packed section of gorse. Tinder dry, it immediately begins to smoulder. I stand up and stamp at it with my foot, then leap back as it bursts into flames. Which, within seconds, are as tall as I am.

Michael and I look at each other.

"Run!" he says.

By the time we reach the road, tracing a furtive path to emerge as far from the spreading inferno as logistically possible, a large crowd has already gathered. Thick black smoke is billowing into the sky and flames are dancing across the top of the gorse. As we scuttle away, we hear the distant sound of sirens.

The blaze is quickly extinguished, the Brook an immediate source of water for the Fire Brigade's pumps, but not before a good half of the Scrubs is reduced to a flat, blackened wasteland. And it's definitely a mistake to be the only two kids on the estate not watching the Fire Brigade deal with the fire, although it's actually an aunt of Michael's who's noticed us scurrying away from a scene which everyone else is heading towards.

Michael's father brings him around to our house that evening.

Once both sets of parents have established that what happened isn't down to malice or wanton destruction - 'Daft pair of buggers' is my father's verdict - they're left with the dilemma of what to do with us. We obviously need to be punished, but there's lately been an outbreak of vandalism across the estate, equipment smashed on building sites and windows broken at one of the schools. This has given rise to an increasingly vocal outcry of anger at both the perpetrators and the apparent inability of the police to catch them. Handing us over, it is agreed, would be likely to provoke a disproportionate reaction all round.

It is my grandfather, I later learn, who proposes the solution.

* * *

I'd been going for about three hours and was on my fourth cup of coffee when I found it.

Beginning with Robert's emails and working back through the last couple of months hadn't thrown up anything out of the ordinary. Correspondence was neatly stored under labels like Agency, Bank, Travel, Insurance, together with matching sub-folders for any Word documents he'd needed to create.

But one file, in a folder marked Personal, I couldn't open. It was titled 'FDS' and, although it had a .doc suffix, when I clicked on it a message box popped up saying 'Incorrect Format'. I tried an ASCII reader, a utility that will display the raw text inside any file regardless of the program which created it. But the screen filled with scrambled hexadecimal code, a low-level machine language which runs behind the normal user interface.

The file, I concluded, was encrypted and yet Robert didn't have an encryption program installed - if there were, I'd have been prompted to enter a key or password when I tried to open it. So Robert had either been sent, or downloaded, an encrypted file which he didn't appear to have the means to decrypt. Decidedly odd, and I copied it across to my PC to take a closer look at later.

Then I had an idea. Going back to his emails I entered 'FDS' into the search box. If he'd received the file as an attachment I might be able to identify the source... 'No matching items found' was the response. I loaded his web browser and opened the 'Favourites' tab, checking word patterns for a match.

There was nothing.

Robert's settings for his browsing history and cookie cache - a sort of collection of tags from each website visited - wiped them clean whenever he logged off the internet. Not that unusual, my own browser was configured the same way and more a security precaution than concern about prying eyes, but it wasn't making things easy.

I decided on the sledgehammer approach.

I fired up the ASCII reader again. This time I typed in a wildcard pattern, which would open every text-based file on the hard drive and look for any contiguous instance of those three letters. Fortunately, this was a combination of consonants not likely to occur frequently, but would still probably be a lengthy process.

I hit the return key to get it started and went through into the kitchen for yet one more cup of coffee. Then, on my way back to the study, I was struck by a thought. Sitting down, I opened my email program and began to type.

"Any idea what this format is?" I asked Vic. "And is there any chance you could open it?"

I attached the FDS file and pressed 'Send'.

Sipping my coffee, I watched the screen as a succession of files opened and closed, a tech version of watching paint dry. After about fifteen minutes, the phone rang.

"Where did you get this file?" asked Vic. Like most techies, social pleasantries weren't his forte, but even for him this was abrupt.

I explained the situation in terms more general than specific. A friend of a friend had died and I'd been asked to take a look at his computer.

"Okay," said Vic. "Well, what you've got there is a PGP file. Pretty Good Privacy. Ever heard of it?"

"No."

"Right..." He paused. "Most governments designate it military grade encryption. In Russia you can get ten years just for having a copy on your PC and in the Middle East... Well, you really don't want to know."

"Seriously?"

"I've no idea why your friend had it installed, but-"

"He didn't," I interrupted. "Have it installed, I mean. There was only a folder with that file inside."

"Whatever it is," said Vic, "it's probably bad news. I'm not going to speculate about what he might have been into, but I doubt it was anything good. Particularly as it's disguised as a Word file."

"So there's no chance you can open it?"

"Richard," a slight tetchiness now creeping into his voice, "the bloody CIA couldn't open it."

"Right," I said. "Okay. And thanks for the heads up. I'll shred it."

"Anytime, Richard."

"Bye."

But before I could put the phone down, a ping came from the PC's speakers and a file opened up on screen.

* * *

My grandparents live on the other side of the city, also on a council estate, but one of sharp contrasts to ours. Theirs had been built in the nineteen thirties and to a design more elegant than utilitarian, concentric circles spread outward from a leafy park intersected by a dozen or so avenues, like spokes on a wheel. And where our house seems little more than one of a succession of boxes, its exterior pebble-dashed and whitewashed, theirs is a construction of gables and brickwork, some of it - surrounding the doors and windows - quite intricate. Even as a child, it strikes me that their house has been designed by someone who'd imagined living there themselves, while ours is simply a solution to a problem. I am puzzled - given the March of Progress we are always being told about at school - why it isn't the other way around.

Mr McKenzie is somebody I've thought about a lot over the years and I'm probably not alone in that. He and his wife live next door to my grandparents and not only are they referred to as 'Mr and Mrs McKenzie' by their neighbours, it is also how they address each other. In public, that is, but I doubt anyone would be surprised to discover they did so in private. They are the only people I know who don't speak with a local accent and who are regular churchgoers.

While most of the neighbourhood are skilled working class - fitters, engineers, machinists, skills acquired via the armed services or apprenticeships - Mr McKenzie leaves the house every morning dressed in a formal black jacket, pinstriped trousers and a bowler hat, carrying a briefcase and an umbrella. His job is, depending on who you ask, to do with either the Law Courts or the Town Hall. But rather than singling him out as an oddity, this invests him with genuine respect. People from quite a distance around call on Mr McKenzie for advice when having to deal with the council over some matter or are faced with a complicated form to complete and never find themselves treated as anything other than equals.

Mrs McKenzie serves on various church committees, is active in the Women's Institute and for all the patronising attitude these organisations can sometimes bring to bear on the needy recipients of their good works, you won't hear - my grandmother would say - a bad word spoken against her.

I never discover their story, what brings them to a Midlands council estate in postwar Britain. A fresh start after a scandal, illicit love escaping the bounds of convention, were Mr and Mrs McKenzie actually Mr & Mrs McKenzie? I'm sure the truth is far more mundane, but as a child I'm not intrigued enough to enquire and wouldn't be told, anyway.

* * *

The contents of the file were a jumble of text and control characters. In this unformatted state, it was difficult to understand in what context. From the file-path listed on the screen I saw it was a Word document named 'Memo', buried in a nest of sub-folders under the general heading Misc.

I stared at it for a moment, then brought Windows Explorer back up. Burrowing down to the file's location, I highlighted it with a mouse click and copied it over to my PC, where I double clicked on it. It opened up in Word, as the ASCII reader continued its search in the background.

It was a list of URLs, user-names and passwords. The opening ones were bank accounts, I assumed, Lloyds and NatWest. A few building society names I recognised, followed by what looked to be estate agency organisations. But at the bottom was a lengthy web address which ended in fds.ru, not exactly explicit, but it indicated the site was hosted in Russia. I copied the URL into my browser and pressed Return.

A blank white screen appeared. There was no hint of anything in motion, no progress bar or spinning arrow to reassure the user they weren't forgotten, that in the background cogs were turning. I studied the URL, comparing it to the text I'd pasted in and checking I hadn't inadvertently clipped a character off.

Then, after half a minute or so, a bevelled box began to draw itself in the centre of the screen. I got the idea. Anyone casually or accidentally arriving at this page would stare at a blank screen for a few seconds and then probably shrug and move on.

I wasn't exactly sure what I felt about that.

The animation concluded with the appearance of two text entry fields, one labelled 'User' the other 'Password.' From the Word document, I copied in 'ms4912' and 'fel!&26'. At least he'd had the sense not to use 'password' or '123456'. As I typed in the last digit, a button appeared. I clicked on it and the white background shattered like breaking glass, a thousand shards falling to the bottom of the screen.

"Sorry to see you back ms4912' was the unexpected greeting and, across the top of the screen, golden letters in Gothic script spelt out *'Felo de Se'*.

* * *

It's a Saturday, but everyone's all dressed up. Michael and I in school uniform, his dad and mine wearing suits, all in deference to Mr McKenzie who - weekend or not - wears pinstripes and a bowler hat.

We meet in a car park on the eastern side of town, an area I'm not familiar with.

"Good morning, boys," says Mr McKenzie.

"Good morning, sir," I reply. I usually address him as Mr McKenzie, but I'm eager for him to know that I understand the severity of this matter.

"Good morning, sir," echoes Michael.

"What you boys did was very serious," continues Mr McKenzie, his tone sombre but not unkind. "We know you didn't intend what happened, but actions have consequences." He pauses. "Society has a duty to protect itself, its citizens, from the irresponsible minority."

"Yes sir," we both say.

"We're going to show you something today," Mr McKenzie tells us. "Something which I hope will stay with you in the coming years, should you ever again contemplate a thoughtless course of action whose outcome you cannot determine. And for you to understand what the consequences of that might be."

We all follow him out of the car park and around the corner, where we find ourselves walking alongside a high wall. Whilst no taller than many of the buildings in the city - the Town Hall, the Guildhall - the facade has not been rendered, and the thousands of bricks seem to both to exaggerate its scale and suggest a labour to some ominous purpose.

Turning right at the end of this road, both Michael and I gasp. Facing us is what appears to be the entrance to a medieval castle, huge stone turrets on each side of wooden gates which must be at least twenty feet high and fifteen feet in width, studded with large black iron bolts. The outline of a door can be made out in the gate on the left, and Mr McKenzie bangs on it with his fist.

It swings open.

* * *

I knew it was a legal term of some kind and my first thought was this might be some conveyancing or land registry related site, maybe a discussion and advice forum for estate agents or property developers.

It took only a few seconds to dispel that idea.

That it was a special interest site was obvious, a box on the right-hand side of the screen was titled 'Members Currently Online' and headings across the page included 'Chat Rooms', 'Messaging', 'Forum' and 'Resources'. I clicked on a tab marked 'Your Account', thinking this had to be some kind of weird kink adult hookup site. Nothing else seemed to make any sense.

And the page that opened appeared to confirm this. It gave Robert's contact email address as a Hotmail account, one that I hadn't come across anywhere on his hard drive. I quickly changed that to a Hotmail account of my own, which I used when logging onto temporary sites to avoid getting buried in spam. I didn't want my visit to this site triggering an email trail after his death, particularly if the police were going to be digging around.

I also learnt he'd been a member for eight months, with four months left to run on his subscription. Which, I noted, was paid by a transfer from an ABN AMRO account, in the name of David Jones.

I sat back and stared at the screen.

A Dutch bank account in a false name, quite the elaborate setup for an occasional lascivious fling. The rest of the info didn't offer more by way of enlightenment, so I returned to the Homepage.

I clicked on Chat Rooms.

The page offered two choices 'Area' or 'Interest'.

I selected 'Area' and a list box of countries appeared. I clicked on 'United Kingdom' and in a pop-up screen, half a dozen usernames were listed above a button labelled 'Enter Room'.

I considered.

There weren't enough members in the room for my entrance to pass unnoticed and until I understood what was expected from 'ms4912', it probably wasn't a good idea to start interacting.

I closed the window and exited back to the Homepage, this time clicking on 'Forum'. A list of usernames scrolled down the screen in apparent date order, subject headings colour coded, I guessed to signify whether unread, viewed or replied to.

I opened up the thread and a virtual envelope rack appeared. A click of the mouse on each one lifted the flap, and the message slid out, formatted in a copperplate font.

'Insurance companies have started to catch on,' the first one read. 'You need to be really smart now.'

Click.

'I dread my kids believing I've abandoned them. It has to look like an accident. I thought about a car crash but I'm terrified I'll lose courage at the last minute, maybe leave myself helplessly paralysed.'

Click.

'Drowning's supposed to be peaceful, right? And people drown every day.'

Click.

'Question from a newbie. If I go Felo de Se's buddy route with this, what happens if I don't think the buddy's appropriate? Is there an opportunity to get to know each other first?'

I realised I'd been holding my breath for quite a while now. I let it out slowly, sinking back into the chair.

And Alan Bradshaw had been worried about a bloody note!!?

* * *

The gaol has been closed for a while, but that doesn't make our tour any less disturbing. In fact, the presence of inmates might have gone some way to lifting the pall of depression which hangs everywhere. We're all conscious of the ghosts of prisoners long departed, as the clanging of doors being slammed shut echoes along empty corridors.

Mr McKenzie sits each of us alone in a cell for just the slightest taste of the desolation so many must have experienced in here. After that, he leads us down into a dusty basement where a massive cylinder the width of the room is positioned against the far wall. Approaching, we see that planks have been fitted at twelve-inch intervals into the length of its surface.

"The treadmill," says Mr McKenzie. "God knows how long it's been since it was last in use," he shakes his head, "but not long enough for many poor souls."

We follow him out into a walled courtyard, circular and perhaps twenty yards in diameter. On the far side, wooden steps lead up to a small building with a gabled roof, set away from the main prison block.

"The exercise yard," says Mr McKenzie. "Prisoners would be brought out here for half an hour every day and walked around in pairs, although silence was strictly enforced."

He pauses.

"Condemned prisoners were exercised individually," Mr McKenzie tells us, "and always kept separate from other inmates for the three clear Sundays between sentence and execution."

He points to the small building at the top of the wooden steps.

"At some point during those three weeks," he says, "it would be made known to them that was the Execution Shed. That the last steps they would ever take would be across this yard and up that stairway."

We are silent as we follow him back inside and find ourselves at the far end of one of the gaol's long narrow wings. Mr McKenzie opens a cell door and leads us through it.

It's at least twice as large as any of the other cells we have been in.

"The condemned cell," says Mr McKenzie. "The prisoner is never alone during those last weeks. Two prison officers would stay in here with him, day and night.

"On the morning of his execution, the Governor, a priest, the hangman and the hangman's assistant all enter the cell. The hangman binds the prisoner's arms behind him with a leather strap, tips a glass of whisky into his mouth and opens the cell door. The two prison officers take an arm each and march him through it."

Mr McKenzie steps out into the corridor.

"The prisoner expects to be led from here out into the courtyard and up to the Execution Shed. But..."

Mr McKenzie is standing by a large bookcase, set opposite the cell door. With what seems to be just the slightest push of his hand, it rolls away to one side, revealing an archway. Through it we see a scaffold, complete with a leather encased noose hanging down from above.

"The prisoner is walked straight through onto the trapdoor. In his fist, the hangman has concealed a silk hood, bunched tight, and which he now shakes open and pulls down over the prisoner's head. His assistant releases the lynch pin from the trapdoor lever as the hangman positions the knot of the noose under the prisoner's jaw. He then crosses to the trapdoor lever," Mr McKenzie moves over to it himself, "checks the prison officers are clear of the drop and..."

Mr McKenzie wrenches the lever and, with a mighty clatter, the trapdoor falls open.

He looks over at us.

"The time taken between the prisoner stepping into the corridor," he said, "and the trapdoor opening was rarely more than five seconds."

Behind me is a crashing sound and I turn around.

Michael has fallen to the ground in a dead faint.

* * *

Felo-de-se

1: a person who commits suicide or who dies from the effects of having committed an unlawful malicious act.

2: an act of deliberate self-destruction.

Etymology:

Medieval Latin. Literally: evildoer in respect to oneself.

I closed the dictionary and stared out over the bay. I'd poured myself a large whisky and found a packet of Marlboro in the pocket of Veronica's Barbour jacket, the one she always wore when she disappeared off for a walk.

Quite the little detective today.

I had known that sites like this existed. Or rather, sites that facilitated end-of-life options for the terminally ill. Euthanasia was illegal in England - in most countries - but doctors and nurses, who believed helpless cases in extreme pain should be an exception to the law, could be found to deliver a lethal injection.

But this...

I sat back and drew on the cigarette.

From what I could discover, this was an organisation not only for those with a terminal illness but also anyone who'd decided they'd had enough. Its purpose was to shield those left behind from both the sense of not being worth living for and being penalised by insurance companies. For a hefty subscription charge, Felo de Se created scenarios for either a natural or accidental death and supplied whatever might be needed to expedite that. The deal was that you engaged with three other members before your turn came around, like some macabre chain letter.

So... What was I going to do about it?

I stubbed the cigarette out, tossed the butt over the

balcony and took my drink back inside.

The ASCII reader had finished its search. The only reference to FDS on the hard drive was in the file I'd opened and the only traces would be the Hotmail account and the Dutch bank he'd paid the subscription from. But I'd found no evidence of either on his laptop and I doubted anyone else would. In fact, the encrypted FDS file was more likely to act as a lightning rod for any suspicions, channelling them towards an uncrackable solution. After that, the probability was they'd skim the Word files and drawing a blank there, call it a day.

And all for the better, I decided. Claudia was certainly taking comfort from the belief that Robert's death was an accident or, at worse, misadventure. Plus, Alan's business would struggle to survive without the insurance payout.

I opened up the Word document and snipped out the lines with the FDS password, username and login. Closing it, the file date and time stamp now reflected my altered system date prior to Robert's death.

I copied it over to the laptop's hard drive, replacing the original. I powered it down from the mains, put the cotton gloves on, reconnected the motherboard and internal power supply, then screwed the cover back in place. Finally, I slid it into the carrier bag, picked up the phone and dialled Alan's mobile.

He answered immediately.

"There's nothing there you need to worry about," I told him, and the relief coming down the line was almost palpable.

"You sure?"

"I've given it at least as good a going over as anyone else is likely to," I said. "I couldn't find anything on there that even hints he was planning to take his own life."

"I'll come over and pick it up now," said Alan, and then paused. "Thanks Richard, I really owe you for this."

More than you might imagine, I thought.

After he hung up, I turned back to my PC, still logged into the Felo de Se website. I sipped the last of the whisky and then moved the mouse over to the 'Logout' button. I was about to click on it when the speakers made a 'Ping' sound and a box labelled 'New Message' popped up in the centre of the screen.

I must have stared at it for at least twenty seconds, before cautiously sliding the mouse onto it and clicking.

'Hello there,' read the text which appeared. 'Noticed you

were online. Thought I'd just check we were still on for the first week of August.'

It was signed 'Herostratus'.

* * *

Fortunately, Michael hasn't damaged himself, and when we get him to his feet, he is more embarrassed than injured. Mr McKenzie goes off to fetch a glass of water and during his absence I see Michael's father and mine exchange looks - expressions which reflect what I overhear him say to my mother when we return home.

"All a bit over the top, if you ask me," he tells her. "It sent shivers down my spine, so God knows what it did to those poor little sods."

But it's all polite smiles and gentle remonstrations of lessons learnt and future behaviour as we part company outside the gaol.

And they are right, it's something which never will escape my mind.

Although, in a gaol so deserted and dusty, I doubt the woodwork of the scaffold would be so polished, the tiled walls scrubbed so bright or the trapdoor lever have kept that gunmetal sheen. Would the rope appear so bristled and waxed, or that brown leather sleeve encasing the noose actually glisten as it caught the light?

But this is the image that rises from my subconscious at moments not of fear, but of comfort or reassurance. It also comes with an aura of physical wellbeing, not in any sexual sense and certainly lacks any connotations of autoerotic asphyxiation one might imagine conjured from such a scenario. Simply a warm, dull, inner glow.

Our heads, for the most part, busy themselves with patterns. From the almost comedic insistence of trying to construct a face from virtually any random visual image to dealing with the nuances of the most complex social interactions, this is the low machine hum of our consciousness. Survival all along the evolutionary chain has been dependent on the subliminal processing of data on the basis of fight or flight, a process which at the lower cortex level we call instinct and at the higher levels, sixth sense or presentiment and little creates a greater feeling of unease than the intellect choosing to overrule it.

Yet perhaps equally disquieting are those individual jolts of memory which appear to persist for no reason, like stills from a film with a plot beyond recall. Scenes which at first seem so inconsequential - two figures on a platform viewed through the window of a railway carriage, a mother cradling her baby in a hotel lobby, an old man sipping ice cold orange juice at a pavement cafe on a hot summer's day... But rather than fading with the passage of time they are enhanced by it, light and shade intensified, colours deepened and all while the claw marks of love, pain and passion have long healed over.

It's hard not to have the sense they will one day coalesce, for a thing lying in wait...

* * *

I figured there was plenty of time for a quick shower before Alan arrived. But climbing the stairs to the living room after drying myself off and dressing, I realised he was already here, out on the veranda and talking to Veronica.

"Saffy says to give her a call," he was telling her. "I think she was wondering what you two had planned for the eclipse."

"For t'eclipse?" echoed Gillian, broadening and mocking Alan's accent. "'Appen we'll be down beach lad, wi' rest of town."

Through the window I saw Veronica stiffen, but Alan simply smiled.

"Well, I'll look forward to seeing you there, Mrs Brown," he said, "and hope that on that occasion you'll have managed to restrain yourself from starting so early. I assume Mr Brown, as ever, will be otherwise engaged?"

That wiped the smile off her face, but before she could respond, Veronica had taken Alan by the arm and was leading him through into the living room.

"I've got your home number," she was telling him, "but I'm not sure what I've done with Saffy's mobile. Would you write it down for me?"

"Oh, hi Richard," said Alan, seeing me standing there and

then scribbled on the notepad by the telephone, as Veronica and I stared at each other.

"Don't you think," I said softly, "that it might be an idea to get some food into her?"

Veronica nodded and went back outside.

"Sorry about that," I said to Alan as we walked to his car.

"You'd be amazed," he smiled, unlocking the doors with the press of a key fob, "how many middle-aged women in this town can only make their lives bearable by staying sozzled from lunchtime onward."

"I think that was a one off," I told him as we pulled out of the driveway. I explained about Gillian's promotion.

His silence as I finished was non-committal.

"Anyway," I shrugged, "what did you want to see me about?"

"I've a problem," he said, "with Belle Meadow."

* * *

Two years ago, Alan and Robert Pascoe had bought *Mulberry House*, a fifteen room Edwardian 'Gentleman's Residence', about a mile out of town. They'd picked it up for a song, not only because of its dilapidated condition but also a lack of access and the unlikelihood of planning permission ever being granted to remedy that.

The existing unpaved track leading to the house passed through a bluebell glade and a copse, both habitats supporting enough protected wildlife to guarantee a battle royale with the environmentalists at even the whisper of bulldozers moving in. As a commercial enterprise it looked a nonstarter and word around the town was that the two of them had drastically overplayed their hand.

But this proved to be merely the beginning of a carefully choreographed campaign. The planning permission they applied for was not for a hotel, but a nursing home. The West Country has a disproportionate number of the elderly - it's a favoured retirement area - and care home accommodation is in drastically short supply. The original idea had been to robustly lobby local and district councillors themselves, but Saffy's unexpected flair for dealing with bureaucratic obstacles presented them with a more subtle option.

Saffy wasn't selling herself cheap here and her price had been to employ her brother, Ratko, at the letting agency. She couldn't stretch herself to do both jobs properly, she told them, and nepotism was the last thing this was. He was a hotel manager in Croatia, spoke fluent English, but most of all she trusted him.

In the end Saffy had her way, but her brother wasn't a popular choice around the town. His manner was abrasive, to say the least, although the general consensus was that for all his faults, he got things done. But best not, Veronica warned me, to refer to him by his local nickname of 'Ratty' within earshot of his big sister.

With the letting agency now on the back burner, Saffy's first hurdle had been the access to *Mulberry House*, and she filed a change of usage application before the planning committee. Veronica and I went along to the hearing for moral support, the presence of Alan and Robert considered perhaps too much a portent of what might be waiting further down the line.

Although the unpaved track weaved through the wood, the house itself was no more than a hundred yards from the coast road, the other side of a field known as Belle Meadow. This field had already been purchased, Saffy informed the committee, and if planning permission would be granted for a two-lane byway to run from the main road to the driveway of *Mulberry House*, only fifty square metres of woodland, from the existing seventy-five acres, would need to be incorporated into it.

"It's not simply the desecration of our countryside, which is the issue here," stated a member of the committee. Saffy had clashed with Keith Thompson on previous occasions, she'd told us, and it seemed she was correct in anticipating this was where the stiffest opposition was likely to come from today. "The increase in traffic also needs to be taken into account."

"Because of isolated location," Saffy told him, "we would

use minibus to ferry staff from town. And bear in mind, this is not hotel - no guests arriving and leaving on daily basis. Residents there for good."

"Even so," Thompson continued, "there will be visitors. The volume of traffic generated by family members visiting their loved ones shouldn't be assumed insignificant."

Saffy nodded and picked up a slim cardboard file from the desk in front of her. She flipped it open and removed a single sheet of paper. Putting on her glasses, she peered down at it.

"Your mother," she said, eventually glancing up at him. "She in nursing home, correct?"

"I'm sorry?" Thompson was staring at her with a furrowed brow.

"Your mother," Saffy repeated. "Is in Willow Vale Nursing Home, near Truro." She paused. "Would you like me to read out how many times you visit her in last twelve months? So we might have better idea of volume of traffic to expect?"

"That is *outrageous!*" Thompson tried to gather himself. "I am not the one appearing before this committee today."

"Actually," said the Chairman softly, giving a sideways glance over to where a smiling reporter was scribbling furiously away into his notebook, "probably best to know when to stop digging."

Permission was granted and the first hurdle cleared.

* * *

Like a lot of rural golf clubs, this one on the outskirts of St Hannahs owed more to a need for exclusivity than a love of the sport. A hefty yearly subscription ensured a venue where only the right people rubbed shoulders.

"I'm a member because I bloody well have to be," Alan told me, as we pulled into the sandy car park. The club bordered the edge of the Burrows, dunes and clumps of marram grass surrounded the clubhouse. "It's where most of my business gets done and you can always find a quiet corner for a chat."

Alan signed me in and we walked through to the lounge. He nodded greetings to most people we passed on our way to the bar, where he ordered us both a pint of the local bitter. As they were being poured, he turned to a man standing alongside.

"Hello Dennis," he said, and then indicated me with a nod of his head. "I don't know if you've met Richard Hanson?"

We shook hands.

"Dennis Nelson," he said. "You've *Cliff Dene*, I understand?"

"Yes," I told him.

"So, what brought you to St Hannahs?"

* * *

At first we think we've taken a wrong turn. The place is more like a hotel than a hideaway and a sign at the bottom of the driveway saying 'The Grange' *certainly seems overly ornate for a private residence. But there are no other cars in sight and as we sit hesitantly in front of a building more gothic mansion than manor house, the door opens and a figure walks down the steps.*

"Hello," he says. "I'm Paul, Lee's business partner."

Although he's only slightly above average height and of slim build, he exudes the quiet confidence of someone used to things being done his way.

There's also something familiar about him.

"Have we...?" I begin slowly, but Veronica cuts me off.

"Pembridge Villas," she says. "And far too long ago."

Paul nods.

"Lee explained," he says. "I'm very sorry for your loss."

"Thank you."

"Let me show you where you'll be staying. It's okay," he adds as I turn toward the car, "I'll get someone to bring your luggage through."

He leads us towards the front door.

"There's a separate entrance around the back, which you'll probably prefer to use," Paul tells us, "but in case you do come in this way..."

We follow him into a large hall and then left into a narrow passageway.

"Is this a hotel?" asks Veronica, and Paul shakes his head.

"It used to be," he says, "and was when Lee first owned it, but we run courses here now."

"Courses?"

Paul's smile has a touch of humour to it.

"Management courses. Here we are."

At the end of the passage is a door with a 'Strictly No Admittance' sign on it. A numeric keypad is fixed to the wall beside it.

"I had these fitted the third time I had to get the locks changed because Lee lost her keys. It's five, five, four, nine at the moment, same on the outside door, but if you'd prefer something different it would be no problem to reset them."

"It's okay," I tell him.

"I've filled the fridge and larder," as the door gives a click and opens, "but if there's anything else you need, let me know and I'll put it on the daily shopping list."

We step into a sizeable living room, floor to ceiling French windows open through into a walled garden.

"Lee has the entire wing," he tells us. "She says to make yourself at home." He indicates the phone. "Pick it up and press nine for an outside line, zero to speak to someone here. Otherwise, you'll be left to yourselves."

"Thank you," I say to him.

He nods and leaves.

We plan on staying for a week and are still there a month later. Decompression is how I come to look back on it. Away from the sympathetic expressions, the awareness of everyone walking on eggshells around us.

This kind of grief isn't something which ever really fades. It's always there and always will be, ready to hit you with undiminished ferocity. But the occurrences grow less frequent and you learn to recognise them in each other, know when to reach out a hand or slip an arm around the shoulders.

We begin to function again.

Eventually we decide we should go back up to London, that things need to move on.

"Can we buy a place here?" asks Veronica on our last day. "Just to..."

She gestures with her hand and I understand what she means. The Cornish peninsular may feel like the edge of the world, but you can throw a bag into the car in London knowing it's only hours away. I understood why Lee had her 'bolt-hole' here and I know there'll be times we'll need one too.

"Sure," I tell her.

Properties don't come on the market that often, Paul tells us. Nothing has been built in the actual town since the seventies - all of St Hannahs is under a Preservation Order - and most houses change hands by word of mouth and at a premium. But he'll keep an ear out for us, he says.

It takes three years.

* * *

"A friend owned a house here," I tell him. "We came to visit and fell in love with the place."

"A not unfamiliar story," smiled Dennis.

"Amongst other things, Dennis is Chairman of the Board of Governors at St Anne's," Alan told me, before turning back to him. "We've just been chatting with one of your teachers, Gillian Brown."

"She's a friend of my wife," I explained.

"That's right," Alan continued. "They were celebrating her promotion."

"Well," Dennis gave a disparaging smile, "there's nothing official yet. We've other candidates to interview tomorrow. But she's been Acting Head of the department for six months now and done an excellent job."

"I'd have said that's more of a reason to go for someone else," said Alan.

"I'm sorry?" asked Dennis, somewhat taken aback.

"If you already have someone who can do the job," said Alan, "going for the most promising external applicant gives you the best of both worlds. Particularly somewhere like here."

Dennis was shaking his head.

"I don't understand?"

"The whole world and his brother would love to live in Cornwall," said Alan. "Whenever we advertise a job, the CVs from up country are way more impressive than you'd expect for what the position involves. We've had some real talent injected into the business over the last few years."

He took a sip of his beer.

"And if they don't live up to expectations, well, it's no problem getting rid of them after a three-month trial, because there's already someone to step straight back into their shoes." He shrugged. "I mean, they won't be leaving Cornwall for Birmingham or Leeds because they're pissed off at missing a promotion, will they? And it's not like there's anywhere else for them to go down here."

"That's a bit... Darwinian," said Dennis, dryly.

Alan shook his head.

"It's never a bad idea to keep your people on their toes, Dennis. And," he added, "I saw that piece in the *Western Gazette* about school league tables in Cornwall - probably wouldn't hurt to have some ammunition ready, along the lines of fresh ideas and broadening horizons, if St Anne's keeps on slipping."

Dennis was staring at him.

"Just a thought," smiled Alan. "Anyway, what are you doing for the eclipse?"

"We're having a barbecue at the house," Dennis told him. "Friends and colleagues welcome. Why don't you and Safranka drop by?"

"I don't think we've anything planned," said Alan, "so we might well do that."

Alan led me over to a table in the far corner of the lounge.

"I'll bear in mind," I said quietly, as we sat down, "always to stay in your good books."

"Aye lad, thou should think twice about crossing us Yorkshire tykes," said Alan, thickening his accent to the extent that Gillian Brown had, before adding *sotto voce*, "Especially if you're a mouthy fucking sow."

"So, Belle Meadow?" I prompted him, after the waitress had taken our order.

"The contractors are due to go in on Monday," he said.

Normally I'd have offered congratulations, the first tangible result of a long hard battle, but this *tête-à-tête* suggested that probably wasn't the appropriate response.

I waited.

"You've heard about those Travellers who turned up last week?"

I nodded. From Emblyn, I'd gathered that at least once a year a group of Travellers arrived in St Hannahs, setting up camp in some farmer's field on the outskirts of town until a warrant could be applied for, issued and executed. Usually they moved further along the coast, but sometimes found another field on the opposite side of the town and the whole dance would start over.

It wasn't too hard to guess what had happened.

"They're camped in Belle Meadow?"

Alan nodded.

"Since yesterday morning."

"How long is it going to take you to get a warrant sorted out?"

"Too long." He gave a wry smile. "It appears Keith Thompson has stuck his oar in."

I stared at him. Keith Thompson was the committee member who Safranka had clashed with during the planning application. And clashed with so very publicly.

"A word to the magistrates via the old boy network, and suddenly it's like wading through treacle," said Alan, shaking his head. "And I've heard that as the Travellers were being evicted from Seagrove Farm yesterday, they got a whisper that if they moved to Belle Meadow, then things might go a little easier with them. Well, for a while at least."

I stayed silent, digesting this.

"You know, one of my reasons for going into partnership

with Robert Pascoe," Alan said, "was that he was one of them. I knew that come hell or high water, they'd never fuck him over. But now, with Robert gone..."

He let his voice trail off and shook his head again.

"It also seems that the insurance policy his wife stands to collect on doesn't have a suicide clause in it. Financially, it won't matter two hoots to Claudia whether the coroner decides if Robert topped himself or not, she can just sell her share of the business to some national chain looking to get a foothold down here. Who'll then spend the next few years gently - or perhaps not so gently - easing me out."

He sighed.

"So, I'm really up against it at the moment, Richard. And I was hoping I could ask you for a favour."

"Of course Alan, anything I can do to help."

"I'd like you to go and talk to the Travellers for me. I need to pay them off."

"Sorry?"

The waitress appeared with our food, giving me a chance to recover from my surprise. I'd been half expecting him to ask me for a loan to tide him over, and part of me wondered if Alan hadn't structured the conversation to create that impression. It's a lot easier to get someone agreeing to a big favour when they've been anticipating a massive one...

We waited silently as she fussed with the cutlery and condiments. When she'd finished, Alan leant forward again.

"It really is my only way out," he told me and then gave a sigh. "Ratko went down there to see them earlier today," he said. "That was a mistake - my mistake. There's a whole... culture thing going on with eastern Europeans and Romanies, apparently."

"What happened?"

"Let's just say that it didn't play out well. And now I've been tarnished with the same brush." He paused. "What I need is a middleman with some business nous, diplomatic skills and who I can trust." He shrugged. "And it's not like I'm exactly spoilt for choice in this town, am I?"

"So, what do you want me to do?"

"Offer them two grand to move on. I'm not bothered where to. They can go over the hedge into the next bloody field for all I care, as long as they're out of Belle Meadow before Monday."

I nodded.

"I'll go and see them first thing," I told him.

"Thanks, Richard." He visibly relaxed. "If it does seem to be a question of money, then go higher, use your judgement."

"Okay," I said, picking up my knife and fork. "I'll play it by ear."

* * *

"You know," said Alan reflectively, as the waitress took away our empty coffee cups and replaced them with two brandies, "I think the real reason I get so wound up by people like Gillian Brown is a suspicion that they might be right."

"In what way?"

"Oh, I don't know..." He sat back in his chair. "That perhaps things have fallen into my lap all too easily. And then along comes a reminder of how quickly it could all fall apart."

He gave a short laugh, shaking his head.

"Sorry," he said. "God, the last few days must have really got to me. I'm usually not this maudlin."

"Having doubts about yourself," I told him, "isn't being maudlin, Alan. It's reassurance that life hasn't transformed you into a self-satisfied arsehole." I shrug. "Not yet, at least."

He grinned and shook his head.

"You've never struck me as someone who doubts himself," he said. "'Still waters run deep', as my mother always used to say." He smiled. "And for a successful businessman, you do occasionally come across as surprisingly philosophical."

"As I'm forever telling you, I got lucky. Right place, right time is all. And whatever face we choose to present to the world, most of us have somewhere in our head where we can find sanctuary when we need it." I shrugged. "If we're lucky, that is."

"If we're lucky? What would you have to...?" He broke off, his expression suddenly stricken. "Oh Jesus, Richard, I'm sorry - I..."

His voice trailed away

"It's okay," I told him.

"No, it's not bloody okay. Here I am wallowing in self pity when..." He shook his head. "I can't imagine how you ever deal with something like that."

"But you do," I tell him. "Slowly, eventually. You either discover or create the mechanisms you need."

"Which are?"

"If I told you," I said, "you'd never believe me."

His expression became quizzical.

"Aye, lad," I smiled, mimicking Gillian Brown's earlier mockery of his accent. "There's nowt as queer as folk."

Alan softly laughed.

* * *

I was a solitary child, living as much in my imagination as reality. Which is something - even at an early age - you learn to keep to yourself. Most aberrations are regarded as a vulnerability by the pack instinct which surrounds you from the playground to the care home and, for all the superficial congeniality you may encounter in life, this is a zero-sum world.

I don't recall ever having an imaginary friend. If I did, they obviously proved as transient as the real ones. But the rabbit hole I did fall down - and perhaps never fully emerged from - I was led to by an alter ego.

I suppose to some degree we all fantasise about the world being other than it is, whether spurred on by regret or indulging a daydream. This was neither, more akin to tally marks on a cell wall... I grew up in a home in which the only books were cheap paperbacks, torrid covers promising more than the mores of the time ever would have allowed. No music that didn't come from the BBC's Light Programme and anything else by way of culture via that sturdy cabinet in the corner of the room. Switched on for Children's Hour at five o'clock and staying on until the last strains of the National

Anthem died away and the screen exploded into static.

I - as they say - made my own entertainment.

In retrospect, I'm astonished at the complexity not only of the worlds I created but by how I sustained the multiple storylines and relationships within them. I have wondered if there was some kind of idiot savant element involved, but it's more likely down to the remarkable ability to assimilate and assemble which all children possess - effortlessly becoming bi or tri lingual in multi-national households is probably the most common example.

The dangers of stepping sideways into a parallel existence are more insidious than simply losing touch with reality. When the consequences of your actions in the real world can be shrugged off by slipping into a fantasy one, life's lessons quickly begin to pass you by. I think it was repeating the same mistakes which finally began setting off alarm bells. Approaching puberty, my instincts started to lean more toward changing my circumstances than escaping them and eventually came the realisation that my best exit strategy was education.

But most solitary vices which have served a purpose are hard to let go of entirely, even when the purpose they've served finds itself redundant. Paths not taken, I would continue to persuade myself, and choices not made needn't be anything more than an insightful mirror for the soul to gaze into.

So...

Veronica and I are staying on Ischia, in the Bay of Naples. This is our first real holiday since the honeymoon. Ronald and Marjorie are taking care of Emily and we have each other exclusively to ourselves, something of a rarity over the past year. I'm sipping wine on the hotel terrace while Veronica dresses for dinner. Across the water, city lights are sparkling in the twilight and Vesuvius is a dark shadow rising high in the background.

It's a location exotic enough to almost beg the question of how I've found myself here and hard to escape the answer of by good fortune rather than talent. How would things have gone if Veronica hadn't fallen pregnant? How tenuous would the bonds between us have shown themselves to be?

I don't so much reflect on the life my alter twenty-three-year-old self - Rick strikes me as more appropriate than Richard - would most likely be leading right now, as allow myself to slip into it.

Rick's probably a graphic designer at some magazine or second-rate advertising agency, being constantly nagged by a girlfriend for spending more time with his art than her. And knowing deep down that he does so because if he lets it go, he'd have to accept that this life he was living would now always be the life he'd be living. That...

I'm drawn back - surprisingly reluctantly - to reality by Veronica stepping outside. I rise and we silently take in the view before she slips her arm through mine and we enter the hotel restaurant.

But the die is cast.

And now, with every minor triumph in my life - or occasional flash of hubris - I indulge the notion that a shitty parallel world need not be too many quantum leaps sideways. Years pass, Rick inhabiting a life which at times is as elaborately constructed as the one I'm actually living and at others a fast forwarding blur..

A succession of jobs in advertising are accompanied by an equal succession of relationships. Both expect more from him than he is prepared to give or take seriously. And eventually he is unable to see the point of trying.

There's a period spent working on set designs for fringe theatre groups, but it never pays enough to cover the rent. Benefits can only make up so much of the deficit and so he enters the world of squats. There's always an intent to somehow get his act together, but time keeps slipping by.

There are spells on building sites during the summer, temporary office work during the winter. Every few years an exhibition at a library in Holloway or a community centre in Dalston, where a sufficient number of his paintings sell to convince him that one day he'll make it and there's always a piece in the local rag complimentary enough to foster that delusion.

And there am I, to watch over it all.

From the balcony of a Gstaad ski lodge, I witness an argument in a DHSS cubicle in Stoke Newington. Fifty thousand feet above the Atlantic and sipping champagne at twice the speed of sound, the latest amour disintegrates in a maelstrom of clothes, books and LPs hurled down the stairs of a Kentish Town squat.

It's not perpetually downhill. A chance meeting in a pub leads to the role of part-time art lecturer at a North London college. Not enough to make ends entirely meet, but another member of staff emigrating to Canada is looking for someone to take over her share of an Islington housing co-op. Which lifts him out of the world of slumlords and squatting.

And, as an additional sweetener, I bring into his life Francesca McCaffrey.

Some people you can be around for months and a year later they'll be out of your head for good. I'd known Francesca for less than forty-eight hours, not in any intimate way, but she'd been someone who, for whatever reason, sticks with you. She'd arrived one day at Pembridge Villas looking for somewhere to stay. A guy in the house was away for the month, I recall, and she'd briefly used his room.

There was just something about her that gelled with me. She came across smart and sassy and there'd been real chemistry between us. In retrospect, so many relationships seem to have been less about who and more about where and when... Francesca was the wrong time and the wrong place, but I'd always wondered how it might have played out if things had been different.

I manoeuvre Francesca back into Rick's life during a sojourn in Fort Lauderdale, staying in a borrowed beachfront condo on Galt Ocean Drive. A squadron of pelicans skimming the surf, parading beach bunnies in the first year of the thong.

In her forties, she appears by chance at Rick's college, a life model who becomes an occasional tumble. Life's dealt Francesca - quickly Frankie (Rick and Frankie has a ring to it, T-Birds and Pink Ladies or a wiseguy and his moll) - as many hard knocks as Rick. The sassy smarts are still there, if now with a delivery more wary than cocky. Frankie is independent enough and Rick irresponsible enough for what could just about be perceived as a relationship to need no formal basis. But the chemistry of that first meeting slowly reasserts *itself and eventually she moves in with him, good for each other in their very different ways.*

The thing of it was though, and despite what I'd said to Alan about sanctuary, the only emotion I feel towards Rick these days is envy.

* * *

All was in darkness when Alan dropped me off back home. I guessed Veronica and Gillian had gone into town for a meal. I let myself in, poured a large scotch, and took it down to the study. I had something to tidy up and knew I'd feel more relaxed about it with Veronica out of the house.

I brought my laptop out of 'sleep' mode but instead of the usual login I selected the ID 'admin2', a username suggestive of an account set up for maintenance but was actually a front. It was from where I signed into the *Felo de Se* site, but that wasn't its sole purpose and from the desktop I logged into Hotmail.

I'd half a dozen Hotmail aliases. Often a website requires an email address before granting access and afterwards will bombard you with spam. To prevent my main account from getting clogged with junk mail, I directed that traffic to where I could periodically run my eye over it before dragging it across to the recycle bin. The Hotmail accounts I'd created were graded by how frequently I thought they'd need checking. This one I went into once a day.

Sometimes twice.

I'd last heard from Carin about a week ago. She'd be in London at the end of the month, as arranged, but was thinking of taking an extra few days in England and coming down to St Hannahs for the Aidan McShane exhibition. Which would suit me best? Or what about both?

I was still working on my reply. Deluding myself that leaving it a while longer was more down to prudence than prevarication, I exited the Hotmail account, took a sip of whisky, and clicked on *Felo de Se*.

* * *

A year after Emily's death, I found myself for a while

in London alone. We'd planned to sell the house - too many memories to live with, said Veronica - but it was proving a task easier to shelve than face. Eventually, we bit the bullet. I went back to London to handle the sale and Veronica to Los Angeles, staying with Lee for however long this was going to take.

Which turned out to be less time than we'd thought. We received an offer only a couple of days after it was listed, well below the asking price, but the housing market was in one of its periodic slumps. Plus, this was a cash buyer who wanted to be in by the end of the month. Once contracts were exchanged, I had the furniture put into storage and checked into a hotel until we completed. Veronica had been right. There were too many ambushes lying in wait there.

But an open-ended stay at a decent central London hotel in August proved trickier than I'd expected. Eventually I found somewhere in Bloomsbury, off Russell Square, and began occupying my days with rediscovering the British Museum and my evenings at the theatre or cinema.

I'd been there for about a week - with probably another to go, according to my solicitor - and was having a pre-dinner drink in the bar, half skimming the listings pages in *Time Out* and trying to filter out a dozen or so women around a group of tables on the other side of the room. Not that they were particularly raucous, but it was obviously a reunion of some sort and each new arrival was greeted with cries and laughter. Eventually, I was aware of them gathering themselves together, rising and drifting out in twos and threes. But one of them, I noticed, had hesitated and, looking in my direction, spoke to the woman next to her. As the others left, she walked over towards me.

I looked up quizzically as she reached my table.

"Excuse me," she said, and there was the barest hint of an accent there, "but is it Richard?"

I studied her carefully before nodding. There was something familiar about her, I just couldn't...

"You probably don't remember," she smiled, almost bashfully. "My name is Carin. I used to visit Pembridge Villas when..."

"Carin!" I rose to my feet. "Of course. I'm so sorry, I was miles away and..."

I let my voice trail off as we embraced and then stood back from each other. The inevitable appraisal by two people who hadn't seen each other in decades rather than years, camouflaged by smiles.

"You're looking really well," I told her, truthfully. "How long has it been?"

"Over twenty years, I think," she smiled. "And not so bad yourself."

"So, what are you doing here?"

She gestured toward the women leaving the bar.

"College reunion." She shrugged. "We do this every year."

"Do you still live in London?"

"Amsterdam. But I teach at Leiden - History of Art."

"You're a lecturer?"

That bashful smile again.

"Professor."

"Wow!"

She gave a shake of her head.

"Sorry," she said. "I must go. We have taxis booked for the restaurant."

"Are you staying here?" I asked.

"Yes."

"Me too." I hesitated. "Look, would you like to have a drink later? When you get back."

Her gaze was steady before slowly nodding.

"Yes," she said. "I'd like that very much. But I don't know what time that will be - these evenings do go on."

"I'm in room 422," I told her. "Ask Reception to call me and I'll come down to meet you in the bar."

"Okay," she smiled, and leant forward to peck me on the cheek. "See you later."

* * *

But it was, I reflected as I sat back down, perhaps

opportune that Carin had to leave almost immediately, allowing me a chance to gather my thoughts.

Because our last parting hadn't exactly been on ideal terms.

In the summer of 1970, Carin spent a lot of time at Pembridge Villas. I'd first known her as the girlfriend of a dealer there, a romance which didn't last long. It was a breakup, according to house gossip, which she'd not taken well and been caught on the rebound by another guy who lived there. That fared almost as badly, but one night I'd been at the house when she'd turned up looking for him.

This was during one of Veronica's trips abroad with Lee, promoting the TV series she was starring in. I'd escorted Carin around the pubs in the area, trying to find who she was searching for. The combination of my resentment at Veronica's absence, Carin's emotional fragility and at least one drink in each bar, lead to a situation perhaps not inevitable but certainly characteristic of people hurting. At the end of the evening we'd taken brief but intense comfort in each other's arms, which became even briefer when Lee's promotional tour was cut short and Veronica arrived home to discover the two of us in her bed.

The first I knew of her return was waking up to flailing fists around my head. I was aware of Carin trying to restrain her, eventually with some success. Grim faced and steely eyed, Veronica stood with folded arms as Carin quickly dressed. Finishing, Carin turned to me with a questioning expression, but when I couldn't meet her eyes, she gave a sad shake of her head and left.

Then the recriminations began, loud and furious, and ten minutes later I was out on the pavement. There'd been a couple of nights sofa surfing, but with the new term almost six weeks away, I quickly realised this couldn't go on. Scraping enough together for a train ticket to the Midlands, I returned home.

The last time I'd seen Carin had been shortly after Veronica and I had reconciled. She was at the house with Veronica's *bête noire* Claudia, upset and again looking for the guy she'd been trying to find that evening. It appeared that having got her pregnant, he'd now disappeared. Given the intensity of the emotions flying around that day, I'd quickly made myself scarce.

So, that summer had been a pretty wild ride for her, and one that my own role didn't emerge from exactly covered in glory. In fact, I was already regretting my invitation. At best, this was going to be a walk down a memory lane constructed almost entirely of eggshells. I was becoming tempted to ignore any phone calls to my room that night - if we encountered each other by chance the next morning, I could always claim to have fallen asleep.

But it wasn't a phone call.

* * *

The knock on the door had something perfunctory about it and because it was still relatively early, I'd answered it expecting maid service, offering to turn down the bed.

But Carin stood there.

"Hello," she smiled. "I thought I would surprise you."

"Come in." I opened the door wide and she stepped through into the room.

"The girls went on to a club," she said. "I feigned a headache."

"Right," I told her, "I'll get my jacket."

"Actually," she said, "it's rather crowded down there now - and noisy. I think a convention has just checked in." She shrugged. "Which is why I came up."

"Okay... Well, have a seat." I indicated one of the armchairs, but instead she walked over to the window and stared down into the street.

"You have a nice view," she said as I opened the minibar. "From my room, it's a courtyard full of dustbins."

"What would you like?" I asked.

"Vodka and tonic, if that's possible?"

It was. I made myself a whisky and dry ginger as she

moved over to the bed and sat down.

"Do you still live in London," she asked, "or are you visiting?"

I explained about the house move, without going into the reason behind it.

"Veronica? That night, that's who...?" She let the sentence trail off with a shake of the head and I nodded.

"Crazy times," she said, but with a smile.

"And you?" I asked, handing her the drink.

"Oh, we ended up together in the end," she smiled. "And still are."

Carin kicked her shoes off, leant back and brought her right foot up and across to rest on her left thigh, slowly massaging the sole with her fingers.

"Sorry, those heels were killing me." Her skirt was riding high. "Although we both travel a great deal with our work, spend a lot of time left to our own devices."

Our eyes met.

"Shall we skip the small talk?" she said.

* * *

It was an hour later before we finally left each other alone, clothes scattered across the floor and sheets crumpled at the foot of the bed. She lay with her head on my chest and my arm around her shoulders, her breathing soft enough for me to wonder if she'd slipped into sleep.

Then she stirred and slowly raised herself up.

"I should get back to my room," she smiled.

I began to protest, but she put a finger against my lips.

"I'm sharing," she said. "I can do without the bitchy gossip."

She slid out of bed.

"Do you and Veronica have children?" she asked, picking her clothes up from the floor.

"No," I said, an entire world of omission encapsulated in that little word. But in a few minutes our lives would separate again, probably for good.

"You?" I enquired politely.

"Saskia." She rummaged in her handbag, found her wallet and then slid out a photograph.

"I'll use your bathroom for a minute, okay?" as she passed the photo over.

It was a portrait of a young woman in her late twenties, smiling at the camera from a table on what looked like a restaurant terrace, blue sea and an even deeper blue sky behind her. But as I stared, the blood flowing through my veins seemed to have turned to ice.

Saskia could have been Emily's twin sister.

* * *

I stared at the photograph, unmoving and almost unblinking, until I heard the bathroom door open. I thought I'd experienced pretty much everything that pain and loss had to offer, but the realisation that the consequences of paths not taken, of choices not made, did not exist entirely in the abstract brought bile rising into my throat.

But I forced a smile as Carin stepped back into the room.

A smile she returned.

"I'm glad we've had this, Richard," she said. "I've often..."

"Can I see you again?" I interrupted. "Perhaps the next time you're over here?"

She studied me carefully.

"This will never be any kind of romance," she said slowly. "You do understand that?"

I nodded.

Reaching into her bag, she took out a small notepad and pen and handed it to me. I scribbled my email address and phone number and passed it back, strangely relieved that the onus was now on her. That maybe I'd been spared the embarrassment of vain pursuit.

"It won't be soon," she told me. "But I'll be in touch."

We embraced and then stepped apart.

"Au revoir," she smiled.

As the door closed behind her, I lowered myself down onto

the bed. Her scent lingered and I buried my face in my hands.

* * *

We've seen each other every summer since and God only knows what draws me back there. Certainly I've no intention to meet Saskia, which would have been unbearable beyond belief, but once a year we contact each other through the Hotmail account I'd given her.

She explains to her friends that she and her husband are staying with an elderly relative in Parsons Green, and we both check into a hotel at least a mile away from where the reunion is being held. To give her story credence, I pick her up from the restaurant, an indistinct figure waiting outside in a black cab.

There's nothing by way of tenderness between us - during the day we're careful not to touch. There are no pecks on the cheek or hands finding each other's during a stroll. All physicality is reserved for our return to the hotel and it lasts long into the night, on her part dark and savage and perhaps providing a hint of why she returns year after year. But whatever the nature of this relationship might be, exchanging confidences has no role to play.

The previous August, I arrive in London a couple of days before Carin. I want to browse the bookshops in Charing Cross Road, I've a shopping list of CDs and there's the Summer Exhibition at the Royal Academy.

It's in one of those secondhand bookshops that I strike pure gold, an out of print copy of The Harmonious Circle *by James Webb. This is a book I've been after for years and although I haggle over the inflated mark up on the original cover price, I'd have been happy to pay pretty much anything he was asking.*

I'd never had a lot of time for the occult or the paranormal, but George Gurdjieff had interested me since my late teens, when I'd read Peter Ouspensky's In Search of the Miraculous *and* A New Model of the Universe. *Conventional Christianity never suggested more than state sponsored superstition and the eastern mysticism in vogue back then held no appeal for me, culturally or emotionally.*

But Gurdjieff's teachings - at least as interpreted by Ouspensky - seemed to touch a spiritual nerve while retaining day-

to-day pragmatism. In the early seventies, a few friends visited a retreat in the Cotswolds run by Kenneth Walker, a British soldier and mathematician who had been one of Gurdjieff's pupils and was continuing his work. I'd been impressed by how they'd turned their lives around and made plans to spend time there myself. But events - parenthood - had intervened.

Webb's book was a definitive account of Gurdjieff's beliefs and how they played out amongst his close followers. Back at the hotel, I decide to treat myself to a few chapters before dinner. I take the book out of my bag and lay it on the bed, flicking on the TV for white noise as I wash my face and brush my teeth. It's tuned to an American satellite channel and a biography of Bing Crosby is in progress.

Finished at the sink, I kick off my shoes and sit down.

On screen, Crosby is telling an anecdote about the death of one of his children's pets, a white mouse. The boy had been inconsolable and one of Crosby's friends suggested that they needed to create closure. When his daughter's guinea pig had died, he said, they'd held a mock funeral.

So Crosby and his son began to work at this, lining an old shoe box with black silk, making a shroud for the mouse and finally digging a grave out in the garden. After gathering the rest of the family together around this, the two of them went back into the house to collect the makeshift coffin.

And as they lifted it up, the mouse opened one eye.

Crosby's son stared down at the mouse, then out through the open doorway to the figures gathered at the little grave and then once more down to the mouse. It gave another twitch. He looked up and his eyes met his father's.

'Let's kill it,' he said.

I smile and reach for the book.

And picking it up, I realise that I no longer have the slightest interest in anything it might have to say.

Initially, it is an odd moment, almost inconsequential. There's the inclination to shrug and move on, yet somehow this impulse has both the air of a salesman's smile and the glint in a guilty partner's eye about it. Then suddenly this moment is no more inconsequential than an Ace of Spades flicked from the bottom row of a gigantic house of cards or the first domino sent tumbling.

The realisation that my cognition has just been subtly rewired without even the pretence of logical process or emotional resonance brings no sudden flash of illumination, no lightning bolt of understanding. There is more the sense of bearing witness to an unravelling, a short circuit in the projector... And now, faced with a blank screen for the very first time, comes an awareness of repair mechanisms rummaging through the pigeonholes of science and philosophy in a frantic attempt to cobble together just about anything to fill this empty vista and dreadful silence.

Is rational thought and reason simply the toolbox of sanity, stitching together a coherent internal narrative? Einstein's relativity theory would have time slowed to a standstill - and all space contracted to a single point - at the speed of light, which, after all, is the status quo of the quantum world. Are space and time nothing more than artificial constructs of a consciousness attempting to unpick reality?

Chuang Tzu dreamt he was a butterfly...

I have the sense of rooms folding flat behind me as I leave them, panoramas of lakes and mountains evaporating into nothingness as I turn away.

I consider what hoops I've jumped through, what tricks been made to perform. Rags to riches, unbearable loss, a love which to the rest of the world must seem as something thrown back by a funhouse mirror. So who is the ringmaster cracking the whip here, where are the audience hidden? And what other attractions does this performance hold in store for them? What new surprises - to outdo the last surprises - will be waiting down the line?

I sit on the bed and try to gather my senses. One of the few worthwhile lessons taken from the excesses of the sixties is that flashes of insight are not well served by analysis. Better to let them burrow their way down into your psyche unhindered, allow them to nestle there for a while.

When they're in need of your attention, you'll know about it.

* * *

More people depart this world by their own hand than are accounted for by warfare and malicious intent combined. That wasn't always the case, far from it, and it does beg the question of just exactly how well adapted to modern life we might be. Because what the statistics don't reveal is that in the main, these are not figures conjured from despair or remorse.

For the last year, I'd been pretty certain that what happened in my London hotel room was the Doppler effect of that final clear, bright light bearing down on me. And while *Felo de Se* might seem part of a pattern slipping into place, it was never more than a catalyst. I'd followed through on Robert's arrangements with 'Herostratus' because I'd stumbled across them when they were already in play and who knew what alarms had been rigged to sound if they were derailed?

But with that now out of the way, I had no further use for the site.

I'd taken up surfing a week after discovering *Felo de Se*. Veronica was forever badgering me about my sedentary lifestyle and - once past the initial surprise of my arriving home one afternoon carrying a surfboard - continued to be encouraging. Experience, I dare say, suggesting there was a good chance of the board taking up permanent residence in the garage once the novelty had worn off.

Joining a local surf club, I took weekly lessons in the techniques needed to ride a wave. But once I'd mastered the basics, the rest was little more than an alibi for the morning, not too distant now, when I intended to go down to a deserted cove, change into my wetsuit and leave my clothes neatly piled on the beach. Then, laying face down on the board, I would paddle so far out towards the horizon that there would be no possibility of ever returning.

I slid the mouse to the top right of the screen and clicked on 'Settings'. A range of options appeared, the bottom one was 'Close Account'. I took a sip of whisky before highlighting and clicking it. A message box popped up. 'Are you sure?' it asked. 'This action cannot be undone.'

I clicked on 'Yes'.

The screen flickered and then, in imitation of an old cathode tube TV set turning off, gave a crackle of static and a burst of bright light in the centre, before fading to darkness.

* * *

I've always been an early riser, enjoying that part of the day when it feels as if you have the world to yourself. Veronica's late to bed and even later to rise, although if she's stirring first thing then I'll leave a coffee by her bedside. But as I slipped out from under the covers, she was still sleeping off her night out with Gillian.

I showered, made bacon and eggs to set me up for the morning ahead and took them out onto the veranda. As Gillian had reminded us the day before, we probably have the best view in St Hannahs and the sharp chill of dawn had rendered it crystal clear. Sailboats bobbed in the harbour and even distant container ships, heading for the Bristol Channel or South Wales seaports, managed to have a touch of romance about them.

I ate slowly, considering my options. I'd learnt from Alan that the Travellers were working up at *The Grange*, tarmacking the driveway. I was reluctant to drag Paul into something which didn't involve him, particularly if they hadn't yet finished the job there. So, as I mopped up the last of the egg yolk from my plate with a slice of bread, I made the decision to head over to Belle Meadow and hopefully catch them before they left.

I took Veronica's Land Rover, figuring the less ostentation the better. At that time of day the roads were empty, but halfway there I realised I'd forgotten my mobile. I knew that Veronica - breaking down once on Dartmoor after being equally forgetful - kept a pay as you go phone in the car. Flipping the glove compartment open, I quickly found it with my fingers and slipped it into my pocket. But what my fingers also came across was a pack of Marlboro Lights.

Officially, Veronica and I quit smoking about a year ago and if either of us did occasionally catch a lingering whiff of tobacco on the other's breath, the silence was conspiratorial.

But a sudden yearning for that nicotine rush had me turning into the next Viewing Area, a series of lay-bys which had been extended back from the road to allow tourists to pull over and savour the Atlantic vistas.

This morning I had it to myself. Leaving the engine running, I slipped the cigarette between my lips and waited for the cigar lighter to pop out. Once lit, I climbed out, crossed the road and perched on the sea wall.

Its effect was immediate and after an abstinence of at least a couple of weeks, it felt like chasing the dragon. But the dizziness was more pleasurable than nauseous and I smoked the rest of it slowly, savouring every draw.

It wasn't until I stood up that the full effects really hit. I made my way back to the car on increasingly unsteady legs and realised I needed to sit down again. I left the door open as I slid in behind the wheel, waiting for the fresh air to clean out my lungs before moving on.

* * *

Belle Meadow wasn't what I'd expected.

The caravans which circled the campfire could have come from another era. Wooden and ornately carved, their bright paintwork glistened in the morning sunlight and at the far end of the field, horses were grazing. Everywhere was neat and tidy, I saw none of the strewn rubbish Traveller sites had become notorious for. As if to emphasise this, each caravan had a wide broom resting beside the step to the door. Washing lines ran between the caravans, an assortment of brightly coloured garments rustling in the breeze.

I stepped out of the car, then hesitated. There was no sign of life, and I wasn't sure what the protocol might be for announcing oneself.

"Hello," I called out.

No response. After a few seconds, I decided to try knocking on one of the doors and started walking over to the nearest caravan.

A door opened and a woman stepped slowly down to the

ground.

It would have been impossible to be certain of her age - anything over sixty. Her face, although not heavily lined, had the texture of old parchment and was stretched tight over a fine bone structure. Her hair was silver, coiled down her back to her waist, but it was her eyes that were her most striking feature - a deep amber, almost russet, a colour I'd never seen before and her stare was both unblinking and impassive as she studied me.

"Hello," I repeated and carried on towards her, conscious of attempting to make my gait appear as unthreatening as possible. "My name's Richard Hanson. I was hoping to talk to someone about..."

I hesitated, struggling for a neutral tone.

"About the situation here." I chose my words carefully. "And perhaps come to a mutually beneficial arrangement."

She continued to stare, but then broke into a smile. Her teeth, I noticed, were stained deep yellow with nicotine.

"Please," she said, indicating the caravan, and turning climbed back inside. Following her, the first thing that registered was a rich aroma of spices and oils, blending in a way that felt both exotic yet familiar.

The second thing was that the interior seemed far more spacious than my initial impression would have suggested. She indicated a quilted bench running along one wall. She sat opposite, and we faced each other over a low table on which had been arranged a plate with a thick slice of black bread, a samovar and two china cups and saucers.

"Please, drink," she said. It sounded more like a command than an offer, and so I nodded.

I'd expected to be introduced to - possibly - her husband, but she seemed in no hurry to leave and fetch anyone else. It occurred to me that this might be exactly who I should be talking to. I knew nothing of how Romany society was structured. For all the swaggering and braggadocio displayed by the males, maybe the real authority lay in a matriarchy.

"What I was..." I began, but she silenced me by lifting her

palm.

"Please," she repeated. "Drink."

Not wishing to seem disrespectful towards what was perhaps an important ritual, I raised the cup to my lips. Unexpectedly sweet, but not unpleasantly so.

"Your hand," she said, reaching out with hers.

"Sorry?"

"Hand," she repeated, and inwardly I groaned, the situation instantly obvious. Everyone else left for work and here I was, ambushed by some 'cross my palms with silver' old crone, who probably couldn't believe her luck that such an easy mark had walked right into her parlour. But she held me by the wrist and, with a surprisingly steely grip, turned my palm face up.

She studied it carefully and then began to trace along it with the forefinger of her free hand. Suddenly - almost as if she'd been burnt - she snatched it away.

Then, with a shake of her head, she rose and left the caravan.

* * *

I waited perhaps four or five minutes. With the passage of time, the mingled scents in the caravan became more pungent, almost cloying. I couldn't see a window to open, but a hinged shutter on the opposite wall would probably let in some fresh air. I stood, walked around the table and pushed at it. It was stiffer than I expected. I thought there might be an unseen catch, but before I could examine it more closely, there came the sound of voices from outside.

Finally, I said to myself, someone's returned. Then the shutter, seemingly with no effort on my part, opened fully.

The campsite was bustling. The horses which had been grazing at the far end of the meadow were now tethered only a few feet away and being rubbed down by two young girls. Flames from the fire were licking around a cauldron, into which vegetables were being scraped from a cutting board by an elderly woman. Alongside her squatted a teenage boy, skinning a rabbit with a blade that looked more weapon than kitchen implement.

A group of men were clustered together. One knelt, creating some design in the soil with a long stick. The others gathered around him, staring downward. All were smoking, some drawing on thin cheroots, the rest of them clay pipes. A woman with her back to me was also taking in this scene, hand on hip and her hair jet black ringlets tumbling over her shoulders. An elaborately embroidered silk blouse was tucked into a flowing skirt that reached the ground.

All were dressed Romany style and much more so than might be expected. Rather than trousers, some of the men wore rough corduroy breeches, fastened below the knee into gaiters. The young girls were clothed in calico shifts. The teenage boy...

The Land Rover! Where was the Land Rover?

Certainly nowhere to be seen on the campsite. I dropped my hand to press on my jacket pocket and felt the keys against my skin. Turning my head towards the road, I half expected to see it disappearing around the curve of the headland, but then I froze, all thoughts of cars and keys and theft instantly wiped from my mind.

There was a road there, but it wasn't the one I'd arrived by.

Tarmacked but hardly more than a track, it followed the course of the headland but with no markings - no centre line, no cats-eyes. And no sea wall either, where I'd sat to smoke a cigarette, minutes or eons ago. Then I heard the sound of an engine approaching and raised my head, both knowing and fearful of what I was about to see.

It was a grocer's delivery van, box-like in its antiquity, and I watched its slow approach, almost mesmerised. As it disappeared from view, I returned my gaze to the campsite. The woman had turned and was staring at me.

Despite the jet black hair and features which couldn't have been more than twenty years old, there was no mistaking those amber eyes.

She smiled, and with a clatter the shutter slammed down.

* * *

This sudden extinguishing of bright sunlight gave my

eyes no time to adjust, the caravan was effectively plunged into darkness. With my hand trailing against the wall, I felt my way to the rear and opened the door. I stepped down to the ground and staring wildly around would probably have seemed something of a maniacal figure to any observer.

The Land Rover was parked where I'd left it by the entrance. Everything else was as it had been before I'd entered the caravan.

"Nothing is set in stone, certainly not the future and sometimes not even the past."

I whirled around. The woman was behind me, stepping down from the empty caravan which I'd left only seconds before.

I found myself breathing heavily.

"I don't understand," I told her.

"The path can be changed," she said. "But only if you are certain of where your steps first went astray."

"Look..." I began, but without breaking her stare, she raised her hand to silence me.

"Life is meaningless, wealth is worthless, death a comfort. If you would have things otherwise, think of when you first persuaded yourself of that which you did not believe. Hold that moment in your mind's eye as if it were a precious stone and reflect on its many facets. Then bring it back here tomorrow, at noon."

She turned and began to climb up into the caravan as I stared after her.

"Noon tomorrow," she repeated without turning, pulling the door closed behind her, "if you would have things otherwise."

* * *

A multitude of possibilities swirled around my brain as I drove away, the most obvious being that she'd spiked my drink.

Except I was sure she hadn't.

In my youth, I'd probably ingested most hallucinogens known to man, and none of them had produced effects so powerful in such little time. Or rather, effects which also dissipate this rapidly, leaving no residue.

Not a drug, then.

Perhaps she'd somehow hypnotised me. Not something I knew much about, other than it involved suggestion and I couldn't recall even a hint of that... Unless it was a combination of the two, some kind of sedative to make me suggestible and then induce a trance. Valium wipes short term memory clean. Except - glancing at the dashboard clock - I'd been there less than twenty minutes. The rest of my memory seemed just fine and the last thing I felt was sedated.

I stomped on the brakes and swerved into the Viewing Area where I'd parked earlier. I really needed to think this through. I took Veronica's pack of cigarettes from the glove compartment and lit one with the cigar lighter.

Drawing on it deeply, I walked back over to the seawall again.

Even if I had been drugged or beguiled, what about worthless wealth or death a comfort? If that had been a cold reading, it was a bloody impressive one...

* * *

Veronica was in the kitchen, dicing vegetables on a cutting board and I had a sudden flash of the scene I'd witnessed from the caravan. My nostrils flared, as if to catch a hint of spice and oils...

I shook my head.

"Hi," she said. "You were out early."

"Had a couple of errands to run," I told her, as she came over to give me a kiss. There was only a fractional hesitation as her lips left mine, a whiff of *eau de Marlboro,* I guessed. She said nothing and her expression didn't change, but she'd probably be checking her glove compartment at some point during the day.

"Want a coffee?" I asked.

She nodded as I took a box of filters out of the cupboard. The TV, mounted on a bracket in a ceiling corner, was tuned to a news channel but I wasn't really paying attention as I scooped ground coffee beans out of the tinfoil pack.

"Did you ever read any of his stuff?" asked Veronica. "When you were a kid?"

"Sorry?"

"Peter Matthews, the children's author. He's died."

I glanced up at the screen. The newsreader's voice came over a black and white video clip, which I realised was a kids' TV series from the sixties.

"Yes, I did," I told her. "I used to like them a lot."

'As with several children's authors popular in the nineteen fifties and sixties,' said the newsreader, 'his work had lately attracted criticism regarding gender and racial stereotypes. Only last year, Islington Council removed his books from local libraries.'

"I could never get on with them." Veronica shrugged. "Like they say, girls were either packing a picnic basket or being rescued. But sometimes I do wish they'd give it a bloody rest, rewriting the past never solved anything."

I gave her a sharp look - Veronica's the most intuitive woman I've ever known - but she only shook her head as she finished with the vegetables.

The TV screen switched to a portrait photograph, superimposed with 'Peter Matthews, 1920 - 1999'.

"Everything okay?" asked Veronica, catching my expression as I stared at the TV.

"Yes," I told her, turning back to the coffee. "It's just a bit sad, that's all."

"I imagine a lot of people are going to be dusting off old hardbacks this afternoon," nodded Veronica. "That's the thing about authors from childhood, isn't it? They seem to have that same feel in memory as someone you actually knew."

True enough, I thought. I'd known him as Herostratus.

* * *

For once, Veronica was up and about before me. I'd worked late the previous night, going through my PC and transferring what I didn't want to outlive me into a separate folder, ready for shredding at a single keypress. I'd already cancelled most subscriptions for magazines or online services. Bank account usernames and logins, insurance policy details and anything else Veronica might have to deal with, I'd given her on a Zip floppy a few weeks ago, 'Just in case'. I'd also emailed Gerry about the Jag, offering him a hefty finder's fee if he managed a quick sale.

Cleaning up the crime scene in advance.

For most of the evening I'd kept the gypsy's words well to the back of my mind - I was returning to the campsite, I told myself, because I'd promised Alan I'd do this for him. Anything else had the feel of abstract rationale, those deals you make with yourself when you're desperate for things to play out in a certain way... Prayers of the secular, Veronica used to call them.

But while I showered and dressed, I couldn't shift the events of that fateful night at Pembridge Villas. If I'd walked down those stairs with Carin, would Emily be alive now? Would Saskia have grown up with me as her father?

But more than anything else, what the hell had really happened during that visit yesterday...?

Heading for the front door, I realised Veronica wasn't alone, that there were voices coming from outside. I glanced at my watch, hesitated, and then stepped into the living room where the panoramic view across the bay also took in most of the veranda.

A red-eyed and visibly upset Gillian was being consoled by Veronica and it didn't take much of a guess to work out why.

The outer door was open and their voices clear.

"Did they give you any explanation at all?" Veronica was asking, as they sat beside each other on the cushioned wooden bench.

Gillian brushed away a tear with the back of her hand.

"'Taking all factors into consideration', was all they bloody said." Gillian shook her head, as if still numb with disbelief.

Veronica slipped an arm around her shoulders and gave her an affectionate squeeze. I found myself rigid as a statue, aware I was in their direct line of sight, that the slightest movement could attract their attention.

Veronica's attention.

"They have to be more explicit than that," Veronica told her. "You must know some of the Governors personally. Why don't you give them a ring, try to find out what happened?"

"Oh, we all know what's happened," said Gillian bitterly. "Ticking all the PC boxes is what's happened. Believe me, everyone knows what's really going on here, but none of them will tell me that to my face."

"You don't know that," said Veronica. "You should try to-"

"Twenty bloody years," Gillian broke in. "That's how long I've been there, that's how much of my fucking life I've given them. And I was the best Head of the department they'd ever had, even though it wasn't official. Everybody said so. Everybody!"

Gillian half turned her head towards me and I quickly stepped out of her line of vision.

"Oh, Gillian," I heard Veronica say softly.

"And I'm supposed to carry on and..."

Gillian's voice broke off and there was silence. Cautiously, I inched back to where I'd stood a few seconds before.

They were locked in an embrace, Gillian's lips pressed against Veronica's and their arms around each other.

As silently as possible, I crossed the room to the front door.

* * *

The traffic was heavy. Saturday was the holidaymakers' changeover day and with the upcoming eclipse, St Hannahs was packed to the gills. I found myself becoming increasingly tense at the realisation that I might not be arriving there by noon. But once through the town, the coast road was free flowing and the time I'd lost was easily made up. According to the dashboard clock, it was three minutes to twelve when I pulled into the Travellers' site.

Where it was obvious that something was very wrong.

The campfire was still the centrepiece of the camp, but the wooden caravans were nowhere to be seen. In their place was a collection of motorhomes, their appearance neglected at best. A fierce-looking dog, at a glance mostly Alsatian, was chained by its collar to a tree stump, being taunted with a long branch by a group of small children. A woman, borderline obese in sweatshirt and jogging bottoms, broke off from hanging similar garments on a washing line to stare at me.

Two men standing by the fire were also staring. My instinct was to immediately reverse back out into the road, but whatever might actually be happening here now, this scene in front of me was what I'd expected to see - and deal with - the previous day.

Hesitantly, I got out of the car, wishing I'd come in the Land Rover again instead of the Jaguar.

As I did so, the door of a motorhome opened and two more men stepped down from it. Instinctively I knew not to mention the woman I'd met, that whatever happened yesterday had been nothing to do with this.

Revert to plan A.

"Hello there," I said with a smile, although no one was looking friendly.

"What do you want here?" asked the youngest of them. The door of another motorhome opened and an older man, perhaps in his sixties, walked over to join us.

"I'm a friend of Alan Bradshaw," I answered. "Who owns..." I gestured around the site. "He asked me to come and speak with you."

"We already send one coney packing," said the young man. "You got plenty nerve coming here."

I raised my hand.

"Look, there doesn't need to be any trouble," I told him. "I'm only here to make you an offer. It's a good one, but if you're not interested, no problem - I'll be on my way."

"That's what the other bastard said." He was shaking his head. "Then the maskers turn up while we're away working."

"Sorry...?"

"The police came." The older man was careful to enunciate

his speech clearly. "When only the women and children were here." He eyed me steadily. "So nobody believes your Mr Bradshaw."

From which I gathered that Ratty had handled the situation with his usual tact. There was a shout, words I couldn't distinguish from one of the kids who'd been tormenting the dog, a sullen faced boy of about ten. He shook his fist at me.

"Police chase him into woods," said the old fellow. "Talk to his mother about Social Services."

I made a snap decision.

"Five thousand," I told him. "In cash, if you're gone today."

Alan had said two, but screw him. He wasn't standing here surrounded by the fruits of his brother-in-law's diplomacy.

The old man hesitated.

"We have two more days' work here. Tarmacking. We don't finish, we don't get paid."

"I'm not saying leave St Hannahs," I told him. "I don't care about that. The money's for moving out of Belle Meadow."

He considered for a few seconds and then nodded.

"We make deal," he said. "Come back with money in two hours and…"

The left side of my head exploded in pain, I think I might actually have screamed. The old man shot his hand out, grabbing my arm as I toppled backwards. He continued to hold me steady as I sank down onto one knee, dimly aware of consternation all around. Turning my head, I saw the boy who'd shook his fist at me standing no more than a dozen feet away, wearing an evil smile and holding a metal slingshot.

The belligerence of the surrounding crowd evaporated instantly. One of the men shouted angrily and made after the boy, but he'd already turned and scampered into the trees behind him. The others were exchanging nervous glances and backing off, separating towards the different motorhomes.

The old man dropped onto his knees beside me, took what was a surprisingly clean white rag from his pocket, and held it gently against my temple. It came away soaked with blood.

"Little bastard get hiding of his life when we catch him," he told me softly. Wiping at the blood, he peered at the wound and then gave a nod. "Is not too bad, won't need stitching," he said, and then - to what must have been my dubious expression - added, "What you feel is shock, not damage. Just hold cloth there until you bleed no more."

He seemed to be right. After a few minutes, with the flow all but dried up, I rose unsteadily to my feet.

"You okay to drive?" he asked, and I nodded.

My head was starting to work again, and I realised it was a Saturday, which meant I wouldn't be able to get the cash I'd promised out of the bank. I did some quick calculations - I had Alan's two thousand, maybe fifteen hundred in the safe at home and a collection of credit and debit cards to raid an ATM with. If any of that proved a problem, Rod at *The Barque* would cash a cheque for me. But I'd need more than two hours for sorting all of that out, and - after Ratty - I didn't want this guy to think I was stalling.

"I'm going to go and have this looked at," I told him, raising my hand to my head, "and I've no idea how long I'll have to wait in A&E. So let's make it five o'clock, okay? But if I am late, I'll still be coming."

"I understand," he said, nodding.

"And you'll be ready to leave when I get here. All packed up and engines running."

He nodded again.

"You come, we go," he said.

"Right," I said, fishing in my pockets for my car keys. "See you later."

* * *

I steered the car back onto the coast road and headed towards St Hannahs. The blurry vision I'd initially suffered, when whatever had been in that slingshot collided with my head, was clearing and a sharp pain down the side of my face at least made it unlikely I'd nod off. There was a Viewing Area ahead and it seemed a good idea to pull in there and clean myself up before arriving home. I was in two minds about the hospital, I figured I'd dose myself with a couple of Solpadol tablets and then see what I felt like after I'd sorted the money out.

The Viewing Area already had a vehicle parked in it, so I decided to try further along. It was a beat up Volkswagen campervan, one of those sixties models with a split windscreen and a V-shape on the front. A woman stood beside it, holding her hand over her eyes, shielding them from the sun as she looked out across the ocean. As I drove by, I casually glanced into the rear-view mirror. Whether it was delayed shock or sublimated disbelief which prevented me instantly registering what I saw there, I don't know, but it was a good two or three seconds before I slammed the brakes on.

The woman standing by the campervan was Francesca McCaffrey.

Frankie!

* * *

Ronald and Marjorie's retirement present to themselves is a villa on Tenerife. For Ronald's seventieth birthday Marjorie has organised a surprise party, family and friends fly out to wish him well and grab a few days in the sun. Emily brings her boyfriend Jason, they met at university and it seems to be getting serious between them. He's a nice kid, Veronica and I concur, she could do a lot worse.

I return home early. I'm in the process of selling the business and things have reached a crucial stage. Veronica, Emily and Jason stay on, flying into Gatwick a week later. They collect Emily's Audi from Long Term Parking and drive to the ticket barrier. A quarter of a mile away a helicopter, just fitted with an external fuel tank for a non-stop delivery flight to its new owner in Finland, is lifting off. At the barrier, Emily inserts the ticket three times with no success before Veronica says 'Look, give it here', gets out of the car and strides over to the kiosk to ask the attendant to let them out.

One of the bolts fastening the external tank to the helicopter had been over-tightened, was the finding reached by the Inquiry. Its integrity is now weakened to the extent that the vibration on take-

off causes it to shear. At five hundred feet, the weight of the tank proves too much for the remaining bolts and it breaks loose. If it had landed on the front of the Audi, the inquiry concludes, it would have shattered on the engine block where the heat would almost certainly have exploded the fuel, turning a tragic accident into a disaster.

Instead, it impacts the roof and flattens the passenger compartment.

* * *

I sat motionless for a few seconds, aware of an irate driver behind me waiting for oncoming traffic to pass so he could pull out around me. With the road clear, I reversed back to the Viewing Area, swung the car through a hundred and eighty degrees and stepped on the brake to leave me parallel parked alongside the VW.

Frankie was nowhere to be seen.

The woman! The woman was nowhere to be seen, not Frankie. The only place Frankie exists is inside my head, a construct of neural pathways and synaptic switches. *You've just been knocked half unconscious*, I told myself. *Is it any surprise your brain's filling in blanks for you?*

And is that what it was doing yesterday?

Filling in blanks?

This was ridiculous. I'd no idea what was happening here, but I was obviously in no fit state to be behind the wheel. I needed to call Veronica, she could get a cab over here and drive me home.

I got out of the car and flipped my mobile open. Dead, battery zero percent. I was sure it had been fully charged this morning... Maybe the woman I'd seen had a phone which she'd let me use.

I heard a sound and looking up from the screen, I saw her step out from behind the campervan. But this time I couldn't make out her features. My vision was beginning to blur again. And not only blur, it was surrounded by an inky blackness that began closing toward the centre, the sensation now one of entering a long tunnel.

Then my knees buckled and the ground rushed towards me.

CARIN

Carin DeWit usually had better things to do with her Saturdays than return to college. But following a firm word from her tutor, concerning the lack of attribution in her last essay - and with a deadline for the next one only two days away - she'd decided that a few extra hours spent in the library wouldn't go amiss.

The influence of Japanese art on Van Gogh was something she'd struggled with, an irony which didn't escape her, given her parents' initial reluctance to allow her to study in London and the Van Gogh Museum less than an hour from the family home in Amersfoort. But a morning spent with the volumes of Vincent's letters to his brother, she hoped, would provide some heft to her arguments. He'd written to Theo almost daily, leaving behind possibly the most chronicled journey through inner turmoil and soul searching by any artist in history. If she couldn't pick over the bones of that to find support for her hypothesis, she told herself, then perhaps her parents were right. Maybe History of Art wasn't the path she should be on.

It took longer than Carin expected, but eventually she managed to weave a series of extracts and quotations into her own text and create the impression that the latter had been constructed from the former and not the other way around. How convincing an impression she'd learn when the essay was handed back to her...

It was mid-afternoon when Carin finally left the library and headed towards her Halls of Residence. This evening, she and two girlfriends had tickets for *Rosencrantz and Guildenstern Are Dead* at the Old Vic, a play she'd enjoyed reading but never seen. The plan was to grab a bite to eat somewhere near Oxford Circus before taking the tube to Waterloo, but - finding herself with time on her hands - Carin thought she might look in a few shops on her way home.

She heard the demonstration before she saw it, chants of *'Hey, Hey, LBJ, How Many Kids Did You Kill Today?'* over that low rumble of sound which always accompanies a mass of people on the move. Turning the corner, she could see that it stretched the entire length of Oxford Street. Amsterdam had also held demonstrations against the conflict in Vietnam, but none on this scale. She guessed the numbers were swollen by recent revelations of the Americans secretly waging war in Cambodia, the outrage had been worldwide.

Carin stood on the pavement watching it pass, impressed not only by the volume of the crowd but also its diversity. Although mostly young people, scattered amongst them were families with small children in pushchairs and some quite elderly couples. A teenage girl, walking alongside the march, smiled at Carin and handed her a leaflet. She stared at a photograph of a Vietnamese child, crying in the arms of a mother who had blood running down her stricken face.

Impulsively, Carin stepped off the pavement and joined them.

* * *

Carin slowly worked her way into the centre of the crowd. It felt safer there than by the fringes, under the scrutiny of the many police officers stationed along the route. They walked for perhaps another two hundred metres, before she realised the police were directing a section of the march ahead of them off into a side street. She hesitated slightly, noticing this a middle-aged woman laid a reassuring hand on her arm.

"It's alright," she told Carin. "They split us up going into Grosvenor Square. The roads aren't as wide as this one."

They turned the corner, beginning to slow as they were funnelled through the narrower street. Not realising this, the crowd behind kept moving forward and Carin was suddenly at the crest of a surge about to press into what had become an almost stationary wall of people.

Then everything seemed to happen at once.

Trying to keep her balance as she was being pushed along, she was at first unaware of the commotion in front of her. But looking up she saw mounted policemen, three abreast, moving through the crowd towards her. What on earth were they playing at, thought Carin, couldn't they see what was happening here? One of the demonstrators decided to draw their attention to the surging mass of people behind them, raising the placard he was carrying to point down the street. Afterwards, Carin was never sure if this had been a gesture misinterpreted or simply the excuse the police had been waiting for, but the coordination with which the officers drew their long batons suggested the latter. A blow caught him square across the head and, as he crumpled, the screaming started.

That at least had the effect of halting the movement behind them, but so abruptly that Carin, who'd been pressing backwards, lost her balance completely. She tumbled to the ground, aware that the police were not only indiscriminately lashing out at the crowd around them, but that their horses were breaking into a trot and heading straight toward where she lay. She began to scream, hooves only an arm's length away, surely about to come crashing down on her head...

She gasped as a dead weight landed on her, knocking the breath out of her body. She tried to struggle as she realised that she was being held down, but a voice in her ear told her to keep still. She complied, stiffening like a board as the body on top of hers moved forward, covering her shoulders and head, pressing her face down against the cold asphalt. There was a flurry of movement all around. Her eyes were tightly closed but she could hear iron-clad hooves striking the ground only inches from her and Carin's nostrils were filled with an animal stench, horse sweat and faeces. Then the sounds echoed away, and the weight rose off of her.

She tried to stand, but halfway up stumbled as someone crashed into her from the side. But a pair of hands were on her waist, steadying her, and she found herself being lifted and pulled back tightly against the body behind her.

"We have to get away from here," said the same voice which had told her to be still, "before they turn around. Can you stand by yourself?"

The arms loosened their grip. Carin took a tentative step forward before turning her head to look over her shoulder. He was perhaps a year or two older than her, his expression full of concern.

She nodded.

"Okay, come on," he said.

He reached for her hand and led her away.

There was chaos everywhere. People were stumbling around holding their heads, a young woman was kneeling down beside a pushchair, crying. Car windows had been smashed, and she felt broken glass crunching underfoot as they crossed the road. They passed a policeman unconscious on the ground, his helmet rolled a few feet away and he was bleeding from the back of his head. Someone in a duffle coat knelt to help him, she recognised him as one of the lecturers from the college but couldn't remember his name.

"I saw that." A middle-aged man on the pavement was looking at her and pointing down the street from where they had just come. "I saw what they done. You lot didn't do nuffin'." He was shaking his head in disbelief. "They just fackin' charged you."

She stared blankly at him as they passed by. The boy she was with occasionally looked back over his shoulder but didn't stop moving until they reached the entrance to a narrow alleyway where he turned around, apparently looking for someone behind them.

"Claudia," he yelled.

Then they were on the move again, into the alley. Her eyes couldn't adjust quickly enough from the bright sunshine, so she let him lead her along in almost total darkness, until they emerged into the dazzling light of Oxford Street.

* * *

"Are you okay?"

She nodded, before realising he was addressing someone over her shoulder. Carin half turned as a girl moved passed her, she and the boy embraced.

"I really thought your number was up there." The girl shook her head as they stepped back from each other and he

111

gave her a smile. The side of Carin's face, which had been pressed against the ground, was throbbing. She raised her hand to her forehead and gasped as it came away covered in blood.

"It's okay, it's not as bad as it looks," he told her. "Let's go for a coffee and get you cleaned up."

They began to walk along Oxford Street. Crossing the road, it struck Carin what an attractive couple they were. The boy was good looking with longish curly hair brushing his collar but the girl was stunning, as tall as her friend and with a lithe figure, olive skinned and raven haired enough to suggest Spanish or Italian heritage.

They entered the *Egg & i* where Carin often went with friends from college, and the girl took her hand, leading her into the Ladies.

"No, it's alright, she just slipped," she heard the boy saying as the door closed behind them. "She'll be fine."

The girl opened a cubicle door and made Carin sit down, while she ran cold water from the tap over a handkerchief. She dabbed away at the cut and then gave Carin a smile.

"It's stopped bleeding and I don't think you'll need stitches," she told Carin, handing her the handkerchief. "But you should keep that pressed against it for a while."

"Thank you," said Carin, standing up. And then totally surprised herself by bursting into tears.

The girl hugged her for a few minutes, holding her close until Carin had pulled herself together.

"I'm so sorry." Carin shook her head, admonishing herself. "How silly you must think of me."

"Of course not."

"I was really frightened." Still shaking her head.

"It's alright."

"I was down on the ground," said Carin. "The horse's feet were coming right at me and I thought they would break my head open." She felt the tears start to well again, but this time controlled herself. "And then your boyfriend threw himself over me. He saved me."

"He's not my boyfriend," the girl told her. "We're friends, good friends, but not a couple."

"Oh," said Carin, finding herself inexplicably gratified by that. Or perhaps not so inexplicable - a flash of him pressing down on her, all enveloping...

"I'm Claudia, by the way," the girl told her.

"Carin."

"Okay Karen, shall we..."

"Carin." She interrupted. "C-A-R-I-N."

"I'm sorry."

"It's okay." Carin found herself smiling for the first time. "I'm used to it. In England, no one knows of the Dutch name."

"Shall we have that coffee?" Claudia raised her palm. "If you'd like a little longer to collect yourself, that's alright, there's no hurry."

Carin shook her head, and they went back out into the restaurant.

"This is Carin," said Claudia, as they sat down at the table. "And Carin, this is Kit."

"So, you are my knight in armour." Carin gave him a shy smile. "Isn't that what you say?"

"Knight in shining armour," Kit replied, smiling back at her.

"Are you on holiday here, Carin?" asked Claudia.

"I'm a student," she told her. "I am studying History of Art at the Central London Polytechnic."

"Oh, over the road here," said Kit.

"Yes." She shrugged. "I came in today to use the library. Leaving, I see the March, see it is against the Americans in Vietnam. I joined in. We turned off Oxford Street and then..." She broke off. "Why would the police do that? There was no violence."

"It's unofficial policy to keep political demonstrations as violent as possible." Kit shrugged. "Back in the fifties, CND marches attracted a broad cross-section and so..."

"Broad cross-section?"

"People from lots of different backgrounds."

"I understand."

"The Government didn't like the appearance of unified opposition," said Kit. "So, the police got the nod to put the boot in." He sipped his coffee. "What happens is that on the next demo, the women with pushchairs and kids don't come back, but the blokes do, looking for payback. And whatever's being protested about gets buried under accusations of mindless thugs attacking the police."

"You seem to know a lot about it," said Carin, and Kit gave another shrug.

She finished her coffee.

"Where do you live, Carin?" Claudia asked her. "Will you be okay getting home?"

"The Halls of Residence are only around the corner. I'll be fine." She stared at Kit. "You really did save my life, you know?"

Carin reached into her bag, pulled out a pen and a small spiral notebook.

"I've arranged to meet some friends," she told him, "and with all of this trouble, I think it might worry them if I am late."

"That's okay," said Kit. "It was good to meet you, Carin."

"But I would like to thank you properly," flipping the notebook open, "and the least I could do would be to buy you dinner." She gave Kit that same shy smile again. "If you would like that?"

"Yes." Kit returned her smile. "I'd like that very much."

She began to scribble.

"This is the phone number. Ask for Carin in room twenty-three if I don't answer."

She tore the page out and passed it across the table. "The best time to call is between six and seven."

Carin stood up. "Goodbye and thank you again," she said. "Bye bye, Claudia."

From the pavement outside, she had one last look at them through the window. Claudia was leaning forward, speaking intently, but Kit was simply staring at the scribbled phone number Carin had given him. Then, with a smile, he carefully folded the sheet of paper and slipped it into his pocket.

Carin felt a warm rush.

* * *

'The least I can do is buy you dinner!' Carin inwardly winced. *Jesus!* When was the last time she'd thrown herself at someone like that? Certainly long before she'd learnt the hard way if that was all you were offering, then that was all that would be taken. She'd might not have been herself, Carin mused, but it hadn't been that much of a knock to the head.

Her friends had been all concern when she'd returned to the Halls of Residence, Kate cleaning her cut with Dettol - God, that had stung - before dressing it with a sticky plaster. Lucy asked if she was sure she still wanted to go out tonight, if she didn't feel up to it there'd probably be someone who'd take the tickets. They could stay in, most Saturday evenings BBC2 had a World Cinema film on. But Carin told them she'd be fine, that she was really looking forward to it.

Carin played down exactly what had happened, telling them she'd taken a shortcut behind Oxford Street and been caught up in the violence, rather than explaining how she'd actually joined the demonstration. She wasn't sure why, all of her friends were against the Vietnam War and a lot of them had stories of the protests they'd been on. A gashed head from a police charge at a demo might almost be worn as a badge of honour.

Was it because she didn't want to talk about Kit? Didn't want all the drama of the afternoon inevitably embellished in their minds, especially with feelings she herself wasn't sure about.

But they were feelings that wouldn't leave her alone. Throughout the evening at the theatre they kept flashing into her mind - the weight of him pressing her down, the strength in his arms as he lifted her...

'Oh, snap out of it!' she told herself as she prepared for bed. He's forgotten about you already, a silly little girl who stumbled

into his life for twenty minutes and needed taking care of. You'll never see him again, and today will fade into just one more dim recollection of what might have been.

Carin slipped under the covers, restless in the dark before eventually soothing herself into sleep.

* * *

She slept late the next morning, woken by a knock on her door.

"Carin - phone!"

"Okay - who's calling?" Her speech slurry as she pulled the bedclothes to one side and sat up. But whoever had been at the door was gone.

Carin climbed out of bed, put on her dressing gown and stepped into the corridor. The payphone was three doors down and the tiled floor cold under her bare feet. Picking up the handset, she swallowed to get some moisture into her dry throat.

"Hello?"

"Hi. Is that Carin?"

Recognising the voice, she swallowed again.

"Yes."

"It's Kit - from yesterday." He hesitated. "How are you feeling?"

"I'm okay."

"You seemed pretty shaky when you left. I thought I'd check to see that you were alright."

"Thank you." *Don't gush, don't gush!* she told herself. Slowly: "And for what you did yesterday - I don't know what would have happened to me if you hadn't been there."

"That's okay, I'm just glad I was." A slight pause. "Look, are you doing anything tonight?"

"I've nothing planned."

"Would you like to go to a concert? I've tickets for Leonard Cohen at the Albert Hall."

Her heart rose at the first sentence and sank at the second. Her last boyfriend had played his LP all the time...

Not something exactly conducive to a happy relationship, she'd always thought, and eventually been proved right.

"I was supposed to be taking you for a meal," she reminded him. "As a thank you."

"Maybe we could grab a bite to eat afterwards," he said.

"Okay," she told him, "I'd like that very much."

They arranged a time and place to meet and hung up, leaving Carin with the rest of the day to fret over what she should wear and the things they might talk about.

* * *

"So, what did you think?" asked Kit, as they exited the Albert Hall onto Kensington Gore.

"Not as depressing as I expected," said Carin.

Kit laughed.

"Well, I'll take that as a ringing endorsement."

"No, I meant..." She broke off, smiling and shaking her head.

"It's okay, I know what you meant." He put his arm around her shoulders to steer her out of the path of a passing couple, letting it linger there a few seconds longer than necessary. She leaned into him until he lowered it and then slipped her arm through his.

"I liked the song about Joan of Arc," she told him. "And the one which was a letter to a man who had stolen his wife. But I don't know what he meant when he said that he left his songs empty so we could put into them what we wished." She shrugged. "Isn't creativity supposed to be the other way around?"

"D. H. Lawrence once said 'Trust the art, never the artist'."

"And I'm also not sure what that means."

"That perhaps some great works of art - or music, or literature - owe more to instinct than intellect. Leaving their creator as baffled as anyone else... Yet that's who we turn to for explanations."

Carin nodded.

"Okay, I can see that." She squeezed Kit's arm. "But it's

still a thin line between being insightful and being pretentious, right?"

"Right," grinned Kit.

"So what do you do?" she asked him. "Are you a student?"

"No." He shook his head. "I'm a writer."

"A writer?"

"Nothing too impressive so far," he smiled. "Articles in the underground press and I've written a short play for a street theatre group that's being put on at the Roundhouse." He gave a slight shrug. "But Lee Munro's in it."

She turned her head to look at him.

"I'm guessing an English girl would be impressed by that?"

"An English girl," he told her, "would be going weak at the knees right now."

"So this Lee...?"

"Lee Munro."

"She is an actress?"

"Yes. When she was a kid, she was in this British TV soap called *The Hendersons*." He paused. "She's filming a detective series at the moment, which hasn't been shown yet."

"And she wanted to be in your play? Okay, maybe I am a little impressed."

"We've been friends for a while." Kit shrugged. "And we live in the same house. In fact, it was Lee who got the tickets for tonight. Leonard gave them to her at a party last week, but she couldn't make it this evening." He grinned. "And if I told you why, you'd think I was really name dropping."

Carin stayed silent, feeling what might have been just the tiniest pang of jealousy.

"But to pay the rent, I have a stall at Kensington Market," he said.

"Really?" Carin knew the market well, a three story warren of stalls and boutiques stretching along Kensington High Street. She'd been taken there by friends on her first weekend in London and it had reminded her of Waterlooplein Market in Amsterdam, but an indoor version. She still went over there maybe twice a month. The clothes, mainly Afghan and Indian imports, were cheap and she loved browsing the antique and craft stalls. "What do you sell?"

"Leather belts and bags, mostly."

"Do you make them yourself?"

"No, a Brazilian couple I'm friends with."

"They don't want to sell the bags and belts themselves?"

Kit hesitated.

"They need to keep their heads down - they're in the country illegally." He shrugged. "And trying to get the fare together to go home. We split the money the stall makes, after expenses." He gave a rueful smile. "But it's looking as if they'll be here for a while yet."

He stopped walking and turned to her.

"Would you like to come back to my place for coffee?" he asked. As Carin hesitated, he added, "It's only on the other side of Hyde Park, a thirty-minute walk. And I'll get you a cab home afterwards."

"After what?" asked Carin with a wry smile.

"I didn't mean..." began Kit, but Carin turned, lifted herself onto tiptoe and kissed him on the lips. Resting his hands on her shoulders, he pulled her close.

"I've enjoyed tonight very much," Carin said to him, as they eventually moved apart, "and I'd really like to see you again. But I'm not going to sleep with you on a first date."

"You know, technically," Kit said to her, as they walked along by the park railings, his arm back around her shoulders, "this could be considered our second date."

"Which would make the next one our third," smiled Carin, "and I have no rules about that at all."

* * *

Carin hoped he'd ask to see her the following evening. Her Van Gogh essay was due to be handed in tomorrow morning and getting the damn thing finally behind her would be a good excuse to unwind.

"I'm going to be busy over the next few days," he told her. "But do you want to go to the pictures on Friday?"

They were standing outside the Halls of Residence. Men weren't allowed in after nine o'clock, and only in the lobby whatever the time of day.

"The pictures?" She smiled quizzically. "Whose pictures are those?"

"I meant would you like to go to.."

"I know what you meant," she broke in, laughing. "I was only teasing you."

They stepped into the shadows away from the doorway and kissed. His hand cupped her breast and she leant into it. His other hand moved lower, giving her a moment of uncertainty. She was about to reach down and take it in hers when the sound of approaching voices allowed her to gently push him back.

"I should go inside," she said.

"I'll call you later in the week," he told her.

"Bye," she said, as two girls from her floor pretended to be fiddling with the lock.

All three of them watched him walk away, then one of the girls held the door open for her. The other looked at her with a smile and a raised eyebrow.

"We were just saying goodnight," shrugged Carin.

"Hey," she said, still smiling. "He can say goodnight to me any time of the day."

* * *

The week dragged. Even her tutor's B plus scrawled in the top corner of her returned essay - at least a grade higher than she was expecting - seemed anticlimactic, with Friday evening looming large in her mind.

"There are a couple of films I'd like to see," Kit said when he telephoned. "*I Am Curious, Yellow* is on in Victoria and *2001 A Space Odyssey* is showing in Leicester Square."

The first, recalled Carin, had controversially been banned in the United States for obscenity. The latter she'd gone to with a girlfriend two weeks ago and been completely baffled by.

Kit seemed to sense her hesitation.

"A friend has tickets for Ballet Rambert," he told her, "if you'd prefer that. *L'Apres-midi d'un Faun.*"

Carin had never been to the ballet, but of the three options it was the one she plumped for.

"It's at the Cochrane Theatre," he said. "On Southampton Row. Do you know where that is?"

Carin didn't.

"Okay," said Kit. "Let's meet at Holborn tube station. Say seven, and we'll go for a drink first."

Carin wasn't like a lot of the girls she knew, who always arrived late for a date because they didn't want to seem too eager. But she did get annoyed if she found herself having to wait.

"Sorry," said Kit, when he eventually appeared. "The train stopped for fifteen minutes, no explanation or..."

He broke off as he realised she was staring at his face.

"It looks a lot worse than it is," he smiled.

There was a plaster over his left eyebrow and a discoloured bruise on his cheek.

"What happened?" she asked.

"I was helping a friend out in a garage," he told her. "A petrol can exploded."

"How did *that* happen?"

"Carelessness, really," he said, taking her hand and leading her out onto High Holborn. He was also, she noticed, walking with a slight limp.

"Look," said Carin. "Are you going to be okay sitting down for the evening?"

"I'll manage," he said, "but a couple of large whiskies first wouldn't hurt."

They found a pub across the road from the theatre. Carin insisted on getting the drinks while he sat down.

"Give me the tickets," she said to Kit, putting the glasses down on the table.

"Sorry?" he said.

"The tickets," she smiled, and with a puzzled expression

he handed them over. She returned to the bar and interrupted a conversation between two youths, offering them the tickets. One of them took his wallet from inside his jacket. She shook her head, but he insisted, handing over a pound note while the other hastily finished his drink.

"I overheard them saying they'd hoped to see the ballet, but that it was sold out," she told Kit, as she sat down at the table. "I explained that we weren't able to use ours."

"And why is that?" asked Kit.

"Because we will finish these drinks," said Carin, "and then go back to your house, where I am going to take care of you."

Which she did.

* * *

It wasn't the first time Carin had felt this way, but never so quickly. And as much as she cautioned herself not to get swept away here - infatuation had masqueraded as love before in her life - Kit increasingly began to govern her thoughts.

The morning after that first night they spent together, Kit went over to Kensington Market and Carin returned to the Halls of Residence, to shower and change. They'd made no plans, but Carin was careful to make sure she had enough toiletries and underwear in her bag to see her through the next few days. Then, taking the Tube to South Kensington, she easily found Kit's stall. He seemed busy and so she walked about the building for an hour or so, waiting for him to close up.

For a while she took a seat at a coffee bar, watching him through a gap between two stalls, but from where, given the bustle of the market, it was unlikely he'd catch a glimpse of her. When she'd first arrived at his stall, Carin thought the leather bags and belts - although excellent quality - were overpriced, yet as she sat and watched, he seemed to do a brisk trade. But she soon realised that it wasn't the expensive items he was selling, it was beaded wrist bands and packets of incense which sold the most. He also appeared to know most of his customers, greeting them with a smile and by name. Some girls he was being obviously flirtatious with and she felt pangs of irritation at the way a few of them looked at him when his gaze was turned away.

Oh, grow up, Carin! she told herself. Would you want Kit to see you batting your eyelids when you're late with an essay? Or, allowing herself a smile, haggling with a boy at a stall like this?

We all do what we have to do to get by, and so why pretend otherwise?

* * *

The entrance to Rustin Close wasn't exactly blocked off, but a strategically placed truck meant that any cars attempting to enter had to pull over and be checked. The only pedestrians being allowed through were residents or press.

Carin and Kit waited across the street, while Lee Munro had a word with the uniformed security guard. He turned away, spoke briefly into his walkie talkie and then nodded. Lee gave them a wave. They crossed over to join her and together the three of them entered the Close.

Carin was immediately struck by the contrast of the buildings. Houses at the entrance to the Close, while not exactly gentrified, had their doors and windows brightly painted and the brick walls looked freshly scrubbed. Those further away had a dingy appearance, dusty and dirty.

"They've given them a mud wash, darling," said Lee, noticing Carin's head moving back and forth. "Certainly got that late forties, post-war dreary look off to a tee, haven't they?"

Carin assumed the question was rhetorical, but nodded anyway. They walked on, to where a dark green Rolls Royce was parked and which in Carin's eyes couldn't have seemed more out of place here. A middle-aged man, portly and shabbily dressed, was posing for photographers on the pavement.

They joined a cluster of onlookers on the other side of the road.

"'E's not as tall," said one woman, hair in curlers under a cotton headscarf.

"Not as skinny, either," said her friend.

"Creepy little bugger though, isn't 'e?" said the first woman. "At least they got that right."

"Be back in a minute," said Lee, and made her way through the small crowd to where a young couple were standing just slightly to one side of the photographers. In fact, almost as if they were waiting... Carin suddenly realised that the shabby clothing both of them wore was decades out of date, but had blended so well into the surroundings as to seem unremarkable.

The man greeted Lee with a smile and they pecked each other's cheeks. With a gesture of his hand, he introduced Lee to the girl he was with and, as they also exchanged pecks, Carin was startled by the realisation that she knew him. Or rather, recognised him. He was an actor who had been in *A Man for All Seasons*, one of her favourite films. He'd played the courtier who betrayed Thomas More, she recalled.

As Lee spoke with him, he looked in their direction and then gave a slight shrug. Lee broke off talking as the man being photographed - obviously another actor, decided Carin, but she couldn't place him - came over to join them. He and Lee embraced, and as the couple now moved into position for the photographers, he also looked over as they exchanged words. He combined a smile with a small shake of his head - practised regret, thought Carin, easily dispensed - and then turned his attention to the reporters who'd gathered around, holding their dictaphone recorders out to him.

Lee came back over the road.

"John says he'll have a word if there's time at the end," she told Kit. "But Dickie's only talking to the national press today."

"What if," asked Kit, "I threw in a blow job?"

Lee giggled.

"Don't think so." She gave a shake of her head. "You know," she said, "there might well be a story here around the edges of the production."

"What do you mean?"

"John told me they're having to film inside number seven, because the people in number ten wouldn't move out. Even though the production company offered to put them up at a hotel for the duration of the shoot, all expenses covered." Lee shrugged. "Might be interesting to find out why."

"Is the house number so important?" asked Carin.

They both turned to her.

"Ten Rillington Place," said Kit, "is one of the most infamous addresses in Britain."

* * *

"This is Carin. Carin, this is Lee."

Carin had been slightly nervous about meeting Kit's actress friend, but she actually seemed very nice. Lee rose from the sofa and with a smile gave Carin a kiss on the cheek.

"Lovely to finally meet you," she said. "Kit just can't shut up about you."

Carin found herself blushing, but also wondered about Kit's slight hesitancy to that. As if there were some undercurrent here.

Don't overthink it, she told herself.

"I've made the changes you suggested," Kit said to Lee, handing her a sheaf of papers. Kit had explained to Carin that he and Lee had created a one woman play, *The Mystic Leeway*, based on the memoir of Frances Gregg, an American poet. She'd been a friend of Ezra Pound, known Yeats and Jacob Epstein among many other distinguished artists and writers of the inter-war years. Moving to England in the thirties, she had been killed in an air raid during the Second World War and her work now was almost forgotten.

"We were hoping to get it put on at the Edinburgh Fringe last year," Kit said. "But in the end, it all fell through."

The playwright Arnold Wesker, Kit told her, ran the Roundhouse, an experimental arts venue in Camden Town. Carin adopted an expression of wide-eyed interest, even though she'd been there herself just a few weeks ago, on a blind date to a T-Rex concert. An occasion probably best glossed over in present company, she reflected. *The Friends,* Wesker's own play, was being staged there at the moment, continued Kit, but he'd left one night open for a charity event, an evening of music, poetry and drama to raise money for Palestinian refugees. Wesker had suggested to Lee that she construct a fifteen minute vignette from the original script - there was always a chance it might catch someone's eye and lead to greater things.

Carin sat on the sofa, listening to them discussing Kit's changes, but her attention soon wandered. She was fascinated by Lee's room. Large enough to hold a bed and two leather sofas without feeling cramped, the walls were covered with old movie posters and chipped mirrors advertised long obsolete grooming products. Free standing vases were filled with ostrich feathers and the entire length of one wall taken up by clothes racks.

Carin picked up a magazine from the coffee table and began flicking through it. *OZ* it was called, she'd seen it on newsstands but never bought it. The text seemed to be printed over multicoloured illustrations, how could anyone be expected to read...

Then she found herself staring at a complete contrast to this. A double page spread of a stark black-and-white photograph of a naked woman. A twenties flapper, thought Carin, taking in the Gatsby turban and period...

Carin froze. *She* had a penis!

Her instinctive reaction was to shut the pages and get the damn thing as far away from her as possible.

But she didn't.

She simply stared.

And as she did so, she felt an eroticism enveloping her and one unlike anything she had ever experienced before. It wasn't desire; it didn't even seem to emanate from her sexual core... Its grip on her was almost *psychic,* its intensity a manifestation of all which seemed forbidden. In later years, she would describe this moment as less a door being opened than the sense of a key being turned in the lock of a door she had yet to find.

"Carin?"

Kit's voice startled her back to herself.

"Yes."

She closed the magazine and laid it down on the coffee table.

"Shall we go over?"

"Sorry - I was miles away."

"There's a movie being shot just around the corner from here, starting today. Lee thinks she might be able to get me an interview."

* * *

John Hurt had given Kit a regretful smile as he stepped into yet another Rolls Royce, arriving at what only an hour ago had been a typical West London street, but was now very much a film set. Trailers, probably dressing rooms, thought Carin, had been delivered and long cables snaked from generators in through the door of number seven.

"Dickie's invited me to a reception at a hotel in the West End," Lee had said to Carin, after Kit had gone over to chat to a group of West Indians standing on the pavement outside number 10. "Trust me, more hard work than glamorous, but he's a director as well as an actor and it's a chance to buttonhole him about *The Mystic Leeway* - see if I can get him to come over to the Roundhouse for the Palestinian benefit."

She'd given Carin what seemed to be the mandatory kiss on the cheek when saying hello or goodbye to almost anyone, told her it had been lovely to meet her and disappeared into the Rolls with the other actors. Kit was still talking and Carin found herself hesitant to join him. She'd noticed when he first approached them they'd appeared wary, but now everyone was smiling and chatting freely and she was conscious her presence might rupture that mood.

Kit broke off the conversation as a carpenter began unscrewing the front door. Looking across the road he saw Carin standing by herself, gave her a smile and turned back to the man he'd been speaking to.

"Thanks Gus," she heard him say, as the door was now replaced with a far shabbier one. "Good talking to you."

Carin crossed the road to meet him halfway. He looked around quizzically.

"Lee has gone to a hotel with Dickie," she told him. "To

127

'buttonhole' him. Is that like a blow job?"

Kit burst out laughing.

"No, it's..." Smiling, he shook his head. "It's something completely different."

"And were you serious - about what you'd 'throw in' for an interview?"

"I've done worse."

Kit was still smiling.

"So..." Carin wasn't sure what she was about to say here.

"Oh, come on," grinned Kit. "You wouldn't mind, would you? If it got me the interview? And a tryst with a famous movie star, that'd be something to tell your grandkids about."

Carin stared at him, wide-eyed.

"*Me!*" She shook her head disbelievingly. "You were talking about *me!*"

He turned her towards him, pulled her close and silenced her outrage with his mouth.

"You've a lot to learn," he said eventually, "about English humour."

She slipped her arm through his as they began walking back to the house.

"So," she asked, "was Lee right? Is there an interesting story there?"

Kit hesitated.

"I'm never comfortable," he said slowly, "talking over what I'm about to write." He paused. "It's that you tend to formulate fresh ideas differently in conversation. And if you've been trying to explain what you might not have a handle on yet yourself, it can all feel a bit stretched out of shape by the time you sit down at the typewriter."

"Okay," said Carin.

"Once I've got it on paper," continued Kit, "I'm happy to go on about it until the cows come home. But until then, things seem to work out better if I keep everything in my head."

"Type it out," Carin told him. "Let me read it and then we will go home with the cows."

"This," said Carin, putting the sheets of paper down and looking up at him, "is really good."

"Thanks," said Kit. "I'm quite..."

"I mean *really* good," broke in Carin, surprising herself with her intensity, having to pause before continuing. "I'm not trying to flatter you - I know you said that you were a writer, but..."

She let her voice trail off, still staring at him.

"But anyone can pick up a pen and a piece of paper, right?" smiled Kit.

Carin didn't respond, but that was exactly what she'd been thinking. These days, it seemed everyone who wasn't a musician had to be a poet or a writer. And also, that if this was a self illusion Kit had needed to bolster his ego, then she would have been happy to play along.

At first, anyway.

"I think I should do a rewrite," he said. "There are a couple of paragraphs that need tightening."

"To me, it's fine as it is," she told him.

"At five hundred words, it could be a bit long."

"You counted the words?"

"No," he shook his head. "I know roughly how many words fill a page, so it's easy to calculate. I won't be more than a dozen out."

"And that matters?"

"Yes. Newspapers and magazines work in terms of column inches. If a piece is too long, they might still buy it, but then chop the copy to fit. I like to think I'd make a better job of that than a sub editor with a deadline."

Carin began to read the article again.

What Kit had discovered from the tenant of number ten the reason they had turned down the film company's offer to be put up in a West End hotel was that by vacating their house, even temporarily, they would lose their right to be rehoused.

The property was a slum, Kit had learnt, riddled with

damp. Plaster was falling from the ceiling, wallpaper peeling from the walls. Everyone in the house - about ten residents in total, all West Indian and including three children - was waiting for the council to rehouse them, but if they moved into a hotel, they'd lose their priority status, going back to the bottom of the list when they returned.

'We all got a handout from the film people,' another tenant told Kit, *'but it's not handouts we need, it's someplace decent to bring up our kids.'*

Kit's piece reflected on the irony of a production company dressing the exterior of a street because it didn't meet their visual concept of the poverty which actually existed within its households. *'Building a reconstruction on a back lot at Elstree is one thing,'* Kit had written. *'Shoehorning real people, with real problems, into a mock film set is something else entirely.'* The Rolls Royce ferrying the cast off to a West End reception also got a mention.

"You know, the film company will not be happy with this," said Carin, finishing it for the second time. "Or the actors."

"Tough," shrugged Kit. "If they could have been arsed to talk to me for ten minutes, then I'd never have got around to meeting Gus."

"Your friend Lee hoped that... Dickie, she told me his name was, would help with your play."

"He'll have decided about that long before my article gets published," said Kit, then added, "If it gets published."

"Do you have anywhere to send it?" asked Carin.

"It's more dropping it in than sending," Kit smiled. "Let me have another go at it and then we'll take a walk."

* * *

Their destination was a house on Ladbrook Grove, not too far away. Kit rang the doorbell and after identifying himself to the intercom, the door sprang open with a loud click. Carin followed Kit down a dingy staircase into the basement, where he knocked on the first door they arrived at.

Carin was getting used to stylish living rooms in

dilapidated buildings. Two boys sat opposite each other over a dining room table, on which was a large reel-to-reel tape recorder and a microphone. On a Chesterfield sofa, two girls were sitting side by side. One, small and pretty, was leaning forward and looking uncertain, if not nervous. The other - Carin at first hadn't been sure if this was a boy or a girl - had a half smile on her face and her arm draped along the back of the sofa. Under her stare, Carin found herself uncomfortable in a way she usually only felt with men when she was conscious of their eyes undressing her.

"Hi Mick," said Kit softly.

One of the boys at the table turned, smiled and held up five fingers, indicating the interview was almost done. He had long tight curls, what they called an afro. Lots of boys were now getting their hair permed, but this looked natural. It didn't have that frizz which comes without the weekly care regime none of them could be bothered with.

Carin reflected she'd had doubts about the girl on the sofa not because she was especially masculine, but because boys these days were so feminine. You had to look twice at anyone with longish hair and no make-up or boobs.

There was only one spare seat in the room, an armchair. Kit indicated for her to take it, but instead she perched herself on one of its arms. As Kit sat down, she rested her arm on his shoulder and crossed her legs, aware of her skirt riding high on her thighs. *You want to look?* she thought to the girl sitting opposite. *Well, here's an eyeful.* An image of the flapper from *OZ* magazine flashed through her mind, then was gone.

"So what are your immediate plans, Steve?" asked Mick.

"We've already laid down three tracks," Steve told him, "and we're booked to play at Phun City in July."

Obviously a musician, decided Carin, but not famous because she didn't recognise him. Also, she quickly gathered, not particularly interesting either.

"Thanks Mick," said Steve eventually, as the interview more tailed off than reached a conclusion. "I really appreciate it, man."

"No problem," smiled Mick. "Glad to help out."

"So the piece will be in the next issue?" asked Steve as he stood up.

"Sure." Mick leant forward and switched off the tape machine. "I'll drop a copy round to you before it hits the streets."

"Cool," said Steve and his girlfriend rose from the sofa with an expression bordering on relief. He gave the others in the room a nod of farewell before shutting the door behind them.

"Sorry about that," said Mick to Kit. "He just turned up and after kicking him out of the band, I figured I owed him one."

"That's okay," said Kit, then smiled at the girl. "Hi, Veronica."

"Hi Kit."

"We're not in a hurry," Kit said to her, "and you were here first."

"We'd pretty much done," said Mick, "before Steve arrived."

"And the longer you let that guy stay," Veronica gave a shake of her head, "the harder he is to get rid of."

She reached into her bag and pulled out a wad of leaflets. Peeling one off, she offered it to Carin before handing the rest to Mick.

Women's Defence League, read Carin.

"The Free School let us have a room every Thursday night," Veronica told Mick, "if you want to send someone along."

"And it's what - Judo, Karate?" asked Mick.

"No." Veronica shook her head. "None of that coloured belts, bowing shit. It's how to put some bastard who grabs you in a dark alleyway down on the ground and make sure he stays down. We've got an ex-commando taking the classes, it's all about using what you've got - a key, a nail file - and going for the eyes and balls."

"Women's Defence League is a bit..." Mick was shaking his head, "militaristic, wouldn't you say? You know, perhaps something a bit more hip might have greater appeal."

"Like what?"

"I was thinking maybe," Mick shrugged, "'Pussy Power'?"

"How would you like," Veronica had him fixed with an icy stare, "a demonstration of the skills we've acquired so far?"

"Why don't I cover it?" Kit turned to Carin. "We could go along next week - you give it a try and I'll write it up from a mainstream perspective."

"Okay," said Carin and gave Veronica a smile. "Let's see what you can show me."

Slightly bemused, Veronica rose to her feet.

"It starts at seven thirty," she told him, picking up her bag. Then, after a slight pause, "How's Emma? I haven't seen her around lately."

"Nor have I." Kit's response was casual and smooth. It was the unmistakable barb in Veronica's tone that had Carin's ears pricking up. "So I wouldn't know."

"Say hello, if you do bump into her," said Veronica who, as she opened the door, turned back to Carin.

"When I'm on the other side of this," she rapped on the door with her knuckles, "those two are going to warn you about me." She smiled. "You should listen to them."

The door clicked shut behind her.

* * *

"Who's Emma?" asked Carin. And in that same overly casual tone, she realised, that Kit had answered Veronica with.

"A girl I used to know," said Kit.

They were walking back to Kit's house, her arm through his, Carin enjoying the easy intimacy. And not something she wanted to break, but...

"A lover?" she asked.

Kit's forehead furrowed slightly.

"'Lover' isn't really a term we use much in England," he said. "We're a bit staid in that respect."

"Right, unlike us Lutherans," said Carin. "Okay... So, is Emma someone you used to wake up next to?"

"'Girlfriend' or 'a girl you went out with', tends to be the..."

Kit broke off, catching her expression.

And then nodded.

"Lover," he said.

"What happened?"

"The usual, I suppose." Kit shrugged. "We were really young when we met, time passed, the things we had in common became fewer and fewer." He shrugged again. "While the list of things we disagreed about got longer and longer."

"Like what?"

"Politics, mainly. She comes from a very left wing, politically engaged background - her family are hardcore communist activists. Which was something she became more involved with, as I grew less interested."

"You were in the thick of it at the anti-Vietnam War demonstration," she said. "That's not indifference."

Kit's hesitation was only fractional.

"I was thinking about doing a piece on it for Mick," he said. "The changing nature of political activism. Plus," he added, "you were there too and you're not politically engaged."

"How are you so sure of that?"

"Because that's something I was into at the deep end." He stopped and turned to face her. "Trust me, I *know*."

They began walking again, Carin unsure of what to say next.

"You do care," said Kit eventually. "And you do get angry about the right issues when it comes to what's wrong with the world. But there are limits to what you'd do to go about changing things."

"And Emma...?"

Kit stayed silent.

"You make it sound very cerebral," Carin said. "All very well reasoned. But the heart doesn't really work like that, does it? And sometimes it's those very opposites in our nature which create the strongest attraction. Doesn't..."

"We slept together the night we first met," interrupted Kit, "because she wanted to get her virginity out of the way. And figured I was someone who wouldn't be too bothered that wasn't going to lead to a romantic relationship. Cerebral enough for you?"

"And how did that work out for you both?" asked Carin.

Kit began to laugh, shaking his head.

"So, do you still see her?" Carin struggled to get that neutral tone back into her voice."

Kit shrugged.

"We have the same friends, so we'd find ourselves in the same pubs, at the same parties," he said. "But she's at university now, Oxford, so not that often. She comes home for the weekend occasionally - or used to," he corrected himself. "Like Veronica said, she's not been around for a while."

"And you don't miss her?" pushed Carin.

"It burned bright for a while," said Kit. "But it burnt out. So, no is the answer to your question."

"Good," said Carin.

Carin wasn't exactly sure why this felt less reassuring than it should have done, but she took his hand, squeezed it and they walked on in silence.

* * *

But by the next time she saw Kit, Emma had - slowly - faded from her mind.

"Are you sure it's okay for me to come with you?" she asked, as they met at Notting Hill tube station the following Thursday. "I understand that this is work for you - my being there won't cramp your style?"

"Of course not," he told her. "What guy wouldn't want to watch his girlfriend wrestling lesbians?"

"So I'm your girlfriend, am I?" she smiled.

"Are you?"

She sighed.

"Looks that way, doesn't it?"

The Women's Defence League wasn't what she'd imagined. First of all, it hadn't been Veronica in charge but a woman in her forties named Frances, who had more the air of a librarian about her than militant feminist. But, she explained to Kit once the class was underway, she'd been the victim of an assault a couple of years ago and was determined never to let that happen again.

"Most of the women here have been through some form of trauma," she told him. "Rape, domestic abuse, targeted because of their sexual orientation. I wouldn't want you to write this up," she added dryly, "as some kind of women's lib fad, because it's not. We've all learnt the hard way that what it's about is survival."

Meanwhile, Carin was listening to an introductory talk from Veronica. This, she gathered, was given at the start of every session for the benefit of first timers and to reinforce the message for regulars.

"The best form of defence is to not put yourself in danger to begin with. And that's not just about staying away from dark alleys or being out by yourself late at night. If you're going to be sexually assaulted, then statistically you're likely to know your attacker, either as a friend or a date. You have two problems there. The first is that things will start to escalate because you'll try to reason with them, rather than physically resist straightaway. But their reasoning will be centred on '*women always say no when they mean yes*'. The second is because you know them, the police will be inclined to believe you went along with it but then changed your mind afterwards.

"So fight back right from the off. And hard - literally teeth and claws. Get physical evidence under your fingernails and leave enough bites and scratches on his face so that no one could ever believe what happened was consensual." She paused. "And if all else fails, void your bowels. Trust me, that puts a damper on even the most determined assault."

Next, they were handed over to Terry, an ex-soldier.

"If in doubt," he told them, "run. If you're wearing high heels, kick them off and leave them behind. Take one of these with you when you go home tonight," he indicated a cardboard box full of the kind of whistles used by football referees, "and never worry about using it - the last thing an attacker wants is attention being drawn to him. Don't be afraid to scream, but scream 'Fire' not 'Rape'. People will come running to the first but not want to get involved with the second."

He considered them.

"You're not heroines," he said, softly. "And I can't make you into one. You're vulnerable women and if an attacker does get his hands on you, the odds are with him. But there are things you can do. You've always got a weapon of some kind - a key poked into the eye, a ballpoint pen rammed up his nose into the brain. So keep those in a pocket where they're close to hand."

They paired up and practised what he showed them. Not the choreographed jujitsu moves Carin had half expected to spend the evening practising and knew would fly straight from her mind in the immediate panic of being grabbed from behind, but the techniques of vicious infighting, intended to startle and shock.

"That was," said Carin, as they walked back to Kit's house, "more interesting than I thought it would be."

"Never let it be said," nodded Kit, "that I don't know how to show a girl a good time."

"The man who was teaching us," said Carin. "The soldier. I liked him, he was nice. Firm but respectful." She shrugged. "It's generous of him to give up his evening like this, to help."

"Three years ago," said Kit softly, "his daughter was raped and murdered." He shook his head. "On her way home from school - she was fourteen."

Carin turned to him, open-mouthed.

"Frances told me," he continued. "Terry takes one of these classes most nights of the week, all over London."

"Oh, God!" she said.

"I think she was worried I might not treat this seriously. Perhaps even play it for laughs."

"But you're not going to, are you?"

"No," he said. "I'm not."

* * *

To write the article from a woman's perspective, reflected Carin, definitely made the piece more effective and she'd certainly contributed her fair share to it. But she was still startled when Julie, one of the girls on her course, came over to her table in the cafeteria at college holding a copy of *Time Out* magazine. And was looking at her in a way she never had before.

A way no one ever had, really, thought Carin.

"Oh wow, Carin!" she smiled.

Carin took the magazine from her. She hadn't seen the finished copy, she assumed Kit would write it as a piece of straight reporting, although she had expected to be heavily featured.

But it was her name on the by-line, not Kit's.

Women Fight Back by Carin DeWit.

After lunch, she went out to a newsstand on Oxford Street and bought her own copy. Back at college, she took it into the Ladies to read. How ridiculous was that, she told herself, of all the things to be furtive about... In the cubicle she read it twice, initially full of anxiety about what Kit might actually have said in her name, but the second time was with a warm glow of satisfaction.

It was a first person account of an evening spent at the WDL. What its aims were and the background to its creation. It lamented the need for its existence, praised the dedication of those running it and suggested that a woman could learn more about taking care of herself over the course of one night there, than by working through the entire spectrum of coloured belts in the more esoteric martial arts. Survival is not a sport, the article concluded.

"I just thought it worked better that way," Kit told her that evening, when they met in *Finches* on the Portobello Road. "And I took it to *Time Out* because it's a weekly mag with a much higher circulation. Plus," he added, "Mick still seemed to have that whole 'Pussy Power' thing in his head. I really couldn't trust him not to rewrite the piece with that slant to it." He stared at her. "You didn't mind, did you? My using your name?"

"No, but I wished you'd told me first. It was a little startling to discover it, but it's okay." With a smile, Carin gave a slight shake of her head. "I'm a feminist icon around college now, you know?"

It was true. All afternoon she'd caught people in the corner of her eye, if not actually staring at her, then giving her the same kind of look Julie had. Preconceptions being upended, she realised. She'd even overheard in passing a whispered conversation about 'militant lesbian groups', which had brought a smile to her lips.

And when, a week later, Kit's article on Rillington Place appeared, her stock truly rocketed. This time Kit had given her a heads up that it was coming out, mentioning that Lee had got hold of a packet of photos a press photographer had taken that day and Mick had bought the copyright on one of them. She gasped when she saw it.

It must have been when Kit was over by number ten, talking to Gus. *'From left to right'* ran the caption, *'Richard Attenborough, Judy Geeson, John Hurt, Lee Munro and friend.'*

Carin was *'and friend'*.

She didn't recall her and Lee standing that close to the others, then realised it was the bunching effect of a telephoto lens which had made her appear to be such an intimate of the stars.

IT might not have been a big read on campus, but it only needed one fan. A group of girls came up to her at the end of the last lecture of the day and she was handed a copy, folded open at the article.

"This *is* you, isn't it?" asked the girl who'd given it to her.

Carin nodded.

"You're friends with Lee Munro?" asked another.

"My boyfriend lives in the same house as her," she told them. "We do know each other, but I couldn't really say that we are friends."

"Well," said the first girl, shaking her head but with a friendly smile, "aren't you just full of surprises?"

It was the beginning of what seemed to Carin an idyllic summer, Kit her entrée to an endless stream of cutting-edge culture. Days filled with fringe theatre, *avant-garde* movies, experimental music and all bookended by mornings and evenings of lovemaking, as languid or passionate as the mood took them.

She'd planned to go to Amersfoort for the summer, but now decided to stay in London. The college made provision for overseas students not returning home - circumstances ranged from family difficulties to political upheaval - and she'd be able to keep her room on until Autumn Term started in September. Kit suggested she move into Pembridge Villas until then, but Carin worried about her parents' letters being returned marked 'Addressee Unknown' if she moved out. That was an argument she really wasn't ready for yet and part of her, instinctively, still clung to the idea of holding onto somewhere that was uniquely her own.

Because as much as they spent their time together, it was Kit's world they were spending it in.

The clubs he took her to she would never have discovered by herself, the parties they attended she would never have received an invitation for and she would never have found herself wandering freely backstage at the Roundhouse or Rainbow Theatre while Kit went in to see the musicians, some of them household names. These 'underground' magazines he wrote for, she thought, might not sell many copies but must carry a lot more influence than she'd realised.

She was ambivalent about introducing him to her friends. As much as, Carin admitted to herself, she wanted to show him off, she couldn't help contrasting the conversations she was listening to around Kit's friends with those in the college bar. Everyone was about the same age but there was - not a seriousness, or even a maturity, perhaps 'awareness' was the word she was looking for, to the discussions at Pembridge Villas. By comparison, what she heard from the girls on her floor now struck her as little more than frivolous chatter.

But they were pestering her to meet him and so she decided to ask Kit to the end of term College Ball. Hopefully, she thought, it would be too noisy for any sustained conversation and if it followed the pattern of other dances she'd gone along to, then her friends would be too drunk to be taken seriously, anyway.

Which was how the evening played out. Kit was charming, he danced with most of her friends, with good grace he allowed himself to be pestered about what it was like to live with a famous actress and fielded at least one - that she noticed - clumsy advance with adroitness and humour.

"Jesus," he said with some relief, as they stepped out onto the pavement and looked for a taxi, "I thought they were going to eat me alive in there."

"Tonight," she smiled, "that's my job."

The evening, she believed, as a cab pulled over to the curb, had been a real success.

* * *

"Carin - do you have a minute?"

It was a Saturday morning and Carin was about to leave for the day. Since the end of term dance, the Halls of Residence had virtually emptied. The only girls remaining were almost exclusively foreign students like herself. But Janet was English, from York, recalled Carin, and she'd managed to get a job at the National Gallery for the summer.

"Of course," said Carin, stepping back into her room. Then, registering Janet's uncertainty, added, "What's the matter?"

Janet waited until Carin closed the door.

"Look," she said, "I'm really not sure that I should be doing this…" She paused. "And I'll completely understand if you tell me to mind my own business."

Carin shook her head.

"Why would I say that to you?"

Janet took a deep breath.

"Do you know Steph Manning? She's a third year doing Politics and Economics."

Carin thought.

"Yes," she said slowly. "Tall, blond - wears an Afghan coat, even when it's sunny."

Janet let a smile flicker across her lips.

"That's her." All serious again. "She was at the dance the other night. With her boyfriend."

Carin was beginning to find Janet's pauses irritating.

"He plays in a band," Janet eventually continued. "Who're into all kinds of things, apparently."

"All kinds of things?"

"Drugs." Janet shrugged. "Not only pot. Acid and speed, too."

"Okay," said Carin slowly. "But I don't..."

"When he saw you and Kit together at the dance, he told Steph that Kit was their main dealer."

"What!" Carin stared at Janet, shaking her head in disbelief. "That's ridiculous."

"They score from him over at Kensington Market, according to Steph. He's got a stall there. Supposedly selling belts and stuff, but that's just a cover."

Carin sank down onto her bed.

"Like I said, tell me to bugger off if you want." Janet shrugged. "I don't know what you're into and I don't care - that's your business." She took another deep breath. "I only figured that if you didn't know, then you ought to. Okay?"

Carin looked at her wordlessly.

"And you didn't, did you?" said Janet softly.

As Carin continued to stare blankly, Janet sat down and slipped an arm around her shoulders.

* * *

Janet offered to go over to Notting Hill with her for moral support, but Carin forced a smile and said she'd be fine. Janet seemed to have found a role she was enjoying perhaps a little too much and there were things which Carin wanted to discover only by herself.

And anyway, Kit was at Kensington Market today - doing

whatever it was he did over there.

Carin positioned herself at the same coffee stall where she'd watched him after that first night they'd spent together. But this time, armed with the context she now had, there could be no mistaking what was happening here. The constant stream of customers buying packets of 'incense' far outnumbered those casually browsing the belts and bags, who mostly checked the price tag and moved on.

Another mystery solved.

She left after half an hour with no doubt at all in her mind, but what else might be going on that she didn't know about? The house at Pembridge Villas was only a twenty-minute walk along Kensington Church Street, but her steps became more hesitant the closer she got.

It's not that he'd actually *lied* to her, Carin told herself, but of course that wasn't true, was it? At best, it was a lie of omission - if he was really selling those bags for his friends, he was making a pretty poor job of it - and how could that be anything other than deceit? And what place did deceit have in a relationship?

But before confronting him, she decided she was going to have a good rummage around his room first. Her resolve strengthened as she climbed the stairs at Pembridge Villas, the lock in his door handle hadn't worked properly all the time she'd known him. You usually just had to give it a sharp twist and sure enough, it swung right open and...

Carin froze, staring at the figure in the room, his back to her as he knelt, flicking through Kit's bookshelf.

"Who are you? What are you doing in here?"

He whirled around at the sound of her voice, almost stumbling as he rose.

"Oh hi," he said. "It's Carin, isn't it?"

She recognised him as someone who lived in the house. She'd met him with Kit a few times - in the kitchen, passing in the hallway.

"What are you doing in here?" she repeated.

"Um, there was a book Kit said I could borrow sometime. He wasn't in, so I..." He shrugged. "I was going to leave a note."

"What book?"

He hesitated.

"Tim Leary. *The Politics of Ecstasy*."

Not a book Carin recalled seeing here.

"I don't believe you," she told him. "Get out."

"Look," he began awkwardly, "I..."

"Get out!" She stepped to one side, indicating the open doorway with her hand. After he passed through it, head slightly bowed, she pushed it shut behind him.

And then turned back to the room.

* * *

"Carin!"

Kit paused in the doorway. His surprise at seeing her changed to uncertainty as he caught her expression.

"Is everything okay?" he asked.

Then he registered that on the low table in front of where she sat was a bundle of letters, held together with a thick rubber band.

"On balance," said Carin quietly, "I'd say not."

"Why are you going through my things?"

He came into the room, closed the door behind him and stared down at her.

"Because it seems that I have no idea who you are at all." Carin let out a long breath and shook her head. "One of your *customers*," she left a slight pause after the word to emphasise it, "at Kensington Market is the boyfriend of a girl I'm at college with."

Kit continued to look at her, silently.

"Which made me wonder what else I didn't know about." She stood up, slowly. "So, does that answer your question?"

"Carin," he said carefully. "If you've read the last ones, then..."

"Oh, I've read all of them," smiled Carin, tapping the envelopes with her fingers. "And helpfully in date order - I could go straight from one thrilling instalment to the next."

"It's over," said Kit.

"Does Emma know that?" Carin pulled the top envelope free and offered it to Kit. "Because this is not the kind of letter a girl writes when things are over. Not unless she's lost her grip on reality." Carin felt her voice rising, but didn't care. "So, is that what this is, Kit? You being pursued by a crazy ex-girlfriend? Is that what you expect me to believe?"

"I haven't seen her for months," said Kit. "I've no idea where she even is?"

"And if you did?" demanded Carin. "If you did know where she was?"

Kit simply stared at her.

"Oh, you bastard," said Carin, shaking her head at him and fighting back the rising tears. "You bastard."

She let the envelope fall to the floor and pushed by him out of the room.

* * *

Reaching the landing on the floor below, Carin slowed, expecting to hear Kit behind her on the stairs.

But there was only silence.

And no sound other than the echo of her own footsteps as she descended the lower flight into the hallway. She waited there a few seconds, her hand resting on the banister before looking back over her shoulder.

Nothing.

No longer able to subdue the tears, she sank down onto the bottom step and buried her face into her hands. They could at least have held off until she was outside, instead of making an exhibition of herself here and…

"Are you okay?"

Carin stared up at the figure standing alongside her, recognising him as the artist who had a studio down in the basement. Kit had warned her about bothering him, apparently he could be bad tempered if interrupted in his work.

But he didn't look bad tempered now.

He looked concerned.

She pulled a handkerchief from her pocket, dabbed at her eyes and nodded.

"What's happened?" he asked gently.

Carin found him easy to talk with, kind and understanding as he listened to her disconsolate - and probably incoherent - account of what she'd discovered today. As her words eventually petered out, he took her hand and squeezed it.

"You need to let this settle down," he told her. "Wait until tomorrow and then come back and talk to him. You'll both have had time to think and things might look different by then."

Carin seriously doubted that. But she nodded and almost managed a smile.

"Why don't you go home," he said. "Let me get you a cab."

Carin started to protest, but he raised his hand.

"It's okay," he smiled. "I'll cover it."

He gave her hand a last squeeze and stood up. Carin finished dabbing at her eyes as the sound of his footsteps faded, but then became aware of someone coming down the stairs behind her.

Kit!!

Standing, she whirled around. But it was the boy who'd been in Kit's room when she'd arrived. To borrow a book that wasn't there.

"Carin..." he began, but she sighed with exasperation.

"I've nothing to say to you," she told him, adding archly, "Except that Kit is back now, so feel free to go and knock on his door."

"Please," he said. "You can't tell anyone you found me in Kit's room."

She shook her head dismissively, but then slowly froze as she caught his expression.

"You've no idea," his eyes were fixed on hers, "what could happen to me if you did."

* * *

"A policeman!" Carin stared at him, disbelievingly.

"*Jesus!* Keep your voice down." Cagily, he glanced over his shoulder, although seated in the far corner of an almost empty pub, it seemed unlikely they'd be overheard.

"Look..." she faltered. There'd been so much to take in that his name escaped her.

"Andrew."

"Okay." She took a breath

"He's a Chief Superintendent," said Andrew. "And he has me completely by the balls."

"But..." Carin shook her head. "Your own father?"

"What - blood thicker than water?" He gave a tight smile. "Don't you believe it."

Carin was silent.

"Things were just about bearable while Mum was here," he continued. "But she died five years ago, and that's when it got really bad. He had no idea how to show his feelings and thought I was a wimp because I did. '*You need toughening up*' has been his bloody mantra for as long as I could remember and with Mum gone, there was no one to stop him. I was sent off to boarding school, but that was more an institution for dumping problem kids." He gave a shrug. "Anyway, after a year I ran away."

"Where did you go?"

"I was living on the streets in London for a while, then I stayed at this commune type place in County Durham. Eventually, I headed down to Cornwall and tried to get some bread together by dealing hash and acid to the weekend ravers. But I got busted down there."

"Busted?"

"Arrested. I was looking at a couple of years in Borstal, or at least a spell at a Detention Centre. Anyway, while I was on remand, Dad came to see me. He could pull some strings, he said, and probably get me probation, but there'd have to be changes. 'Like cutting your bloody hair,' he told me. 'You look like a tart'. I ended up living back at home for two years, knowing that I only had to step out of line once for him to have a word with my Probation Officer and I'd find myself banged up."

"That's terrible," said Carin. "What kind of father would do such a thing?"

"Oh, we're just warming up here," he told her, with that tight smile that was actually more of a grimace. "Last year, my probation ended and so I moved out. In this country you're an adult now at eighteen, which meant there was nothing he could do about it. I got a bedsit in Earl's Court and found some casual work with a couple of bands, as a roadie."

He paused.

"Six months ago, I was walking home from the pub when a panda car pulls up alongside me and two uniformed coppers jump out. They push me up against the wall and frisk me, saying I'd been acting suspiciously, which was bullshit. One of them sticks his hand in my pocket and takes out an ounce of Lebanese Red, which definitely hadn't been there before. They handcuff me, take me to Paddington Green Police Station and start giving me the third degree. There's enough dope to charge me with dealing, they tell me. Which, as a second conviction, could see me sent down for five years. Unless I begin cooperating, of course - who am I buying from, who am I selling to?"

He took a packet of Benson and Hedges from his pocket and offered it to Carin. She shook her head.

"After a couple of hours," he said, lighting a cigarette, "I'm left alone to mull things over. Then guess who comes into the room?"

"Your father?"

"Spot on. I'm not surprised, I'd figured that when they eventually realised who I was, they'd get onto him. And at first I'm actually relieved - the pigs might not have a problem fitting up someone they hadn't liked the look of and dragged in off the street. But a senior detective's son would be something else."

He drew on the cigarette.

"'There's evidently been some kind of mistake,' he tells me and I'm thinking those two woodentops who picked me up are probably shitting themselves right now. Then he puts a folder he's carrying down on the table and opens it. 'But while it's getting sorted out,' he says, 'and as you're here, are these faces familiar to you?'

"One by one, he slides photographs from the folder across the table towards me. They're surveillance shots and all of people I'd known when I'd been living in Cornwall."

Andrew drew deeply on his cigarette.

"I looked up and nodded. 'Of course they are,' said Dad. He pushes more photographs across, but these include me. They were taken a couple of years earlier, on the campsite in Cornwall where I'd stayed.

"'Come on,' he said, 'let's get you out of here before too many people clock your face.'"

Carin stared at him silently.

"I'm pretty sure you can guess the rest," said Andrew.

"He wanted you to spy on them? For drugs?"

Andrew shook his head.

"Politics. Although anything I could turn up on that score would be a useful bonus for the Drug Squad."

"Politics? I don't understand?"

"Aidan McShane - down in the basement?"

Carin nodded.

"Back in Ireland, his family is heavily involved with the IRA, deep into what's kicking off over there right now. And Emma Brownlow's into all kinds of left wing shit. Her parents have a Special Branch file on them a yard thick."

At the mention of Emma, Carin stiffened, the letters she'd read still raw in her mind.

"So..."

"We go back home - well, to Dad's place. He tells me that the people they're interested in are either living at this house in Notting Hill or are regular visitors there. I get a list of places they hang out, where I can 'accidentally' bump into them again, renew old friendships. The aim is to move into the house. 'What if there aren't any rooms there?' I asked. 'Don't worry about that,' said Dad. 'I'll make sure that there are.' Meanwhile the ounce of dope stays an open investigation."

"And so you work for the police." Carin considered. "Do you see them every...?"

"I don't see them at all," Andrew interrupted. "I've nothing to do with any of them, except my father, and I can't even be certain that he's told anyone else about me. And we never meet. We use a dead drop on Parliament Hill."

"A dead drop?"

"Like a hiding place - he leaves messages there, things he wants me to find out about. Then I leave the replies. I have to check it once a week."

"Or...?"

"Nothing stated, but it's obvious that my open investigation suddenly becomes very active."

Carin hesitated.

"Why are you telling me all of this?"

"I'm pretty sure," said Andrew slowly, "that Kit and Aidan are beginning to suspect something. The last time I was out with them, the vibe I was getting..."

He shook his head.

"Have you thought about telling them what you're being made to do?" she asked. "I'm sure that once they knew why..."

"Do you know what the bloody IRA do to informers?" he interrupted harshly. Then his voice softened. "Carin, if you tell anyone about this, that you found me searching Kit's things, I'm dead." He stared at her. "I'm not being over dramatic here - they'd kill me."

Carin stared back at him.

"What are you going to do?" she asked after a few seconds

"The plan is to disappear." He hesitated. "I've got a job on the cards, as a roadie with a band doing the Isle of Wight Festival in August. Straight after that, they're touring the States and I don't plan on coming back from there."

"What about your father?"

"I'll have a head start - and try finding someone at a festival that size." He shrugged. "Then once I'm on the other side of the Atlantic..."

He shrugged again.

Carin digested this in silence.

"About today," asked Andrew. "Are you going to say anything?"

Carin shook her head.

"No," she said. "As long as you promise not to inform on Kit." She thought about Aidan McShane, who'd been so kind to her just a short while ago. "Or on anyone here. That you do as you say. Go away with this band and disappear."

"I promise."

"How can I be sure you'll keep your word? After this morning?"

"I wasn't looking for stuff on Kit," he told her. "I was trying to find out where Emma Brownlow was."

"Emma Brownlow? Why?"

"I'm not sure." He hesitated. "There's a lot going on in London that isn't getting into the papers - have you heard of D-notices?"

Carin nodded. Kit had explained to her how the Government could stop newspapers reporting stories for reasons of national security.

"That spate of gas main explosions lately..." He stared at her, letting his words tail off.

"They were bombs?" Carin shook her head, wide-eyed. "And Emma Brownlow is involved?"

"I'm not sure whether she is or not," said Andrew, "but I'm guessing Special Branch thinks so. And with the way things are these days, that comes down to the same thing." He sat back in his seat. "If they can get her into court with the right judge, she'll be going away for quite a while."

"And does Kit know about all of this?"

"I've no idea what Kit knows." He arched an eyebrow. "I think most people gave up trying to work out what was going on between those two a long time ago."

Carin stared at him evenly.

"If anything happens to Kit," she said, "I'll tell people

everything I know. But if you go away and make a new life for yourself, this conversation will stay between the two of us."

"I'll be gone in a few days," he told her.

Carin rose from her seat and left the bar.

* * *

The next week was the worst of Carin's life.

She barely ate, hardly slept and with no classes to occupy her, time fused into an endless daze. She thought of returning home to Amersfoort, but that would now involve explanations she really couldn't face. Janet was avoiding her, probably feeling Carin had cast her in the role of a wicked messenger. And there was some element of truth in that, Carin reflected. If Janet had minded her own business...

If Janet had minded her own business, then what?

Then she and Kit would still be together, is what.

Was blissful ignorance that bad? Who knows how it all might have played out if they'd been left to their own devices? She'd run the scene in Kit's room over in her mind dozens of times, at first in a rage but then more reflectively. Hadn't she backed Kit into a corner over Emma? she finally asked herself. He'd opened the door to his room and walked into a barrage of accusations. Who wouldn't react badly to that? And he was right. The last of those letters were postmarked months ago. But why had Kit kept them, if they didn't mean anything to him? But then, didn't she have a sheaf of old love letters locked away in her bedroom at home? Aren't things that once mattered hard to let go of, even if life has changed? They could have been happy together, she knew that. If she hadn't known about Emma, hadn't pushed so hard, then perhaps Kit would have seen that too.

And round and round and round in her head it all went, day and night.

She didn't care about the drugs, she decided. He was just doing what he had to do to get by until he could make a living from his writing. For goodness' sake, what a prissy little bitch she'd been about it! In Amsterdam, it wouldn't even have been illegal and probably won't be here in a couple of years.

What really worried her was what she'd learnt from Andrew. Carin had been truly shocked by what he'd told her - student demos and protests were one thing, but bombs! If he was right about Emma, then could Kit get dragged into it too?

That she needed to go back over to Notting Hill was the conclusion Carin eventually reached. She couldn't leave things like this. She would apologise for the childish way she behaved, tell him she understood if he didn't want to see her anymore. That she had no right to pass judgement on how he chose to live his life, past or present. She'd find out if Andrew had left the house and if he hadn't, then any deal they'd made was off, and she'd warn Kit about him.

And perhaps then, with the turmoil in her mind finally settled, she might go home for the rest of the summer. Hug her parents, wallow in sympathy from friends, try to get her head together for the upcoming term and quietly mourn an *intrigue* which had proved far more fraught than she ever could have imagined.

* * *

So, it seemed one thing that Kit had got around to during her absence was fixing the lock. She'd knocked a couple of times to no response, nor was there any sound of movement inside. Taking hold of the door handle and tentatively - mindful of the last time she'd entered this room uninvited - turned it and pushed.

It was unyielding.

Carin didn't know whether to feel annoyed or relieved. Reaching into her bag, she took out a notepad and pen and - not sure at all about what to say - simply scribbled 'Please call me'. She signed her name, thought about adding 'I miss you' but decided against it. If Kit did call her, it was a conversation likely to go better if he was as uncertain about her feelings as she was herself.

She slipped the note under his door and made her way back down the stairs. But just as she reached the landing below, she heard footsteps behind her.

"Carin!"

Turning to see Andrew standing in an open doorway, she shook her head in exasperation.

"You're not supposed to be here," she told him, anger creeping into her voice.

But he simply stared at her.

"Things became complicated," he said, quietly but intently. "We need to talk."

With a nod of his head, he indicated the door to his room. After a moment's hesitation, she followed him inside and he pushed it shut behind them.

"Complicated how?" she asked.

"Special Branch found out where Emma Brownlow's staying - over in Camden Town. Harcourt Close, number twelve."

"So...?" Carin was still angry. "How does that complicate things?"

"It's a house rented by a couple named Anna Grant and Dave Simmonds. Who are probably behind the bomb attacks."

"So Emma Brownlow is involved?"

"Who knows?" Andrew shrugged. "The thing is, Special Branch is going to raid the place. But before they do, they want plastique planted inside. Just to make sure."

"Plastique?"

"Plastique explosive."

Carin stared at him, speechless.

"They've asked me to talk my way into the house and somehow hide it as surreptitiously as possible. Failing that, there's a shed in the yard. It's kept locked, but the key's under a flowerpot by the door." He shook his head. "It doesn't matter where, the dogs are going to sniff it out. Wrapping it in something from the rubbish bin - a magazine or takeaway box - likely to be covered with their fingerprints would be all the evidence needed." He hesitated. "Once that's done, I'm supposed to phone Emma Brownlow's parents and tell them where she's staying. Apparently they've been going mad trying to find her."

"But why would they want you to do that?"

"They obviously have the Brownlows' phone tapped. Once they hear that call, not only will they know the explosive's been planted, they can put a tail on them and time the raid to scoop them up at the house as well." He shrugged. "Those two have been a thorn in a lot of people's sides for a long while."

He paused, staring at Carin's expression, and then gave a wry smile.

"Don't worry," he said. "I'm not doing it."

"So... What are you going to do?"

He hesitated.

"Will you help buy me some time?" he asked.

* * *

For the fifth time in as many minutes, Carin counted off the number of stops remaining. Now it was only two, Kentish Town and Tufnell Park. The carriage was still crowded and so she decided to stand up and make her way through to the doors as soon as the tube train started moving again. She'd already seen people struggling to get through the crush before the doors closed and wasn't going to let that happen to her.

She had enough to worry about.

Andrew had drawn her a map of the dead drop and drilled the directions into her head a dozen times. 'It's no more than a fifteen-minute walk,' he'd told her, which had looked about right to Carin after she double checked the route in her London A-Z. Turn left out of the tube station, cut across to Highgate Road and then onto the footpath around the back of the Lido. There was a litter bin by the third bench along. When she was certain no one was paying her any attention, reach underneath and lift the loose paving stone. Take out the package and replace it with his letter. Leave in the opposite direction, follow Mansfield Road over to Belsize Park Underground Station, a twenty-minute brisk walk at most.

But most importantly, dump the package at the first opportunity that came her way - rubbish bin, wasteland, even over a garden wall if there was dense shrubbery on the other side.

It had all sounded so simple.

* * *

"What I'm planning on doing," Andrew had told her, "is to get rid of the plastique and then make the phone call. The house gets raided and if they do find anything there, well…" He shrugged. "That'll be down to them, not me."

"What will happen to you?" asked Carin.

"I'd planned on picking up the stuff from the dead drop and leaving a letter saying that I was going to be out of London for a couple of weeks. That I needed to be certain nothing was pointing at me over this. And also that I'd met a girl - after everything I'd done, I figured I'd earned a break and so I was taking some time out to be with her."

"Eventually they will learn you tricked them," said Carin, slowly, "but you'll have the head start you wanted."

Andrew nodded.

"The problem is that the band I'm roadying with are leaving for a recording studio in the country tomorrow, to finish off their new album and rehearse before the festival and the US tour. If I want this job, then I'm going to have to go with them. But the plastique won't be there until the night after next." He stared at Carin. "I can still make the phone call, but I won't be able to collect the stuff or leave the letter."

"*No!*" Carin shook her head vehemently. "I'm not getting involved in this."

"Once it's done," Andrew said carefully, "all of this ends. I'll be gone and the cops will get their fingers so badly burnt that it's going to be a while before they try anything like this again. Emma, if she's got any sense, will disappear and Kit won't get tangled up in some mess on account of a torch he's carrying for an old girlfriend."

Maybe, thought Carin. But maybe he'll decide to disappear with her.

"Or perhaps he isn't." Andrew shrugged. "Look, I don't know what's happening with you two, but I'm guessing it doesn't need any more complications." He stared at her. "This is the only way I can think of to give all of us a chance to get clear of this mess."

Carin bit her lip.

"What would I have to do?" she asked.

* * *

The path leading away from the roadway was illuminated, but barely. Pools of light cast from ornate Victorian streetlamps were separated by stretches of darkness in which anything could be lurking. Or anyone. What had she been thinking, coming here by herself at this time of night?

She counted the benches along the path. At the third one, she lowered herself down at the far end, next to the litter bin. Carefully, she looked around her. Other than a car passing on the road below, there was silence and she had no sense of movement nearby. She reached under the bin and tugged at the loose edge of the paving stone. It lifted away easily. Reaching inside, her fingers felt a package tightly wrapped in plastic. She replaced it with Andrew's letter, put the package into her bag and slid the stone back in place.

Slowly she stood up and then gave a start - had she heard a twig crack underfoot?

Swiftly, she began to walk towards the road. After a few paces it was either nervousness or instinct which made her look over her shoulder, and she gasped as a bulky figure stepped into the band of light she'd just left.

Jesus! How stupid had she been?

Quickening her pace - and with visions of herself being dragged into the dark undergrowth - she could see that she had perhaps fifty metres or less before she reached the road. If the footsteps came anywhere near she would scream, surely someone would be close enough to hear? But would they come to help, in the big city who wants to get involved...?

Carin turned her head again and *Christ!*, he was barely a few metres behind her. She broke into a run, hearing his footsteps also quicken.

"Hey," she heard him say, "wait."

Not on your life! she thought. The road was no more than fifteen metres away now and she gathered her breath to scream. Whether there was anyone around or not, it might at least scare him off or...

From behind her came a cry and the footsteps stopped. Turning, she saw that he had dropped onto one knee and was clutching at his chest with both hands. Under the halo of the last street lamp, Carin could see him clearly. He was about fifty, well dressed in a suit and tie. Their eyes met as his face grimaced in pain.

"Tablets," he gasped. "Inside pocket."

She actually took a step forward, a natural instinct to help, before reason kicked in.

He was chasing you!

With one last look - slowly he crumpled to the ground - she turned and ran.

* * *

She'd been tempted to do nothing. If it wasn't a ploy, then he'd be one less predator the women of this city would have to worry about. But at the first telephone kiosk she came to, Carin dialled nine, nine, nine and told the operator she thought a man was having a heart attack and where he was. When pressed for details, she hung up.

Kismet!

Carin walked briskly, but not so fast as to seem in a noticeable hurry. The last thing she wanted was to draw attention to herself. She was breathing easily now, as the exertion - and fright - of a few minutes ago subsided. And a glimpse of her reflection in the window of the tube station ticket office reassured her there was nothing untoward about her appearance.

There'd been several opportunities to get rid of the package, but she hadn't. Sitting on the station platform waiting for the next southbound tube, she slit one end open with her thumbnail to examine it, before carefully placing it back in her bag.

Once again, Carin found herself counting two stops to her destination - Chalk Farm and Camden Town. She would disembark there, turn right onto Camden High Street and follow the directions which she'd memorised from her London A-Z to Harcourt Close.

Where she would commit the wickedest act of her life.

GILLIAN

"Okay, Gillian - I think that just about wraps it up."

Ted smiled and closed the folder on the desk in front of him. The interview had been as perfunctory as Gillian had expected, the members of the panel she knew well and had anticipated problems from only one of them, the School Bursar.

Linda Haversham, suspected Gillian, harboured a grudge from an incident which had taken place a few years earlier. The mother of a year eight pupil had been soliciting special attention for her daughter on the grounds of her supposed dyslexia. When Gillian contested this - she knew the child well and during her career had dealt with various manifestations of learning disorders - the mother produced a letter from a child psychiatrist confirming the diagnosis. *'Whilst accepting this opinion,'* a frustrated Gillian scribbled across the report, *'let's not draw the conclusion that dyslexia and indolence are mutually exclusive.'* She'd handed the paperwork into the office and let the whole episode fall from memory. It was a week later that a colleague quietly informed her that the girl was Linda Haversham's niece and that anything destined for filing passed through her hands.

Which certainly explained the brusqueness which had continued ever since.

But, Gillian reassured herself, Linda's presence on the panel was little more than token recognition of her role as head of administration. The voices that really counted belonged to the Headmaster and the Chair of the Board of Governors. Ted she knew she could count on one hundred percent. He'd effectively mentored her throughout her entire time at St Anne's and Gillian was confident of his full backing. When Derek Keyworth, Head of English, received his prognosis six months ago and sadly informed everyone that - even if the course of chemotherapy he was about to embark on proved successful - he would be unlikely to return to the school, Ted had no hesitation in making her the acting department head. And Dennis Nelson she also knew socially, he and Tim regularly played golf together. It was only the other week that he'd told her husband how impressed the

Governors were by the way she'd stepped into the breech.

"Thank you, Ted," she smiled back at him.

"Obviously, we've other people to see," he said carefully, and Gillian nodded. External candidates were mandatory for most public sector roles, if for no other reason than to dispel any accusations of nepotism. Even if, nine times out of ten, the job went to who everybody always knew it would. "But," shrugged Dennis, "hopefully we'll have some good news for you within the next few days."

"I'll look forward to hearing from you," she said.

With a last smile for everyone, she rose to her feet and left the room.

* * *

Gillian Brown wasn't fazed by job interviews. Unlike most people, who found them nervous affairs, Gillian discovered at an early age that what transpired during them seldom had any bearing on their outcome.

She'd supported Tim through university with a succession of secretarial jobs, mostly temporary work covering periods of illness. Back then, employers rarely filled career positions with young married women, the expectation being that any investment in skills would be rewarded by an early departure to begin a family. If women were to be found in these roles, they would be the ones with children now out in the world or whose expectations of family life had long ceased to give cause for concern.

Gillian would change jobs four or five times a year, attending up to half a dozen interviews during each interim period. Initially, she'd approached these with a degree of edginess, but the more of them she got under her belt, the less that played a part, until finally evaporating completely.

There was no pattern to these interviews at all, she discovered. She would spend an hour in what seemed to be complete simpatico with a potential employer, even be given a tour of the office, only never to hear from them again. And then for a curt ten minute question-and-answer session, concluded with a brusque dismissal, to be followed up with a request to start the following Monday.

She learnt a lot in those years. Less about the day to day running of an office, anyone with half a brain could pick up all you needed to know about that in a week. But about people. Or more specifically, about power. Not the power which descends from on high, but its interplay at ground level, where individual strengths and weaknesses are tested and exploited in the pull and push of departmental interaction.

Gillian quickly gathered that while barely concealed chest beating machismo may appear to be the default setting for the workplace, its superficiality is easily undermined by manipulative innuendo or delicate sabotage. And whatever shit you might have to put up with while engaged in those guerrilla incursions, Gillian learnt from her colleagues, every pat on the bottom can be repaid with a spoonful of spittle in the coffee cup.

The plan had been that once Tim qualified, they would start a family. Or rather, that was Tim's plan - Gillian had no intention of spending the best years of her life washing nappies. She'd coo along with the rest of them at family gatherings, but nothing gave her greater satisfaction than handing the little bundle of joy back to its sunken eyed mother. And whatever deficits Gillian might have in the maternal feelings department, she strongly suspected she was far less alone with them than conventional wisdom would suggest.

So, informing Tim that she'd stopped taking the contraceptive pill - which had been the sensible course of action whilst he was a student - what she actually did was to cancel the prescription from their local GP, but then register with a Family Planning Clinic on the other side of town. At least she had the satisfaction of knowing that all of Tim's antics in bouncing up and down on top of her would be literally fruitless, and indeed, that was the only satisfaction she did derive from an act Gillian had never known to be anything other than uncomfortable and degrading.

That there was pleasure to be found she was in no doubt,

her own explorations once Tim had rolled off of her and begun to snore supplied confirmation of that - *if you want something done properly* - but she doubted any man could furnish what she seemed to need and the alternative didn't bear thinking about. She was astute enough to understand there must be a fair amount of suppression or sublimation or whatever the latest trendy word for it might be, happening here, but so what?

Since when had insight ever been a path to equanimity?

* * *

If Gillian's career path had been planned with almost military precision, then her teenage years were boot camp. Her father had insisted she leave school at fifteen - a year before she could take O-level examinations - explaining there were plenty of jobs for factory girls and that with overtime she'd be able to start bringing home some good money.

Gillian dug her heels in at that and, for once, her mother backed her up. They compromised with a twelve month course at the local College of Further Education, working for a City and Guilds certificate in typing and shorthand. 'She'll never be out of a job with that behind her,' Mum had reassured her father and eventually he conceded. But only, she later discovered when overhearing a snatch of conversation between her parents, because her mother had persuaded him that she was more likely to snare a better class of husband in an office than a factory.

Well, whatever works, thought Gillian, but it was a lesson well learnt. Don't expect even the people who love you to look out for your best interests. You always have to make sure that there's something in it for them.

As Tim studied, Gillian's Open University English course became an object of amusement for both her own family and Tim's. But she'd been happy to play along with that, confident it would become the foundation of all she intended to construct.

"Well," she'd smile, at those interminable family christenings, wedding receptions and Christmases, "I have to find some way of passing the time while Tim's buried in his books."

She could perhaps learn to sew, her mother-in-law once commented rather brusquely, and that there were endless night school classes on household crafts such as re-upholstery and embroidery. 'Oh, I've never been good with my hands,' Gillian had replied sweetly, 'and you know what they say about your brain - use it or lose it.'

She'd selected an English degree for what she perceived to be its general purpose nature and because it was the subject she'd enjoyed most at school. Grammar had driven most of her friends to distraction, but she'd loved it. The changing nuances of language through conjugation and declension, the rigid structures they adhered to. And to enjoy literature not simply for the worlds it created an escape into, but to grasp and wonder at each and every element of their construction.

Gillian thought long and hard about where her best prospects might lie and eventually concluded either the NHS or education. Being public sector institutions, they at least paid lip service to notions of gender equality and both operated a national salary scale, no minor consideration given the notoriously low wages on the south west peninsular.

In the end, she'd plumped for education. Her only two options in the NHS would have been nursing or administration. The first she knew from the experiences of school friends would involve a training period comprised of bedpans and night shifts. The second, from her own observations during visits to the hospital, seemed little more than subservient lackeys in the minor fiefdoms of doctors and consultants.

Tim did raise an unexpected amount of resistance to her enrolment at Teacher Training College, perhaps taken aback at how her OU degree - fused with a preference for mature students - easily trumped her lack of traditional educational qualifications. She guessed this uneasiness was being fuelled by his mother, and this echo of her own father's notions of her *'getting ideas above her station'* only steeled her resolve.

This was only a contingency, she reassured him. And most likely she'd fall pregnant before completing the course and drop out to become the full-time housewife and mother they both knew was the role which would serve them best.

Suitably swayed, Tim gave his reluctant consent.

* * *

Ironically - given the skulduggery which had delivered her here - Gillian proved to be an excellent teacher. Pupils instinctively respected her no-nonsense attitude and reserved their less restrained behaviour for the classrooms of members of staff who considered the best approach to the teacher pupil relationship was being mates.

It helped that English was largely a subjective forum. An author's intent and judgement on his or her execution, was something she threw open to debate and not much in life gave her greater pleasure than watching those little minds blossom. When even the troublemakers began to realise their lives were not unique, that everything they believed or were disturbed by echoed back through the ages under one guise or other. She was opening a world for them, she liked to think, and whatever life might have in store further down the line, a world that could always be a refuge of sorts.

Even now, when the mothers and fathers she met at parent teacher evenings had been those first children she'd taught at St Anne's, she still took satisfaction in her work. It had not grown stale for her, she'd not become - like so many of her colleagues - browbeaten by the increasing interventions of government, with the Department of Education's ever-changing array of shifting curricula and movable targets. Gillian had her own goals, and she steered towards them unswervingly.

And now Head of Department!

She was genuinely sorry for Derek. She liked him both as a colleague and a friend. But life goes on and she knew that she'd more than earned the position.

Gillian glanced at her watch as she walked through the foyer and down the steps to the main gate.

'Come over when you're finished,' Veronica had said to her. 'We'll have a few drinks to celebrate.'

Which had sounded a great idea.

* * *

Gillian hadn't really known what to make of Veronica when the Hansons first arrived in St Hannahs. That they were well-to-do was obvious, but they weren't flash with it. At least, not like so many who arrive from up country and think that everything here is for sale, including friendship. They spent their money locally whenever they could and had been generous with local appeals - a trip to Disney World for a child with terminal cancer, the vicar's Sure Start programme - and all whilst insisting on anonymity, which of course sent the word around like wildfire. But on the downside they were friends with the Bradshaws - Alan Bradshaw she'd never been able to abide - and spent time at *The Grange*, which the actress Lee Munro had an interest in and so naturally sparked prurient rumour amongst all those excluded from that circle.

And it was through Sure Start that she'd really got to know Veronica. Jenny Warwick had been a breath of fresh air for St Hannahs as far as Gillian was concerned, although there were still some - and not just the usual suspects - who balked at the thought of a female vicar. But Jenny'd been something in the City before her modern day 'flash of light on the road to Damascus' moment and brought a can do / take charge ethos to any project she undertook. Which Gillian, who'd rarely stepped inside a church other than to witness the rituals of birth, marriage and death, found an instant rapport with.

Gillian assumed Jenny got her involved because many of these girls sitting in the Church Hall, cradling crying babies with expressions of almost bewilderment, had so recently left her classroom. In some cases she'd been one of the few figures in their lives who'd been both authoritative and supportive, and Gillian guessed that the smart as a whip Reverend was using the lingering imprint of that to subconsciously reassure them they weren't on their own here.

That people cared.

Veronica Hanson was the other side of that coin, more

often than not to be found sitting with a girl at a table outside, sharing a cigarette - and occasionally something stronger, Gillian suspected - her head thrown back in laughter or crouched forward listening intently to a young mother's hesitant words. Later, Gillian might catch her in serious conversation with Jenny.

The Reverend Warwick, Gillian came to realise, knew how to put a good team together.

After Jenny locked up the Hall for the morning, Gillian and Veronica had got into the habit of going for a coffee. It developed into an easy companionship, even if one based on differences rather than similarities and as such didn't expand into each other's wider circle of family or friends. We shy away, reflected Gillian, from introductions which need to be accompanied by explanations. But equally, confidences one might worry about being subjected to the tittle-tattle of group dynamics are more easily exchanged *vis-à-vis,* and gradually both began to look forward to these regular exchanges.

* * *

"Again, I'm so sorry." said Gillian. "Being rude to someone's guest and in their own home. That really is unforgivable."

Veronica dismissed her apology with a small smile and a shake of her head.

The taxi dropped them at the harbour and Veronica slipped her arm under hers as they crossed over the road to *The Barque's* restaurant entrance. Gillian was tempted to say she was okay now, that she could manage, but then discovered she was comfortable with the intimacy.

And she *was* okay. The black coffee she'd drank after the departure of Veronica's husband and Alan Bradshaw had definitely done its job. And the sassy lightheadedness she'd experienced was, Gillian assured herself, as much down to the euphoria of her promotion as the wine. But as steady on her feet as she now felt, it was still a relief to sink down into the chair which the waiter pulled out for her at their table.

"So how long has it been going on?" asked Veronica, as they settled themselves in. "This feud between you and Alan Bradshaw?"

Gillian stared at her and then sighed.

"It was soon after he'd moved down here. He was working for Connaught & Brown, the estate agents in Truro, and we'd just put our house on the market. We were hoping to buy the place which we're in now." Gillian leant back in her chair. "The first time we sold a house we did it sole agency and what a mistake that was. You know how that works, right?"

Veronica nodded.

"They put bugger all effort into it for us," said Gillian. "It doesn't matter who buys it or how, they still get their two percent. And it took ages to sell."

Gillian broke off as the wine waiter came over. Almost in unison they motioned him away, then caught each other's eye and smiled.

"So, we weren't going to make that mistake twice," continued Gillian. "We put it with Pascoe's here in St Hannahs but also with Connaught and Brown, which is how we first met Alan Bradshaw. The agreement was that whichever agency made the introduction to the eventual buyer would get the commission."

A waiter arrived with a carafe of water, and Gillian paused while Veronica filled their glasses.

"About a week later, Tim's sitting in there having a drink," Gillian nodded toward the Lounge Bar, "and this couple start walking over to him. He doesn't recognise them, but they're with one of Tim's clients. Suddenly, Alan Bradshaw, who's been drinking at the bar, steps in between them and says to the couple, 'This is Mr Brown'. The man sticks his hand out and Tim - like an idiot, but I'd probably have done the same if I'd had it sprung on me - shakes it."

Gillian took a sip of her drink.

"Apparently, they'd been going around the estate agents all day, which is how Bradshaw recognised them. We found out later they'd casually mentioned to Tim's client that they were looking for a house, and he'd told them about our place. They seemed interested, so he'd brought them down to *The Barque* to meet Tim."

"I see," said Veronica quietly.

"That handshake cost us eighteen hundred quid," said Gillian. "So, in my book, that made Alan Bradshaw a devious shit and he's done nothing since to convince me otherwise." She shrugged. "I'm sorry, I know he's a friend of yours, but..."

She let her voice trail off.

Where do you begin, Gillian reflected, to encapsulate what you can't articulate without sounding well, to be frank, a bit unhinged? The row over the house sale could have been put down to getting their fingers burnt by some wide boy - that's life and life's lessons come at a price. But from day one, she'd had the feeling that there was something more in play here. It wasn't only how his understated faux bonhomie and overplayed Yorkshire pragmatism insinuated him into both St Hannahs social life and business community. It was that he was so obviously trying to be all things to all people and, for some reason, nobody could see through that. Gradually he'd managed to have his hand in everything, he'd wheedled his way into Pascoe's and look how that had turned out. His wife - and wouldn't Gillian like to know *her* story - was mopping up all the small self-catering properties, with that absolutely *odious* brother of hers strutting around town like he was...

Gillian became aware Veronica was staring at her. She smiled and shrugged.

"What does Tim say?" asked Veronica.

Gillian rolled her eyes.

"Tim says that life is too short." She grimaced. "I say that for some people, it's not bloody short enough."

Veronica laughed, but Gillian shook her head.

"I'm sorry, that was really inappropriate." She sighed. "Given recent events."

"Did you know Robert Pascoe well?" asked Veronica.

"We were at the college together. Even went on a few dates." Gillian smiled. "Lots of unsure fumbling on the back row of *The Rialto*, for which I was the envy of my friends."

"He would seem to have been a complex character," suggested Veronica, carefully.

"Not always. When we were young, he was a lovely man. Good looking, charming, fun to be with. He could have had his pick of any girl in town."

"What's your take on what happened?"

That bloody wife of his! flashed through Gillian's mind, but she stayed silent. *Something* had happened, something around the time of that business of Claudia Pascoe and *The Grange*. And it wasn't just to do with money, were the whispers. There'd been speculation about her and Paul Chapman, who had bought out her share to set up *Executive Action*. It seemed they'd known each other before either of them had arrived in St Hannahs and even the gradual realisation that Paul was gay hadn't done much to quell the rumours. Simply made them more disturbing. But it was from then on that the change in Robert was noticeable - the smile always more forced than natural and stay away from him if he'd had a skinful.

And this, Gillian cautioned herself, *was the circle that Veronica moved in, so be careful what you say here.*

* * *

The restaurant phoned a cab for them, dropping Veronica off before taking Gillian home. She'd insisted, despite Veronica's protestations, on paying for the meal.

"It's my celebration," Gillian told her, "so my treat."

With Tim not due back from his golfing weekend until Tuesday, they'd arranged to meet for lunch on Saturday. There was a message from Tim waiting for her on the answerphone - they'd arrived okay, the hotel was really nice, they were about to go for something to eat. He hoped the interview went well, he was sure it did, all his love and...

Gillian pressed the delete key before the message finished playing and walked through into the kitchen to make herself a coffee. But before reaching for the kettle, she hesitated and then returned to the living room. Opening the drinks cabinet, she poured herself a large scotch and carried it over to the coffee table in front of the sofa. She kicked off her heels and stretched before picking up the remote and switching on the stereo. A light classical compilation CD was already inserted and the sound of the *Flower Duet*, from Delibes's *Lakmé*, filled the room.

Gillian lowered herself down on to the sofa and closed her eyes, resting her hands together in her lap.

She didn't often have the house to herself and so she might as well make the most of it.

* * *

The phone started ringing as she was about to leave the house, and she was tempted to let it go straight to answerphone. She hadn't got back to Tim since his call on Thursday, so he was probably checking everything was okay. Or more than likely, it was one of those cold callers so persistent about double glazing or insurance. But after hesitating only slightly, she walked through into the living room and picked it up.

"Dennis!" She smiled, glad she'd answered the call. He'd said that he'd get back to her as soon as he could. "How are you?"

She listened for a few seconds and then shook her head.

"Tell me yourself? I'm sorry, I don't understand - tell me what?"

The next two minutes left her stunned. Literally. It was as if the words and phrases he was speaking - '*the board were impressed but*' - '*Prunella Pozniak*'- '*Shoreditch*' - '*brought out of special measures*' - '*league tables*' - needed to be rearranged to make any sense to her.

But eventually it sank in.

"Of course, it doesn't mean that your value as a member of the team is regarded in any way less," he was saying, and even in her dazed state, she recognised the hurried tone his conversation was adopting. Without a word, or listening for a second longer, she carefully placed the handset back down in the cradle.

Suddenly nauseous, she ran to the bathroom but bent over the toilet bowl she could only retch, the taste of bile rising to her mouth. She stood, breathing deeply, then washed her face and rinsed out her mouth.

What would people think? What could she say to them?

She considered cancelling her lunch date with Veronica, but then pushed the thought out of her mind. Throughout every struggle to get where she was today, she'd never once backed away from anything and she wasn't going to start now. Plus, she knew that the longer she put this off, the harder it would become to eventually deal with.

She redid her makeup, tidied her hair. Gillian studied her face in the mirror for any trace of the turmoil which was raging inside and then, satisfied, picked up her keys and left.

She'd driven on autopilot before, but never, she realised as she found herself pulling into Veronica's driveway, to this extent. She couldn't remember a single detail of the journey, her head a jumble of rehearsed responses and choreographed reactions as she contrived to construct a narrative from which she could emerge with at least a vestige of dignity. But *'All schools need an alibi for Ofsted these days'*, sounded every bit as hollow as *'They can't appear too incestuous if they're going for Academy status'*.

"Gillian - what's happened?" At the door, Veronica's face was a picture of concern. So much for the blasé approach, thought Gillian.

It was out on the balcony that the tears began.

"Did they give any explanation at all?" Veronica asked, as they sat side by side.

Gillian found herself repeating the phrases Dennis had used, and at least Veronica found them as meaningless as she had.

"They have to be more explicit than that," Veronica told her, slipping her arm around Gillian's shoulder and giving her a squeeze. She continued to comfort her as sorrow transformed to anger.

"I was the best Head of Department they'd ever had, even though it wasn't official," said Gillian eventually. "Everybody said so. Everybody! And I'm supposed to carry on and..."

"Oh Gillian," said Veronica.

And then, without the slightest warning to herself of what was about to happen, Gillian leant forward and covered Veronica's mouth with her own.

* * *

Gillian hadn't realised she'd fallen into a slumber until an awareness of movement in the room opened her eyes. Veronica placed a glass on a small cabinet by Gillian's side of the bed and sat down beside her, sipping her own drink. Gillian thought about pulling the sheet across to cover herself but instead lazily stretched, enjoying the tension in her muscles.

"I'm guessing that nothing like this has ever happened before?" asked Veronica softly.

Gillian considered.

"When I was thirteen," she said, slowly, "Wendy Garner and I practised kissing once. To find out what it felt like and so that we'd know what to do later. With boys."

Veronica reached down and with her fingers, brushed the hair away from Gillian's face.

"I don't think that counts."

"I suppose not," said Gillian, enjoying the sensation of her hair being stroked. "And you - I'm guessing this isn't...?"

She gestured with her hand, not quite finding the words.

"No," said Veronica, "it's not."

Gillian lifted herself up onto an elbow and stared at her.

"So what happens now?"

Veronica raised an eyebrow.

"Well, experience suggests a wealth of possibilities," she said. "You drop this like a hot brick, pretend it didn't happen and never go near it again. Or, you leave your husband to go and live in a women's collective in Hackney. Or, you tell your husband, he accuses you of being a deceitful bitch, beats you up and throws you out. Or, you tell your husband and he wants a threesome.

Or, you don't tell your husband and consumed with guilt wither away on the vine in the dry heat of repressed desire."

Before Gillian could respond, the telephone began to ring.

"It's okay," said Veronica, "it'll go to answerphone." She hesitated. "Look, what I'm saying is that right now there's no way for you to deal with this on any rational level."

"I'm not sure what you mean?"

"A favourite quote of Richard's, whenever I get into an argument with somebody about religion or morality, is that you can't reason someone out of what they haven't been reasoned into. This isn't exactly the same, but close enough." She reached down, took Gillian's hand into hers and squeezed it. "You can't apply rationality to emotional responses that you don't yet understand, so why even try? Just let things settle - it's surprising what gets sorted out in your head while you're not paying attention to it."

"I don't know if..." began Gillian, but Veronica broke in, giving her hand another squeeze.

"In the meantime, all you need tell yourself is that what happened was exactly what that moment needed. Nothing more and nothing less." Veronica paused. "Dennis Nelson, Prunella whoever... So what do you think about all of that right now?"

Gillian considered and then gave a dismissive shrug.

"Sod 'em."

* * *

Veronica showered first. Gillian sat out on the veranda, as brazen as she'd ever been in her life and enjoying the cool breeze brushing against the film of warm perspiration which still coated most of her body.

She understood the insight of Veronica's advice, wasn't that exactly what she'd done in those early battles with her father and then her mother-in-law? Lock it all away, not because she was hiding from anything but to build the strength to deal with it on her own terms. And more often than not, with her attention elsewhere, her mind had transformed it into something which hardly seemed worth the confrontation.

But not quite yet. Gillian wanted to... Savour was perhaps the wrong word, given the ambivalence which still lingered. Gillian had never experienced anything even remotely close to what had happened when her lips met Veronica's. She'd climaxed immediately, overcome by wave after wave of pure physical euphoria. *At a kiss!* A crisis, wasn't that once a euphemism for it? Certainly more elegant than 'cum', that tacky expression learnt from the pages of the trashy novels she'd occasionally confiscate from year eleven girls. Flicking through them to see if they contained any literary merit whatsoever and never once having her expectations confounded. Cum, there was a verb she could give them to conjugate, what irregular forms might that take through the tenses.

But *crisis*. Yes, crisis summed it all up very well.

She was still smiling to herself when Veronica, showered and fully dressed, came out to join her.

"My," she said, looking down at Gillian. "Don't the pair of us just look like something Manet might have conjured up?"

Gillian showered quickly while Veronica booked them a table for lunch. Her dress had taken less smoothing out than she'd expected and she'd only needed a minute or two with her makeup.

"All done," she said brightly, stepping into the living room.

Where she froze.

Initially, at seeing Sergeant Vanner standing next to Veronica, then again as she registered Veronica's ashen face.

"What's happened?" The words felt almost breathless as they left her mouth.

"It's Richard." Veronica stared at her, numbly. "There's been some kind of accident. He's... He's been airlifted to Derriford Hospital. Sergeant Vanner's going to take me over there."

* * *

"Coma!!!?"

Gillian squeezed Veronica's hand tightly. She'd held it all the way over to Plymouth, in the back of the police car which

- with lights flashing and the occasional siren - had reduced the journey time from the usual hour to under forty minutes. Sergeant Vanner said he needed to see if Richard could be interviewed, but Gillian guessed the real reason they were being chauffeured was that he didn't want Veronica behind the wheel in her current state of mind.

"That's not as drastic as it sounds, Mrs Hanson," the doctor told her. "A medically induced coma is a common initial procedure for head injuries which we've yet to discover the extent of. What it actually involves is sedating the patient, mainly with a course of barbiturates, to reduce brain activity - hopefully preventing further complications."

"So, how long before...?" Veronica let her voice trail off.

The doctor - my God, thought Gillian, she didn't look older than a schoolgirl but she must be competent enough - shrugged.

"That depends on the diagnosis. It would help if we knew the circumstances which caused the bruising to your husband's head, but usually twelve to twenty-four hours. As I said, it's an entirely precautionary measure. The paramedics who attended your husband had intended to take him to Treliske. Purely coincidentally, the Air Ambulance was nearby and so the decision was made for it to detour and bring him here."

Treliske was their local hospital, on the outskirts of Truro. And however much the doctor might be playing down the role of the Air Ambulance, reflected Gillian, those paramedics must have been really concerned to get Richard to Derriford in such a hurry.

And she guessed Veronica was thinking the same thing.

"We've a neurologist on his way in," the doctor continued, doubtless dragged from the nineteenth hole, what with it being a Saturday and all, assumed Gillian. "So we should have a clearer idea of how things stand in about three or four hours."

"May I see my husband?" asked Veronica.

"He's being prepared for the scans," said the doctor, "so I'm afraid not. But obviously I'll keep you updated on any changes in his condition. We've a family room where you can wait, rather than sitting out here. Would you like me to get someone to take you along there?"

Veronica was staring blankly, and so Gillian nodded.

The room was an oasis of soft furnishings. Gillian settled Veronica down on a sofa and had just returned with two coffees when Sergeant Vanner arrived. She sat down alongside Veronica and took her hand again as he sat facing them.

"Well," he said, "we do seem to have some idea of the sequence of events now. As you know, your husband was found collapsed at a Viewing Area on the coast road by a tourist who'd spent the night there in a campervan. Strictly disallowed, of course, but in this instance we're letting that slide because if she hadn't been parked up, there's no telling how long Mr Hanson could have been lying there. He was on the other side of his car and not visible from the road. And fortunately she had a mobile phone, the paramedics were there in under ten minutes - the consensus seems to be that without this lady's prompt action, your husband might not still be here."

"Do you have her details, Sergeant?" Veronica asked quietly. "I would like to thank her."

"She's staying at Petroc now. I don't know for how long, but I'm sure they'll have her contact details if she's moved on."

"Thank you."

"It appears that your husband had just made a visit to the Traveller camp in Belle Meadow."

"I don't understand." Veronica was shaking her head. "Why would he do that?"

"We believe he was acting on behalf of Alan Bradshaw."

Gillian let out a sharp hiss of breath. Vanner either didn't hear it or chose to ignore it.

"You believe?" asked Veronica.

"Two days ago Ratko Novosel - Mr Bradshaw's brother-in-law - visited the site in an attempt to persuade the Travellers to move on." Vanner paused. "By all accounts, the visit didn't go well. We've tried to contact Mr Bradshaw, but apparently he and his wife are away for the weekend. Mr Novosel believes that your husband returned to the camp to offer them a financial incentive to leave."

"What do the Travellers say?" asked Gillian.

"That Mr Hanson spoke with them, and they came to an agreement." Vanner shook his head. "They deny any money changed hands, but they would, wouldn't they? And according to them, your husband left the camp without incident."

"Do you believe them, Sergeant?" asked Veronica.

"When one of my officers turned up there to question them," said Vanner, carefully, "they were packing up to leave. So that part of their story pans out. And if that's the case, then it doesn't really make sense that they'd bear any ill will towards your husband."

"So…?" Gillian was still doubtful.

"Well, they certainly won't be leaving Belle Meadow anytime soon," said Vanner. "Not until we've got this straightened out. Harry Thomas has planted a bloody great skip across the entrance and that's not being lifted until I've at least heard Mr Hanson's account of things." He hesitated. "Which I gather from the doctors is unlikely to be until tomorrow at the earliest."

"Well, I'm staying here," said Veronica. "Until I know something for definite."

"There's a *Future Inn* less than five minutes down the road," Gillian told her. "Where I stayed when my mother was in here." She wasn't going to elaborate on how that played out. "I'll go around to your house with Sergeant Vanner - if that's okay," she said, looking at him and he nodded, "and pick up what you'll need for a few days away from home. I'll drive back over with it, book you a room at the hotel and then see you here."

"Thank you, Gill," said Veronica.

* * *

"Is it alright if I sit up front?" asked Gillian. "Otherwise, I'll feel like I'm being chauffeured and everyone else will think I've been arrested."

"Of course," smiled Vanner.

The pace, while not as frantic as the journey there, was brisk and Gillian couldn't help but smile at the brake lights flashing as they appeared in rear-view mirrors.

"God, you must get a kick out of this, Jack," she said and Vanner grinned.

"Never wears off," he told her.

Gillian turned her head and looked sideways out of the window. In the distance loomed Bodmin Moor, even in summer as desolate as ever.

"Have you been friends with the Hansons for long?" asked Vanner conversationally, and certainly every bit as relaxed as he had the right to be with someone whose pigtails he'd pulled in the playground when they were both six years old. But don't forget what he does for a living now, Gillian told herself.

"A few months," she said, matching his casual tone. "I know Veronica better than Richard. We met at the Sure Start group, at the Church Hall, and seemed to hit it off."

"She volunteers there!?" Vanner couldn't hide his surprise. "I know she's in with that circle up at *The Grange* - Lee Munro, Paul Chapman. I'd have thought she'd be a bit too up herself for the rest of us."

"She's surprisingly good with the girls," Gillian told him. "They do seem to find it easy to confide in her."

Vanner considered for a moment

"And you, Gill? You in with that lot too, these days?"

"Not really." Gillian shook her head. "I mean, no. Lee Munro's come down to the Church Hall a few times to meet some of the mothers - she's a patron of the Trust the vicar set up - and we've chatted." She gave a tight smile. "And that's about it, it's not like we're jetting off to San Tropez together every weekend." She turned to look at him and arched an eyebrow. "Is your interest specific, Jack, or are you just scooping up the tittle-tattle us girls pass along the time with?"

Vanner chuckled.

"No," he said. "It's just that... If you start rubbing shoulders with that crowd, then watch yourself."

"Any particular reason I should be concerned?" Gill asked dryly and Vanner shook his head.

"No, I've never had any problems with them," he said. "Just a general observation that the glitterati have a tendency to chew people up and spit them out. And I have to say, Gill," half turning his head toward her and then back to the road, "that you really don't seem yourself."

"In what way?"

"I'm not sure. But we've known each other a long time..."

She turned her head to stare once more out across the moor.

"Jack," she said softly, "you've no idea who I've been today."

* * *

"It's an open-ended booking," Gillian told Veronica. "With the hospital so close, they're used to that. And a family room - double bed and pull-out sofa." She shrugged. "I wasn't sure whether you'd want company, have relatives coming down, or needed to be alone."

Veronica reached out and took Gillian's hand. She was about to speak when the door opened and the doctor they'd spoken to earlier stepped into the room.

"Mrs Hanson," she said. "We have the results of the scans. Would you follow me, please?"

She led them through a maze of corridors and then knocked on a door, pushing it open without waiting for a response. They walked into what seemed to be half office, half consulting room. A middle-aged man wearing scrubs rose from behind a desk, greeting them with his hand outstretched. Against a side wall was a large light board, holding what appeared to be a series of X-Rays.

"Mrs Hanson?" he asked questioningly, looking back and forth between them.

Veronica shook his hand.

"Yes," she said. "And this is Gillian Brown, a family friend."

"I'm Stephen Drake, a senior consulting neurologist." He indicated two chairs in front of his desk. "Please, take a seat."

"Your husband," he began pursing his lips slightly, "presented us with quite a conundrum, at first. We couldn't understand how a superficial blow to the side of the head could account for his condition."

"Superficial?" asked Veronica, although it struck Gillian that the really loaded part of that statement was 'at first'.

"Yes, there was bruising, but no fracture." He studied her for a second. "Mrs Hanson, has your husband been suffering from headaches or blurred vision recently?"

Veronica shook her head.

"No. At least not that I'm aware."

"Right." He seemed to consider. "What about displaying uncharacteristic forms of behaviour?"

Oh God, thought Gillian. *Oh God!*

"Uncharacteristic...?"

"Reacting to situations in a manner you wouldn't expect? Forgetful, perhaps to the extent of having whole chunks of memory missing? Or misremembering events, even referring to shared experiences of which you have no recollection."

"I don't understand," said Veronica quietly.

Dr Drake slowly rose from his chair and indicated the light board.

"I need to show you something," he said.

* * *

Gillian stood outside the cubicle and listened to the sound of retching. *Jesus*, it seemed incredible that it was only hours ago that she'd been doing the same...

White faced, Veronica emerged and closed the door behind her.

"I have to go back and see him," she said. "Everything he told me went in one ear and out the other. I need to know..."

"It's okay." Gillian laid a hand on her arm. "I've got it." She paused. "They're going to do more tests on Richard over the next few days and then they'll start to bring him out of the coma. You remember that, right?"

Veronica nodded.

"So, if there're any more developments, they've both our mobile numbers. We'll go back to the hotel - neither of us has eaten since breakfast and we won't be any use to anyone if we're faint from hunger. While we eat, I'll take you through what the doctor explained and then we'll work out what we're going to do next. Alright?"

It took longer to pay for the parking ticket than it did to drive to the hotel. Maybe they should walk back over in the morning, thought Gillian. She gave Veronica the key card so she could go to the room and freshen up, while she organised a table for two in the restaurant and ordered a large gin and tonic. By the time Veronica joined her, less ashen now with the minimum of lipstick and blusher, Gillian was on her second.

As they talked, Veronica appeared to remember the discussion with the doctor in the manner of re-watching a movie you saw long ago - you can't actually recall what's coming next, but as each scene unfolds it springs up intact in memory.

The tumour was inoperable but could hopefully be kept in check by chemo and radiography. The tests they were going to carry out would determine exactly how impaired he currently was. And while that would give them a more accurate basis for prognosis, Veronica had to prepare herself for a difficult road ahead. But most of all, what they should consider was how lucky Richard had been. Whatever had caused that blow to the head and brought him to the ICU meant they had caught the growth at an early stage. Perhaps only months later it could have proved fatal without even being diagnosed.

They finished the meal and considered each other.

"Gillian," said Veronica, "thank you so much. I really don't know how I would've managed if you hadn't been there."

"Don't be silly," said Gillian, almost adding that anyone who'd been there would have done the same. *Indeed!*

Veronica seemed to sense her hesitation.

"When Richard and I first met," she said carefully, "and he was trying to get his head around exactly what the nature of this relationship was going to be, one of the questions he asked me was *'Is this something you do or is this someone you are?'"*

Gillian waited.

"Thirty years later, we're still hanging fire over me getting back to him about that." Veronica shrugged. "Things can be as nebulous for as long as they need to be."

Gillian reached across the table and with a smile squeezed Veronica's hand.

* * *

Over the next few days Gillian travelled back and forth between St Hannahs and the hospital, while Veronica spent most of her time at Richard's bedside. Veronica's only other contact with the outside world was a call from Alan Bradshaw, to ask about visiting Richard. Somewhat icily, Veronica suggested he wait until they had brought Richard out of the coma. The plan was that once he was conscious, he'd be transferred to the Cottage Hospital in St Hannahs, where he was to stay under observation before hopefully being allowed home.

That wasn't the only relationship which had become decidedly frosty. Only the Travellers knew for certain what had happened during Richard's visit, but Chinese whispers had him in a coma at Derriford Hospital by their hand. And newcomer or not, as far as the townsfolk were concerned, he was one of theirs. Refused service in the pubs and shops and their exit from Belle Meadow still blocked by Harry Thomas's skip, tempers were fraying.

On the Tuesday, Veronica decided to return to St Hannahs. There was no change in Richard's condition, she told Gillian on the phone, and it was expected to be a few days before he regained consciousness. She'd be of more use at home, she continued, getting the house ready for Richard - there was a possibility that at some point he'd be wheelchair bound and so she needed to get people in to make sure the place catered for that. And probably a stairlift, who knew how steady Richard would be on his feet at first...

Gillian let her carry on. A busy mind was better than a worried one.

As she arrived at the ICU to pick Veronica up, she found her chatting to Jack Vanner.

"The Sergeant's just waiting to see Richard's doctor," Veronica told her and gave a tight smile. "As well as everything else, we're still trying to get to the bottom of that lump on Richard's head."

"Okay if I grab a coffee before we leave?" asked Gillian. "I'm parched."

"Of course, I could use one myself," said Veronica, and turned to Vanner. "Sergeant?"

"I'm fine, thanks," he told her, just as the door opened and the doctor stepped out into the corridor.

Gillian and Veronica walked along to the hot drinks machine.

"About the promotion?" Veronica looked at her. "Still sod 'em?"

"Sod 'em, indeed," smiled Gillian, and then shrugged. "Life's too short, right?"

"If you're not wrong about things," said Veronica, "odds are she'll be gone in a year. And if you are, well, maybe you should give her a chance."

"I know," said Gillian. "In fact, Dennis Nelson's having a barbecue tomorrow. For the eclipse. I wasn't going to go but..."

"Easier to face people over a burger and a glass of wine, than on the first day of term?" Veronica nodded, before adding, "I'd completely forgotten about the eclipse."

"Come over," said Gillian. "It's an open invitation and everyone would love to see you."

"I'll try," said Veronica. "I've one or two things going on in the morning, I could be a bit busy."

On the way back to the ICU, Gillian paid a visit to the Ladies. Entering the Unit she found Veronica in conversation with Vanner.

"And there's been enough ill feeling in the town over this already," she caught Veronica saying and Vanner nodded.

"Goodnight ladies," he said, as if about to leave, but then

turned back to them. "Oh, one more thing, Mrs Hanson?"

"Yes, Sergeant?"

"Your husband's car. The keys were in the ignition, but we couldn't get it started." Vanner shook his head. "At first we thought that it might have broken down, that maybe that was the reason Mr Hanson had pulled into the Viewing Area. So we arranged for Bob Northcott to collect it on a trailer."

Although there were a few petrol stations in and around St Hannahs, Northcott Motors was the only actual garage.

"But it turns out it's fitted with some kind of anti-theft device," continued Vanner.

"That's right." Veronica nodded. "There's a sliding panel on the consul, with a keypad behind it."

"Bob was most impressed," said Vanner. "Says he's never seen anything like it. But he needs the space and so if you could arrange to have it collected, he'd be grateful."

"Of course, Sergeant, I'll get that sorted out tomorrow."

"I'll pick it up, if that makes things easier for you," said Gillian. "On the way over to the Nelsons' barbecue. Tim can drop me off at Bob Northcott's, follow me back to your house and we'll go on from there. I'll pop the keys through the letter box."

"Thanks Gill, I really appreciate it," Veronica nodded. "But just put the car in the garage and leave the keys in the glove compartment. Our garage locks itself when you close it," she added, catching Vanner's raised eyebrow. "And tell Bob that I'll settle up with him as soon as he sends a bill."

"I don't think he's too worried about that," Vanner told her. "He was just pleased to help. And if you ladies would excuse me, I need to get back to St Hannahs."

"Of course," said Veronica. "Goodnight Sergeant."

* * *

Gillian wasn't used to automatics. In fact, she'd only ever driven them on holiday abroad, where trying to change gear with her right hand proved far more confusing than driving on the wrong side of the road. But the Jaguar was easier to handle than she'd expected, and with Tim right behind, shielding her from impatient drivers as she tentatively arrived at and departed from junctions, the journey from Northcott Motors to *Cliff Dene* was uneventful. Pulling into the driveway, the garage doors opened automatically and she cautiously inched inside.

With a sigh, she turned off the engine

There was a lot about the last few days Gillian wasn't sure of - and wouldn't be for quite a while, she suspected - but Veronica's advice about St Anne's was sound. So, she told herself, show up today with a beaming smile and prove to absolutely everyone that being a team player was yet one more of her admirable qualities. Qualities, she was confident, the school would be in dire need of, as Ms Prunella bloody Pozniak discovered the realities of transplanting Shoreditch into Cornwall.

Okay.

They'd have to stop off on the way over to pick up a bottle.

'Anything cheap and cheerful,' Dennis had told her, 'it's only going in the punch.'

Gillian lent over and swung open the glove compartment. Before she could drop the keys in, she noticed a bottle and raised an eyebrow. Richard wasn't someone she'd had pegged as a secret tippler. Curiously, she pulled it out and examined the label. German schnapps. The bottle had been opened but barely touched.

She shrugged.

That would do. It would save a trip to the off-licence and, making a note of the brand, she'd get a replacement for Veronica the next time she was in town.

Without giving it another thought, she closed the garage door and walked down to where Tim was parked at the roadside.

JACK

The first time there'd been a VIP - political, that is - visit to St Hannahs, Jack was on tenterhooks for days. It had been the Prime Minister opening an old winding shaft building re-purposed as a 'Visitor Centre', celebrating Cornwall's history of tin mining.

The PM actually spent most of his day at a GCHQ satellite ground station situated a little further along the coast, a structure which dominated the skyline whilst remaining conspicuously absent from any maps of the area. Its primary function was communications eavesdropping and most of the funding for its construction had come via the US National Security Agency. Its location was the point where TAT-3 - the third transatlantic undersea telephone cable - made landfall back in the sixties. And for all the secrecy, most of the personnel stationed there were readily identified in St Hannahs' bars and restaurants by settling their bills with credit cards bearing no actual identification.

Naively, Jack had expected to be consulted by the PM's security team prior to the visit, but their indifference to his offers of help bordered on the downright rude. It appeared all that was required of the local force was to hold back the crowd and keep the traffic flowing, leaving the Special Branch Section Two officers to swan around flashing their holsters in imitation of the poncey actors they'd seen on TV who made their job seem exciting.

It was a mistake Jack never repeated.

"Do what they ask you to do, but otherwise stay out of their way and let them get on with it," had been Jack's instructions to his own officers on all subsequent visits. Because when the shit hit the fan, as one day it inevitably would, he was determined they'd not be caught in the spray.

So, tomorrow's visit he'd initially been almost blasé about. Jack skimmed the itinerary without it really making much sense to him, but Carol explained - and for once this didn't go in one ear and straight out of the other - that the Secretary of State for Northern Ireland had been married to the artist and that these paintings had been created in St Hannahs over thirty years ago. All of them were now in private collections around the world and so this was the first time they'd ever been exhibited together.

"The gallery opening *and* the eclipse are a big deal for the town, Jack," said Carol. "It's not just about art. It's well known that he played an important role behind the scenes of the Good Friday Agreement."

"Seriously?"

"Aidan McShane's family had been staunch Republicans throughout the Troubles," Carol told him. "Between the two of them, they got a lot of people sitting down together at the same table."

At that, Jack decided he'd pay a visit to the gallery, maybe first thing in the morning. It wouldn't hurt to see if a local nose might sniff something out of place.

And speaking of something out of place...

* * *

Jack had known Gill Brown, on and off, for about as long as he'd known anyone. A Cornish childhood might sound idyllic, but both of them understood what the reality could be - a cluster of mundic council houses tucked away behind even the backstreets. Their lives seemed to have bumped against each other on and off ever since, first school and then college. She'd taught both his girls at some point and rarely a month passed by at St Anne's without some act of vandalism to be investigated. So, while much remained unspoken, each of them appreciated what it had taken for the other to make their way to where they were now. Mutual respect sounded a bit grand, he'd always thought, more like having the feel of each other.

Jack knew he'd walked in on something as soon as Gill entered the living room. It wasn't that they were both freshly showered in the middle of the day, they could have returned from a run or finished one of those exercise classes it seemed every woman of a certain age in St Hannahs was signed up to these days. No, it had been the expression he'd caught on Gill's

191

face before she registered him there, before it clicked what he was telling Mrs Hanson.

Sated was the word that came into his mind. And while it had never occurred to him that Gill was a woman with something bubbling away on the back burner - and St Hannahs had its share of those - the initial impression was definitely of someone who'd just been taken off the boil.

As regards the Hanson woman, well, Jack wasn't sure what to think. He was aware she was friends with Lee Munro and there'd been plenty of whispers around town about what went on up at *The Grange*. But in all his years in St Hannahs he'd never had cause to regard them as anything more than rumours and that was fine by Jack. As far as he was concerned, she came down here for privacy, didn't stick her nose into other people's business or rub their faces in hers.

But over the last few days, that moment had become as niggly as a loose tooth which you just can't leave alone. Jack took no prurient interest in the foibles and idiosyncrasies of St Hannahs social life, it was all simply filed away as backstory to potential flashpoints and flareups. The scales finally falling from a cuckolded husband's eyes or a wife deciding enough was enough. Domestic arguments, as any good copper will tell you, are rarely about what's being argued over.

Gill's husband was up country on a golfing trip this weekend, Jack recalled hearing, returning today. And while Jack didn't know Tim well, he did come across as the sort who'll do just about anything for a quiet life - always, in Jack's view, a sure-fire guarantee of never getting one.

Jack wondered if he'd any idea what he might be coming back to.

* * *

Jack knew Derriford well, he'd met Carol there when she'd been a Ward Sister. Lots of coppers married nurses and it wasn't only because their paths crossed so frequently. There's a mutual understanding of the havoc shift work wreaks on personal life and of what it's like to arrive home after a day you can't bear to talk about.

He made his way up to the ICU and waited while a student nurse went to find the doctor. There was a calmness, almost a serenity, about the Unit which took him by surprise, more used to the bustle - at times chaos - of Casualty. But wherever you were in a hospital, there was always that something which your senses latched onto. Same as a gaol, there's a tangible presence that lingers, sometimes even after you've stepped back into the outside world.

Further along the corridor a door opened and Mrs Hanson appeared. She was heading home to St Hannahs, she told him, hopeful of Richard's early return.

"I need to talk to the doctor about a couple of things," he said, "but if you want to wait until I'm finished, I can save you the price of a taxi."

"Thank you, Sergeant." She managed the first smile he'd seen on her face since he broke the news about her husband to her. "But Gillian's picking me up." And as the door to the ICU opened, added, "Well, speak of the devil."

Vanner and Gill Brown exchanged greetings.

"Okay if I grab a coffee before we leave?" asked Gillian. "I'm parched."

"Of course, I could use one myself," said Veronica, and turned to Vanner. "Sergeant?"

"I'm fine, thanks," he told her and, as the two ladies left, the doctor appeared in his office doorway and nodded at Vanner.

"Sergeant," he said, and Jack followed him in through the door.

"How is he?" Jack asked.

"We're keeping him in an induced coma while we carry out more tests. And given his condition, we'll be bringing him out of that slowly - it's unlikely you'll be able to speak with him for at least a day or two."

"It's a tumour, I understand?"

The doctor nodded.

"I'm afraid so." He paused. "And inoperable. Radiation

therapy and chemo are options and both have a high success rate in slowing further growth, but…"

Jack didn't press further. He'd learnt from Carol's time in the ICU that long-term prognosis for brain tumour patients was on a par with reading chicken entrails and that the outcome was rarely positive.

"This blow to the side of his head - what can you tell me about it?"

"In itself, unlikely to have caused him to lose consciousness. My guess would have been that he either struck it on something on his way down or when he hit the ground."

"But definitely a result of blacking out, rather than the cause of it?"

"Given the circumstances, I'd say almost certainly, but without actually being there…" He gave a shrug.

"I understand. Thank you, doctor."

Jack turned to leave and then hesitated.

"If Mr Hanson does regain consciousness sooner than you expect, would you have someone contact the police station in St Hannahs? We really do need to speak to him as soon as possible."

"Of course, Sergeant."

Outside in the corridor, Mrs Hanson was sipping from a Styrofoam cup.

"Did you find out what you needed to?" asked Mrs Hanson.

"I'm not sure," Jack began cautiously, "that we'll ever get to the bottom of what happened at Belle Meadow. But whatever did, I don't believe it's why your husband's in here."

"So…?"

"I'm inclined to let the Travellers move on. I'll have another word with them but, unless they give me good reason not to, I imagine they'll be gone by tomorrow." He studied her carefully. "Would you have any strong feelings about that, Mrs Hanson?"

She seemed to consider, as Gill Brown made her way down the corridor towards them.

"Nothing's going to change what's happened." She

returned his stare, then shrugged. "And there's been enough ill feeling in the town over this already."

Jack nodded and was about to leave when he remembered Bob Northcott's message about Richard Hanson's car. He listened, only half paying attention, while she and Gill sorted out between them who was going to be picking it up, and then he wished them a good evening.

* * *

Jack had already decided that this would be his last year in the job. Although he was only fifty, if you threw in his time as a Cadet that gave him the thirty years' service requirement needed. It also qualified him for a two-thirds final salary pension and that would be more than enough.

He'd been giving it serious thought for a while, even before that conversation last Christmas with his father-in-law. Brian had owned Petroc - a local holiday park - for over fifty years, growing it from a campsite in a field rented from a farmer to a twenty-five acre complex of Scandinavian Lodges and mobile homes. They still kept the touring pitches for caravans and campers, although Jack guessed this was more down to sentiment than the bottom line. It didn't hurt to be reminded where you came from.

Jack always assumed Brian would eventually sell out to one of the big national leisure companies. At seventy, he had the appearance of a man ten years younger and the energy of one twenty, but even he couldn't keep going forever. He'd receive offers at the beginning of every season, eye watering amounts to Jack's mind, but Brian always said that he'd think about it when the time felt right.

After Boxing Day lunch, they'd walked into St Hannahs for a drink at *The Barque*. Watching the hunt gather had become something of a ritual over the years and - being one of the few things Brian and his daughter disagreed about - it had been just the two of them. Jack was ambivalent, he liked the spectacle and sounds of it all, the scarlet tunics, yelping foxhounds and the thin yet evocative call of the horn.

But it was becoming more and more an occasion for confrontation. Last year, hunt protesters from the cities - used to being treated as little more than irritants by rural communities - had returned to their cars to find them buried in slurry. Jack believed it would be sooner rather than later before someone got really hurt and was glad when Brian, commenting that it was 'a bit nippy today', suggested they took their drinks through to the lounge bar instead of going back outside.

"I've had an offer," Brian told him as they sat down at a table by the window. "The sort of offer they say you can't refuse."

"Congratulations," said Jack.

"Well, I'm still thinking about it." Brian was uncharacteristically hesitant. "At the end of the day, it's all about what you've built rather than what it might be worth." He took a sip of his drink. "What are your plans for the future, Jack? Long term, I mean?"

"Policing's a young man's game," Jack told him. "It's why most leave as soon as they've got the years in for a decent pension. Unless you want to climb the greasy pole," he added. "Get political."

"And you don't, do you?" Brian smiled.

Jack shook his head.

"Left it a bit late, even if I did," he said. Not that his face would fit anymore. The force was recruiting from the universities now, rather than the armed services. Neither had been Jack's route in, but he knew that he was already regarded as a dinosaur.

And as much by the ranks above as below.

"Ever considered a career in the leisure industry?" asked Brian, a half smile on his face.

Jack stared at him silently.

"Strikes me," continued Brian, "that you and our Carol would make a good team. Her handling the staff, you taking care of day-to-day business."

"Brian," said Jack carefully, "I'm flattered by the offer, but we've nowhere near enough cash to match-"

"Let me worry about that," Brian broke in. "Look, at some point, everything will be going to Carol anyway, right?"

Jack was silent. Carol was an only child.

"And we could come to some sort of arrangement in the meantime," Brian told him. "If you were interested, that is." He shrugged. "It would mean a hell of a lot more to me to have something I felt I still belonged to - and that I knew was in good hands - than a fat bank account."

"I'd have to talk it over with Carol," said Jack slowly, "but..."

Almost bemused, he shook his head and smiled.

"Merry Christmas," said Brian.

* * *

The gates to *The Grange* were open, unusual in Jack's experience. He knew they used some kind of motion sensing malarkey, which let them know up at the house when a car was approaching. You rarely had to wait long, but this was the first time he could remember driving up and straight in since *Executive Action* had been running the place.

Jack always had the sense there was something just not quite right about *The Grange*. For one thing, it should have dominated the town, a neo-Gothic mansion constructed on the highest cliff tops along this part of the coast and indeed, it was unmissable on the skyline for miles around. But once you actually came into St Hannahs itself, a peculiar topography of hillside and ridges - which, although lower, were located closer - obscured it from view, which seemed in itself metaphor enough for Jack in his more notional moments. A looming presence, out of sight, so out of mind, he'd once confided to Carol when they were courting and she'd teased him mercilessly about it, delighted by this fanciful side to him which she'd never imagined.

Jack knew better.

The original house had been constructed in the nineteen twenties as a country retreat for a London businessman, James Carrington. A bit of a card by all accounts, which, coupled with a service record that had seen him awarded the highest military honours for his actions at Ypres, created a popular persona locally, even amongst the shopkeepers and hoteliers who occasionally made the mistake of allowing him credit. 'But he always came good in the end,' Jack recalled his grandfather once saying, 'and that's what matters.'

During the Second World War, Carrington had been involved in some shady scheme involving petrol coupons. He'd seemed to take his arrest philosophically, even extending his wrists for the handcuffs with a jovial 'It's a fair cop, guv.' But when he discovered that the charge sheet read 'Actively Hampering The War Effort', he'd become subdued very quickly. He definitely wasn't himself, the locals agreed during the days leading up to the case being heard. And when he failed to present himself in court, the magistrate reluctantly issued a warrant for his arrest.

He'd made things easy for the constables who arrived at *The Grange*. The front door was unlocked, and they found him sitting in a wicker chair on the veranda, his service revolver caught by a finger in the trigger guard as his arm hung loosely down, his brains across the wall behind him. A full tumbler of whisky sat on a table beside him, to all appearances untouched.

Since Jack first heard the story as a teenager, he'd wondered about that glass of whisky. Why pour it if he wasn't going to drink it? At the last minute, did he worry it would appear he'd needed Dutch courage? Or was the opposite true? Did it come to him that perhaps the alcohol might weaken his resolve and that he should act quickly?

What must it have been like, thought Jack, sitting there knowing you were watching your last sunset and casting your mind back along the paths which had led you to this moment?

* * *

The Grange remained empty during the austere post-war forties. A Labour Government's punitive taxation regime to get the country back on its feet did little to encourage investment into a potential inheritance tax nightmare. So its next incarnation had to wait until the nineteen fifties, which saw it re-open as an Academy for Young Ladies.

Which in reality was one more outpost in a Gulag of establishments intended to keep wayward daughters of the upper-crust out of further trouble, if only by reasons of geography and opportunity. Going by the stories Jack heard from his older brothers while growing up - and tales in the police canteen when he'd first joined the force - this wasn't an entirely successful strategy.

They closed down in the early sixties, when the place was picked up - for a song, as he liked to say - by 'Bunny' Johnson. Bunny was an impresario in the music business, whose speciality was finding good looking, working-class youths able to carry a tune, and re-branding them as teen heartthrobs with names like Ricky Verve or Frankie Tempest. But any swooning fan who managed to meet her idol would be unlikely to have much to kiss and tell about. According to the stories, a weekend at *The Grange* with Bunny and his confidants was a necessary precursor to the launch of their careers and even in an era when scandal could be easily bought off, Bunny sailed pretty close to the wind.

Bunny moved on in the seventies and *The Grange* became a hotel, run by the actress Lee Munro in partnership with a friend, whose family - while not local - had owned a house in St Hannahs since before the war. That was about the time that Jack had passed his Sergeant's exam and St Hannahs was the first promotion to come up. He got to know the two ladies quite well - bounced cheques, a cuckolded husband arriving unexpectedly, the occasional death of an elderly guest - and he'd liked them. Lee Munro, although a well known TV actress, had yet to gain movie star status and she spent far more time here - 'resting' Jack believed was the term - than in later years. But there were none of the airs and graces about her he'd anticipated and surprisingly, for both Jack and the townsfolk had expected this to be a dilettante enterprise, they'd made a go of it.

Until the inquest last week, Jack hadn't known the reason their partnership broke up. Initially, he'd assumed there'd been some kind of falling out, either personally or to do with the business. Although, in the months following Mrs Pascoe selling her share in the hotel, he'd occasionally seen them together and they'd seemed friendly enough. But having to bail her husband out... That must have stung, thought Jack, and it certainly cast a fresh light on Robert Pascoe's death, even if the coroner didn't seem to have made much of it.

Through the grapevine, Jack learnt that Lee Munro had acquired a new partner and that *The Grange* was closing for refurbishment. He'd assumed that only meant it was being tarted up, but when it re-opened a few months later Jack realised it was a whole new ball game. A wing of the house had now been taken over by Lee Munro as a private residence and she was a silent partner in *'Executive Action'*, a business managed by Paul Chapman.

'Executive Action', apparently, offered corporations the opportunity to send their management staff on a residential course specifically tailored to assess their abilities to function under pressure. And then how to develop techniques to cope with rapidly changing situations and best use them to your advantage. Jack had dropped the brochure into his wastepaper bin and given them six months.

Which, pulling into their car park five years later, just went to show how much he knew.

* * *

Jack always made a point of running a Criminal Records Office check on anyone moving to St Hannahs. It was the first piece of advice Tom Ferris - his predecessor - gave him, and it had paid dividends more times than Jack could count.

"The thing about St Hannahs," Tom told him, "is that it's the kind of place which attracts people looking for a fresh start. As well as those who don't want to be found. Neither necessarily means trouble, but it's good to have your card marked."

More than a few dodgy characters had set themselves up in St Hannahs during Jack's time, and he'd made it plain to all of them - discreetly - that he knew what was what. Some had moved on at that, but others just didn't care. There were a couple of ice cream parlours and a tat souvenir lockup Jack was convinced were money laundering operations, but knew he'd never be able to prove that in a million years. All he could do was give the Inland Revenue a heads up and wait them out.

But most watched their step.

The report that came back on Paul Chapman didn't ring any alarm bells. He was ex-army, which was what Jack had expected, and there'd been a few brushes with the law in his late teens. Dust ups between squaddies and locals in dance halls, reading between the lines, pretty much par for the course wherever troops are stationed. But nothing since, other than the odd speeding offence or parking fine. Jack slipped it into the filing cabinet with all the other CRO reports and thought no more of it.

The next day, Jack received a phone call from the Chief Constable of Devon and Cornwall Constabulary. What, the Chief Constable wanted to know, was Jack's interest in Paul Chapman?

Wondering exactly what kind of hornets' nest he might have kicked over here, Jack carefully explained that the bloke had set up a business in town and it was a routine background check to pre-empt any surprises. Jack noticed there seemed to be a delay to the responses he was getting. Less a technical issue, he assumed, than a second handset at the Chief Constable's other ear.

And when Jack finished, there was no mistaking the relief in the Chief Constable's voice. That was fine, he was told. Someone had obviously got their wires crossed. Keep up the good work etcetera, etcetera and then he was gone, leaving Jack staring at the silent receiver in his hand.

He'd thought about it for a couple of days, and then he'd phoned Tom Ferris. Not even for advice, really, just to get Tom's take on it and he'd been halfway through explaining what happened when Tom cut him short.

"Been a while since the two of us got a round in," said Tom. "What about tomorrow? Say about tennish down at the club."

Jack had never played a round of golf in his life, least of all with Tom.

"Sure," he said. "See you there."

Tom had waited until they were at the second hole before he brought the subject up, listening carefully. After Jack finished, he seemed to consider.

"I told you the eldest boy's a DI now, didn't I?" He said. "Up north, in the Lancashire Constabulary."

Jack nodded.

"Last time he was down, he was telling me this story. I can't give you names and places because I didn't get them from him - and I didn't ask - but I've no reason to doubt what he told me."

"Right," said Jack.

"A couple of years ago, in one of the old mill towns up there, a Casualty doctor treats a young teenage boy who's been the subject of a serious sexual assault. The kid's cagey as hell, won't say who did it, but the doc keeps badgering him and eventually gets a name." Tom paused. "It's the local MP."

"Bloody hell," said Jack.

"The doc gets in touch with a DI on the local force and gives him what he knows. There's been rumours for years apparently, but this really does look like an opportunity to nail the sick bastard. They wire the kid up, send him off to meet this bloke again and with a full surveillance team on him - video, directional mikes, the lot. By the end of the night, there's enough of a cast iron case to finally put him away. The DI takes it all to the CPS and waits to hear back from them, a slam dunk he reckons."

As another pair of golfers approached, Tom placed the ball on the tee, straightened up, took a club from his bag and drove the ball two hundred yards onto the green.

They walked on.

"Two days later he gets called into the Chief Superintendent's office, who he finds sitting behind his desk ashen faced. There are two other blokes in there who he doesn't recognise, one of whom tells him to go and get the evidence he's holding on the MP. Every last bit of it. He looks at the Super, who nods. Returning to the office with everything boxed up, it's taken from him and it's explained that the case is being taken over. He has the sense not to ask by who. He's also told that this better be everything he's got because if it isn't, he won't just be out of a job. One of the two men hands him a bank statement with his name on it. The sum isn't insignificant, and he's told that a local crime boss will swear blind he's been on the take for years. The Super won't meet his eyes as he leaves the room.

"He heads down to the hospital, wondering how the hell can he explain what's just happened to the doctor. But when he arrives, the doc takes him into an office and explains he's also had a visit this morning. He's been shown two sworn statements from women who claim he sexually molested them in the examination room. And that unless he hands over the medical records of the boy he treated, he'll be struck off."

Jack was silent as they arrived at the green.

"What I'm saying to you," Tom continued, "is that there are forces at work in this country whose nature we can't even begin to imagine." He reached into the bag for a putter. "And if we've any sense, wouldn't want to. So, unless you've got a *really* bloody good reason to, don't go second guessing nervous Chief Constables. Right?"

Jack nodded.

"Right."

Tom sank the putt in one.

* * *

There were two areas for parking at *The Grange*. For guests, a gravelled area surrounding a fountain at the end of the approach to the house, for staff and deliveries, a paved courtyard around the back. Jack usually parked out of sight, there was rarely any advantage in letting the world know where your enquiries might be taking you. But as Jack circled the fountain, Paul Chapman was already walking down the stone steps at the front of the house and so Jack pulled up at the bottom of them.

"Sergeant Vanner," greeted Chapman, as Jack got out of the car. "Good evening."

"Mr Chapman," nodded Jack, and made a point of looking around. "I was hoping to find the crew that's been working on your driveway."

"They finished this morning." said Chapman, slowly shaking his head. "Told me they'd be moving on," he added, "first chance they got, that is."

"That's what I wanted to talk to them about," said Vanner.

"I heard what happened," Chapman told him. "Or rather, what people say happened. How is Richard?"

"Well, he's still in an induced coma, but the doctor I spoke to expects him to be out of it by the weekend."

He hesitated, then thought what the hell, this bloke was no idiot.

"Confidentially..." He looked at Chapman, who met his stare evenly, "it looks like it was some kind of brain tumour that caused him to black out. So, all things considered..."

He shrugged.

"You're going to let them move on?""

"With a few caveats," nodded Jack. "The main one being that St Hannahs gets dropped from their itinerary, for the next few years at least. There's a lot of bad feeling in town and it wouldn't take much for things to flare up." He paused. "So with that in mind, I was wondering if you might have anything else lined up for them, off the books?"

With a smile, Chapman shook his head.

"It was a one off, Sergeant. We'd been let down by a Truro company and they were our only option. If we wanted the job done this year, that is."

"We're not talking roguish tinkers here," Jack said quietly. "Snaring the odd rabbit and gypsy fiddles around a campfire. The world's moved on - these are not people you'd want involved in your affairs."

"Point taken, Sergeant," said Chapman. "You won't find them back in St Hannahs on our account." He hesitated. "Would you care to come in for a coffee - or maybe something a little stronger?" He smiled. "You look as if you've had a long day."

Before Jack could answer, the radio in his car crackled into life.

"Excuse me," he said, opening the door and lifting the handset. As he listened, he felt his heart sink.

"Sorry," Jack said to Chapman. "But it's about to get even longer."

* * *

Jack had almost reached the art gallery when Tina came on the radio again.

"You'd better get to the Square," she told him, abandoning all protocols of call signs and procedure. "It sounds like a riot's about to break out."

"Exactly what happened?" Jack asked her.

"From what we can tell so far," said Tina, "a Traveller got into the gallery and threw paint over one of the pictures. He made a run for it, but a student working there went after him and yelled to some workmen coming out of a pub. They joined in the chase and caught up with him in the Square. They'd just grabbed hold of him when a van pulled up and half a dozen Travellers carrying pickaxe handles got out. That's when Andy Carter's first on the scene. He parked his car in between them and read the riot act to everyone, while he handcuffed the bloke being chased."

She took a breath.

"But right now, the Travellers are between Andy and his car and aren't letting him through. Word's going around the pubs like wildfire and they're emptying into the streets, so now it's the Travellers who are surrounded."

"What's everyone else's status?" asked Jack.

"Harry's three minutes out, Linda reckons five." She paused. "Do you want me to call Truro?"

Reinforcements.

"I'm almost there, give me a couple of minutes to assess the situation," Jack told her, trying not to sound hesitant - never a good signal to send out to officers under pressure.

There must have been at least thirty people in the Square when Jack arrived, clustered in the western corner. He pushed his way through the crowd to find Andy gripping his prisoner by the arm and facing three men standing in front of his car. Not the half dozen Tina had reported, he noted with relief. One of them was the elder who Jack had spoken to a couple of times at the campsite, and while giving Andy a brisk nod, he strode over to him.

"You have to leave," Jack told him. "If this goes any further, you'll be leaving me with no options here."

"That's my son," one of the other men said angrily, but the older one motioned him to silence, staring at Jack.

"The doctors at the hospital," Jack said carefully, "reckon it was a medical condition which put Mr Hanson into intensive care." He paused. "So, I was about to let that go when..."

He gestured behind him, to Andy and the Traveller in handcuffs.

"He's being arrested on suspicion of breaking and entering and causing criminal damage," he told the boy's father. "We'll be keeping him in custody at least overnight, while we investigate those charges and," with a nod towards the still gathering crowd, "for his own protection."

The patriarch seemed to consider this and then nodded. He turned his head to the crowd and then back to Jack.

"So many art lovers," he said dryly. Jack suppressed a smile, he'd been thinking along those lines himself.

"You'll be able to see him tomorrow," Jack told him. "Just check with the duty officer by phone first."

"As you say, Sergeant."

The three of them turned and began to walk back to their van. The crowd, for all its bristling anger, readily parted for them. Jack waited until they'd driven away and then gestured to Andy to put the young Traveller into the back of the squad car.

"Okay, folks," he said to everyone. "Show's over."

* * *

"Will you be going over to the gallery tonight, Sarge?" asked Andy, once they'd got 'Chummy' - Camlo Sterescu still proving too much of a mouthful and Jack really hoped they wouldn't have a chance to get used to it - booked in and settled down in a cell.

Jack shook his head.

"It can wait until morning," he said. He'd just come off the phone with Ruth Weinstock, who with her partner Fiona - it was funny how some days followed a trend - ran the Gallery on behalf of the Trust which owned it. To all appearances, she told him, the damage to the painting looked superficial, but they needed a specialist restorer to take a look at it as soon as possible. As much as Jack was relieved to hear this - if the damage was minimal this might get dealt with by local magistrates instead of County Court, and God alone knew what kind of circus that would turn into once the rent-a-mob 'Do Gooders' turned up - his main concern was security and his next question was, had he actually broken in?

Apparently not, was the answer. One of the cleaners, from the firm contracted to put the final touches into sprucing the place up for the opening, had stepped outside for a smoke and left the door open. The Trust had contacted the insurance company, she continued, and organised a contingent of security guards to be on site from ten o'clock tonight. Jack bet they had. Egg all over their bloody faces already, they wouldn't be taking any chances with the national press arriving in force tomorrow.

When she asked if Jack had any idea as to motive, he was slightly disingenuous in telling her they were waiting until he had a solicitor before questioning him. Before she could pursue that any further, he explained he was coming over there in the morning to conduct a security check of his own. He was sure everything would be okay, but given today's events and tomorrow evening's guest list...

Of course, she told him. She'd look forward to seeing him then.

Jack placed the receiver back down on the handset,

wondering exactly how long this was going to take to work its way up the chain of command. And also what he was going to say about it.

On his desk a bulky, official looking A4 envelope was waiting for him. He opened it to find a copy of the forensic lab report on Robert Pascoe's computer, the original having been sent to the coroner. Most of it was taken up with a file list printout of the contents of the hard drive, which, for all the sense it made to Jack, might as well have been written in Sanskrit. But a half-page summary sheet told him just about what he'd expected. There was nothing on there that gave any indication of a state of mind contemplating suicide. And although the FDS file was a mystery - a lot of technical gobbledegook as to why they couldn't open it - the fact that a program needed to either create or decrypt it wasn't installed on the machine and apparently never had been, suggested it probably wouldn't have much light to throw on the circumstances surrounding his death.

A toss-up between misadventure or suicide, concluded Jack, fitting the sheets back into the envelope.

The phone rang.

"Sergeant Vanner?" Tina's voice sounded uncharacteristically prim and formal.

"Yes, Tina."

"I have the Chief Constable on the line for you, sir."

Jack let out a sigh.

"Put him on," he said.

FRANCESCA

The house was a surprise.

From the outside - and Francesca had passed by a couple of times - it looked as rundown as the rest of the street. Rows of decaying townhouses, their grandeur long faded and now, she'd been told, packed God knows how many to a room with recent immigrants from the West Indies and Ireland. If this was the better life they'd come in search of, reflected Francesca, their previous one must have been grim indeed.

But as she pushed open the front door and stepped inside without knocking - the correct protocol, an old boyfriend had once told her with a smile, for arriving at both a Country House and a tenement - she walked across a floor which was carpeted, rather than the bare boards or cracked tiles she'd expected. And a hint of fresh paint, she noticed, lingered in the air.

Francesca had been told there was a communal kitchen and, hearing voices coming from the rear of the building, followed the sounds down a short passageway to where a door was ajar. Tentatively, she pushed it fully open to find a couple, in their early twenties, she guessed, sitting at a large wooden table.

They broke off their conversation and looked up at her.

"Hello," she said. "I'm looking for Paul."

The girl stood up.

"Is it about a room?" she asked.

Francesca nodded.

"I'll go and see if I can find him for you," the girl smiled.

"Would you like a coffee?" asked her companion. Francesca usually only drank tea, but aware that being awkward did little for first impressions, nodded.

"Thanks," she said. "Love one."

"I'm Aidan," he told her. "Pleased to meet you."

There was a soft Irish lilt in his voice, unlike the harsh tones of her grandparents, whose accents had suggested Belfast. Their past was a closed book and one, Francesca had learnt at an early age, seemingly best left that way.

"Francesca," she told him, adding, "Where is it you're from? My family's from the north, but I was born over here."

"Dublin," he told her. "Or more accurately, a small village a couple of miles south of there. Do you take milk and sugar?"

She said yes to both and then turned as the door opened.

The girl had returned with a man of about their own age. Initially he appeared to defy her expectations, his hair was cut short, he wore a crisp white shirt and his black trousers had a sharp crease. But his manner was casual enough and he was - Francesca couldn't help but notice as they shook hands - very good looking.

"Hi, I'm Paul," he said. "You're trying to find somewhere to stay?"

"Veronica, a girl I met last night at the Women's Defence League," she told him, "thought there might be a room here."

"Where are you staying at the moment?"

"The YWCA, on Great Russell Street."

"You've just moved to London?"

"Yes." She hesitated. "My dad died a couple of years ago - my mother's taken up with a new bloke and... Well, things didn't exactly work out between me and him." She shrugged. "It seemed time to make a fresh start."

"Where are you from?"

"Bristol."

"Do you have a job here?"

Francesca shook her head.

"I've applied for at least half a dozen. I can do typing and shorthand." She hesitated. "But when they see..."

She gave another shrug.

"That you're living in a hostel, they're not interested," said Paul.

Francesca nodded.

"But I've got money," she told him. "Savings. Enough to get by on for a while."

"We don't have a room right now," Paul continued. "But we might be able to help you out."

"Are you thinking of ...?" Aidan's voice trailed off as he turned to look at Paul.

"We're not sure if he's actually left yet, are we?" shrugged Paul.

"No great loss if he has," said the girl.

"We had someone staying here," Paul told Francesca, "who might've moved on. But his rent's paid until the end of the month."

"So, let her stay in the room," said Aidan, "and if he comes back, she can crash downstairs until we sort something else out." He turned to Francesca. "I've two rooms down in the basement. One of them I use as a studio, so you'd have to be out during the day. But there's a daybed in there, which is comfortable enough to sleep on."

"That's brilliant," said Francesca. "Thank you."

It was far more than she'd hoped for.

* * *

Francesca had little by way of personal possessions and when she returned to the house, Paul helped to carry them upstairs.

"I've brought a chest of drawers up from my room," he told her. "I don't really need it and if you can manage with that until we know what's what, then we won't have to mess about with his stuff."

"It's not likely he'd leave all his things behind, is it?" she asked. "I mean, if he's not coming back?"

"You'd be surprised," he smiled, "what people walk away from."

"Have you managed this place long?"

"I don't," he said. "I just help out when Lee - she's the one who looks after the house - isn't here."

"Well, who should I pay the rent to?"

"Like I said, this room's paid up to the end of the month. So let's wait and see what happens."

"Okay, thank you," she smiled.

Leaving, he turned back to her at the doorway.

"If you're looking for office work, your best bet would be the temp agencies," he told her. "Head down to Holborn or the

Strand. You'll get paid weekly in cash, instead of a monthly salary. And if a business likes you, there's a good chance of being taken on permanently - if that's what you want."

"Thanks."

After he left, she spent half an hour or so sorting the room out. There was space in the wardrobe for the few dresses and skirts she'd brought. Hanging her coat on the back of the door, she folded the rest of her clothes away into the chest of drawers.

A table pushed against the wall in the far corner seemed to have served as a desk. She tidied a sheaf of loose papers off to one side after giving them a cursory inspection and finding little of interest. A stack of paperbacks, the top three - *Steppenwolf*, Kafka's *The Trial*, a collection of D.H. Lawrence's essays - proved typical and she couldn't see herself returning to them unless she had trouble sleeping.

Francesca went downstairs to the kitchen, made a pot of tea and sat at the table with *The Evening News*. Her new housemates drifted in and out, names were exchanged and eventually - as she'd hoped - a couple of girls asked if she fancied joining them down the pub, where, after a few tentative exchanges, they immersed themselves into gossip as if it were a hot bath on a cold winter's day.

* * *

Linda and Kath shared a room on the top floor, Francesca discovered.

"Just as friends," added Linda, quickly. "Not like, well, you know...?"

Francesca shook her head, puzzled. Linda and Kath exchanged a look, then Linda turned back to her.

"You really haven't been here long, have you?" she smiled.

Most of the people in the house were involved with the arts, they explained. It was owned by the actor Don Mayberry - she'd heard of *him*, right, and Francesca nodded - who rented rooms out while it was being renovated.

"My boyfriend works in the ticket office at the National Theatre," Kath told her, "and when I had to move out of where

I'd been living, a friend of a friend told him about Pembridge Villas. It's supposed to be just for actors, musicians and writers, but when I explained to Lee what was going on in my life, which I really won't bore you with, she took pity on me and let me have the room."

"Lee?"

"She's a friend of Don's, who looks after the place for him. An actress." Linda shrugged. "She's got a room here, but we hardly ever see her, unless there's a problem with the plumbing or something."

"Linda and I have been friends since Primary School," Kath told her. "When she decided to come to London too, I said she could move in with me."

"How did you find yourself here?" asked Linda.

"I met a girl called Veronica, at a self-defence class." Francesca took a sip of her drink. "When she found out I was living in a hostel, she said she'd have a word about my being able to stay here. So I came along this afternoon and saw Paul."

"He takes care of things when Lee's not here," nodded Linda. "Another friend of Don Mayberry." She and Kath exchanged smiles, and Francesca gave them a puzzled look.

"You have to be pretty broad-minded staying here," said Kath. "Don't get me wrong, it's a great place to live - no creepy landlords, crummy kitchenettes... My last house, I found a spyhole in the bathroom."

"*Jesus!*" said Francesca.

"So, whatever other people are into behind closed doors is just fine by me, as long as I'm left alone, right?" Kath fixed her with a stare. "But it helps to know what's what."

Francesca slowly nodded.

"Same again?" asked Linda and without waiting for a response, picked up Francesca's glass.

"Do you smoke?" asked Kath, while Linda was at the bar.

"Sorry," said Francesca, "I'm afraid I don't. But I saw a machine in the corridor by..."

She broke off, as with a smile Kath raised her hand.

"No, I meant *smoke* - hash?"

"I've tried it," said Francesca cautiously, "but I can't say that I really got on with it." She shrugged. "All that happened is that I felt dizzy and ate about a dozen Kit Kats."

"Me neither," grinned Kath. "I'm always going to be a gin and tonic girl. But it goes on a lot, in the house. Just hash and acid," catching Francesca's expression. "Lee's pretty strict about that - any hard drugs or dealing and you're out."

"That's not a problem for me," Francesca told her.

"Here we go," said Linda, returning with a tray of drinks.

"I like your wallet," Francesca said, watching Linda put her change away. "I've never seen one like that before."

Linda handed it over to her. It was a leather billfold that opened in both directions, each of which revealed different compartments. But when you unfolded it again, there were even more compartments. Francesca really couldn't see how it worked.

"A bloke in the house has a stall at Kensington Market," Linda told her. "I got it from there, if you'd like one?"

"I think Kit's away at the moment, though," said Kath.

"Kit?" queried Francesca.

"A boy who lives in the house," explained Linda.

"Right," said Francesca slowly. "Any idea when he's likely to be back?"

"No, but I heard that Richard's looking after the stall while he's gone. " She smiled at Francesca. "Richard is Veronica's boyfriend."

"Boyfriend?" Francesca stared from one of them to the other and shook her head. "Sorry, I got the impression that..."

Both of them regarded her with amusement.

"As I said," smiled Kath, "it helps to be broad-minded."

* * *

The first thing which struck Francesca about Kensington Market was that incense did a really shit job of covering up the aroma of cannabis, its pungency permeated the entire building.

It was an incongruous feeling as you stepped in from

the ordinariness of Kensington High Street and moved deeper inside. Passing stalls of Afghan coats, cheesecloth shirts and dresses, beads and bangles, the ambience became more eastern bazaar than London market.

The stall she was looking for, Linda had told her, was upstairs at the back and selling mainly leather bags and belts. But as she soon discovered, that didn't really narrow things down much. Eventually she found it because she recognised Richard from the house, he'd passed her on the staircase the previous evening after she'd returned from the pub with Linda and Kath. They'd exchanged smiles and Richard's eyes had lingered long enough for her to suspect that if she'd turned her head, she'd also have caught him checking her out from the rear.

"Hi," she said to him.

"Hi." She could see that he recognised her but was struggling to remember where from.

"Francesca," she told him. "We almost bumped into each other on the stairs last night."

"Right," he said, returning her smile. "You've just moved in?"

"Yes," she nodded, adding. "I met Veronica a couple of nights ago and she had a word with Paul for me."

"She said - at the Women's Defence League." His smile widened. "So, is that what you're into? Women's lib?"

"I'm not sure what that even means," she told him, keeping her eyes on his, "but a girl all alone in the big city needs to know how to... handle herself."

"And that's what you are - all alone?"

"At the moment." She paused. "I'd been hoping to bump into Veronica in the house, to thank her properly."

"She's away for a few days. Working."

"What does she do?" asked Francesca. "It never really came up when we were talking."

"She's Lee Munro's PA," said Richard.

"For such a short sentence," said Francesca slowly, "there's an awful lot I don't understand about it. PA?"

"Personal Assistant," grinned Richard.

"And Lee Munro is who manages the house?"

"Yes, but she's also an actress," Richard told her. "She's just finished a TV series and there's a lot of promotional work right now. A PA takes care of the day to day hassles which come with that."

"Okay," said Francesca. "Wow! Beats working in Woolworth or sitting at a switchboard. I..."

She broke off as a customer approached.

"Just a sec," Richard told her, turning to the teenage girl who was smiling at them. "Anything I can help you with?"

Francesca backed away and pretended to examine a fringed leather bag, not wanting to make a potential customer feel crowded. The girl was speaking softly, whatever she was saying too low for Francesca to catch, but Richard nodded and opened a small drawer by the till. He took out two small, square paper packets of incense, identical to the ones on display, she noticed, but perhaps these were of a different fragrance. And apparently quite a bit more expensive. The ones on sale in plain sight were labelled two and sixpence, but the girl received only a small amount of change from the two pound notes she handed over. As he closed the drawer, Richard glanced in her direction and, feeling herself caught staring, Francesca turned her attention back to the bag she was holding.

"If you like that," he told her, coming back over, "I could do you a special deal."

"Bet you say that to all the girls," she said tartly, hanging the bag back onto a hook.

"I do," he said.

"Not exactly a special deal then, is it?"

"Everyone's special," he smiled. "You just have to find out how."

She gave a short laugh and shook her head.

"Well, aren't you just the silver-tongued devil," she said and then, as his grin widened, arched an eyebrow. "Don't you *dare!*"

"So, what kind of bag are you looking for?" he asked.

"Actually," she told him, "it was a wallet I was after."

She described the billfold that Linda had shown her, and Richard nodded. He went to the back of the stall where there was a tray of purses and pulled one free, handing it to her.

"We've only got it in black, right now," he said. "If you wanted a different colour, I could put an order in."

"No, black's fine," she told him. Opening it, she was fascinated yet again by the myriad compartments that folding and unfolding revealed.

"Clever, isn't it?" smiled Richard.

Francesca nodded her head.

"It's like a magic trick you think you'll understand the next time you're shown it, but never do. How much is it?"

"Seven and six usually, but with housemate's discount..." He shrugged. "Call it five bob."

"Thanks." She took her purse out of her bag and gave him two half crowns.

"Was there anything else you wanted?" Richard asked, and there was something about his phrasing which made Francesca give him a quizzical look.

"Do you need to score?" he added.

"Oh," said Francesca, pieces suddenly falling into place. "I..." She managed a slightly embarrassed smile. "I've smoked hash a couple of times, but I'm not really sure about how to..."

She shrugged.

Richard pulled open the drawer and took out one of the packets labelled as incense. He unfolded the wallet, slipped the packet inside, folded it closed and handed it back to her.

"When I'm finished here," he said, "I'll drop by your room and show you how to build a joint. Or roll a few up for you."

"If we'll ever be able to find it again in there," she told him. "How much do I owe you?"

"That's okay, I'll look on it as a loss leader. Once you're enslaved to the demon weed and dragged down into a world of vice and iniquity, I'll extract my recompense many times over."

"Right." Francesca nodded. "Thanks for the heads up, I'll be back home about six."

"Catch you later," he smiled, moving over to a young couple examining a suede satchel.

* * *

Francesca had only been back in her room for a few minutes when there was a knock at the door. Opening it, she found a girl standing there, her expression of nervousness switching to surprise as she registered Francesca in the doorway.

"Hello," said Francesca. "Can I help you?"

"I..." she faltered. Then, with a slight shake of her head, the girl seemed to gather herself. "I was looking for Andrew. Is he here?"

"Andrew?" Then she remembered the paperwork she'd tidied up on the makeshift desk belonging to the room's previous occupant. "He's away."

The girl looked so discomforted at this that Francesca stepped back, opened the door wider and with her hand gestured for her to enter the room.

"Do you know where to?" asked the girl as Francesca closed the door behind them. There was only the trace of an accent, she definitely wasn't English but it was her phrasing rather than a lack of fluency which gave it away. Dutch or Swedish maybe...

"Sorry." Francesca shook her head. "Apparently, he's paid the rent until the end of the month, but nobody's really sure whether he's coming back or not." She hesitated. "I'm Francesca. I was stuck for somewhere to stay and so Paul said that I could use the room until we found out what was happening."

"Carin," said the girl. "I am a friend of Andrew." With a sigh, she laid a folded newspaper she was carrying down on the table as if it were a great weight. "He told me he planned to go away, but I hoped he hadn't left yet." She stared at Francesca. "I really need to see him. Do you think someone in the house might know where he is?"

Before Francesca could answer, there was a sharp knock at the door.

"Excuse me," she said to Carin, and crossed the room to open it.

"Hi," said Richard.

Francesca stood to one side to let him enter and caught the flicker of surprise as he saw Carin.

"Hi Carin," he smiled, and Carin nodded back.

"Carin's trying to find Andrew," she explained. "Any idea where he could have gone?"

Richard slowly shook his head.

"Have you tried in *The Elgin* or *The Duke of Wellington*?" he asked Carin. "He's in there a lot, might have said something to somebody."

"I don't know where they are," Carin told him. "I thought perhaps that someone here would be able to help."

"Unlikely." He stared at Carin's expression of dismay and then gave a small nod. "But worth a try. Come on," he said to her, "let's go and knock on a few doors and if not, it'll be a good excuse for a pub crawl."

He looked over at Francesca.

"Do you need me to, ah...? Sort out what we were discussing earlier?"

Francesca smiled.

"It's okay, there's no rush," she told him. As they turned to leave, she smiled at Carin. "Good luck. I hope you find him."

Carin paused, then reached into her bag and took out a small spiral notebook. She scribbled on a sheet, tore it out and handed it to Francesca.

"My phone number," she said. "And where I live. If Andrew comes back or you hear anything about where he might be, would you let me know?"

Francesca nodded. Carin managed a smile and then they were gone.

And leaving behind, Francesca suddenly noticed, Carin's newspaper. Well, too late to go running after them and anyway, she hadn't seen a paper today. Sitting down at the table, she unfolded it. *The Evening News*.

It took a couple of seconds to realise that it wasn't today's edition. The headlines were still going on about that shooting over in Camden Town. A separate story ran under the photograph of a severe-looking man in his early fifties. *'Family, friends and colleagues mourn the death of a senior detective'*, began the piece in bold type. Other than the fact he'd been found collapsed on Parliament Hill, near the Lido, the rest of the column had little more to add.

Francesca folded the newspaper and dropped it into the wastepaper bin.

* * *

Francesca was beginning to think of Linda and Kath as a double act. This was her third day in the house, and she'd yet to encounter one without the other. When she arrived in the kitchen, Linda was pouring coffee while Kath buttered toast. There was a sleepy-eyed contentment about the pair of them which for a second had Francesca wondering about their assertion of 'nothing like that' before putting the thought out of her mind with a slight shake of the head.

This house really was getting to her.

"Would you like a cup?" asked Linda, raising the coffee pot.

"I'd love one," said Francesca. "Thanks."

"Did you hear the kerfuffle last night?" asked Kath, as Francesca sat down at the table.

"Kerfuffle?"

"We're in the room next door," said Linda, bringing the coffee over and sitting down across from her. "But I'd have thought you'd have known about it halfway down the street."

Francesca shook her head, silently looking from one to the other.

"Veronica came back unexpectedly," Kath told her. "She was supposed to be away for the week, but something got cancelled and so she arrived home early."

"And found Richard in her bed with another woman,"

said Linda. "We had to listen to the whole thing - screaming, shouting, his things being thrown down the stairs and out of the window."

"I thought that..." began Francesca and then broke off. What she'd actually thought, given all she'd heard about the couple, was that Veronica's most likely reaction would have been to simply get undressed and climb in with them.

But obviously not.

Linda nodded at her hesitancy.

"I know," she said and shrugged. "I don't think anybody's ever been sure what's going on there... But whatever it is, it's certainly not as open-minded or *avant-garde* as they all pretend, is it?"

"No," said Francesca, slowly. "No, it's not. Who was the woman?" she added. "That Richard was with?"

"We couldn't really hear," said Kath. "And it wasn't like you could stick your head out and take a look. "

"She was out the door pretty sharpish," Linda told her. "And no surprise there, given the mood Veronica was in."

But Francesca had a good idea of who it might have been.

* * *

Security was tighter than Francesca expected, but on reflection that made sense. A building full of single young women would probably have an irresistible pull for some sick minds if there weren't effective deterrents in place. She had to announce herself at a speaker grill on the wall by the main entrance and rather than the door clicking open, a uniformed female security guard came over to scrutinise her through the plate glass before allowing her inside.

Even then, she had to wait in the foyer while a receptionist spoke on an intercom. Seemingly satisfied, she turned to Francesca and nodded.

"Take a seat," she told her. "Miss DeWit will be down in a second."

It was actually five minutes or more until Carin appeared, dressed for the street in a brown leather bomber jacket and also wearing wraparound sunglasses.

"Hello," she said cautiously. "It's...?"

"Francesca." She hesitated. "I heard about what happened last night - I just wanted to make sure that you were okay."

Carin removed the sunglasses. The left eye, swollen almost closed, was bruised yellow and blue. Francesca gasped.

"It was an accident," Carin said softly. "Veronica threw a punch at Richard. I tried to grab her arm and she caught me with her elbow." She gave a wry smile. "Although I don't imagine she's too sorry about it."

"Have you had that looked at?" asked Francesca.

Carin shook her head.

"Come on," Francesca told her. "I'm taking you to Casualty."

Outside on the pavement, Francesca considered. University College Hospital was the nearest and by the time they'd walked over to Oxford Street to get a taxi, they could have made it there on foot.

"It's not far," said Francesca. "About ten minutes. Will you be okay?"

Carin nodded.

* * *

Sunday lunchtime was probably the best time to show up at a Casualty Department in Central London, reflected Francesca, as a nurse led Carin off into a curtained cubicle. Friday and Saturday evenings could resemble a war zone and the working week came with its quota of industrial accidents. But only a few patients, kitted out for football or keep fit, nursing twisted ankles or sprained wrists, had been in the queue ahead of them and they'd been quickly dealt with.

As was Carin. After half an hour, she emerged wearing a very impressive black eyepatch and a rueful smile.

"Is everything alright?" asked Francesca.

"No bones are broken and the eye is not damaged," Carin told her. "But it's very badly bruised. The worse thing," she continued, as they stepped outside onto the pavement, "was having to explain how it had happened. The doctor was very nice, but she was determined to make sure that I was not in an abusive relationship - walking into a door was not going to cut the ice." She sighed. "But in the end she accepted that it wasn't intentional. Only embarrassing."

"What did happen? Look, sorry," Francesca gave a shake of her head at Carin's frank stare, "but I'm not being nosy. I'm just worried for you." She paused. "Do you want to go and get a drink?"

"*God, no!*" Carin shook her head vehemently. "Alcohol is the last thing I need right now."

"Okay, what about a coffee or tea?" asked Francesca and after a few seconds' hesitation, Carin nodded. They turned onto Tottenham Court Road and immediately opposite was a small cafe.

"Let's try there," suggested Francesca.

They found a table and a waitress came over to take their order.

"How long do you have to wear that for?" Francesca indicated the eyepatch.

"I don't." Carin shrugged. "But it's this or the sunglasses. And it's better to look like a pirate, I think, than an actress whom no one knows pretending she doesn't want to be recognised."

Francesca laughed.

"Actually, it looks good on you," she said. "You might start a trend."

The waitress returned with a pot of tea for Francesca and a coffee for Carin. When she had finished laying everything out for them, Francesca leant forward and rested her elbows on the table.

Carin seemed to consider her and then sighed.

"We went to three or four pubs," she began, "where Richard thought someone might know where Andrew was. I'd told Richard that Andrew had worked as a roadie in the past and when I last saw him, he said that's how he was planning to spend the rest of the summer. So these were pubs where people in the music business - road crew mainly - hang out. In the last one, a sound engineer said that Andrew was with a band who were staying at a farmhouse in East Anglia, rehearsing before... I'm not sure how you would say it, playing live?"

"Going out on the road?" suggested Francesca. "Doing gigs?"

"Yes." Carin nodded. "Apparently this farmhouse is well known to groups, there is a recording studio there. He told us that a band playing in a club around the corner had used it earlier in the year and would be able to give us directions. So, we go to the club."

She took a sip of her coffee.

"We have to wait for the band to finish, and so we have a drink while we wait. *Another* drink, because we've had a drink in every bar we've visited, but I'm not drunk, although perhaps a bit..." She gestured with her hand.

"Mellow?"

"That sounds about right." Carin nodded. "After the performance, we go backstage and talk to them. Richard explains why we're there and, sure, that's no problem. They write down the address of the farmhouse and how to get there." Carin paused, then looked up and met Francesca's eyes. "Before we left, they offered us a smoke, a joint they had been passing around and it seemed," she shrugged, "rude not to take it. After they'd been so helpful, you know?"

Francesca remained silent.

"Except..." Carin shook her head. "I don't think that it was a joint. I think it was something else, something a lot stronger. And with the drink..."

"So that's how...?" began Francesca, but Carin broke in.

"I wasn't too out of it to not know what I was doing," she told her. "But perhaps enough to enjoy what I was doing. Even without the alcohol and whatever, I'd probably..." She shook her head. "Richard had been really nice to me. And it's been a while since anyone else has."

"It's okay," Francesca said, softly. "I get it."

"Just a shame he forgot to mention the Wicked Witch of the West. I was asleep when she arrived." Carin raised an eyebrow. "'Here we go', I thought, 'your first bad trip'. It took a while to realise she was actually there, I kept expecting her to disappear in a puff of rationality. Two minutes later, I was heading down the stairs with a black eye and clutching my underwear in my hands."

Francesca was softly laughing, shaking her head.

"But you got the address you needed?" she asked.

Carin nodded, reached into her bag and passed over a sheet of paper.

"This is in the middle of nowhere," Francesca told her, studying it. "On the Norfolk Suffolk border between Bungay and Beccles. You'll have a job getting there using public transport."

"I will manage," Carin told her, reaching out for the paper.

"Can I ask," said Francesca, "why it matters so much for you to find this Andrew?"

Carin shook her head.

"I'm sorry," she said. "It's really personal. But there's something that he has to know and only I can tell him."

"It's that important to you?" asked Francesca.

"Yes," Carin nodded. "It is."

"Just after I moved into the hostel," said Francesca, "I had to go home to Bristol to pick up some stuff and sort a few things out. One of the girls there had a car. She let me use it for a fiver and a tank of petrol. She told me I could borrow it anytime." Francesca indicated the sheet of paper Carin was still holding. "As I said, it really is the middle of nowhere, but driving we could be there and back in a day."

"Why would you do that for me?" asked Carin, slowly. "A complete stranger?"

"Because I know what it's like," said Francesca, meeting her eyes, "to be alone in a foreign country needing help. I was at my wits' end once, but then somebody was there for me. So, I'm sort of thinking of this as a debt getting repaid, if that makes sense?"

Carin studied her and then slowly nodded.

"Thank you," she said.

* * *

With Francesca driving and Carin navigating from an old AA membership yearbook they'd found in the glove compartment, they made good time. Until they reached the warren of country lanes criss-crossing the Suffolk and Norfolk border, that is, whose existence the Automobile Association seemed unaware of and where signposts at road junctions proved an exercise in contradiction.

"Aren't we supposed to have just come from here?" asked Francesca, staring at the name sign as they entered a small village and Carin shook her head in bewilderment. But after enquiring at the village shop, which also served as a post office, the directions Carin had been given were corrected and they discovered they were almost at their destination. Half a mile further along, they turned left into a country lane, even narrower than the one they were on, and after a few hundred yards came to a five-bar gate with 'Orchard Farm' carved into it.

At the end of a long track they arrived at a courtyard, surrounded on three sides by low-slung buildings. Their appearance was far more modern than Francesca had expected, shiny brickwork rather than the earthen exterior more common to East Anglia. As they pulled up, a door opened and a young woman dressed in jodhpurs and leather riding boots walked over to where they were parked.

"I'll have a word," said Carin, stepping out of the car. The girl seemed friendly enough, thought Francesca - country folk can be prickly when it comes to strangers - and pointed towards the rear of one of the buildings.

"Come on," said Carin. "The studio's round the back."

There was another parking area behind the building. A couple of VW campervans and a larger American Airstream caravan sat outside what had the exterior appearance of a barn, although a set of panelled double doors had a red light flashing over them.

Carin looked at Francesca, who shrugged.

"I suppose we just wait," she said, but then turned her head at the sound of a door opening. A young man of about twenty stepped down from the Airstream, staring at them as if not quite believing his eyes.

"Carin?"

* * *

"So," Andrew indicated the eyepatch, "what happened?"

"Something I'm becoming a little weary of repeating," Carin told him, "so perhaps we could leave that until later."

"Sure," he said and gave her a smile. "It's just really good to see you."

They were sitting at a pull-down table in the Airstream, Carin and Francesca sipping tea, Andrew with a can of beer. Carin had made the introductions, Francesca wondering what he might make of her staying in his room, but he'd simply shrugged.

"The rent's paid until the end of the month," he told her. "Someone might as well use it."

It was obvious to Francesca that the eyepatch wasn't the only thing that Andrew was itching to talk to Carin about and so finishing her tea, she stood up.

"I've been sitting down for the last three hours," she explained. "I need to stretch my legs."

But once outside, Francesca wasn't really sure what to do. There didn't seem anywhere obvious to take a walk, and she worried that hanging around the main building might be construed as snooping. And God forbid she'd be mistaken for some groupie! But before she could make her mind up, the flashing red light changed to a steady green and the door opened.

The figure that stepped through them didn't match any of her expectations, as rock musician, farmer or country gentry. He was about thirty, she guessed, shortish hair and wearing what appeared to be the trousers and waistcoat of a pinstriped suit with an open-necked shirt.

"Hello," he smiled. "You're new."

"Hi." She indicated the Airstream with a nod of her head. "Just with a friend visiting a friend."

"Right," he said, reaching into his trouser pocket and taking out a flat, silver cigarette case. He flicked the lid up with his thumbnail and offered it to her. "I'm Colin."

"Francesca," she smiled, and pulled one of the cigarettes out from under the strap. "Thanks."

He struck a Swan Vesta and, as she leant forward, shielded the flame from the slight breeze with his hand.

"Do you live here?" she asked.

"Oh, good Lord, no!" He shook his head. "I'm out here doing a story."

"Story...?"

"Or stories. *'Where The Sixties Have Left Us'*" He grinned at her puzzled expression. "I'm a journalist, with *The Observer*. We're running a series on the social changes of the last decade - music, the arts, politics, education - and where they might lead us."

"Right," said Francesca. "That must be interesting?"

"A rock band on a Norfolk farm, rehearsing seditious anthems under the influence of mind-bending chemicals... I don't recall anyone predicting that ten years ago. So, yes, putting together a plausible scenario of where we could be in 1980 has its challenges." He drew on the cigarette and blew a smoke ring. "What do you do?"

"At the moment, nothing." Francesca shrugged. "I've only just moved to London and so I'm looking for a job. But secretarial work mainly, typing and shorthand. Quite boring," she added with a smile, "by comparison."

Colin was staring at her.

"So you came up from London this morning?"

Francesca nodded.

"When are you planning to go back?"

"This afternoon," she told him. "I've only got the car for today."

"If it's not too much of a cheek to ask," he was still staring, "would there be any chance of a lift?"

"I'm not really sure..." began Francesca uncertainly.

"I lost my licence last month," he interrupted. "One for the road proved one too many. And you would not believe what I had to go through to get here - train to Norwich, bus to Bungay, taxi here. That was two days ago and I'm still recovering." Sensing Francesca's continuing hesitation, he added, "I'll pay for the petrol and buy dinner at this great restaurant I know in Epping Forest."

"You really are desperate, aren't you?" smiled Francesca. "Okay, I suppose it would be cruel not to."

"Brilliant, thank you. What time were you thinking of leaving?"

"I'm not sure." She gestured toward the Airstream. "I'll go and check with my friend."

"Right. I'll get my stuff sorted out, so I'll be ready to leave as soon as you are."

As she walked back over to the caravan, Francesca felt a little lightheaded. It struck her that she wasn't as used to cigarettes as she'd once been and, letting it fall from her fingers, she ground it underfoot.

And rather than knocking on the Airstream door, she sat down on the step for a minute.

* * *

The voices inside were faint but audible.

"There's no way you could've known," she heard Andrew say. "Jesus, it was dark, you were spooked - no one would blame you."

"If only I'd stopped and helped." Carin's tone was contrite. "Things might have been different."

"No," said Andrew. "Things would've been exactly the same, with me still completely under his thumb. But how it's worked out now..." He paused. "There's no reason I can't return to London, nobody else is going to be interested in me."

"Are you sure? What about Camden Town?"

"Well, in the end, that wasn't anything to do with me, was

it? Looks like they were right all along. Plus, they'll have their hands full with the major fuckup it's all turned into."

Andrew hesitated.

"Look," he said. "Thanks. For coming all the way out here to let me know. You didn't have to do that."

"It's just that..." Carin's voice lowered and Francesca had to strain to hear. "I'm so sorry about how I acted towards you before. What you did. Being under all that pressure and yet determined to do the right thing, when it would have been so simple for you to take the easy way out. And all the while knowing that you'll never get any credit for it." She paused. "Not many people would have done that."

"Carin, it wasn't..."

"And all I could think about was myself," Carin steamrollered on. "I was such a judgemental little cow about it all. I'm really sorry."

"That's okay," said Andrew.

"And I've been thinking about you a lot since then," she told him, her voice softening.

There was silence for a few seconds, followed by the sound of creaking and a gasp.

"Is the door locked?" asked Carin breathlessly.

Francesca rose to her feet and walked quickly away.

* * *

Francesca sat in the car wondering why she hadn't brought a paperback or magazine with her. Why had she assumed she wouldn't find herself with time on her hands? Picking up the AA book Carin had left on the passenger seat, she flicked through the maps at the back, trying to work out exactly where they were.

There was a knock on the window and she looked up to see Colin standing there, a small leather holdall slung over one shoulder by a strap.

"Sorry," she said. "It didn't feel like I could interrupt them."

"Must be serious," he grinned, "for a two hundred mile

231

round trip."

Francesca smiled and shook her head.

"Why don't you stick your bag in the boot," said Francesca. "And is there anywhere we could get a cup of tea?"

"Sure."

The last door in the building on the left of the courtyard opened into a farmhouse style kitchen, with a large oak table in the centre. Colin filled a kettle and lit a gas ring on the cooker.

"Whereabouts in London do you live?" he asked.

"I'm staying in Notting Hill at the moment," she told him. "But it's looking as if I might have to find somewhere else."

"I'm in Islington," he said, spooning tea leaves into a pot. "Like Notting Hill, it's a bit grotty but definitely on the way up. When I bought the house I had friends shaking their heads over it, but now they're envious that I could make a killing on the place."

"Have you always been a reporter?" Francesca asked.

"Left school at fifteen," he said, "to work as a tea boy at the Nottingham Evening Post. Which is why," he smiled, "this will be one of the best cups of tea you've ever tasted. Reporters might have a reputation as boozehounds, but trust me, it's a decent cuppa waiting for them back in the newsroom that really gets you into their good books."

Francesca returned his smile.

"And from there, I clawed my way up to a by-line on a Sunday national."

"I'd assumed it was the kind of job you'd need to go to university for."

"It's the kind of job that pays by results," said Colin. "Full stop." The kettle began to whistle and he poured boiling water into the teapot. "The best advice I ever had was from my uncle, who worked in advertising. He'd started in the post room of a large agency in the late forties, and now he's the chairman. He told me that if you think you've a talent for something, then take anything on offer to get in through the front door. Once you're inside, there'll be chances enough to impress who you need to."

He shrugged. "And he was right."

"So, did you find the story you were after here?" asked Francesca.

He gave the contents of the teapot a stir and put the lid on.

"We'll, there's always a story. It might not be the one you came for, and you might not know what it is until you're back in the office, going through your notes and listening to the tapes. But, like a sculpture inside a block of marble, it's there waiting for you."

"You make it sound..." began Francesca, but then broke off as the door opened and Carin stepped into the kitchen.

"Hi - this is Colin," said Francesca to her. "He'll be coming back to London with us."

Carin gave him a hesitant smile and turned back to Francesca.

"Can we talk?" she asked. "Outside."

With an apologetic shrug to Colin, Francesca followed Carin out.

"I've decided to stay here," she said, after the door closed behind them.

"Okay," said Francesca, then added, "Are you sure?"

Carin nodded.

"We'll be back in London at the end of August," she said. "Or Andrew will. I'll probably be going home to see my parents for a week, before the new term starts."

"Well, I'm glad things have worked out for you both," said Francesca carefully.

Carin hesitated.

"Andrew says it's okay to stay on in the room. And that if you haven't found anywhere else by the time he gets back, don't worry. He'll sort something out."

She handed Francesca a ten pound note.

"For the car," she said. "And the petrol."

"That's too much," protested Francesca, but Carin pressed the note into her palm and closed her fingers on it.

"Thank you," she said. "For being such a friend when I

really needed one." She smiled. "And I'll pass it on." She leant forward, kissed Francesca on the cheek and was gone.

Francesca went back into the kitchen, where Colin was pouring out the tea.

"Well," she told him. "Looks like it's just two for the road."

* * *

"Does your wife mind you being away so much?" asked Francesca, once they'd navigated the country lanes and arrived at a road wide enough to have a white line running down the centre and she could switch to autopilot.

"I'm not married," he said, and then added, "I'm gay."

"Okay," said Francesca, uncertainly.

Colin turned his head to stare at her.

"You know what that means, right?"

"Of course I know what it means," she told him tartly. "It's Bristol I'm from, not the last century."

He chuckled softly.

"It's just..." She shrugged. "Not something I'd have guessed."

"Because I don't conform to a stereotype?"

"Because I thought you were being a bit flirty back there."

"You can enjoy banter without sexual attraction, you know. In the main, gay men get on well with women, as confidants - lesbians and straight guys, not so much." He paused. "Has misreading the signals disappointed you?"

Francesca hesitated for a second and then laughed.

"Yes," she told him. "A bit."

"Your friend?" he asked. "What's the story there - reconciliation or rebound?"

"I'm sorry?" Francesca gave him a sideways look.

"Women rarely take point in the mating game," he said. "At some level, they instinctively understand the attraction passivity holds for men. As a rule, they only set out in pursuit when they've something to lose or something to prove."

"And you got all that from a twenty second glimpse into her life, did you?"

"Yes, I did," he told her. "Because that's my job." He hesitated. "What are your plans?" he asked. "About finding work back in London?"

Francesca shrugged.

"I'll try the temp agencies to get some ready cash. I've heard they're a good way to find something permanent, if a company likes you."

Colin seemed to consider.

"This driving ban. What the last few days have shown is that I really need someone to drive me around for a few weeks. Interested?"

"Sorry?" Francesca couldn't keep the surprise out of her voice.

"I'll pay you fifteen quid a week, cash in hand. Plus meals. And if you're stuck for somewhere to stay, I've a spare room you can use until you get yourself sorted out."

"Are you serious?"

"Like I said, there's this series I'm working on. Women's lib, gay rights, black power - whether it realises it or not, this country's at a crossroads right now. What I'd also had in mind was to send someone along a couple of days before I turn up, to spy out the lay of the land. I'll only be shown what they want me to see, told what they want me to hear. So, what I need is an idea of what's going on at the grassroots level. What the word is around the campfire, not the throne room."

"So you'll know what questions to ask?"

"Or not to. If what's being presented to the world is a facade, there's little to gain by setting off alarm bells."

Francesca considered.

"Why me? You must have a newsroom full of eager young reporters champing at the bit?"

"Well, for one thing, I'm not sitting here stamping my foot onto an imaginary brake pedal every time we approach a bend." He smiled. "I'm the world's worst passenger, but for some reason I seem okay with you behind the wheel. Plus, any journalist I send in there is going to have their own agenda or angle." He shrugged. "I don't mind giving anyone's career a leg up, but not if it's queering my pitch."

"A good title for the article on gay liberation," said Francesca, dryly.

"See," Colin told her. "You're getting into the swing of it already. Give it some thought, but there's no rush for an answer. By the time we're back in London will do fine."

Francesca smiled, seeming to consider as they drove on in silence for a while.

"I suppose as a reporter you get to hear a lot of things ordinary people never find out about?" she eventually asked.

"Scandal, you mean?" He nodded. "If Joe Public only knew half of what really went on, there'd be a bloody revolution."

"This business in Camden Town last week." Francesca gave him a quick glance before turning back to the road. "There's got to be more to it than what's been in the papers, right?"

"What makes you say that?"

"Gun battles in North London between police and gangsters." Francesca shook her head. "All because *armed* police turned up at some student digs. This is England," Francesca gave another shake of her head. "Don't tell me that police with guns are on the streets without a bloody good reason?"

Colin hesitated.

"Those gas explosions that happened recently…"

"Some sort of corrosive effect on rubber seals," nodded Francesca. "They all need to be replaced."

"They were bombs," said Colin. "The gas leak story was to stop people panicking."

Francesca gave him an incredulous look sideways and then snorted.

"Oh, come on!" she said. "*Stop people panicking!!?* You'd be a damn sight more likely to panic at the thought of your cooker blowing up than some office in Whitehall being bombed." She shook her head. "Stop people realising how bloody incompetent the police are at catching them, more like."

"You'll get no argument from me on that score," he told

her.

"But your paper went along with it, the same as all the others," she said. "The cover up, I mean."

"We had no choice. Have you heard of D-notices?" he asked.

"D-notices?"

"An official request from the Government to the press, asking them not to publish information relating to national security."

"But it's a request, right? Not an order or an actual law? You could have ignored it."

"As a rule," Colin let a smile play around his lips, "it's not a good idea to get MI5 seriously pissed off at you."

"Okay..." Francesca considered. "And that's what happened with the Camden Town story?"

"No." Colin shook his head. "In fact, there're no reporting restrictions at all. It seems to have gone down exactly like the police say it did."

"Which was?"

"The security services got a tip off where the suspected bombers were staying and Special Branch organised a raid. As armed officers approached the house, a well known East London villain was - it appears coincidentally – parked on the same street. There's no word about what he was doing there, but he was sufficiently spooked by the cops to get out of the car with a gun in his hand. Shots were exchanged, he was killed outright. The mother of one of the girls in the house, who she was visiting, caught a stray round and also died at the scene." Colin sighed. "All very tragic, but if ever a situation screamed cock-up rather than conspiracy, this was it."

"Okay." Francesca slowly nodded. "Truth stranger than fiction, I suppose."

"You have no idea," smiled Colin, "how often you learn that in this job."

"And yes," said Francesca.

"Yes what?"

"Yes and do I get to wear a chauffeur's cap?"

* * *

"So, you've found a job?" asked Paul and Francesca nodded.

"It's only temporary," she said. "I'm working for a journalist who lost his driving licence. Ferrying him around and being a general dogsbody." She gave a shrug. "But it could lead to something more permanent."

"Great," he said, before adding, "And it's live in?"

Francesca caught his expression.

"Don't worry," she smiled. "There's no chance of anything like that. It's all above board, believe me."

"Okay," nodded Paul. "Just that in the big city, you need to be careful."

"I know," she told him. "And thanks for the concern. But he's got a spare room I can use until I find a proper place of my own, which is one less thing for me to worry about."

"Right. Have you heard anything from Andrew? What his plans might be."

"As far as I'm aware," said Francesca, "he's coming back at the end of the month. Carin said he's working at the Isle of Wight Festival, something backstage."

"Carin?"

Francesca nodded.

"Yes, she was going there with him."

"Okay," said Paul, looking thoughtful. "I'd better hang fire on the room."

"And thank you." Francesca leant forward and raising herself up onto tiptoe, kissed him on the cheek. "For everything you did for me - I really appreciate it."

"Glad to help," said Paul. "And look, if things don't work out, come back and see us. We'll always be able to sort something out for you."

"Will do," smiled Francesca.

* * *

"Follow me."

On her arrival here, the commissionaire had struck her as

238

unnecessarily brusque and after keeping her waiting for twenty minutes his manner displayed little improvement. Without pausing for a response, he turned and walked away along the corridor. Francesca rose and followed, catching up with him as he rapped with his knuckles against the last door on the right and pushed it open.

It was a large room, dominated by a circular table, which could easily have seated twelve people. At the moment it was occupied by just six, their chairs arranged in a semicircle from the nine to three o'clock positions. Facing them at six o'clock, a seventh chair was pulled back from the table, as if awaiting her. The only face she recognised was Brian Maddox, and he indicated the empty chair with his hand.

"WPC McCaffrey," he said, with a half smile that was no doubt intended to put her at ease. "Please, take a seat."

Five of them were in uniform, lending their posture an exaggerated formality. The sixth wore a well-tailored suit and by comparison there was almost a languid air about him. Francesca guessed he would be the one to watch out for. Although middle-aged, there was a boyish look about him, still lean and with a fringe resisting being brushed to the side.

She turned her attention back to Maddox, slightly disconcerted that the Special Branch officer was actually in uniform and wondered what to make of that. But he continued to smile as he addressed her.

"Everyone here's read your report and first of all, congratulations. Your lack of experience in undercover work doesn't appear to have proven much of a hindrance."

"Thank you, sir," she said.

"As you're probably aware, there's going to be a full inquiry into exactly what happened in Camden Town. We appreciate that your understanding of that... incident is secondhand, but we'd like to hear it all the same."

"Sir..." she began hesitantly, then paused as the figure sitting directly opposite her raised his hand. He was, she suddenly realised, the Commissioner of the Metropolitan Police.

"As Detective Sergeant Maddox said, we've all read your report. But I think what we're looking for here is less an itinerary of events and more a feel of why it happened." He sat back in his chair. "So, we were hoping you could take us through the last few months in a more informal manner." He smiled and gestured around the table with his hand. "I know this isn't a setting that exactly lends itself to that, and I do have an idea of how intimidated you're probably feeling right now. But no one is trying to catch you out here, WPC McCaffrey."

"Yes sir."

"So… You were stationed at Forest Road, Walthamstow, when DS Maddox approached you?"

"Yes sir. My duty sergeant told me Special Branch was looking for a young female officer to go undercover in West London. Someone whose face wouldn't be known in that area. He asked if I'd be interested and so of course I said yes."

"Of course?"

Francesca shrugged.

"I assumed that if I did well, there'd be a chance it would lead to other things."

"And that's how you met DS Maddox."

"Yes sir, he came over to Forest Road. He explained that what had been reported in the press as a series of gas mains explosions was actually a bombing campaign carried out by a left-wing terrorist group. And that this group was connected to the shootings in Camden Town."

"Had you been aware of this?"

"No, sir." Francesca shook her head. "Like everyone else, I believed what I'd read in the newspapers."

"Very well. Please continue."

"DS Maddox explained that one of their informants had disappeared immediately after the Camden Town shootings. They had reason to believe that was by his own choice, but needed to confirm that. And if possible, by infiltrating the same circles he'd been moving in."

"The risk didn't deter you?"

"No sir."

"And so…?"

"DS Maddox and I created a back story for my role. He drove me around Notting Hill for a few days, showed me the house where his informant had been living, the pubs and cafes he'd frequent. We went through the files of the people he wanted me to meet and worked on a strategy for how I might best insinuate myself with them."

Francesca continued to explain how she'd used the self-defence club to strike up an initial meeting and how things had developed from there. For the next half hour, she was questioned at various points by most of those sitting around the table, all except the civilian who seemed, if anything, to be quietly bored by the whole procedure. Until:

"And it was through Carin DeWit that you eventually tracked him down?" The civilian spoke for the first time.

Francesca nodded.

"Yes, sir."

The civilian turned his head to stare at DS Maddox.

"By the time we were in position to make contact, he'd left for the festival on the Isle of Wight." DS Maddox shrugged. "Little chance of finding him in the middle of a crowd that large, but thanks to WPC McCaffrey we knew he'd be returning to London straight afterwards. I issued a warrant for his arrest to protect his cover for when we picked him up, which we did almost immediately after his arrival back from the festival."

"What had been the problem?"

"Just burnout, really." Maddox shrugged. "He'd been under a lot of pressure from us, plus he had personal stuff going on. A month away from it all seems to have straightened him out."

The civilian was staring at him.

"Burnout isn't uncommon, in fact it's more to be expected than not," he said eventually. "But coming back from it… Generally, when someone's done, they're done."

"Who knows?" Maddox gave a shake of his head. "Maybe he's more resilient than most. Plus, he seems to be in a stable relationship now. He's set up home with Miss DeWit." He glanced over at Francesca. "And I believe she's expecting."

Francesca smiled.

"Okay," she said. "That explains a few things."

"It was at this point you encountered Colin Savage?" asked the civilian.

Francesca related meeting Colin and his job offer on the car journey back.

"I know they say you should never look a gift horse in the mouth," smiled DS Maddox, "but my God."

"I can't take too much credit, sir," said Francesca. "It was his idea to have me infiltrate these organisations. All I did really was..." She shrugged. "Foster the impression that I shared his views by asking a few telling questions, I suppose you could say."

"A Trojan horse inside a Trojan horse," smiled the civilian, slowly shaking his head. "You should learn to take credit for what you stumble into, WPC McCaffrey, if only to balance the occasions when diligence and insight will reward you with nothing."

"Yes sir," she said.

"Well," said the Commissioner, "I think that just about..."

"Actually," broke in the civilian, turning to look at him. "If I may?"

The Commissioner nodded, and he turned back to Francesca.

"So, what did you think of them?"

"I'm sorry, sir?"

"These various groups you infiltrated." He paused. "Undercover work rarely plays out to our expectations. Whatever notions we might set out with, whilst living in close proximity it's not unusual to develop a simpatico..."

"I thought they were dangerous," broke in Francesca, then added, "sir."

He sat back in his seat and smiled.

"Go on," he told her.

"With criminals they're, well, criminals, aren't they?"

Francesca was conscious of choosing her words carefully. "It's all a bit cat and mouse. They know what the law is, we know they've chosen to break it, they know that at some point they'll be going away for that whether..."

She hesitated, suddenly uncertain.

"Whether it's for something they've done or not?" smiled the civilian.

"Oh, for God's sake, Sandy," said the Commissioner, angrily.

"Sorry for introducing *realpolitik* into the discussion," was Sandy's dry response. Turning back to Francesca, he nodded. "But I take your point. These are not criminals *per se*, but people indulging in criminal acts for political ideology, rather than monetary gain."

"My dad always said," Francesca spoke quietly, "that there'd never be a revolution in England. And that the public would never be stupid enough to vote in the communists. But these people aren't deadbeats - they're going to be teachers, lawyers, civil servants, broadcasters. You don't need victory at the ballot box - or barricades on the street - when you're going to have that kind of influence."

"I think you'll find, young lady," said the Commissioner primly, "that as people grow older, their outlook grows more circumspect."

"Not after they've had drugs planted on them or been pulled into an alley and given a quiet kicking for their political beliefs, they don't," said Sandy. "Circumspect is the last thing they become." He paused. "WPC McCaffrey's assessment is absolutely correct. These people are dangerous in ways society has yet to fully comprehend and treating them as petty criminals is fighting fire with fire."

"As opposed to what?" asked one of the uniformed officers.

"Fighting fire with water?" suggested Francesca.

Every eye in the room turned to her and she could feel the beginnings of a blush creeping up her neck. But Sandy was smiling at her and not unkindly.

"Have you returned to normal duties now, WPC McCaffrey?" he asked.

She nodded.

"This was good work," he told her. "Only someone who's been at the sharp end can understand the pressures this kind of operation puts on one. You've handled yourself exceptionally well."

"Thank you, sir," she said to him.

"I'll show you out," said Maddox, rising.

Francesca stood up. She supposed that given the assemblage of braid and brass in front of her she should salute, but - as they'd all turned away to talk among themselves - she settled for a brief nod in their direction. No one seemed to notice other than Sandy, who casually returned it. She followed DS Maddox out of the room and waited until he'd closed the door behind him.

"He's right, it's good work you've done here," Maddox told Francesca, before fixing her with a reproving stare. "But if you want to get on in this job, don't ever again side with an outsider against your own senior officers."

"I'm sorry, sir," she said to him. And then, tentatively: "Who was that, sir? The man they called Sandy?"

He seemed to consider for a second.

"Alexander Beaumont," he told her, "is the Assistant Director of MI5."

Francesca's mouth dropped open.

"To tell you the truth, I'm not at all sure what he was doing here," Maddox continued. "We and the Met are handling Camden Town and the rest of it seems pretty low key to warrant attention from that level. But for some reason, he's definitely taken an interest." He paused. "And probably the less we know about why that is, the better."

"Yes sir," said Francesca.

Maddox thanked her once again, confirmed that if any loose ends showed up over in Notting Hill she'd be available to resume her role, and wished her all the best.

* * *

Stepping outside onto the pavement, Francesca was experiencing a peculiar mix of emotions - satisfaction tinged with a sense of anti-climax at returning to normal duty. Sensations distracting enough for her not to be aware of a sleek Rover saloon pulling up alongside and so when she heard her name being called, she turned with a start.

The rear window had been wound down and Sandy Beaumont was looking out at her.

"Are you free right now?" he asked.

Numbly, she nodded.

"Thought I'd give you lunch," he said. "Over which, I was hoping we could discuss where your obvious talents might find a more suitable home than Forest Road nick."

The car door swung open.

VERONICA

Children born to the wrong parents have an instinct for each other. Falling so far from the tree, I've always been able to sense that rootlessness in others in the same way that I've never been mistaken about the prim and proper housewife on the other side of the room, demure at her husband's elbow and smiling along at his jokes with dead eyes.

It's no secret my father hoped for a boy. Given the choice, most fathers in the fifties would have plumped for a son and heir. But on discovering it would not only be ill advised but life threatening for my mother to fall pregnant again, Ronald was reduced to working with the material at hand.

Apparently the options were Petronia, Sharon, Veronica or Saffron and so, on the whole, I think I got off lightly. Rhonda had also been briefly considered, but although hacking it phonetically didn't make the final cut. Mostly I grew up in a more choreographed version of the rough and tumble of Ronald's own childhood, he mistaking my tomboy outlook for a child's natural instinct to please, rather than the busted flush in the nurture versus nature stakes it actually was.

Adolescence is the point where tomboyishness ceases to be a winsome trait and begins to give rise for concern. Unsurprisingly, my mother twigged first, correcting my father's use of 'Ronnie' - his pet name for me - with 'Veronica', her tone increasingly sharper as time passed. We had 'the talk', the whole business of periods, intercourse, childbirth and 'the change' laid out in its chronological inevitability. Well, we'll see about that, was my initial reaction and only fuelled my resistance to dresses, ribbons and engaging with my boisterous cousins in any manner other than fisticuffs.

And doubtless leaving my father reflecting on the wisdom of being careful what you wished for.

* * *

"So, how are you settling in?" asked Lee.

"Okay," Veronica told her. "It's a bit tricky switching mindsets from visitor to local, though."

"Oh, you'll never be a local," Lee grinned. "Your grandkids

248

might, if you're lucky, but don't bank on..." She broke off. "Oh, shit!"

Veronica reached out and took her hand.

"It's alright," she said, squeezing it. "You can't tiptoe around me for ever."

"I know. But..." Lee shook her head.

Tyler - whose role Veronica has yet to fathom - turned the same bland expression she'd worn all afternoon from Lee to Veronica and then back to Lee again. This was Lee's first return to The Grange *since Veronica and Richard moved into* Cliff Dene. *So given the fair amount of catching up to do, it's little surprise Tyler's attention had wandered.*

"I hear you and Claudia are now ladies who lunch," smiled Lee. "How's that working out?"

"Okay," said Veronica. "We get on."

"'Course you do - there was never any reason you shouldn't."

"I know." Veronica shrugged. "I suppose when you're young it's easy to... be judgemental." She hesitated. "I'm not so sure about that husband of hers, though."

"Robert?"

"Yes," nodded Veronica. "Richard and I have been at a few dinner parties where things got pretty fraught." She stared at Lee. "They say you never know what's going on in any marriage, but I'd have thought Claudia would have been the last person in the world to put up with that kind of crap." She hesitated again. "I was thinking of saying something. At lunch, perhaps, when it's just the two of us."

Lee turned to Tyler

"Darling," she said to her. "Do you think you could make us some iced tea? Suddenly I'm absolutely parched."

"Of course, Ms Munro."

They waited in silence until Tyler was out of the room.

"What I'm going to tell you stays between us, okay?" Lee's voice was low but taut. "Not even Richard can know and certainly Claudia must never find out that I've spoken to you about this."

"Okay..."

"Occasionally - and by occasionally I mean a couple of times

a year and after he'd been drinking Robert - could be... 'Quick with his hands' was an expression I once overhead my mother use, in a conversation with a neighbour about someone's husband."

"He... hits her?" Veronica exclaimed.

"Well.... Let's just say he could get a little rough."

"Jesus!"

Lee hesitated.

"You know Claudia had to sell her share in this place? To bale out Robert's business?"

"Yes." Veronica nodded. It's a story she's heard more than once.

"Things were pretty sour between them for a while after that." Lee shrugged. "Claudia loved running The Grange. She once told me it was the only thing in her life that didn't feel like it had been handed to her on a silver platter. Oh, in public she was the supportive wife, but behind closed doors... Anyway, after that she moves into a separate bedroom. Which," Lee raised an eyebrow, "does not go down well at all. Until eventually, after a session in The Barque, Robert arrives home one night demanding his conjugal rights. And when Claudia refuses, takes them."

"Jesus Christ!" Veronica stared at her in astonishment. "You mean he raped her?"

"If we're talking consent, then to all intents and purposes, yes." Lee gave a slow shake of the head. "After Robert passed out, she called me and I went over to the house, helped her pack a bag and brought her back here to stay. Of course, Paul wondered what was going on, but I explained to him they'd had a row and she'd be staying here for a while, until things cooled down. I daren't let him know what had really happened, right?"

Veronica was silent. Claudia and Paul have been friends since their teens - the vibe might be more siblings than lovers, but you can't mistake that strength of feeling between them. If Paul had been straight, Lee once told Veronica, he would have been the love of Claudia's life and probably vice versa.

"Anyway, there were days of anguished remorse on Robert's part. He'll move out of the house while he has counselling, he'll quit drinking blah, blah, blah. *Eventually he simply wears her down, I suppose, and some sort of relationship does get cobbled back together. Everyone knows she should just walk, but...*"

Lee let her voice trail off.

"*About a month later, Robert gets a new client. A phone call from someone up country looking for a rural retreat. A cash buyer with a seven-figure budget who wants Robert to put together a shortlist, ready for him to come down and view over a weekend. Which Robert does. He contacts the client and they arrange to meet at the first property on the list.*

"*The owners are away for the weekend. Robert's in the house waiting for his client, the doorbell rings and he answers it. But instead of the client standing there, it's three men wearing ski masks. They're through the door before he can slam it shut, he's clubbed to the ground. The house is ransacked, jewellery and antiques are...*"

"I remember that," Veronica broke in. "It was all over the news." Staring at Lee, she shook her head incredulously. "That was Robert?"

Lee nods.

"*It got such massive coverage because of the Suzy Lamplugh case - if you remember...?*"

"Yes. She was an estate agent who went missing after going to view a property."

"*That was quite a few years earlier than this, but still vivid enough in the public mind for the media to have a field day with it. Robert was found unconscious. He had a fractured jaw, one of his arms was broken and a couple of ribs.*"

"Bloody hell!"

"*They were never caught. But the reason his name wasn't given out by the police was because of the nature of the charges if they had been.*" Lee's expression was inscrutable. "*Rape victim anonymity - Robert Pascoe discovered what it was like to be on the other side of a serious sexual assault.*"

"What!!?"

"*All three of them, apparently. And it must have gone on for a while.*"

"Jesus!!" *Then Veronica caught the glint in Lee's eyes. "Are you saying that...?"*

"Paul was away in London that weekend," *she said. "I checked."*

'Well, he would be, wouldn't he?' *flashed through Veronica's mind.*

"So, other than Robert Pascoe being left seriously fucked up, I've no idea what's been playing out between the two of them in terms of guilt, redemption or recrimination," *Lee told her. "But I doubt Robert's laid a finger on her since."*

The door opened and Tyler came back into the room carrying a tray.

"Excellent timing, darling," *beamed Lee. "For once."*

* * *

Everyone's room here is awash with photographs, except mine. I'm sure a wall covered with brightly coloured snapshots of smiling progeny or sepia portraits from a simpler time brings its comforts, but it also seems redolent of job done. Game over, move along now.

As if we need reminding.

I've only the one print, from when Emily was perhaps five. It was taken by a street photographer as the three of us were seated outside a cafe in Minorca, the first 'bucket and spade' holiday we'd been on. Neither Richard nor I cared much for basking in the sun, but as dutiful parents believed Emily would enjoy it and of course she did. I'm reading a week-old copy of the *Daily Mail,* which at home I wouldn't be caught dead with but out here is exchanged like contraband. Emily is on Richard's knee. He's steadying a cup of orange juice at her lips and it's a scene of such tranquillity and contentment that it is the only gateway I need into the world of memory.

People wondered about Richard and I a lot, and for the most part we let them. We knew the kind of love we shared was different from the love most people understood, less rooted, more tactical, always ready to be up and on the move at a moment's notice. We also set great store by intuition. Other than the purely practical, our conversation was rarely peppered with rationale. Explanations, as Lee once observed, the vampires of creativity.

One of the first things we discovered we had a shared taste for was French New Wave cinema. I don't doubt there was a degree of pretentiousness about this, but we genuinely enjoyed the iconoclastic freshness in contrast to what Hollywood had on offer in those days. What delighted us more than anything was its willingness to bring matters to an abrupt end. With little by way of audience conscience regarding the tidying of loose ends, *'Fin'* could flash up on the screen seemingly without rhyme or reason and that would be it. Often, according to Lee, it was because that was the point at which the filmmakers ran out of money, which made overheard speculation as we left the cinema - generally along the lines of the transient, unresolved nature of life being reflected on screen - all the sweeter.

I don't recall what our first argument was actually about, something trivial no doubt, but the feeling of growing more and more heated, as I sat across the table from him in the kitchen of Pembridge Villas, is as fresh as if it were yesterday. Then, just as I felt fit to burst, Richard met my eyes and said, *'Fin'*. Almost instantly, I was shaking with laughter rather than anger.

I imagine all relationships have their safety valves - the ones that last, that is - and this became one of ours. A watchword to let the air out of the squabbles and dust ups of daily life, *'Fin'* would always steer us clear of the pointless minor victories or concessions which slowly begin to push the two of you apart.

Few other people got it but, as I say, they didn't have to.

* * *

"Sure you don't want a lift?"

"Honestly, the night air will clear my head," Veronica said to Gillian. *"And I'll feel a lot less guilty about that strawberry shortcake if I've put some effort into walking it off."*

Gillian laughed and the engine sparked into life as she turned the key in the ignition.

"Good night then. See you next week." She closed the window

and Veronica sent a wave into Gillian's rear-view mirror as the Volvo pulled out of The Barque car park. Then, with a surreptitious glance around her, she stepped back out of the light and reached into her bag.

She and Richard officially quit smoking a few months ago and mostly Veronica had been okay with it. But the one she missed almost as much as that one after sex was the one following a good meal. Confident she wasn't being observed, Veronica lit up and savouring the roughness in her throat and lungs, she waited for the light-headed rush. My God, she thought, once it was a furtive spliff you sneaked out for. Who'd ever have believed that one day it would be a bloody Benson and…

She caught herself, suddenly aware of a figure moving across the car park and instinctively cupped the cigarette in her palm to hide the glow. Whoever it was, their steps were uncertain and, after almost stumbling, they dropped onto one knee by the wheel of a parked car.

'Bloody hell!' Veronica shook her head. But God only knows how many times in her younger days some Good Samaritan had gently steered her away from whatever perils lay in wait for a drunken stupor. She crushed the cigarette under her heel and stepped forward.

"Hello," she called out. "Are you alright?"

As the figure turned towards her, she realised he'd been reaching under the wheel arch to retrieve a small metal box. Then the moon emerged from behind a passing cloud and she recognised Robert Pascoe.

"Robert!" Definitely not Veronica's favourite person in the world, but she managed a smile. "Are you okay?"

He stared at her, recognition slow to arrive and when it did he simply grunted. He was, Veronica realised, almost paralytically drunk and that what he was holding was a key safe.

"Do you need a hand there, Robert?" she asked as he rose. "Are you feeling alright?"

Robert smiled, but there was nothing amusing about it, absolutely nothing at all. He stepped towards her, his expression *unlike any she had seen on his face before.*

"So, it's you." His voice was somewhere between a sneer and a snarl. "No surprise to find you sneaking about in the shadows, is it? Fucking dykes and queers..."

And with a sudden chill Veronica realised exactly how off kilter Lee's take on Robert Pascoe actually was. That it's not conscience or guilt which has kept Claudia by his side, but the knowledge of what she'd be releasing were she ever to let him slip free of the leash she's been handed.

"Who else is there?"

Robert's voice dripped with menace and Veronica reached into her pocket, fingers scrambling for her door key and her head a jumble of memories from practice mats in Notting Hill half a lifetime ago.

"It's just me, Robert," she said, surprised by how calm and natural she managed to sound. "Sneaking a cigarette," she added, attempting to turn a confrontation into a conversation. "We're supposed to have given up."

His laugh was a short bark.

"Lies and secrets. That's all you people know, isn't it?"

He was breathing heavily and had her almost backed up against the wall.

But a wall, Veronica realised, which has a packed restaurant on the other side of it. Reaching out, she splayed her fingers against his chest and pushed.

"This isn't funny, Robert," she told him, "and if you take one step closer to me, you're going to discover just how loudly I can scream."

Robert laughed.

"If you think that..."

He broke off with a gasp as an arm came snaking over his shoulder and tightened around his throat. Veronica stepped backwards and found herself pressing hard against the wall as Robert struggled. Whoever had the sleeper hold on him was half obscured by shadow, half by Robert's writhing body, but after only ten, perhaps fifteen seconds, his struggles ceased and he was lowered to the ground.

"Are you okay, Veronica?" asked Paul.

* * *

To my surprise, having always accepted the adage of 'out of sight, out of mind' when it comes to society's attitude towards the elderly or infirm, most residents here receive a steady stream of visitors. Over breakfast one morning I mention this to Janice, who has the room next to mine.

"It's not like this is a Retirement Home, dear," she tells me. "With us, they've a light at the end of the tunnel."

Paul is my most frequent visitor, the only person I'm close to who still lives in St Hannahs. He drops by every few days, brings magazines wrapped around a half bottle of Bushmills and a pack of Marlboro. I'm sure both can be detected on my breath, but no one ever says anything - not that finger wagging would carry much weight this late in the game.

Lee's first visit was conducted under that anonymous persona created to allow her as normal a daily life as possible. A retired headmistress, you might think, or perhaps something in local government, an air of professional brusqueness about her which discourages engagement.

I understand the purpose it serves on the street but...

"Oh, give the girls a thrill," I tell her. "Let a bit of glamour into their lives."

So now when Lee arrives all the young care assistants cluster around her, holding out their phones to capture a moment that won't seem real unless it can be documented and shared, their excitement turning to sweet shyness as they thank her and leave us to ourselves. I'm sure her visits incur great inconvenience, but it's always something she makes light of, as if regular trips to Cornwall when you're based in Los Angeles aren't really much more than popping out to the shops.

She mostly entertains me with celebrity tittle-tattle, currency for the girls whenever I might need a special favour. And, as ever, Lee hoovers up all around her as unconsciously as breathing, plankton on the surface of the sea of life.

Arriving for a recent visit, she catches me lying on the bed, resting. As I lean forward to raise myself and she reaches out a hand to steady me, there comes the sound of breaking wind.

Our eyes meet.

"When you recycle me for the final days of Mother Teresa," I tell her dryly, "you might want to leave that bit out."

She bursts into tears and for a minute is inconsolable. I take her in my arms as she buries her head into my shoulder and sobs, until an incongruous flutter of muscle memory reminds us of what these old bodies had once done to each other and we gently pull apart.

"I didn't..." she begins, but I shush her with a kiss to the lips.

"It's alright," I tell her. We, the nearly departed, often find ourselves comforting those we're about to leave behind and draw a strange, inexplicable strength from it.

* * *

"He'd been causing a ruckus inside," Paul told her, as with trembling hands Veronica lit another cigarette. "And there was the feel about him of not being done for the night, so I followed him out." He gave a shrug. "I've an idea what he's capable of."

"So have I." Veronica met Paul's stare and caught a flicker of something between interest and surprise in his expression. "Lee told me what happened, after Claudia had to sell her share in The Grange."

Paul nodded.

"The thing about self-loathing," he said, "is that it doesn't stay directed inward for long."

"What are you going to do?" she asked him.

"What I should have done a while ago," he told her. "Do you have a problem with that?"

Veronica swallowed. Later, she'd reflect that this moment, with all the significance contained within, should have the sense of a great weight about it, but it doesn't. If anything, her head feels strangely light.

"No," she said. "No, I don't."

Paul nodded towards the car park entrance.

"Go and keep an eye out while I get him into his car. Cough if anyone's coming."

Without looking behind her, Veronica walked over to the pavement. A minute later, Paul joined her.

"What happens now?" she asked.

"Nothing that involves you," said Paul. "Did you drive here tonight?"

Veronica shook her head.

"A friend picked me up from home. She offered me a lift back, but I decided to walk."

"So off you go then." He gave a half smile to her quizzical expression. "You won't have to worry about looking surprised if you genuinely are."

"And...?"

"You left the restaurant, said goodnight to your friend and walked home. You saw nothing out of the ordinary."

"Are you..." began Veronica. "I mean, will you be okay? Are you sure you don't need any help?"

Paul reached out and laid his hand against her arm.

"You didn't see Robert tonight," he told her, softly. "And you didn't see me. That's all I need from you."

"Okay," she said, although for some inexplicable reason Veronica now seemed frozen to the spot in a scenario her right mind should have her run screaming from. But as Paul turned and walked over to Robert's car, her feet, as if possessed by a will of their own, finally started out along the pavement, towards the sanctuary of Richard and home.

* * *

"I want to confess," I tell Mrs Speller, who's the head honcho here. I'd give you her official title if I could, but I struggle to keep pace with the hoops the organisation which runs this place needs to jump through to remain politically correct. Yet one more phrase Orwell would have delighted in - *Ministry of Love, Ministry of Plenty...*

"I'm sorry?"

"I wish to go to Confession."

258

She turns her gaze from me to the computer screen on her desk. It's been the third party in every conversation I've had in this room and I've come to think of it as a little devil sitting on her shoulder, whispering away into her ear.

"There's no mention," squinting at the screen, "of Catholicism in your file."

"Unfortunately, I lapsed," I tell her, giving a sad shake of my head. "But as of late I've - obviously - time on my hands for reflection." I smile. "And now I'm ready to make my peace."

Her lips purse.

"If it's spiritual comfort you're seeking," Mrs Speller speaks slowly, "then Reverend Harding is here every day. I'm sure he'd be more than willing to speak to you personally."

I'm sure he would too. Betting heavily on Pascal's Wager, the clergy assume unquestioning devotion here and consequently we tend to be saddled with their most dim-witted representatives. Which is a shame, despite being as secular as they come I've always enjoyed a good to and fro with the God botherers, but the Reverend Harding would have been too much like shooting fish in a barrel.

He's recently featured on the front page of our local newspaper, having translated both the Lords Prayer and Twenty-Third Psalm into textese, the form of Newspeak - it really is remarkable how prescient Orwell has proven to be - which young people use to communicate with each other. I doubt the sight of those smug features basking in his mediocrity did much for sales and I've certainly no intention of handing over my spiritual wellbeing to anyone who derives satisfaction from making a virtue of illiteracy.

"I think the sanctity of a church would be more appropriate," I tell her and she hesitates, the cogs in her mind doubtless clicking through the *realpolitik* consequences of pissing off someone who has Lee Munro on speed dial.

"There's the issue of parking," she says, and I give a nod. I can hardly manage half a dozen steps unaided and car parking for St Hannahs has been almost entirely relocated to a Park and

Ride scheme on the outskirts, nearly as far from the centre as we are.

"St Agatha's," I encourage her, "is no more than a twenty-minute walk. I'm sure one of the girls would be happy to combine an errand in town with wheeling me along there."

She gives a brisk nod.

"Very well." Mrs Speller stares across the desk still convinced I'm up to something, if for no other reason than past form. "When did you have in mind?"

"Given the circumstances," I say dryly, "sooner rather than later, wouldn't you think?"

"Let me see what I can do," she tells me.

I doubt I'll be that fortunate to find a good old hellfire and brimstone whisky-soaked Irish priest, but in all other respects St Agatha's should fit the bill. It's not that I've paid that much attention during the christenings, weddings and funerals which over the years have been - as with most of St Hannahs' population - my only reason for crossing its threshold, but I recall it being identical to every other Catholic Church I've found myself inside of. Incense and furniture polish blends with body odour to permeate its entire expanse and there's enough idolatry on display to suggest undercurrents of something far more primitive than doctrine. Plaster casts of Mary remain a stark warning to the hubris of virginity, whilst her offspring is nailed high on the wall in that sadomasochistic, homoerotic spasm of a Crucifixion. From the Inquisition to pederasty, is it really any surprise they're so fucked up?

But like all good penitents, it's not actually forgiveness I crave but judgement and I want my money's worth.

* * *

Veronica felt guilty about not mentioning Lee's eclipse brunch to Gill, particularly after everything she'd done over the last few days. But Lee told her that as she'd be glad handing the Gallery opening tonight, she was keeping this one for close friends.

And when Veronica arrived here, that did seem to be the case. Kit Franklyn was over from Amsterdam and she recognised Lee's agent Sy, who she'd met a few times. But suddenly Jenny Warwick, in jeans and sans *dog collar*, was mingling with the guests and from then on Veronica found excuses rehearsing away in the back of her head. 'With all the chaos lately, it completely slipped my mind. I only got a phone call from Lee that morning.'

Anyway, Gill was across town at Dennis Nelson's barbecue and with a job of her own to do there. Lee said that as soon as the eclipse was over she was going to get some shut-eye, what with the jet lag from yesterday's flight, and so Veronica was humming and ahhing about joining Gill over there. Lending a touch of moral support and easing her conscience was something she'd tried not to think of as two birds with the same stone.

But at least with so few locals on the Terrace, Veronica was spared the concern and good wishes which, however well meant, can easily become burdensome. Only Claudia came over to embrace her, but silently and as they pulled apart, she'd given Veronica just the slightest nod of the head and an even stare. A gesture she'd thought little of at the time, but, as the morning progressed, begun to think about more and more...

"Veronica."

She turned to see Paul standing there.

They'd not spoken since that night outside The Barque *and Veronica was suddenly cautious.*

"Hello Paul."

"How's Richard?" *he asked.*

"As well as can be expected," *she told him.* "He should be out of the coma in a few days and they're talking about moving him to the Cottage Hospital here for observation. And hopefully he'll be home soon."

"I'm glad to hear that." *He hesitated.* "Could we have a word? Alone?"

Veronica had always thought the expression 'a sinking pit in my stomach' was only a metaphor, but that's exactly what the tight clenching of her muscles felt like as she followed him into the house, through the dining room and out onto a veranda. A wicker table and chairs were placed to overlook the ocean, but neither sat down.

"Is it certain," he asked, "that what's happened to Richard is down to a tumour? Nothing else?"

"Nothing else?"

"The talk around town is that he'd been attacked by the Travellers. And that's what put him in a coma. Vanner's been trying to quieten everything down, but I didn't know whether that was just to stop things from really kicking off."

"Sergeant Vanner thinks there might have been some kind of altercation at Belle Meadow," she said, "but not anything serious. The tumour is the reason Richard's in hospital."

"Word is that he was over at Belle Meadow trying to broker some deal with the Travellers," said Paul. "On behalf of Alan Bradshaw. Did the rumour mill get that bit right?"

"Yes, or at least that's what I found out afterwards. But Richard hadn't mentioned anything about it before going over there."

"Are they good friends - your husband and Alan Bradshaw?"

"Well, they're friends. We've got to know both of them, Alan and Safranka." She paused. "Paul, what's this about?"

He seemed to consider. And then come to a decision.

"A while back - a long while back - I got into some serious trouble serving out in Aden. The army was ready to hang me out to dry, but..." He slowly shook his head. "Another government agency bailed me out. And," a wry smile, "as you might imagine, that wasn't done out of the goodness of their hearts."

"So you work for...?" Uncertain, Veronica let her voice trail off.

"Let's just say I've a skill set some people can find the occasional use for. Which over the years has gone some way to repaying that original debt."

"Paul?" Veronica felt that tightening in her stomach again. "Why are you telling me all of this?"

"Occasionally," he continued, almost as if she hadn't spoken, "in that line of work you come across someone who you think you should keep an eye on."

"Because...?"

"Because sometimes the... The established order, let's say, won't. Sometimes they've a clandestine agenda all of their own, one which they're capable of doing pretty much anything to preserve."

He reached into his pocket, took out two postcard size prints and handed one of them to Veronica.

"Do you know him?"

Veronica studied it.

"Yes," she said slowly. "He was a writer, Peter Matthews. He died last week, it was on the news."

"No, I meant did you know *him* - not know *of* him? Or did Richard?"

"Know him?" Veronica shook her head. "No."

"Are you sure?"

"Yes, of course." She shrugged. "Richard and I watched it together on TV. If he had known him, why wouldn't he'd have said so?"

Paul is silent for a while, as if considering.

"When Matthews was diagnosed with terminal cancer last year, he signed up to a euthanasia website."

"A what!!?"

Paul smiled.

"A site where those who want to end it all find help to facilitate that. It puts them in touch with each other."

"Strangers on a Train," said Veronica quietly.

"Sorry?"

"The Hitchcock movie," Veronica told him. "Two people meet on a train and..."

"Right," broke in Paul. "Well, something like that. Anyway, what it did was to present an opportunity to get close to him. As a simpatico figure."

"You mean you pretended you wanted to commit suicide?"

"Yes."

"And befriended him?"

Paul hesitated.

"We set up a time and place to arrange his suicide. For a fee, the website supplies what would be needed to sanitise most 'exit strategies', as they term it. His was to be a heart attack, caused by the frailty of his condition. Afterwards, I was to tidy everything away and leave the room looking like he'd simply collapsed and died."

He's silent for a few seconds.

"What I actually intended to do," he said quietly, "after he'd gone, was to create a scenario that would establish absolutely no doubt as to who this man was. To let the world know exactly what his life had been about."

"Which was...?"

Paul shook his head.

"A couple of months ago, I saw a program on TV about charity work in Africa. And there was his daughter, spearheading a drive against malaria. Turns out she's someone who's spent her entire life raising funds for healthcare in third world countries, chiding politicians, fighting corruption and banging heads together at the United Nations." He smiled. "And then came the realisation that this was who I'd really be pulling the temple down onto - his family. Certainly not him, he'd be well out of it all."

"So ...?"

"So I just kicked it in the head. Broke off contact with him and stayed away from the site." He gave a tight smile. "And then Robert happened."

"Robert? I don't understand?"

"Robert's laptop was in the boot of his car that night and I realised I had the opportunity to create the perfect narrative for a suicide. So, I copied over one huge flashing sign that this computer needed closer examination and then laid down a trail of breadcrumbs to the website. Nothing too obvious but unlikely to be missed. Once the coroner was shown that, I assumed, case closed."

Paul stared at her.

"Except they didn't find anything," he continued. "And after it became clear that they weren't going to, I logged back onto the site. But I couldn't get in. The password had been changed."

"Changed...?"

"Because I now didn't have a clue what was happening, I decided to blend into the background at the time and place we'd *agreed on. A Lyme Regis hotel, last Thursday lunchtime."*

He handed Veronica the other photograph.

"This is the hotel bar, a couple of hours before Matthews' body was found."

Veronica took the print from him, looked down at it, and then her head was swirling and her breath racing.

"So, like I said, are you absolutely certain about the tumour? Because it seems a hell of a coincidence that just two days after this, Richard was in intensive care."

Veronica stared at him blankly.

Paul took out a packet of cigarettes and her fingers were trembling as she held one for him to light, trying to collect her thoughts.

"Robert's computer," she said. "You rigged Robert's laptop?"

He nodded.

"Alan Bradshaw gave it Richard to check before handing it over to the police." She shook her head. "He was worried there might be a suicide note on it, which would invalidate their insurance policy."

Paul was silent.

"Richard found it, didn't he?" Veronica's voice was barely above a whisper. "Your trail of breadcrumbs. And..."

The words just wouldn't come.

"And," continued Paul for her, "I'm guessing a brain tumour is likely to manifest itself in ways that wouldn't need a medical diagnosis for you to realise what's happening."

Veronica gave a sudden shiver at an inexplicable flash of a table on which was placed a glass of whisky and a revolver.

* * *

I once read that Victorian matriarchs were in the habit of addressing all their parlour maids by the same name, supposedly to relieve themselves of the tiresome chore of committing each one to memory. Personally, I suspect that a sense of comfort in being surrounded by an unchanging world also had a lot to do with it.

I find myself in a similar situation with the girls here,

addressing most of the care assistants as 'dear'. But this was a habit which started with the best of intentions, I was wary of giving offence by mispronouncing a name consisting mostly of consonants. In the main they appear to be *émigrés* from the remnants of the Soviet empire, doubtless being taken advantage of but there are worse ways to be exploited. The problem with habits, though, is that however easy they might be to slip into, they become increasingly hard to disengage from and I do occasionally catch a glimpse in the mirror of how these girls must see me. Robbie Burns may have thought it would be a gift to see ourselves through the eyes of others, but *please*, who was he kidding? Almost the last thing we can bear to be stripped of is self-delusion.

For Katya, I'm careful to make an exception. Both stunningly attractive and a cheerful soul - it's strange how rarely those two go together and even stranger how little is made of that - I'm always pleased to see her when she's on shift. Intimate situations which don't have their origins in mutual pleasure are invariably tricky, but Katya handles getting me set up for the day with exactly the right blend of tact, efficiency and humour.

So, I'm delighted to discover it's she who's been delegated with taking me to Church this bright and sunny Spring morning.

"We are to go straight there and back again," she declares, wheeling me out through the gates. "And Mrs Speller says I am to be careful. That you are bad influence."

"Mrs Speller," I tell her, "doesn't know the half of it."

I'm in a cheery mood today. Elisabeth Kübler–Ross would appear to be spot on with her five stages of grief, but I seem to be experiencing denial, anger, bargaining, depression and acceptance not as phases of a progression but rather options for each day. All can be serene on Monday, only for Tuesday to find me raging against the dying of the light.

"What else did she say?"

I sense Katya's shrug.

"We have talk. I tell her I think is maybe time to move on.

Perhaps college. Train as beautician."

"And what were her views on that?"

As if I couldn't guess.

"Bad idea to rush things. That I have whole life in front of me."

"People who tell you that you have your whole life in front of you are generally those who have most of theirs behind them. The thing is…" I hesitate. "Katya, this is the stretch of it that matters. When you're my age and looking back, you won't be spending much time on your forties and fifties, believe me. You might have a lot of years ahead of you, but it's not like they all carry the same weight."

There's silence for a while.

"Sorry," I say eventually. "I didn't mean to…"

"No, is okay." She reaches down and gently squeezes my shoulder with her fingers. "Sometimes bad influence no bad thing, yes?"

"Yes," I smile.

She leaves her hand where it is.

"Your husband?" Katya asks slowly. "Has been dead long time?"

"Yes," I nod. "A very long time."

"It was illness?"

"A brain tumour," I tell her.

"Is that something sudden?"

"He collapsed and was put into an induced coma, while the doctors worked out the best way to treat him. It was thought that he could be brought out of it after a few days, but each time they tried his condition worsened. The tumour was inoperable and gradually cerebral activity began to fade. After a year, brain stem reflexes were minimal and it was decided there was little point in continuing life support." I shrugged. "So, both very sudden and extremely prolonged, you might say."

"I am so sorry for you." Katya hesitates. "And you never find anyone else?"

"It's complicated." I manage a smile. "In the husband

stakes, no, but then I never went looking."

She digests this and seems about to speak when we simultaneously realise that we've arrived at our destination.

Katya is obviously right at home in St Agatha's, pausing to bob up and down as we enter, and in the spirit of things I make a half-hearted display of crossing myself. She wheels me over to one of two confessional booths side by side and steadies me for the few steps inside. Katya takes almost my full weight on her arm as I lower my knees down onto a cushion.

"Would you prefer a chair?" asks a voice through the grill, and delightfully there is an Irish lilt to it. I reassure him I'll be fine and Katya closes the door behind me.

"Forgive me, Father," I say, "for I have sinned."

* * *

The nurses quietly departed, leaving only Veronica and the doctor in the room.

And, of course, Richard.

Lee had offered to be with her, and Paul, who has been Veronica's frequent companion on her weekly - she's tempted to say pilgrimages - visits, was waiting outside in the car. She's reassured him countless times that his trail of breadcrumbs is nothing to feel guilty about, although she guesses he's going to have to find his own way out of that maze. Veronica understands and appreciates everyone's concern, but the world can celebrate Richard's life next week at the service.

What today needed was the silent testimony of a lone witness.

"You might want to step out for a second," the doctor said softly, but Veronica shook her head. They wouldn't allow her to switch off life support herself - fair enough, she could imagine the legal and moral minefield that could lead into - but she's damn well not going to let them sanitise it for her.

"Okay," the doctor took a breath and walked over to the machines by the bedside. "This is simply to deactivate the alarms," he explained, flicking at switches. He stared at the readouts, seemed satisfied and crossed back over to the foot of the bed.

"Would you like a last moment with him?" he asked.

"I've said my goodbyes," Veronica told him. The hours she's spent at this bedside holding his hand, reading Pynchon aloud, playing Dylan bootlegs…

He gave a nod and moved to the side of the bed.

"I'm removing the breathing tube," he explained. "There'll probably be some reflex activity. It's perfectly normal and nothing to become distressed about."

After the tube was out, Veronica realised this was the first time she'd seen Richard's face in twelve months, there'd always been at least one part of it covered or masked. He was almost unrecognisable, cheeks sunken, lips thin and bloodless.

Which should have made this easier, but doesn't.

Veronica gave a start at a loud gargling sound, then his arms and legs began to twitch. It's the first motion she'd seen from Richard since he's been in here and she looked over to the doctor.

"The body indicating it needs oxygen," he told her. "As I said, purely a reflex action."

He turned back to the equipment. Carefully and with almost exaggerated precision, he pressed a button and then flicked down two switches.

"Life support is now terminated," he said quietly.

If anything, the tremors running through the limbs became even more pronounced and Richard's lips, she noticed, were turning blue.

"It won't be long," said the doctor, his tone somewhere between reassurance and commiseration.

And it wasn't.

After Richard was still, the doctor reached for a stethoscope on the bedside table and listened to his heart. Then he lifted Richard's wrist and felt for a pulse. Gently, he laid the arm back down on the bed.

"It's over," he told her.

"Thank you," she said, "for…" She made a loose gesture with her hand.

"Would you like some time by yourself?" he asked. "You can take as long as you need."

Veronica shook her head and managed a small smile.

They left the room together and separated at the end of the corridor as if, felt Veronica, escaping the complicity of some dark secret. She was thankful for the normality of the day, the chatter of two nurses in the lift descending to the ground floor, a mother exasperated by a bored child in a reception area, a teenage girl indifferently flicking through a glossy magazine. She knew that anything other than the mundane would tip her fully over the edge at this moment.

Paul was waiting at the car and had the sense to be neither listening to the radio nor reading the paper. Just standing there, silent and steady. Without a word, his arms went around her and she erupted, the sobs choking and the tears flooding.

The first tears Veronica has shed in over a year.

* * *

"You were long time," says Katya dryly.

"I'd have been even longer," I tell her, "but my knees were starting to give."

"Three people go next door," she continues. "In the end I go myself, although it has been only two days."

"Goodness," I smile. "And here's me with a lifetime to atone for. Yours got off lightly."

"Ten Hail Mary prayers."

"Well, I imagine that's something quickly managed?"

"Already taken care of." We arrive at a pedestrian set of lights and come to a halt by the kerbside, waiting for the little man to turn green. "I say under breath while I wait for boyfriend to finish."

"Katya," I smile, "you and I really must find time for a chat about the notion of dogma."

From behind I hear a match strike and she passes me down a cigarette.

"Sometimes," says Katya, "I think as well as confessing sin, they should allow us to proclaim virtue."

"And how would that work?"

"'Rejoice Father, for today I help old lady unburden her

270

soul'." Her tone switches from light and airy to deep and sonorous. "'Bless you, my child, eat ten Belgian chocolates'."

I burst out laughing. I'm definitely going to make some kind of provision for her, I decide. I'll talk to Paul on his next visit, get him to set something up to see her through college...

The lights change, allowing traffic to turn the corner, but for us the little man stays red. A car pulls up at the kerb, a shiny new Mercedes saloon. The four occupants are male and I would guess probably not yet out of the sixth form. You can cut the air of self-satisfaction with a knife, even though it's obvious to all that someone's just passed his driving test and been allowed to take Daddy's pride and joy out for a spin.

The driver's window whirls down.

"Hello there," he smiles up at Katya and I don't have to turn my head to sense her pointedly ignoring him.

"Why not park Granny up for a while," he nods towards me, "and come for a ride? We could..."

I flick my cigarette in through the open car window with enough momentum for it to actually bounce off the windscreen. Katya's laughter is ringing, the interior is now all chaos and consternation. 'Get it before it burns the carpet,' I hear the driver cry and then from behind them comes a cacophony of horns as the lights change. With one last evil stare towards us, the driver slips the car into gear and pulls away.

It's at that moment I notice across the road a young police constable, who's obviously witnessed the entire incident. Then, slowly and regarding us with a bemused expression, he begins to walk off. He turns back to us just once, giving a small shake of his head.

There are only two phases of a woman's life when she may act as she pleases and incur little by way of judgement or consequence - as a flighty young thing or cantankerous old woman. She should make the most of them, neither will last as long as she imagines.

Fin.

DA CAPO

Rick rarely ventured out of the studio to paint. Setting up an easel on a city street gathered unwanted attention faster than an empty skip and the countryside wasn't much better, except you couldn't help but wonder where all the bloody people came from.

But it was early yet, the sun barely peeking over the horizon, and that was the moment he was here to capture. In Cornwall there weren't many east facing beaches which also gave you a vista of only sea and sky, but he'd noted this geographical anomaly as they'd driven by on their arrival. A horseshoe cove set into a headland which twisted back on itself should work for him, Rick had thought, and he'd been right. The coastline did continue but not in his immediate line of sight and that's what mattered. Either get down what's there or unload what's in your head - it's when the two start blending it all starts to unravel...

Saskia had paddled further out than on previous days, but was now turning her board to face the beach. She was still the only surfer out there, although probably not for much longer. The forecast was for a hot sunny day and Rick doubted he'd get more than one shot at this. But once he had the essence down on canvas maybe he could work on it back at the studio, what he needed...

He let conscious thought slip away as Saskia rose to a kneeling position, sensing the incoming wave. 'You just know,' she'd told him and he'd left it at that - you didn't need to school an artist about instinct. As Saskia gathered momentum, the wave beneath her rose deceptively slowly and now she was standing, leant forward. Then, dropping under the crest she flipped the board sideways, skimming across a wall of water as the surf broke above her head and came crashing down behind her as if in pursuit. He had set the scene on her previous runs - the stillness of the sky, myriad reflections breaking apart in the spray, the majesty of the ocean - and Rick worked furiously with his brushes to catch Saskia half crouched in the classic surfer's pose of one arm leading, one arm trailing.

And absolutely flying.

It was funny, reflected Rick, how life worked out. He'd never been much for nostalgia, probably down to the past being such a slippery construct in his mind, at least compared to the way others seemed able to resurrect it with ease, dissecting events in their entirety. But over the years, the realisation settled on him that surprisingly few artists were playing with a full deck in the cognition department. Julian, who he'd known since art college and had been one of the leading lights of the YBA, couldn't recognise his own face in the mirror - proso something they called it. He'd walk right by you in the street, cut you stone dead you'd be thinking, unless you knew about it and few did because when it comes down to it, wouldn't you rather be thought arrogant than cuckoo? Sally, who taught at the college, couldn't return from anywhere by the same route she'd taken to get there and what machinations and hoops she'd jump through to prevent people realising she could no more retrace her steps than they could squat down on their living room carpet and take a dump.

Was it these quirks that had fuelled their creativity or, somewhere along the way, had the creative process rewired their heads? Maybe the two fed off each other. An image of Ouroboros always came to mind whenever Rick thought about thinking, that Egyptian icon of a serpent eating its tail.

For Rick, once stuff was done, it was done. Occasionally there might be resonance in memory, a lightning bolt illuminating a landscape on a moonless night for the briefest of seconds, with little chance to grasp the entire vista and none to gather context or meaning. The narrative of his life held fast, the broad brush strokes of who, when and why, but mostly he depended on others to colour in the details.

Where this really worked for him was standing in front of an easel. He'd probably produced as many bad paintings as good ones, he reflected, but they all had a freshness about them which he knew the work of other artists - some far better - often lacked. That alone was worth a Moleskine as much stuffed with the metadata of life as sketches on the fly, never mind being spared carrying grudges or burdened by slights imagined or real.

What was intriguing, in its way, was what stuck and what didn't. When his mind did settle on a memory of its own accord, it never seemed of particular significance. Frankie, for instance, had been in his life for less than forty-eight hours when they'd first met all those years ago, yet he doubted a single day had passed in those intervening decades when she hadn't broken the surface of his consciousness for one reason or another. Whole relationships had sunk without trace in the meantime, Veronica Hewitt had been the *amour fou* to end all *amour fou* and he couldn't even recall her face. *Events, dear boy*, some politician drawled in the back of his mind, *events*.

Yet when Frankie walked into the college cafeteria twenty years later - and simply glancing at her told you those hadn't been tranquil years - Rick didn't have the slightest doubt who she was. Not one iota. He might struggle with students he'd been teaching all year, but as Frankie piled up her tray at the counter, paid at the till and carried it over to a table to sit by herself, Rick stared across the room spellbound.

Leaving his own meal unfinished, he walked over and sat down. Her body language signalled irritation at the encroachment of her personal space, but she didn't acknowledge his presence in any other way.

"Hello Francesca," Rick said softly. "Long time no see."

Her head turned to him at that, a wariness in her eyes, he noticed.

"Rick Hanson," he said. "Pembridge Villas in Notting Hill. You stayed there once, back-"

"Bloody hell," she broke in, staring. "Where the fuck have you sprung from?"

* * *

Turned out Frankie was a life model at the college, had started that same day. It's what she did, she explained, when funds got low.

"In Europe sell my blood, back here get my kit off."

"Do you travel much?" asked Rick carefully, taking what seemed to be the most neutral way forward from that statement. Apparently so, he learnt she spent her summers in England fruit picking and wintered around the Mediterranean, mainly Spain and North Africa.

"Isn't that dangerous," he asked, "for a woman on her own?"

"Everywhere's dangerous for a woman on her own," she said, shaking her head as if dealing with an especially slow child.

It was only then Rick noticed a thin scar running down her forehead into her eyebrow and continuing across her cheek. It was an intriguing face, fine lines and creases seemed to radiate from a central point instead of being tugged downward by gravity. Character so rarely, thought Rick, wins out over time.

"You know," he said, as Frankie reached the end of her meal, mopping up gravy with a slice of bread, "I'd really like to paint you."

"Shit," said Frankie, popping the last piece of crust into her mouth. "I was hoping you were after a shag."

"I'm serious," said Rick. "I'd pay you."

"So am I," Frankie told him. "And damn right you would."

They met for a drink after college, in the pub down the road. Considering the evening was mostly an exchange of thwarted ambition, broken dreams and failed relationships, they found each other surprisingly good company.

"Who were we, all those years ago?" asked Frankie sadly, as they left the bar. "Jesus Christ!"

"I don't remember a lot about those days," admitted Rick. "Or much about anything, really. But I never forgot you. And I always wondered what might have happened if..." He hesitated. "Look, do you want to come back to my place for a coffee?"

"Let's go to mine," said Frankie. "It's nearer."

"How do you know where I live?" asked Rick, surprised.

"Call it an educated guess," she said, slipping her arm through his and leading him along the road toward the college. But they hadn't gone further than twenty yards before she turned into a side street, stopping in front of an imposing town house.

"This is handy," said Rick, trying to conceal his surprise. Frankie reached into her bag, pulled out a bunch of keys and unlocked a VW campervan parked at the kerb.

"Are you going to be okay to drive?" Rick asked her, mentally totting up the number of rounds they'd put away over the course of the evening.

"Drive?" She switched the light on, unfastened her coat and dropped it over the back of the driver's seat. "Who's driving anywhere?"

Richard stared as Frankie peeled her sweater up and off over her head. Then, with a nod, she indicated the unmade bed.

"You should climb straight in," she told him. "In case you haven't noticed, it's cold as fuck in here and my wrist isn't what it used to be."

* * *

Frankie had been as cautious of Rick's hospitality as a stray cat. Initially, she'd only accepted his offer of parking her campervan in his allotted slot at the housing project. He'd been lucky with the flat, he explained, taking the tenancy over from one of the lecturers who'd left for a job in Canada.

"Or was it New Zealand he went to?" he mused. "And it could have been a she."

"Must be weird," Frankie said to him. "Every day full of the same surprises."

She'd spent the first couple of nights in the campervan, only using the flat to shower and do her washing. He'd shown her the empty spare room and explained he wouldn't want anything for it, that she was welcome.

Frankie had shrugged.

"Maybe if I'm still here when the nights start drawing in," she said.

But a few days later, Rick arrived home to find her carrying boxes from the van to the spare room.

"You're right," she told him. "All this palaver of trailing

back and forth is stupid."

Over the months they fell into a routine. He cooked the evening meal, she did the washing. Whenever they had sex - rarely heralded by anything more than a declaration of 'gagging for it tonight, how about you?' - it was in his room.

Things weren't all plain sailing. Sometimes Frankie would disappear into her van for days at a time. The first occasion this happened, a concerned Rick had knocked on the door and then opened it.

He'd been confronted by her sprawled on the bed, surrounded by empty gin bottles and fixing him with a dead eyed stare.

"Get out," she said. Leaving her to it he'd quickly retreated, the therapeutic approach never something destined to play a role in either of their lives. She emerged a couple of days later and things settled back down to what passed for normal.

But one night, about a year after Frankie had moved in and in a post coital haze, she said to him quietly, "I've never thanked you, have I?"

"Sorry?" asked Rick.

"For," Frankie lazily raised an arm to gesture around the room, "all this. What you did for me. And for not dragging any of that love or relationship bollocks into it."

"You're welcome," said Rick.

"Actually," said Frankie, "I still haven't. Not technically."

"That's okay," Rick told her. "It's not like I'm holding my breath here."

He heard her soft chuckle.

"It's alright, isn't it?" she said after a while. "What we've got."

"It is," said Rick, then added, "And more than I ever expected."

She reached for his hand and squeezed it, as they lay silently together in the dark.

* * *

One night the previous year, Rick had arrived back at the

flat to find Frankie sitting in the living room chatting with a young woman. Occasionally Frankie returned home with a troubled girl - her maternal instincts weren't entirely exhausted - although, in her late twenties, this one seemed a little old for a student.

Perhaps another model.

They both stood up as he entered the room.

"Hi Rick," said Frankie. "This is Saskia."

The girl held her hand out.

"I am very pleased to meet you," she said. Her accent was slight, but there.

"Rick Hanson," he smiled.

"Yes," she said. "You are an artist. You also teach at a college here in North London. This I learn from the internet."

"Right," said Rick, slowly, realising she was looking at him in quite a disconcerting manner. There was something familiar about that look, too. Nothing he could put his finger on, but no surprise there.

"In nineteen seventy you were living in Notting Hill, I believe. A place named Pembridge Villas?"

"Is that on the internet too?" asked Rick warily.

"No." Saskia shook her head and gave him a small smile. "It is what my mother told me."

Then Rick knew exactly where this was going.

And also why that look in her eyes had triggered a synaptic flash... He'd occasionally caught it in the bathroom mirror when he'd something weighing on his mind.

"You're Carin's daughter, aren't you?"

She nodded.

"She wondered if you would still remember her. That you were lovers." Saskia hesitated. "If not, she told me to say to you that-"

"It's okay," Rick broke in. "I remember."

And he did.

Mostly, his recollections were a swirl of images and emotions, each - if unchecked - triggering another into a continuing maelstrom. But occasionally a coherent narrative would emerge and when it did, ironically, it would have the clarity of unfolding as if in real time.

But these weren't memories to be particularly proud of. Carin had been on the wrong side of a bad breakup, vulnerable, upset and however much you wanted to dress up what had happened, Rick had taken advantage of her. He wasn't alone in that, but it was still no excuse. He couldn't help but wonder if 'lovers' were a euphemism of Saskia's or whether Carin had embellished their relationship to gloss over bad memories of a summer that had probably lasted far too long.

"Sorry," said Saskia. "I realise that this must be a bit..."

"Dickensian?" suggested Frankie, as Saskia struggled for a word.

For a moment, no one seemed sure of what to say.

"It was really because of my grandfather that I came to find you," said Saskia, eventually. "He died recently."

"I'm sorry to hear that," Rick told her. "And for your loss."

"Thank you." She acknowledged the platitudes with the slightest of shrugs. "Of bowel cancer." She sighed. "Which got me thinking."

"Right," said Rick, uncertainly. "It's always traumatic when-"

"About my health," Saskia broke in. "That illnesses run in families, don't they? That I should really try to discover more about my genetic makeup. To become aware of what I needed to be careful about. Like being tested for bowel cancer every couple of years, to catch it early."

One thing she hadn't fished out of Rick's end of the gene pool was her practicality, but he simply nodded.

"Sure," he said. "We could go through that."

"Actually, love," Frankie said to her, "if you can remember what you were doing this time last week, you've already dodged one bullet."

"I was thinking," said Saskia, "that perhaps we might go for a meal?"

"Well, yes," said Rick, looking at Frankie. "We don't have anything planned for tonight."

"Sorry, I'm covering for Ingrid at an evening class," she told him. Before he had a chance to point out that the college didn't hold evening classes - and who was Ingrid - she took him by the arm and led him out of the room.

"Need a quick word with you first," she said.

Closing the bedroom door behind them, she stared at him and then shook her head.

"Okay, if all she wanted was a heads up on Alzheimer's, don't you think she could have just written you a letter? Do you understand what it must have taken for this girl to travel to a foreign country all by herself, intending to loom up into someone's life like the ghost of Christmas bloody past?"

"I'm not sure what you mean?"

"*Men!*" Frankie shook her head in exasperation. "You're where she's from, right? She wants to know about you. Don't you want to get to know her?"

"Of course."

"Take her to *Romano's* on Upper Street. Just the two of you. No," she said as he started to protest, "what needs unravelling will go better without an audience." Frankie shrugged. "I'll give it a couple of hours and join you both for coffee - on the off chance you won't have frightened her away by then."

* * *

It proved a quick two hours, they found each other easy company. Saskia did most of the talking, understandably, as she'd already discovered a fair amount about him from the internet. *Bloody hell!* thought Rick. He didn't know much about it, but he'd sort of assumed that if you were on there, then it was because you wanted to be, that it was somehow your choice. Anyway, something to look into another day.

Saskia, he learnt, worked as a translator at the International Criminal Court in The Hague. That can't be easy, Rick suggested, and she nodded. The things she sometimes heard were truly appalling and seemed even more so when it was her own voice speaking of them.

"Yet it is also very rewarding," she told him, "to be a part of justice being served."

But her biggest interest in life, she explained, was surfing. Apparently she'd been the Dutch Junior Surf Champion in her teens, and Rick realised that he already had paternal enough feelings towards her to feel proud about that.

"What about your family?" he asked.

Saskia was an only child. Her birth had been difficult, and her mother was advised against another pregnancy. That probably hadn't been too much of a blow - she gave that slight shrug again - Mama was very career minded and Saskia had been mostly raised by her grandparents, who owned an art gallery in Amsterdam. Oma Gerde had died five years ago and, as she'd mentioned earlier, her grandfather just recently.

"What's Carin doing these days?" asked Rick, in what he hoped came across as a casual tone.

Carin, it transpired, was a professor at Leiden University where she taught history of art. Her father - stepfather, she corrected - was a writer.

"He's always been away a lot," Saskia told him. "When I was little he was a journalist, usually working abroad. These days he is a ghostwriter - you know the term?"

Rick nodded.

"He creates autobiographies for minor celebrities. Musicians, actors. So, as you might imagine, he still travels quite a bit."

"Have you always known that..?." Rick gave a shrug.

"That Kit is not my biological father? Yes, since I was a small child."

"Kit?" Kit and Carin. That pairing definitely rang a bell.

"He also lived at that house in Notting Hill."

"Right. Back then things were..." Rick struggled to find a term that wouldn't be suggestive of musical beds.

"Not too late for coffee, am I?"

Frankie sat down at the table and turned her head from

one to the other.

"So, how's it all going?" she asked with a smile.

* * *

Despite her protestations that she'd find a hotel, Saskia slept in Frankie's room that night.

"You okay?" Frankie asked Rick as they lay in bed together, her head resting on his chest after he'd brought her up to speed on their conversation in the restaurant.

"Yeah," said Rick. "If perhaps feeling a bit..."

He sighed.

"Sandbagged?" suggested Frankie.

"Dunno if that's the word for it." Rick shook his head. "I'm just not sure what it is she wants from me."

"I'm the last person in the world to give relationship advice," said Frankie, "but it often seems to me that while most marriages strike a kind of balance, in some of them it's always going to be about each other and in others always about the kids."

"So..."

"So, no prizes for guessing the sort of family Saskia grew up in." She sighed. "And now she's lost her grandad. Who, it sounds like, was the real father figure in her life."

"I'm not sure that being a father is what I-"

"*Jesus Christ!*" broke in Frankie. "She's nearly thirty years old. You're not going to be putting training wheels on her fucking bike or sitting through nativity plays. All she wants is someone older she can trust and who'll lend her the occasional ear. Even you should be able to manage that."

"Okay," said Rick quietly.

"Something good happened in your life today," Frankie told him. "Don't pull it all to pieces trying to make some kind of sense out of it."

* * *

They'd met up for a few weekends since then, but this was their first holiday together. It had been Saskia's idea to travel to Cornwall and Frankie couldn't believe that in all of his fifty years,

Rick had never once crossed the Tamar.

"The surf's brilliant," Saskia had told them, "almost as good as southern Portugal. And Kit's coming to St Hannahs for the eclipse. We could all meet up and I'll go back home with him."

Maybe mull on that closer to the time, thought Rick. So far, there'd been no reunions, only a cautious exchange of good wishes by email and then a mutual sense of leaving well alone.

They were staying at a local campsite, Petroc. If Rick and Frankie did decide to leave early, Saskia could stay with a family friend who had some kind of business running courses for executives.

"I'm not exactly sure what Paul does," she told them, "but Kit often stays there when he is in England."

Rick had wondered if they might get away with camping in lay-bys or up on the moor, but after their first night down here they'd had not so much a run in with the cops as an encounter.

Rick and Saskia had gone down to the beach, leaving Frankie making lunch. On their return, an ambulance was pulling out of the Viewing Area where they'd spent the night and Frankie was talking to a police sergeant.

"What's happened?" asked Rick.

"Some poor bloke collapsed," Frankie told him. "Just pulled in here, got out of his car," with a wave of her hand she indicated a classic Jaguar saloon, "and down he went."

"Heart attack?"

The sergeant shrugged.

"Paramedics don't think so. Perhaps a stroke. And as I was saying to your wife," - both of them let that go - "if it hadn't been for her, he'd probably still be lying there. He was behind the car, no chance of him being spotted from the road."

He paused.

"I'm not going to ask how long you've been parked here," he said carefully. "As you obviously know, there are hefty fines for staying overnight in a Viewing Area, so I'm assuming you'd just pulled over to admire the view and stretch your legs, right?"

"Right," nodded Rick, Frankie and Saskia in unison.

"That being said," the sergeant reached into the breast pocket of his tunic for a notebook and pen, "with this being August - and the eclipse week - pretty much everywhere down here is fully booked."

He began to scribble in the notebook.

"But follow the road around the headland for about a mile and a half," he said, "and you'll come to a caravan park and campsite called Petroc." He tore the page out and handed it to Frankie. "If you give this to them," he told her, "and tell them Sergeant Vanner sent you, they'll see you alright."

"Thank you, Sergeant," said Frankie. He gave them a nod and walked away over to his car.

"Poor bugger," said Frankie, as they climbed back into the campervan. "He didn't look much older than you."

"A very nice car though," said Saskia. "A classic."

"Yeah, but it costs a fortune to keep them running and on the road," Rick told her. "A real money pit."

"And since when did you become motoring correspondent for *Arts and Crafts Monthly*?" said Frankie archly, giving him a sideways glance as she turned the key in the ignition.

Rick considered and then shook his head.

"Dunno," he said. "Maybe it was something I once heard."

* * *

As Saskia waded ashore, gripping the board under her arm and sweeping wet hair away from her face, Rick stepped back and viewed the painting.

He'd had the background ready before she rode that last wave. Sea, sun, sky and a tunnel of cascading surf, all waiting for her. He'd captured Saskia in no more than a dozen brush strokes, a blur of motion twisting across the canvas and yet uniquely identifiable. And he knew he wouldn't be touching this up back in the studio - refinement wasn't what this painting was about. With that same thought in mind, he left in place the grains of sand which had blown onto the still tacky surface. Sometimes it's pristine that works, sometimes rough around the edges.

Like Saskia had said, you just know.

He heard voices behind him, new arrivals at the beach and a spell broken. The sun was clear of the horizon now, its warmth seeping into the air. Saskia strode towards him, a wide smile on her face before turning to sweep the entire seascape with her arm.

"What it is," she laughed, "to be so free."

AFTERWORD

We hope you enjoyed Felo de Se, the second book in the St Hannahs series of novels.

As with most independently published novels, its success is dependent on word of mouth recommendation rather than mainstream marketing. If you did enjoy it, an online rating or review would be appreciated.

Amanuensis (2020) and Corrigenda (2023) are also available.

ABOUT THE AUTHOR

Phil Egner

Phil was born in Nottingham in 1949.

During the late 1960s he was involved with a number of projects that had their genesis in the London counterculture and was a regular contributor to the underground press.

A career in software development followed, primarily as an IT contractor working in both the public and private sectors throughout the UK, mainland Europe and United States.

Home is now a Devon village where his time is increasingly occupied with the St Hannahs series of novels.

Printed in Great Britain
by Amazon